"Intermixing the experience of cinema, literature, anime, comics, and gaming, this is the new generation of science fiction we've been waiting for!"   —Hideo Kojima, game creator

"How far would you go in pursuit of your dreams? What would you be willing to sacrifice? Set in the fascinating universe of _United States of Japan_, this is the story of a handful of people who will do anything to become mecha pilots. The characters are truly compelling, and the world Tieryas created is a joy to discover. And if you come for the giant robots, _Mecha Samurai Empire_ has all kinds and the best robot combat you'll ever read. Seriously, this is a whole new kind of badass."   —Sylvain Neuvel, author of _Only Human_

"Fascinating and entertaining, _Mecha Samurai Empire_ has a fabulous 'what if' premise that imagines an America controlled by Imperial Japan and Nazi Germany—and giant armored robots duking it out in arenas and on the battlefield. I caught myself thinking about the book long after I read it, and anxiously await the next installment."
—Taylor Anderson,
New York Times bestselling author of the Destroyermen series

Ace Books by Peter Tieryas

MECHA SAMURAI EMPIRE
CYBER SHOGUN REVOLUTION

CYBER SHOGUN REVOLUTION

★ ★ ★

PETER TIERYAS

ACE
NEW YORK

ACE

Published by Berkley

An imprint of Penguin Random House LLC

penguinrandomhouse.com

Copyright © 2020 by Peter Tieryas

Library of Congress Cataloging-in-Publication Data

Names: Tieryas, Peter, 1979– author.
Title: Cyber shogun revolution / Peter Tieryas.
Description: First edition. | New York: Ace, 2020. |
Series: A United States of Japan novel
Identifiers: LCCN 2019039582 (print) | LCCN 2019039583 (ebook) |
ISBN 9780451491015 (paperback) | ISBN 9780451491022 (ebook)
Subjects: GSAFD: Alternative histories (Fiction) | Suspense fiction.
Classification: LCC PS3612.I932 C93 2020 (print) |
LCC PS3612.I932 (ebook) | DDC 813/.6—dc23
LC record available at https://lccn.loc.gov/2019039582
LC ebook record available at https://lccn.loc.gov/2019039583

First Edition: March 2020

Printed in the United States of America
1   3   5   7   9   10   8   6   4   2

Cover art by John Liberto
Cover design by Adam Auerbach
Book design by Kristin del Rosario

This book is dedicated to Misa Morikawa,
super agent, who moves mechas and mountains alike

AUTHOR'S NOTE

CYBER SHOGUN REVOLUTION IS A STAND-ALONE BOOK SET IN 2019 OF THE *Mecha Samurai Empire* universe. There are new characters, new conflicts, and a whole new brew of mechas. You don't need to have read either *Mecha Samurai Empire* or *United States of Japan* to read this one, but you do need to know that the Axis forces won World War II back in the late 1940s and that the Nazis and the Japanese Empire divided America in half.

PART I

★

THE CONSPIRACY OF THE SONS OF WAR

REIKO MORIKAWA

★ ★ ★

TAIKO CITY
WINTER 2019

I.

REIKO MORIKAWA HATED THE RAIN. IT REMINDED HER OF COLD, DAMP nights full of regret. But she'd been ordered to Taiko City, once called Seattle by the old Americans, for an urgent meeting of the Sons of War.

Taiko City looked more dazzling on rainy nights. There were skyscrapers gleaming in vibrant neon, vying for attention with flashy brand logos. Advertisements that were the size of buildings flipped between new portical games, Queequegs Coffee, and various sushi chains that were expanding quickly thanks to breakthroughs in the farming of genetically modified super tuna. Many of the pedestrians were dressed in stylish storm kimonos, while others went for z-cloaks that could change optics to match a given season's fashion trends. Motorcycles zipped by in a frenetic dash, their lights echoing like trails from the past. Reiko spotted a patrol of two of the newer Anubis-class mechas that were designed to protect cities so that tragedies like the Kansas Massacre could never happen again. She'd lived through the massacre, barely surviving in her East Kansas apartment when the Nazis carried out their sneak attack on the city.

Reiko shuddered at the thought. She was glad to arrive early for her meeting with the Sons of War so she didn't have to dwell on memories of that day. She, like all the others, had to undergo a ritual cleansing. This meant a washing of hands and feet, then changing into new clothes that included a Noh mask wrapped tightly around her face. Audio recorders were built into each of the masks and acted as a voice recognition system designed to ensure the people behind the mask were who they said they were. If they weren't, tactile probes on the insides of each mask would become needles and kill the intruder instantly. The eye openings in the masks shut as the members were driven to a secret meeting place many kilometers away. Once they arrived, they had to go through another metal detector and be subjected to a full body search at their destination.

The corridors were lit by lanterns. The attendees were asked to take off their slippers when they got on the tatami mats and entered the main hall.

Reiko was one of the forty-seven present, all of whom were wearing Noh masks. The variety of traditional masks had expanded with the growth of the Empire, and the participants wore many types from different regions. The Sons of War usually met in groups of forty-seven, even though there were at least fifty times that number in total.

Reiko was wearing an *onna-men* mask, and she spotted several wearing the ghostly *onryos*. She knew one of them was her friend from her days at Berkeley Military Academy, Daniela Takemi. Daniela had been the one who'd recruited her to the Sons of War and her roommate when the Nazis had attacked Kansas.

"Nice mask," Daniela said.

Reiko replied, "You look very creepy in yours."

"We need all the ghosts we can get on our side," Daniela replied.

"So we can scare the crap out of our enemies?"

"Hopefully a lot more than just scaring."

Reiko's attention quickly went to the member who was wearing a George Washington face mask, white wig, and colonial hat. It was a strange choice considering that the leader of the Sons of War, General Noboru Yamaoka, had vanquished the GW threat over a decade ago in the Irvine Trap. Was there a special significance to its presence at this meeting? There very well could be, since pomp and drama were an important part of these ceremonies.

"Weird, right?" Daniela asked when she noticed the subject of Reiko's attention. "We should tar and feather them."

Reiko grimaced.

"Don't be so nervous," Daniela said. "We've been waiting a long time for tonight."

"I know," Reiko replied, then looked down at her artificial arm that was covered with genetically grown skin to appear mostly natural. She flexed her fingers and said, "It feels like it's been forever since Kansas."

"Forever and a half. But it'll be over soon."

Reiko wasn't so sure.

The meeting began with a hymn and prayer to Ieyasu, first shogun of the Tokugawa shogunate. The old military dictator had united Japan and brought peace to the main island after years of turmoil. He was the de facto ruler of Japan and made all the key decisions. General Yamaoka revered the old shogun, even painting the crest of the triple hollyhock (mon) for his personal mecha when he was promoted to general.

Even though General Yamaoka did not identify himself as such, everyone knew it was him when he spoke at the meeting. His booming voice, his stoic mask, and his impassioned pose left no doubt.

"We are patriots. We are here because we love our country. Our governor bribed his way into power by feeding lies to Tokyo Command. He has never served in the military. He is a liar, a conceited buffoon who has no regard for life. It is because of his lack of leadership that the Kansas Massacre was allowed to happen. And worse, in his attempt to save face, he tried to blame others, including our esteemed intelligence community. So many of our most respected colleagues were unceremoniously dismissed or forced to commit seppuku for sins they did not commit. Now we have incontrovertible proof that he is collaborating with the Nazis. The Nazis, our sworn enemies! We cannot leave the fate of our country in the hands of fools. We have taken an oath to each other to wrest control away from Tamura and establish a new government. Anything less, and we'd be shirking our responsibilities."

The general's voice was mesmerizing as he led them through the crimes committed by Governor Tamura, some minor, others sacrilegious, immoral, and inhuman. General Yamaoka named all the officials and soldiers the governor forced to kill themselves solely for political expediency. The general had firsthand experience of the governor's influence.

Shortly after the Kansas Massacre, Yamaoka had devised the plan to take over Texarkana Fortress in the German Americas. The campaign succeeded beyond the expectations of the political leadership. Yamaoka conquered Texarkana, smashed the infamous Hitler statue that was purportedly the third tallest structure in the German Americas, and broadcast his victory to the world. The Nazis had been helpless against the new Strand mechas that made mincemeat of their biomechs. But rather than follow up their victory with a march all the way to the East Coast, their governor,

Daigo Tamura, incited Tokyo Command to question Yamaoka's intentions. This had led to all sorts of political fallout.

"It's time for us to make our move," Yamaoka asserted. "We've prepared so long for this moment. The poor leadership of those in command has put everyone at risk. The Nazis will never know their place, and even now they're making preparations for a retaliatory excursion against our forces in the Quiet Border. We've tried rapprochement when I was forced to relinquish the eastern half of Texarkana Fortress. Command wants us to give up the western half too, but that's only convinced the Nazis that the Empire is weak. They weren't wrong. Our political leaders have made one mistake after another, starting with our losses in San Diego. No one survives an alliance with the Nazis. Not without the use of force. We will take control of our country before our so-called leaders throw it away."

Reiko knew the implications of what that meant thanks to the Kansas Massacre. The fact that General Yamaoka's attempt to avenge her compatriots had been stopped by Tamura still disgusted her, as did the revelation he'd been paid off by the Nazis. She trembled in rage just thinking about it.

"The commanders of eighteen of the outposts in the ninth section of the Quiet Border have all agreed to be part of the revolution," an officer confirmed.

"The fire chiefs at the thirteen local regions are ready for any contingency in case there's a mishap."

Thirty members went down the list, confirming all those who would take part in the revolution that would follow after the death of Governor Daigo Tamura.

General Yamaoka said, "From here, you will all go to your designated points. The penalty of failure will almost certainly be death for you and your family. But success means we save the country from itself."

"We won't fail!" someone yelled.

Yamaoka nodded, pleased by the boldness. "No, we won't. We have reason to believe security, while tough, will be vulnerable to a coordinated attack. Our inside contact on the governor's staff has given us the exact route with guard detail. For our own security purposes, you will only be informed of your part in the mission. All of your tasks, however trivial they may seem, will be of essence to the mission. For those taking on the brunt of the combat work, I bow in respect for what you are about to do. Though we have taken many precautions and the plan is sound, there is a chance you may not return. Know that you will forever be honored and spoken of with reverence among the Sons of War. I swear that your sacrifice will not be in vain," he said, and bowed.

The meeting ended. Daniela approached Reiko and said, "You have one of the toughest assignments tonight."

"I'll manage," Reiko replied.

"Good luck. Our future depends on you."

"No pressure."

"Does anything shake you?" Daniela asked.

"The chicken dancers at the Bertoli Discotheque," Reiko cheekily replied.

"I'll be sure to get us VIP seats after this is over."

Reiko went to her mecha, the *Inago*. It was a Katamari class, which was much smaller than the average mecha at about ten meters tall. It sacrificed bulk in exchange for increased agility and ease of control. Her piloting controls placed her inside a cube of gelatinous fluid called the Salamander. There, she could move without pain, despite the injuries she'd taken during the Kansas Massacre. The fluid held healing properties that eased her muscles and could actually sense what she intended to do. The Katamari could even be piloted without the use of her hands. She could use her feet, her eyes, her brows, and even her voice, though voice commands made most pilots hoarse in less than half an hour. Reiko piloted via a combination of her legs, eyes, and voice.

The Katamari had a capsule-like helmet and simplified green armor that used stealth optics to blend in with its background. Acoustic microphones, motion sensors, and a variety of other trackers gave Reiko optimal awareness of her environment. She was also given a Skaria Type-19 prototype electromagnetic gun that, when fired, could magnetize and control anything with metal. Another experimental device that she'd long advocated for, the directional plasma shield, made the Katamaris a fierce challenge for any opposing mecha. The shield used a projection of plasma to heat up the air in a given direction, which in turn would be controlled by a magnetic field. The dense heat would cause most projectiles to lose most of their force, or slow down to the point where they would be harmless against the *Inago*'s armor.

As Reiko piloted the *Inago* out of the warehouse, the night felt different. Rain always made the city scintillate. Each building seemed to be weeping.

She knew the details of her mission, as she'd been informed of them before the meeting. There was going to be a convoy of nine security cars with the governor. They were driving over the West Taiko Bridge, which was about eight hundred meters long. It was a cantilevered bridge, with minimal traffic in the evening. Reiko's task was to dismantle two of the security cars.

Her magnetic gun should be able to do that with ease. There were three other Katamaris, each with the same weapon. Reiko knew it was a smart decision to use the Katamaris, since they were part of the city defense and no one would bat an eye to see a group of them moving through the city together. Just in case, though, they'd received fake permits for sentry duty along the Spokane St. Viaduct which would pass basic scrutiny.

That's where she arrived at 20:13 p.m. The governor's convoy wasn't due for another forty minutes. Governor Tamura was stuck in a contentious meeting with city officials about the annual budget and one of their inside sources informed them that the meeting was running late.

Her team was using code names. The three other Katamaris with her were Gold, Blue, and Green. She herself was randomly named Red. They paired up and stationed themselves on opposite sides of the bridge. Green was her principal partner and he was meticulously going over their instructions on the encrypted channel. She recognized his voice as one of the officers who'd spoken during the public funeral after the Kansas Massacre.

"You there, Red?" Green asked.

"I am," Reiko answered.

The 3-D grid of the map visually splayed out on her goggles and she looked at the simulated routes of attack.

"You're from Berkeley, aren't you?" he asked.

"I was there a few years ago," she replied.

"I thought I recognized your voice. I used to serve in Mechtown."

"Same here."

"You were in Kansas during the attack?"

"I was," Reiko answered. "You?"

"I was showing my nephew around the mecha training camps in Kansas," Green said. "His dream was to become a pilot and I was giving him an early tour. We were on the freeway when the Nazi biomechs attacked and destroyed the road. I didn't even know what happened until I woke up in the hospital. They said his death was quick. I couldn't look my sister in the eye. She still hasn't spoken a word since his passing."

He became silent.

Reiko empathized with his pain.

"I used to be stationed in East Moscow," Gold said. "During the winters, it got so cold, the showers wouldn't work 'cause the pipes in our barracks would freeze. Nazis used to take their prisoners and line them up in weird poses along the wall and pour water over them. They'd freeze to death but stay in their strange poses for months. Sometimes they'd snipe at them and make their bodies shatter. I had a buddy who used to sneak over to the western side 'cause he had a girlfriend there. He got caught and the next time I saw him was on the wall with his girlfriend. They had contorted their bodies and shaped their corpses into a frozen heart . . ."

It was hard to imagine what life could be like in the western half of the Soviet Union, where non-Aryans were slaves, and even among pure Germans, a misspoken word would turn you into a political prisoner, subject to the whims of the Gestapo.

"I fought with the general when we took Texarkana Fortress," Blue stated. "We found an underground structure filled with prisoners. But they were more like walking corpses. You had to see the things the Nazis were doing, stitching people together and splicing them with animals. They forced them to breed and tortured the babies in front of their parents. I still have nightmares about what I saw. We didn't take Nazi prisoners. We killed every soldier we caught. We should have kept on going. Governor Tamura should never have stopped us."

Reiko could feel his burning rage, a sentiment many in the Sons of War shared. She knew it was her turn to share. But she didn't want to talk about her own experience as she remembered the Kansas Massacre.

She and Daniela had been transferred to East Kansas after her junior year in Berkeley to get some hands-on experiences along the Quiet Border. Reiko still remembered the moment when she heard the explosions outside her apartment. The whole half of the hallway in front of her blew up. She was knocked to the floor, hitting her back against the wall. Random clusters of debris surrounded her and smoke devoured all free space. She stumbled out of her room. A neighbor who she'd never spoken to was dead, the lower half of his body crushed by a slab of concrete. There was a sharp pain in Reiko's head and she felt something dripping down her cheeks. She tried to touch her face, but her right arm didn't move. She looked down and saw that her hand was covered in blood and the lower part of her arm had been smashed. There was a gasping sound back inside the room. Daniela was lying in a pool of her own blood, badly wounded. Reiko went to her and she was barely awake. "W-what happened?" Daniela asked.

"I don't know," Reiko answered.

"The—" Daniela started to say, but then passed out.

Reiko used all her strength to lift Daniela and put her arm around her shoulder. She stumbled toward the exit, dragging Daniela. Reiko noticed a gap in the wall and looked through it. Outside, there was a monstrosity like she'd never seen before, a black behemoth drowning in fluidic skin that appeared molten and alive. It was taller than any mecha she knew of and the vein-like strands on its surface were wiggling, even wrestling with their neighboring tubes. There were ebony wings that were throbbing in irregular pulses, scar-like fissures rippling across its surface.

"We should get going," Reiko said in the present, trying not to think about the attack.

No one pressed her.

Normally, there would be swarms of security, but officials who were part of the Sons of War had blocked off bridge traffic for the governor's route. Someone from the Sons of War had issued orders so that a police detachment under their command failed to show up. Another official had ordered an electrical blackout caused by an "accidental surge," meaning only emergency lights were being used for the bridge. This meant surveillance cameras in the area were also disabled. The strip of West Taiko City surrounding the bridge was barren of activity and the neighboring apartments had no electricity. Reiko did note there were seven inactive jeeps used by bridge maintenance workers that were parked at the base. Fortunately, they'd all been relieved of their duties for the evening.

As though the gods were with them, the rain cleared up. It was only a quarter moon, but it was bright, and everything seemed aligned in their favor.

"Wiggler on scans," Green said. Wiggler was their code name for the governor.

She visually checked the nine cars in total and replied, "Wiggler confirmed."

The Katamaris were to let the convoy get onto the bridge. About a hundred meters in, they'd commence their attack. According to the intelligence they'd received earlier, the governor's car was the third from the front.

The first car drove onto the bridge and as there was no traffic, they moved quickly. She aimed at her target, the seventh jeep.

"Commencing," she said, and used the magnetic gun to lock on.

There was a perfect sync and the car levitated under her direction. Even though she'd lifted hundreds of cars before, this one was different. Reiko raised the car up high and hesitated. Killing Nazis was one thing. But the occupants of this car were fellow soldiers doing their duty. Even if this was ultimately for the greater good and she'd been aware of what she'd have to do, because the fate of the people inside depended on her voice command, she struggled to give the order.

"Red," Green called.

Reiko released the trigger and tossed the car over the side of the bridge. Almost at the same time, three other security vehicles got the same treatment from the other Katamaris. She locked on to her next target and repeated the same action. She did not know if the personnel inside would survive, but she reminded herself they were doing their duty, just as she had.

The Katamaris all succeeded in the first phase.

She looked at the remaining armored car, which contained the governor. Reiko did not know who was assigned the task of killing him, but assumed it was one of the other Katamaris. Her job was complete. Just as she was about to make her exit, Gold contacted her.

"Something isn't right," he said.

"What's wrong?"

"My target's vehicle didn't register internal heat signatures."

Internal heat signatures would come from human bodies.

"It could be shielded," Blue said.

"I checked. There isn't anyone inside."

"What's that mean?"

But Reiko already knew. "Check the governor's car."

"You think—"

"I don't know."

Gold approached the governor's car and ran a thorough scan. "Empty according to this," he said. "Permission to confirm."

Reiko wasn't sure who he was asking, but she replied, "Granted."

Gold smashed the door off the side of the car and checked inside. "It's empty. The cars are being automatically driven."

"There was never anyone inside the convoy," Reiko replied.

"Why not?"

Reiko took a pained breath. "Because this is a trap," she said, wondering if their mission had already failed. The thought of Governor Tamura escaping vexed her.

On cue, a massive explosion followed and the blast swallowed Gold's Katamari. Reiko thought the governor's car had self-destructed. But her sensors set off an alarm and she spotted a dark mecha racing toward them. It targeted the remaining three Katamaris, which included her own.

Reiko recognized an Anubis class, with its black armored plating and its four arms rather than the traditional two. It was twice their size and held up a massive naginata. Designed for urban warfare, the Anubis was built to be swift and maneuverable. The corps had long planned to upgrade the older Guardian-class mechas. But after the biomechs smashed the Guardians in Kansas like they were cavalry against tanks, the development of the Anubis was expedited.

"I am Major Usagi Higa of the *Suzumebachi*. Identify yourselves," the Anubis pilot demanded.

"Stand down, Major," Green barked back.

"You've attacked the governor. The governor is a servant of the Emperor. Any action against the governor is an act of treason against the Empire."

"Our fight isn't with you, Major. If you stand down, we will not harm you."

In response, the Anubis fired three missiles, each intended for a Katamari. Blue triggered the magnetic gun to steer one of the missiles away. Another came directly at Reiko and she triggered her magnet, trying to use her weapon to steer the missile into the bay. Blue's missile didn't hit its intended prey but rather a piece of the bridge. The ground shook as a huge chunk fell out, causing Reiko's Katamari to stumble and foul her aim. Just as the missile intended for her was about to hit her, it instead flew straight up and around, blasting another segment of the bridge. Green had used his magnet to deflect the missile headed for Reiko, instead of the one aimed at him. With nothing to stop it, that missile smashed into his Katamari and exploded.

"Green!" she yelled. "Green! What's your condition?"

His face came up bloody.

"I'm alive."

The Anubis locked more missiles onto them. Reiko knew that her Katamari was designed as an anti-mecha unit—there was a reason mecha corps had invested a decade and billions of yen in the magnetic gun. Even then, considering the way the initial attack had taken place, she didn't know if they'd survive. In direct combat, the Anubis had too many advantages. But if they could use their environment strategically, there might be a chance. Reiko checked her surroundings. The *Suzumebachi* was too big to be moved by just one magnetic gun. It would take all three of them working in coordination to stand a chance. But before that, she composed an encrypted communication and sent a message to her contact at the Sons of War. "Mission failed. Trap. Governor is not in convoy. We are under attack."

Just then, the part of the bridge damaged by the missile collapsed, dropping fifty meters into the water. There was now a wide gap in the bridge that was too big to jump over.

She had an idea. To Green and Blue, she ordered, "Lock your magnets on the Anubis."

"What do you plan to do?"

"Toss it down that opening. Wait for me to distract it and magnetize on my signal."

She scanned the *Suzumebachi*, checking its customized parts to see if there was any section that might be more susceptible to an attack. Her sensors showed the bridge with its six crew members, sleeping quarters below that with capsule pods, the BP generator humming above, and missile launchers above the chest on the upper part of the *yoroi*. Reiko aimed at a maintenance jeep, lifted it up, and hurled it at the Anubis, smashing it into its flank. The damage was minimal, but Reiko had caught its attention. She raised another jeep and was about to throw it, but the Anubis sprinted toward it and destroyed it with its fist. It then launched itself at the *Inago*. Reiko raised her gun and targeted the naginata it wielded, pulling it the other way. The Anubis tried to hold on and got dragged away by its own exertion. Reiko drove the *Inago* closer to the *Suzumebachi* and raised her electromagnetic pulse to its highest level, pulling it toward her, then flipping polarities to cause a forceful repulse reaction. The *Suzumebachi* fell backward. Reiko opened the guns on her chest plate and let loose a barrage of armor-piercing bullets. Hundreds of them poured into the Anubis.

Major Higa sent her a communication. "What do you think you'll achieve by resisting? You've already failed. The governor knew about your attack and took a different route. More Anubises will be here to back me up."

Reiko knew better than to reply. Higa was buying time.

"I won't hold back any more," Higa said.

The *Suzumebachi* had fumes coming out of its armor, but its third arm popped out front. From its palm, a pole extruded out, then formed a circular shield to deflect the bullets. The Anubis put away its naginata and charged at the *Inago*. Reiko tried to withdraw, but the *Suzumebachi* was too fast, pouncing on her and attacking her with its three arms.

"Red!" Green yelled. "Do you need assistance?"

"Negative, stay put!" she ordered, even as the *Inago* was taking a beating.

The Anubis punched the left flank, then the right, doing an uppercut to her shoulder, and another series of rapid jabs to the *Inago*'s head.

Her portical screamed alarm signs. Auxiliaries were damaged and shielding was down to almost nothing. For a second, she felt dizzy from the battering. But the moment she was waiting for arrived when two punches came at the same time. Reiko quickly evaded backward, the two fists hitting each other. Just then, Reiko used her boosters to accelerate forward, take out her fusion dagger, and slash the wrists of both. One of the hands fell clear off. The second was damaged. The Anubis crashed straight into the *Inago*, knocking them to the ground. Reiko could tell the pilot was furious. Major Higa didn't know about the weak connections on the third and fourth hands. But Reiko did. She'd noticed a faulty lock on the mecha's wrist that would disrupt when hit at the right angle long ago when she worked at Mechtown—and cautioned her superiors about it. Without those two extra hands, it'd be hard for the *Suzumebachi* to deflect the magnet gun. It also had lost its shield.

Reiko sprayed her armor-piercing bullets again, which, at this close distance, had an even stronger impact. The *Suzumebachi* was forced back. It tried to attack again with a furious fist. Reiko projected her plasma shield, which caused a tremendous arc of heat around her. The Anubis was not prepared for the heat, causing its hands to malfunction even more.

"Now," she ordered Blue and Green.

They fired their electromagnetic guns and locked on to the *Suzumebachi*. They pulled and Reiko used her magnet gun to push. Between the three of them, Major Higa was completely helpless. They directed the *Suzumebachi*'s movement using the polarities, and without saying a word, knew the direction they wanted the Anubis to fall. It was almost pitiful to see the way the *Suzumebachi* was being dragged against its will. The Anubis tried to latch on to the ground, do anything it could to prevent itself from being thrown over. But with only two functional arms and the other two being busted, their combined magnetic force was too much for the Anubis.

They were able to drop the enemy mecha into the opening on the bridge. Its two arms grasped on to a rail. Reiko activated the magnetic beam to repulse the *Suzumebachi*, then heard a warning blip. The Anubis had fired eight missiles. Reiko intensified the beam, causing the *Suzumebachi* to drop off the bridge and into the water.

She turned her gun to the missiles, trying to deflect them. Blue was too slow to respond. His Katamari got hit multiple times in the chest. "Blue!" Reiko yelled. "Are you okay?" she asked.

The plating cracked open and the energy levels skyrocketed.

"I don't think so," Blue replied. "My BP generator is overloading."

"You need to eject."

"My ejection controls are broken," Blue said with a panicked voice. "I can't get—" An explosion cut off the communications and left only a husk.

"Dammit!" Reiko cursed as she swung her fists in the air.

Governor Tamura was probably gone, safely hiding, trying to determine who the conspirators were. More Anubises would be arriving soon as well. She checked the status of the other Katamari. Green was badly damaged and she wasn't sure if it could even move. She'd have to tow it. But what about the remains of the other two? Since their attempt had failed, leaving behind any remnants would lead to an investigation. She got her magnetic gun ready to dispose of the other two into the water, then contacted Green and ordered, "Flip open your wheels."

"What do you think you're doing, Red?"

"Towing you back."

Green chuckled. "You're going to tow me through the streets of Taiko City?"

"I am."

"I can't let you do that."

"Don't be silly," she replied. "I see tows all the time."

"Circumstances are different tonight. There's too much at stake."

"We can go back and regroup," Reiko stated.

"They can only regroup if there isn't anyone to hold them back."

"They're going to need as many people tonight as they can gather."

Green paused and took a long sniff. "I'm wounded."

"They have medics."

"Think this through, Red. Dragging me along will endanger the cause."

"The cause might be over tonight," Reiko stated angrily.

"Each of us knew what was at risk. Have faith."

"In what?" she asked. She hated that word.

"That the Sons of War will prevail."

"If they capture you here, they'll torture you," Reiko reminded him.

"Then I have to make sure they don't take me captive."

"That's why I'm taking you with me."

"I appreciate the thought, but I can't let you do that," Green firmly stated.

The communication cut out. Reiko tried to contact him, but he refused to answer.

Green's Katamari exploded.

At first, Reiko thought that the Anubis had somehow destroyed him from below, or that another Anubis was approaching. But her scans showed everything was clear.

Green had used the self-destruct.

She took a frustrated breath, upset at the waste of life. She honored the selflessness in his decision, but they could have found a way. She used her electromagnetic gun and pushed the three Katamaris into the water. Three lives gone, and for what? They'd failed. Did their families know? If not, they'd be finding out soon enough when the secret police, the Tokko, came to investigate them. If they didn't provide satisfactory answers (actually, even if they did), they'd be carted away.

Reiko raced back to their meeting point, wondering if imperial mechas would be there waiting to arrest her. If so, would she make Green's choice? There was no hope if she were imprisoned. The Tokko would torture her until she betrayed everyone around her. Reiko knew too much about their ways to believe she could actually resist. Would she fight anyone who tried to arrest her? If the plot of the Sons of War was uncovered, it would mean the governor's position would become even more solidified. The idea of leaving the country in the hands of a Nazi collaborator sickened her. Her only option was to see this through to the end. Fight until the governor was assassinated, or die trying. *Think, Reiko, think!* The rendezvous spot would most likely be compromised. Her only chance was to find out where the governor was.

But just as she was pondering her next steps, scans warned of multiple mechas approaching. She checked their signals. There were four mechas heading her way. They'd anticipated her. She knew she had little chance, but she had to fight. She checked her armaments. Armor-piercing shells were down to 58 percent and her magnet gun would need a recharge soon. She checked the surrounding environments to find the best place to defend herself.

"Power down your mecha," the opposing pilot ordered her.

"And if I say no?" Reiko asked.

"We will destroy you."

"You can try," Reiko replied.

Sixteen arms attacked her at once. They tore out huge chunks of her armor and destroyed her magnetic gun. Reiko checked the external scans and saw that her mecha would not survive another attack. She grinned defiantly and prepared the self-destruct.

"Once again, we will give you a chance to power down and—"

"Not happening." Reiko cut them off. The Anubises prepared to strike attack again. Reiko activated the self-destruct, but nothing happened. The circuitry must have been destroyed. "Dammit," she cursed.

She prepared herself to go down fighting when suddenly the Anubis across from her exploded. Reiko was confused until she spotted a new mecha approaching. It resembled a bipedal bug, lankier than the others, but had horns protruding from its face like a stag beetle. The segmented limbs gave it the ability to have a snake-like attack, with its arms moving similar to a whip. It was Daniela Takemi's mecha, *Stryder*.

"Reiko!" Daniela called on an encrypted line.

Reiko was stunned to see Daniela on her communicator. "What's going on?"

"I came as soon as I saw your message. Can you move?"

"Barely."

"Get yourself to a safe distance."

Reiko did her best.

The *Stryder* fired streams of boomerangs which weren't just the typical flat airfoils that would fly back to the thrower. Instead, after they reached their target, they exploded, causing a slicing line of fire to slash through her foes.

Major damage was inflicted on the Anubises, who fell into disarray. The *Stryder* sprinted toward them and used her boomerangs like daggers. Within seconds, Daniela had slashed through the combatants, sundering them into slices of mecha sashimi.

"I can't tell you how glad I am to see you," Reiko said. "I thought I was done."

"Not if I can help it," Daniela replied. "We're going to get through this."

"But we failed our mission."

"If we fail doing the right thing, it's not failure," Daniela replied firmly.

Reiko saw her tactical map light up. "There's some heavy fighting north of here."

"Can you move?"

"With auxiliary power. Give me a second to reroute the generators," Reiko said as she tried to get her Katamari moving again.

A minute later, they zipped past buildings and stores to reach a twisted freeway. A series of explosions set off just as they arrived. The fire became a mountain that towered over them.

"What the hell's going on?" Reiko asked as emergency alerts blared at her. Twelve Anubis mechas were approaching them.

"Looks like an ambush. The—wait . . . Someone's coming out from the fire."

A lone figure emerged from the destruction of the freeway wearing an armored suit and helmet. Whoever it was, they were holding a head.

Both Daniela and Reiko targeted their weapons on the individual when someone in the Anubis contacted them. It was Vice Minister Toyoda, second-in-command of the Sons of War. "Easy on the weapons. We've succeeded," he informed them.

"What do you mean, 'succeeded'?"

"After your report, we found where the governor really was. We dispatched our top agent to get him and as you can see, she's succeeded."

"Top agent?" Reiko asked as she looked back down at the agent.

"Her code name is Bloody Mary."

"The legendary Nazi killer is with us?" Daniela asked, impressed.

"She is."

Reiko had not known Bloody Mary was part of the Sons of War, even though it should not have been a surprise to learn it. Everyone knew the stories of how ruthless Bloody Mary was to the Nazis.

"What happened to the other pilots who were with you?" Toyoda asked.

Reiko shook her head, upset to know that Green had sacrificed himself in futility. There was no reason for his death, even though she was touched by his conviction and his willingness to sacrifice himself for the cause. "They were killed."

"That's unfortunate."

Daniela was more somber. "I'm very sorry."

"So am I," Reiko said.

Reiko wasn't sure if she felt relief or disappointment that the battle was over in this manner, but she was glad Daniela was there. Her eyes went back to Bloody Mary, who waited for Toyoda's Anubis to pick her up. Governor Tamura was dead thanks to her. But Reiko had an ominous feeling that something was wrong. She just had no idea what.

II.

"—HAVE DECIDED THAT GENERAL NOBORU YAMAOKA WILL BE THE NEW interim governor until further investigations can be carried out. In this turbulent time, we have faith that the general will lead the nation and determine who carried out this craven attack."

The press conference held by the prime minister had been playing on repeat over all the major portical channels for the past week, carefully monitored by the censorship office.

Governor Yamaoka carried out an investigation that led to evidence of the previous governor's collusion with the Nazis. This included private bank statements and tax reports that had, until now, all been hidden. There was a huge uproar among the public, shocked by the implications. At the same time, inexplicable acts began to make sense, like why the governor had ordered Yamaoka to cease his attack on Texarkana Fortress. The media was working around the clock to connect the dots, some true, some nebulous but within the realm of possibility, with "unnamed sources" providing tenuously plausible links. All of the governor's cronies were arrested. Reiko knew it would not take long for the Tokko to break them down. Reports were announced of a massive conspiracy by the former governor, who had received payment from the Nazis and worked with them to secure his position.

On the kikkai, orbits like SOCIAL were full of effusive praise for Governor Yamaoka, expressing joy and relief at his appointment. There was a clean sweep of the former government, and all the important positions were given to members of the Sons of War. Reiko was asked multiple times what type of role she would like. But even she wasn't sure.

The weeks were a busy blur for Reiko. She met thousands of officials and spent many of her evenings meeting new members of the Sons of War. It was common to see generals and officials from Tokyo Command visit. All of them had been caught off guard by the assassination, which was blamed on American terrorists.

She was relieved when Daniela invited her for a night out in Berkeley.

"I can't take any more meetings," Reiko said.

"Me neither," Daniela replied. "That's why I want to show you the new Cyber Bubble lounge."

"What's that?"

"You ever been to the moon?"

"Remember back at Berkeley, I got so drunk, I jumped in a swimming pool and swore I reached the moon when I swam into its reflection?" Reiko said.

"I remember we had to clean all five pools for a month after you threw up in them. I thought we were getting kicked out of Berkeley for sure."

"Oh yeah. Did I ever apologize for that?"

"No."

"Good," Reiko said with a laugh which made Daniela laugh as well.

The lounge was called Apocalypse Tomorrow. There were pods laid out like coffins in long rows. A pimply teenager with enormous goggles over his eyes asked them, "For two?"

"Yep."

They got into the pods and a gel filled the inside. All of a sudden Reiko was floating in outer space. It was cold and totally quiet. Daniela was next to her.

"This feels so real," Reiko said, but no sound came out.

Daniela adjusted the settings so they could hear each other.

"This is better than any virtual reality set I've seen," Reiko stated.

"Oh yeah, this puts it to shame. C'mon, race you down to the surface."

"How?"

"*Swim* toward the moon," Daniela teased.

They descended rapidly, but Daniela was faster than her. They jumped from crater to crater and marveled at the lunar topography. The Earth was beautiful from this distance.

"There's all sorts of other experiences we can do," Daniela said. "I love the moon and surfing the Banzai Pipeline in Oahu."

"Let's go surfing!"

AFTER THE CYBER BUBBLE, THE TWO WENT TO GRAB DRINKS ON TELE-graph.

"That was a trip," Reiko said. "How'd you find out about the place?"

"I go there often to relieve stress."

"Meetings stress you out that much?"

Daniela stared at her drink. "What do you think about all the changes Governor Yamaoka is implementing?"

"They're great. He's overturning Tamura's corruption and fixing a lot of the wrongs."

Daniela had a sad smile on her face. She was about to say something when they heard a jeering sound. Reiko looked out the window, wondering what it was. More than thirty people were being escorted by the police, handcuffed and walking in a shuffle. People were throwing food at them, mocking them.

"Who are they?" Reiko asked a waiter.

"Traitors from the old regime," he replied.

Reiko recognized the ex-mayor of Berkeley, who'd been convicted of mass tax fraud and bribery shortly after Yamaoka had taken over.

"Oh my god," Daniela said. "That's Watanabe-san."

"Who?" Reiko inquired.

"Pris Watanabe's dad."

"*General* Pris Watanabe?" Reiko clarified. The general was one of the top officers in the mecha corps.

"Yes. Don't you recognize him?"

Reiko had to look more carefully. He used to teach a class on logic at Berkeley and was one of their favorite professors.

Watanabe-san's face was badly bruised with sunken eyes and he was limping forward without saying a word. Someone slapped him hard in the face and another spat at him.

Reiko saw Daniela's frown and clenched fist, and could tell she was about to step out to fight the protesters. Reiko stopped her. She knew it wouldn't look good for Daniela to publicly defend a traitor, especially during this political climate.

"Let's get out of here," Reiko suggested.

Daniela looked like she was going to protest, but fortunately didn't.

They walked up Channing Way to an isolated spot. Daniela asked Reiko, "Why did you stop me?"

"You know why."

"This is a political arrest, since Watanabe-san didn't openly oppose Governor Tamura by joining the Sons of War."

"Maybe. But there must be a good reason for it," Reiko said, even though she wasn't sure if she believed it.

"To shore up power for Governor Yamaoka. You know how many people he's had arrested and executed?"

Reiko was alarmed by her tone. "I don't."

"Or you don't care," Daniela said. To Reiko's shame, she could not deny it. "This is not what I signed up for."

"Change takes time," Reiko said. "You told me that when you recruited me for the Sons of War."

"I'm wondering if that was a mistake."

"Don't be ridiculous." Reiko leaned in. "We did the right thing with Tamura. Now the old guard has to be pushed aside."

Daniela glared intently at a new mob that was passing down Telegraph. "Pushed aside is one thing. This circus is another. Watanabe was part of the mecha corps like us. He deserves better."

"You're right," Reiko stated, remembering how Watanabe incorporated philosophy and logic into mecha combat. "But getting out in front of that mob isn't the way to do it. Let's go through the right channels."

"You and your channels," Daniela said. "What happens when the channels break down?"

"We'll deal with it then."

"I hope so." Daniela sighed.

A FEW DAYS LATER, REIKO WAS SURPRISED WHEN SHE RECEIVED AN INVItation to meet the new governor in Los Angeles. She flew in from Berkeley and went to City Hall in downtown. Governor Yamaoka was in a meeting with a business council, ministers and representatives from Ordnance, Armaments, Economics, Production, Steel, Metalworks, Bradlium, Atomics, and more. Twenty-three men in suits left. She entered the governor's office.

"They're worried about the new five-year economic plan," Yamaoka said. "I needed to reassure them that things will move smoothly and their pockets aren't in danger of getting any lighter."

"Yes, sir."

"Greed can be a powerful tool to control an empire."

"Greed can destroy empires," Reiko pointed out. "Especially if the officials put their own self-interest above all else."

"Empires have hefty price tags to keep running. Sometimes a little greed is a price worth paying, at least in the interim."

"Understood, sir. I assume their oaths of loyalty to you are as unwavering as they were to the former governor?"

Governor Yamaoka laughed. "You have a sharp tongue."

"I've always been told it's dull and round. Though I do have a sharp bite."

"What would you do in my shoes?"

Reiko glanced at his shoes and said, "I'd buy cheaper, more comfortable ones than those. Italian leather is nice, but can wear down your toes."

He took off his shoes and tossed them in the trash can.

"Best piece of advice I've gotten all day," he declared. He sat back down and said, "I heard you were with Major Kinoshita in his last moments."

"I'm sorry, sir. I don't know a Major Kinoshita."

"I believe his code name was Green."

Reiko was startled that the governor was willing to talk openly about that night. "I don't know what you're referring to, sir, but I do associate the color green with tremendous honor and sacrifice."

The governor nodded. "That's good to know and I appreciate your discretion." From the way he expressed his approval, she wondered if he'd been testing her reaction. "I like you, Lieutenant Morikawa, and your service to the Empire is commendable. You'll be receiving an official promotion to the rank of captain, effective immediately. I also want to transfer you into the Education Department."

"Why, sir?"

"Cadets are the lifeline of the Empire. I believe our education system needs reform and I want you to work on changing the system to find better ways of nurturing talent, as well as finding it. I don't want to perpetuate a hereditary system that gives advantages to those who are already wealthy. I want to find the best potential cadets and I believe an officer with your sense of candor can make it happen."

"Understood, sir."

"Good. I have a meeting in five minutes, but travel the country and give me a plan with your recommendations on how to improve matters in, say, two weeks?"

It looked like the governor had concluded his business with her. But Reiko remembered her conversation with Daniela and knew she had more to discuss with him.

"Is there something else, Captain?" the governor, noticing her tarrying, inquired.

"Yes, sir," she said. "It's about some of the arrests that have been happening over the past month."

"What about them?"

"Some of those imprisoned were loyal citizens doing their duty. Even if they weren't fans of the late governor—"

"You don't need to say any more." He searched cautiously for his next words. "Let's just say some of the Sons of War have gotten carried away with their desire to purge the ranks. I assure you we're addressing the matter."

"Thank you, sir."

The captain bowed and exited.

Her first official duty after joining the Education Department was to attend a hanging. The previous minister of education was being executed for laundering funds and misusing her powers to help her friends earn money by exploiting students. Because of the minister's ignoble actions, she would not be allowed the honor of committing ritual suicide.

Reiko found a plausible excuse to skip the execution. She was too busy traveling, meeting with school administrators, principals, and teachers, trying to get a gauge on what steps they'd like to see implemented. Much of it came down to basics. Better pay for teachers and smaller numbers of students per classroom, a relationship that was connected to higher compensation that would attract more teachers. She was amused when she arrived at Yukichi Fukuzawa High School and was given a student parade with three hundred members. Their band was very good and played several popular songs to which the group had perfectly synchronized their march.

"Wait, is this for me?" she'd asked the principal.

"It's for you and the office you represent," she was told.

Everywhere she went, people prepared gifts with elaborate wrapping. She turned them all down, not wanting her decisions called into question. She also declined invitations for fancy dining and banquets in her honor, insisting that things were different with the old minister gone.

Her last stop on her itinerary was out in Dallas, where she had to visit two schools. It was the one-hundred-day mark since the assassination and there was going to be a meeting of the Sons of

War to celebrate their success. It was jokingly being called the "unmasking," as everyone would get to take off their disguise. Being in Dallas Tokai, she did not know most of the forty-six other members, though she knew Daniela was going to be present.

Daniela, who was wearing the same ghostly mask from before, asked in surprise, "What are you doing here?"

Reiko too wore the same mask, which was securely strapped to her face for the duration of the meeting. "A mission for the governor," she replied. "I talked to him briefly about what happened last time."

"What'd he say?"

"He'd look into it."

"Look into it?" Daniela stated skeptically.

"The Sons of War are a big group. Some of the members got carried away."

"And it cost people's lives," Daniela said.

Reiko, hearing Daniela raise her voice, whispered, "People lose lives in revolutions."

Daniela nodded. "Did you know four members of the corps were executed last week after being accused of treason?"

"I did not," Reiko said, as she'd been so busy with her duties.

"One of them was a student of mine," Daniela said. "Her crime was that she didn't bow to one of the ministers in the Sons of War. He interpreted that as treason."

"Really?"

"Yes, really. Let's go talk somewhere else."

"After the meeting."

"But we—"

The chimes rang and the meeting was beginning.

"Afterward," Reiko said.

There wasn't as much pomp for this particular Sons of War gathering. They lit candles to honor those who'd passed away. There was a minute of silence. One of the masked officers, whom Reiko assumed was a senior-ranking member, stood on the platform wearing the mask of an old man with enameled wrinkles. He welcomed everyone.

"We are aware of all the concerns. I've heard of the desire to accelerate the schedule. But we shouldn't be hasty, especially at this critical juncture. We've already attracted the attention of Tokyo Command to an unwanted degree. In order for us to be able to execute the whole plan seamlessly, we have to be extra cautious now and trust the governor."

"How long is enough preparation? If we wait too long, we risk losing everything we've fought for."

"If we move before we're ready, the revolution will be over before it begins."

Reiko listened as they discussed the general outlines of the strategy. She was aware that the reconstruction effort had multiple options that prepared for potential problems. Governor Yamaoka had pored over the mistakes of past revolutions that had failed.

"What about the rumors that someone has killed seven of our members?" someone asked.

That caused a sudden commotion as members were troubled by the idea that someone was targeting them. The uncharacteristic break in discipline and silence irritated the leader.

"We are investigating the matter, but have no reason to believe it had anything to do with the Sons of War. Almost everyone involved is part of the military, and our lives are continually at risk. We have increased security and are trying to determine who is behind it."

"Is it Tokyo Command?"

"Or the Nazis? They'll strike if they sense weakness."

"We've been closely monitoring the border. The Nazis are always on heightened alert, but we have no reason to believe they will attack until the dust settles. From what we've learned, they have major internal issues going on with Field Marshal Lanser, who is agitating for a shift in national policy."

But the questions wouldn't stop as the members wanted more details about the deaths.

Suddenly the member in the George Washington mask started laughing. It was an uncomfortably digitized laugh, sounding more like a hoarse robot than a human.

"What do you find so funny?" the senior official asked.

"All of you. Do these meetings make you feel better?" Washington asked. "Do they help to ease your conscience, knowing your scruples were satisfied?"

"You are out of line, sir."

"Am I?" the George Washington asked.

"Who are you?"

"Don't you recognize the killer you sent out? I'm the one who cleaned up after your plan flopped."

The senior official looked to the security guards. But they were nowhere to be seen. "You're Bloody Mary?"

"That's what some call me," she replied.

All masks turned in her direction.

Suddenly one of the men started screaming. It was an unnatural noise, aggravated by the sound of something happening to his flesh underneath the mask. Other officers began yelling in agony. It took a moment for Reiko to realize that the tactile defense mechanism had been reprogrammed and the needles had been activated, piercing the faces of those who wore them. One man was able to rip the mask off before he expired. His face was a gory pegboard. Most of the others simply fell down dead, their skulls and their faces crushed. Bloody Mary kicked someone in the face, smashing the mask in half. Behind the cracks was an army major Reiko recognized as being in charge of an important armament depot on the Quiet Border. His face had become a scarlet mess.

One of the members raced at Bloody Mary. He was very tall, muscular, and tried to punch Bloody Mary. She kicked him in the groin, took out a knife, and slashed his throat.

"The bigger they are, the bloodier they die," she said as blood sprayed out of him.

"You're supposed to be on our side!" a male voice yelled.

"Which side are you on?" she asked. "All these masks confuse me."

Reiko was surrounded by unmoving bodies. Why was she still alive? Reiko was able to take off her mask, which confused and relieved her. She felt stunned by the situation and instinctively searched for Daniela's wolf mask. It was nowhere in sight. Reiko's hands went for her gun. Unfortunately, she'd relinquished it earlier in the security check. Her breathing accelerated, but she reminded herself there was still her knife missile in her artificial arm. It was a safety measure she'd installed after Kansas as she never wanted to be caught off guard again. The knife missile was made out of organic polymers to blend with her flesh and even had blood circulating through it as camouflage. Reiko's fingers pressed against her artificial arm, which had a panel where the knife was stored.

Bloody Mary turned to her.

"I wouldn't do anything rash if I were you," she warned. "Do you know who I am?"

"The legendary Nazi killer."

"Then you know my rule."

"You always leave one survivor," Reiko said.

"It's your lucky day."

"You call this lucky?" Reiko shouted. "You killed the governor for us."

"Not for you or the Sons of War."

"Then who?"

She didn't answer.

"Why have you turned on us?" Reiko demanded.

"Because I tire of the same cycles. Governor Tamura is dead, Yamaoka takes his place. After Yamaoka is gone, it'll be another pompous buffoon. The powers that be remain the same."

"Governor Yamaoka is different."

Bloody Mary laughed and said, "From my vantage point, they're identical."

"What's your vantage point?"

"Executioner."

Reiko tore away the artificial skin from her arm and ripped two knives from her artificial elbow. The first, she wielded herself, while the second was the knife missile with a portical in it. It observed the trajectory of her eye, analyzed the fighting style of her opponent, and attacked automatically, trying to anticipate the attacks of the target. Drone-like, it was eight inches long and elongated to the length of her elbow.

Reiko attacked Bloody Mary, charging her and slashing with her knife.

Bloody Mary raised her arm and blocked, defending herself with her metal gauntlet. Reiko tried to kick Bloody Mary, but her foot collided with Bloody Mary's chest and made no impact. It was like hitting steel. Bloody Mary took out a knife of her own, a fat blade that looked greedy for flesh. She attacked back, a whirlwind of slashes that took all of Reiko's effort to avoid. The knife missile chose a terrible time to malfunction as it floated in place without moving and Bloody Mary destroyed it before focusing back on her. Reiko searched for an opening, any hint of vulnerability so she could rush in and thrust the knife into a weak spot. Bloody Mary appeared fully protected, but Reiko was certain there would be a point at her neck which she could penetrate. They exchanged knife blows, the smaller blade clashing against the bigger one. It irritated Reiko that Bloody Mary did not seem to be taking the fight seriously. Her movements were subdued, even as Reiko intensified her attacks. They went back and forth, attacking and retreating, avoiding the corpses on the ground.

"I told you I always leave one survivor," Bloody Mary suddenly said, then swung hard with her knife, sundering Reiko's knife in half.

Reiko hurtled what was left of her weapon at Bloody Mary's face. Bloody Mary raised her left arm to deflect it, and Reiko charged her, roundhousing her in the neck.

Again, Reiko's foot met solid armor and she stumbled back, her whole leg shaking from the impact. She felt something pierce her shoulder. She looked down and saw a dart sticking out of her.

"Have you ever killed anyone?" Bloody Mary asked.

"Of course I have," Reiko replied as she felt her muscles weakening. Her legs were wobbly and she could barely stand.

"Then you remember your first kill?"

"My first kill?"

It was eerie that Reiko could not see any emotion beyond the George Washington mask. "My first target was a bureaucrat, a portical pusher. They said he was a traitor, spying for the Nazis. I followed him for a week. Got to know everything about him, where he ate, who he talked to. He was a family man, devoted to his children and his wife. But times had been tough and they were heavily in debt. He passed on information to the German embassy every few months to help ends meet. Four of our operatives were killed because of it. After I confirmed his guilt, I forced him to write a suicide note and hung him from the side of a building. A public execution so that everyone could see. But he pleaded with me every step of the way, begged me to let him see his children one last time. I told him it was impossible. He pleaded to at least give them one last call."

"Did you let him?"

The George Washington face turned to stare at Reiko. "Would you want me to spare the traitor who betrayed your meeting?"

"Traitor?"

"One of your own betrayed you," Bloody Mary said.

Her mind went to Daniela, but Reiko could not believe she'd turn against them no matter what the circumstances. "Who is it?" Reiko asked as she fell to her knees.

"Does it matter?"

"You killed him?"

"Never trust a traitor," Bloody Mary stated.

"What do you think you are?" Reiko demanded, her accusation clear.

"Interesting question, considering you're all traitors."

"We fought to protect the country."

"You fought to secure power for yourselves. You killed just as many people, if not more, than Tamura did in his entire reign."

"That's not true."

"It is."

Reiko remembered Daniela's words, then wondered again where she was. "Do you have proof?"

"A stinking trail of corpses."

"You say that with so much glee," Reiko said in disgust.

"Glee?" Bloody Mary asked, puzzled by the term. "An exterminator doesn't feel anything killing thousands of roaches."

"Humans aren't roaches," Reiko stated.

"You say that with so much disdain," Bloody Mary said, mirroring Reiko's earlier words. "But roaches aren't bad." Bloody Mary pointed at the dart. "You'll start feeling dizzy soon. Don't fight it. It'll only make it worse when you wake up."

"Why even leave a survivor?"

"So that you can escape to tell them."

"Tell who what?" Reiko asked.

"That I will show everyone the hypocrisy of these Sons of War. My revolution won't be one of peace, but death."

"What revolution? Are you working for the Nazis?"

Bloody Mary shook her head. "I follow no man's order."

Reiko wanted to attack again. But she was feeling dizzy and before she could protest, she fell unconscious to the ground.

WHEN REIKO WOKE, SHE WAS LYING IN A HOSPITAL BED. GOVERNOR YA-maoka was sitting across from her. The governor was staring worriedly at her. She tried to get up to salute him, but he immediately shook his head and said, "At ease."

"Governor. Bloody Mary. She . . ."

Reiko explained everything and anger filled her at the memory of what had transpired. It was as though history had repeated from the Kansas Massacre and she was in a helpless situation yet again from forces outside of her control.

She suddenly remembered. "What happened to Daniela Takemi?"

"She was hiding outside the hall."

"So she's alive," Reiko said in relief.

"Alive, but with a lot of unanswered questions."

"What do you mean?" she asked. She had been confounded by security's failure to detect the intruder. The governor's tone insinuated there was more to Daniela's disappearance than just a bathroom stop.

"Right now, she's in a state of trauma. We're focused on her well-being."

"Was she somehow involved with the attack?"

"Probably not intentionally. But we're still trying to determine what happened."

"Will she be okay?"

"Yes. But leave her to us for now," the governor ordered firmly. She wanted to ask further, but realized from his tone it'd be better to wait. "The death of our compatriots is a terrible tragedy," he continued, and for a moment, she could hear the pain in his voice, but he suppressed it.

"I would like to have permission to help lead a force to capture Bloody Mary," she requested.

"We will deal with this Bloody Mary as soon as we can. But right now, we have to be prudent. I can't make a move because there is a bigger end goal in sight."

Reiko was taken off guard by his comment. "Sir?" she asked, partly to confirm she'd heard right.

"The Nazis are already starting to rebuild their Hitler statue at Texarkana Fortress. But this time, it's bigger. They're prepared for an attack. The political upheaval over the past few months means we need to be very careful about any missions involving Bloody Mary. We will exploit it to our advantage. But sometimes, the best way to kill an enemy is to sic another foe on it."

"What other foe?"

"Do you want to avenge your compatriots?"

She thought again of all the dead. "Yes, sir."

"As do I. But I need to know if someone is using Bloody Mary to attack us and if that's the case, determine who it is."

"I asked her directl—"

"And she'd have no cause to tell you the truth. Believe nothing she says. She's been trained to confound, deceive, and cause panic through lies."

"Yes, sir."

"I have a contact in the Tokko. Her name is Akiko Tsukino. I want you to reach out to her and inform her of the situation."

"The Tokko?"

"This is their jurisdiction, and they will be ruthless in their pursuit."

The strategy made sense. Set the Tokko up against Bloody Mary and wait on the sidelines. Again, it showed how General Yamaoka could dispassionately execute his plans without letting anything personal affect him. But she had her concerns. "Is the Tokko agent one of us?" Reiko asked.

"No. But that's exactly why I want you to work with her."

Reiko was alarmed. She'd dealt with the Tokko before. "Can she be trusted?"

"You can make the final determination. But the Tokko have proven very effective when deployed."

"Yes, sir. But they owe allegiance to no one and could easily turn against us if they found out more."

"That's why you will have to tread carefully. This situation falls under the Tokko's purview. They'll be very interested to know why Bloody Mary is targeting the Sons of War. Even without our involvement, the Tokko would be called in. If it's us inviting them in, we can at least try to steer the investigation."

"That makes sense, sir. But . . ."

The general stared at her. "I know of your past dealings with them. What happened to your parents was unfortunate.

She did her best not to show any emotions. "Yes, sir."

But she thought about Daniela's revelation that one of her students had been arrested for not bowing to an officer. Reiko's parents had been charged with sedition for petty charges and arrested by the Tokko. The memory still provoked anger and frustration.

"Agent Tsukino is a very different type of Tokko agent. I firmly believe that she will always act with integrity and not misuse her authority."

She still remembered the Tokko knocking on their front door.

She answered and one of their agents asked with a bright smile, "You're Reiko, right? Can you call your mom and dad?"

It was his smile that haunted her. It never occurred to her that they were there to cause her parents harm. She'd been fool enough to call her parents willingly. "I hope so, sir," Reiko said in the present, still full of regret that she hadn't warned her parents off.

The general stood up. "We will prepare ceremonies for the dead." He put his right hand around his wrist. "There were many officers killed tonight that I was counting on for the coming revolution. We will avenge them all. But we will also honor them by not compromising the greater plan. We will need to determine if there are more traitors among our ranks and change the nature of our meetings."

"How, sir?"

"More security, and perhaps smaller groups. We'll continue later. For now, focus on resting up."

He left.

As Reiko lay alone in bed, dissatisfied by the governor's reaction, she thought of Bloody Mary's parting question. Reiko's first kill happened while she was serving as a munitions officer in her senior year. They'd been tracking the illegal trafficking of black-market goods on the Quiet Border. It was the middle of the night and rain was showering down. Eighteen people were making an illegal crossing. She couldn't even see them without the thermal scanners as the rain was mucking up the sensors. Her commanding officer told her, "Fire."

She'd aimed, locked on, and pressed the trigger. Fourteen of the life signs ceased. She fired again. The remaining four followed. She didn't feel anything other than a surreal sense about the worthlessness of life. There was no sign from the heavens telling her she'd done right or wrong. Their lives ended, and for all purposes, no one gave a damn. Would anyone even miss them?

"Nice shot," was all she heard from her superior, an officer in his forties whose reaction to anyone trying to come over from the Quiet Border was to pulverize them. She had no idea if she'd done what was right. She hadn't even thought to question it in the moment.

At least Bloody Mary knew the man she killed. Reiko had no idea who any of the people she had killed were, and that made her shiver.

BISHOP WAKANA

★ ★ ★

WEST TEXARKANA FORTRESS
SPRING 2020

I.

"SINCERITY LABORATORY" WAS WHAT THE NAZIS CALLED IT. IT WAS A transient torture facility, designed to make any victim "sincere" in response to the interrogator's questions. Bishop Wakana was a relatively new member of the secret police, the Tokko. He'd joined a year ago and had been called in to investigate rumors of a warehouse on the outskirts of West Texarkana Fortress where people went in but never came back out.

Bishop tugged on his z-cloak, which was a 5.9 model and, in its current state, resembled a trench coat. Optical attributes on the clothing allowed him to switch its appearance, color, transparency, length, and even style, from retro to modern. The black coat worked well for him because it allowed him to wear anything underneath.

Bishop had long hair he tied into a ponytail. He was six feet tall, had a muscular frame and stiff shoulders that were used to marching and charging into the thick of things. His nose was round and bulging like a bulldog, though very little escaped the sharp peaks in his brows that focused his vision. He'd inherited his thick black hair from his Japanese father and his piercing brown eyes from his Chinese mother, and had grown up in Kauai speaking both languages at home.

"You find anything?" Bishop asked Yasu, the Tokko technician assigned for tonight's investigation. The Texarkana Police Force (TPF) was waiting outside to check the site, but the two of them had priority. Yasu always appeared disheveled, always wore a suit, and always stank of cigarettes.

"I'm tracking eighteen different types of DNA," Yasu replied. "But half of them have German blood in them."

Did that point to Nazis? Bishop wondered. At a minimum, eighteen people had been tortured here. Were they their own citizens, or members of the German Americas who had tried to defect? Nazis were even more ruthless to defectors than they were to foreign prisoners.

Bishop checked the sensor attachment on his portical for information on the warehouse and selected the "crime-scene" protocols. That meant the portical could start collecting data, running basic forensics, and snapping galleries of high-resolution images which it'd relay to the Tokko database. The records were transmitted directly to his contact lenses, so the feedback appeared in front of his eyes. There weren't any previous records available to them, as the data on German buildings in West Texarkana was incomplete. A cursory inspection with his own eyes showed a series of old conveyor belts, though most of it had been stripped away. Maybe it'd been a packaging company before? It was now an empty space, with spotlights above that'd been used to shine blinding circles on their victims during interrogations.

"How long since they evacuated?" Bishop asked.

"Hard to say without a body or two," Yasu replied.

They'd worked together three times in the past week, and Bishop noted that Yasu took a little too much joy determining how corpses had been turned into their inanimate state. Yasu was extrapolating the events that had taken place at the lab and describing the various methods of torture he detected, from laser scalpels to precision heat incinerators. Bishop wasn't surprised. Even in the Battle of Texarkana Fortress, regular bullets weren't enough for the Nazis. Their bullets delivered hallucinogenic toxins into a victim's blood that warped their minds into whirlpools of horror.

"Find anything useful yet?" Bishop asked.

"Nah, just the standard."

If it turned out to be Nazis, the usual consequence would be a complaint at the German embassy. To which the Nazis would complain something along the lines of, "Technically, West Texarkana Fortress belongs to us, so it's actually none of your business and outside of your jurisdiction, etc. etc." It was a legal rigmarole that made death less important than an irksome footnote no one wanted to deal with.

Bishop had a hard time believing this was all there was to the location. Sincerity Labs weren't this clean. There should be bodies somewhere, maybe on the periphery, buried underneath the fields. He checked outside the warehouse, but didn't find anything unusual except a group of crates. Something about them felt off. He used the extrapolation scanner on his portical. The crates were empty. Were they just for show? Or maybe to cover something up? He pushed them aside. There was a panel underneath, but no lock. Bishop lifted it up and saw stairs going down. He sent a note to Yasu, took out his Nambu heat pistol, turned on his portical's flashlight, and descended. There was an eerie blue light emanating from below. He moved slowly, had his portical check for heat signatures.

None were actively moving, but there was something human down there.

"I'm Bishop Wakana of the Tokko," he stated. "If you resist, I will fire."

In 99 percent of cases, the mention of Tokko broke all resistance. In the 1 percent that didn't, he'd have to fight his way through. What he didn't expect was silence. When he reached the bottom, he saw ten crates full of guns, which in themselves would have been alarming. But what really disturbed him were the four human-sized glass tubes filled with liquid and separated body parts. His muscles tensed and his face crunched up in disgust. Was this the work of the Nazi scientist he'd been tracking, Dr. Metzger? God-damn them. According to Tokko reports, the doctor had already killed a thousand people in his experiments in the German Amer-icas. Bishop felt sick inside, but he did his best to calm his nerves and focus on investigating what had transpired.

He winced when the eyes on the detached girl's head opened. "Can you hear me?" Bishop asked desperately.

But the girl blinked at him a few times before closing her eyes.

No matter how many times he saw the Nazi's handiwork, he had a hard time dealing with it, especially since this girl reminded him of his niece. He looked closer to make sure it wasn't her. It wasn't, but her presence still creeped him out.

Bishop rushed back upstairs and called Yasu, who followed him back down.

Yasu's eyes brightened at the sight.

"This looks like the work of Dr. Metzger," he confirmed.

"Why do you sound so excited?" Bishop asked, having the op-posite reaction.

"Because it's rare to find a treasure trove like this intact."

On the Tokko feed, Bishop read over Dr. Metzger's profile again.

He was a periodontist by trade, though his interest in human biology went beyond tooth structures and gums. Metzger's family came from a long line of American white supremacists. They'd initially welcomed the Nazis, believing they would help purge the other races. But like many, they were disillusioned to learn that the Nazis didn't believe all whites were equal and that German Aryans were of a superior breed. Born in Birmingham, Metzger was thirty-four years of age, and was reported to be involved with illegal arms dealing, providing weapons for insurgents within the USJ. The trafficking was what had put the periodontist into the purview of the Tokko. When Metzger killed one hundred twenty-three people in a biochemical experiment gone awry, he jumped up on the wanted list. But had Bishop stumbled on something bigger than his original case?

Yasu said, "I'm going to need some time with this."

"You want me to call for help?" Bishop asked.

"Hell no," Yasu snapped, indignant at the suggestion. "Just keep the TPF out."

Bishop would deal with the Texarkana Police Force later. He looked at the sundered body parts again, his eyes going to the young girl.

"Over fifty-six people," Yasu said.

"They're not alive, right?" he asked.

Yasu considered the question. "From a medical perspective, no. But from a biological point of view, it's possible their individual parts can be recycled for use."

"What's that mean?"

"It means more or less they're dead, but other humans can still use their limbs as body parts."

Fifty-six dead people. Bishop felt disgusted.

"I'm going to need more time to figure it out," Yasu continued. "But it's all wrapped under some seal called 'Ulfhednar.' Any idea what that might mean?"

Ulfhednar? Bishop shook his head, never having heard of it. "None."

"There's got to be information somewhere around here."

"What about the guns?" Bishop inquired.

"The shipment data says they were being smuggled to Nakajima Airport in Dallas. I'll send specifics to your portical as soon as I have them."

Bishop stared one last time at the bodies before checking the portical time for the next *Shinkansen* to Dallas Tokai. He could make the 16:00 bullet train if he hurried. The lead detective for the TPF was waiting above, and Bishop hoped she would not make too big a deal in a fight over jurisdiction.

BISHOP BARELY MADE IT IN TIME FOR THE TRAIN. AT THE TEXARKANA STA-tion, he boarded the *Shinkansen* using his badge, which gained him free entry on all transit. "Hand and Eye of the Police" was the text printed at the bottom of his badge in the elaborate merging of a visual eye and the Kanji to represent Tokko. He grabbed a seat and strapped on the belt as the train left. News channels on the train's portical display gave a roundup of the daily news, focusing on the tensions in the Quiet Border with the Nazis.

He used his portical to call his niece, Lena. Her mother, Maia, picked up, and Lena was next to her.

"Uncle Bishop!" Lena yelled. She was eight and had the same sharp brown eyes as his late younger brother. "Are you coming home?"

Bishop was elated to see her and tried to get the image of the girl from the lab out of his mind. "Not today," he replied.

"Will you come to my concert this weekend?"

"I'll try my best," Bishop replied. "You've been practicing your Kawada?"

"I can play it blindfolded!" she exclaimed. It was the way his brother had practiced on his violin, and when Bishop had mentioned it to her, she took it to heart and insisted on practicing in the same way. "Did you see the video I sent you?"

"Not yet, but I will," Bishop promised.

"I played perfect twice."

"She's been going to bed late because she's practicing so much," Maia cut in. "Speaking of which, something happened at Lena's school I need to talk to you about. The—"

But just as she was about to explain, Bishop received an emergency call from his boss.

"I have to go, but I'll call you back," he said, and ended the call abruptly.

He received the call from Colonel Akiko Tsukino of the Tokko. Ethnically, she was half-Korean, half-French, and one of the best agents in the thought police. She had lost both her arms to the George Washington terrorists and replaced them with bionic ones, which she used to hunt them down. The GWs called her the "Scourge," as she violently killed so many of them. It was hard to imagine her as a terrorist killer, as she was so cool and calculating in person. Then again, as a Tokko agent himself, he always had to hide who he really was.

"Once you arrive in Dallas, I want you to head to Governor Yamaoka's office," Akiko stated, getting straight to the point.

"The reason, ma'am?"

"Nakajima Airport is under army jurisdiction. Based on Yasu's report, they've uncovered several more shipments from Texarkana."

"That was fast."

"I want you to investigate the shipments, but the army also wants to have one of their representatives accompany you."

"Understood."

"Be careful in your dealings with the army."

"Be careful how?" Bishop asked.

"No matter how friendly or close they may seem, they have their own interests and objectives in mind."

"They want to kick Nazi ass too, don't they?"

"Their definition of kicking ass may diverge from your own," Akiko replied.

The communication ended.

He tried calling back his sister-in-law, but she didn't pick up. Bishop looked at the videos his niece had sent of her playing the violin blindfolded. Lena made several mistakes, but she persisted through to the end. There were more videos of her after her practice session, as she insisted on salted caramel cake and strawberry ice cream. He smiled, as his brother had a sweet tooth as well. While both were in the army, they'd promised each other that they'd one day start their own restaurant. Bishop would make the main courses, and his brother would pick the desserts.

As he was musing, a report came in from Yasu on his portical, comparing the lab victims with photos of all the people Metzger had killed when the biological chemicals he was experimenting with got out of control. The faces of the dead were ghastly, as their skin had decomposed and their muscles had contracted until they'd essentially imploded.

Bishop compiled a preliminary report about his findings for his boss. Hopefully, his superiors could make more sense of it. He'd been up for almost twenty-four hours, so he was tired and closed his eyes, hoping to catch a few minutes of sleep.

A memory attacked him. He breathed hard, trying not to let the feeling of constriction remind him of the past, the time the Nazis had him in chains, needles in his eyes, chemicals injected into his veins to keep him awake for a month without a second of sleep.

Bishop opened his eyes and looked out the window, unable to sleep, watching the crab mechas from RAMDET that protected transit from West Texarkana Fortress to Dallas Tokai. He went back to watching videos of his niece.

AT DALLAS, BISHOP GOT OFF THE BULLET TRAIN AT IDA TRAIN STATION AND headed for the subway.

Every citizen he passed had a profile he could access alongside a summation of their lives that blipped by. He got readouts on economic standings and recent health checks that collated with family history and social strata to determine where any subject would most likely end up and how they'd die. It fascinated him to learn that much of the information was volunteered by the individuals through a portical orbit called SOCIAL. Members posted pictures, thoughts, biographical information, personal beliefs, and could even send private messages that Tokko had access to (detailed filters and searches made it easy to find a subject's thoughts on any topic they'd discussed, and even deleted posts were accessible in a special category). He knew that the guy standing next to him reeking of alcohol and stinky tofu had been fighting with his wife every night for the past week over his baccarat addiction while ignoring his bloody stool caused by his hemorrhoids. The woman sitting across from him was being chased by debt collectors because she'd borrowed money from multiple loan sharks to pay for extra years of education and was suffering from a urinary tract infection which she couldn't afford to treat. A couple across from him was holding a shrieking baby. According to official records, this baby did not belong to them, nor were there any medical logs indicating the woman had been pregnant. There were no adoption papers either. In the past week, both had expressed admiration for old American ideals. He tagged them for the local police to check up on. The train stopped. Several hundred people got off and several hundred more got back on. Passengers were cramming into the Japan Rail Dallas

Tokai, and Bishop Wakana knew everything on file about them. After joining Tokko, he'd realized privacy no longer existed.

He wondered if it ever had.

The world was strange viewed through numbers and statistics. Everyone was open to him, except for other members of Tokko, certain government officials, and those provided special exemptions. Current military members displayed limited information, mostly public data about deployment status and history, rank, awards, etc. He'd always been careful with his portical transactions, to the point where he'd been accused of paranoia by the other members of his platoon. Now, being able to scan anyone's personal messages dating as far back as portical records were kept, he was glad he'd been so cautious.

Stuck between a thousand profiles, he felt compressed in both the physical space and the mental one. So many people were barely keeping afloat, living from paycheck to paycheck. He knew their problems (financial statements and medical history), their desires (portical search records), their friends and enemies (branching message links that showed a tree of their closest connections), and the anesthetic they used to dull the pain (game time, film habits, literary pursuits, and Cyber Bubble programs).

Something must have been faulty with the air conditioner because it was very hot. Bishop wiped away the sweat forming on his brow. His ears instinctively perked up when the automated voice came on and informed them in Japanese and English that they were arriving at his stop in downtown Dallas. He followed the endless blur of faces that vanished as quickly as they had been there.

There was a stretch of downtown on the east exit of the stop that many considered disreputable. Bishop saw tents for the homeless and groups of the poor huddling in doorstops of buildings destroyed by a Nazi attack over a year ago. Some of these people had profiles that registered on his portical, men and women who'd had middle-class lives but, through circumstance, lost everything.

A woman held up a sign that read "I'm a new mom and don't have enough to feed my son. Can you please spare some yen?"

On his portical view, he brought up an older image of the east exit before the Nazi attack. This used to be a nice part of town. That hollowed structure was once the site of his favorite curry pastrami sandwich shop. That series of columns leading nowhere used to be a hospital. Bishop flipped off the past images and made his way to his destination.

FOUR MECHAS WERE STATIONED NEAR CITY HALL, ON GUARD AGAINST ANY suspicious activity. Government officers and military personnel had the heaviest presence near the administrative buildings, many of which were undergoing reconstruction after Yamaoka's ascension. There were massive ads for Gen Igarashi's popular new art gallery, Tanaka-chan the Immortal Space Dog. There were also ubiquitous ads for the new condominiums that would be finished with construction in the next year and promised armored walls to protect against a Nazi attack.

Governor Yamaoka's Dallas office was full of gloriously old samurai armor. Bishop greeted the receptionist and said, "I'm supposed to meet someone from the office."

The receptionist checked her portical and replied, "You can wait in the seat. Someone will be with you shortly."

The chair looked like it had a huge cushion, but when he sat down, he found it hard and uncomfortable. He stood back up and went to look at the display with numerous awards and medals the governor had received.

"Bishop. It's been forever."

Bishop turned around and was surprised to see his former high school classmate, Reiko Morikawa. Her profile came up blank. Was she the army representative?

"Reiko?" he called, surprised by her presence. "I'm honored you remember me."

She laughed. "Don't be silly." Reiko had long hair that was so dark, the purple almost looked black. She wore a thin black coat that reached down to her knees.

They had been in the same homeroom and had often gotten into vocal debates about politics. They'd hung out on a class trip to Hokkaido and the main island, where Bishop had acted as culinary guide. Even back then, he had a passion for cooking exotic dishes and serving them up to his friends. Reiko had a discerning palate and often gave the best suggestions. Over the next few years, they'd sent each other messages and chatted from time to time over SOCIAL about food and restaurant recommendations before drifting apart.

"What are you doing here?" Bishop asked, wondering if Agent Tsukino had known they were acquainted.

"I used to be one of the general's adjutants," she replied. Which was one of the most prestigious positions to have and would explain why her profile was private. "I never thought of you as a Tokko agent."

"Me neither. You piloting mechas?"

"I have a Katamari. But I haven't been able to drive her as much as I'd like to have. I've been working with the governor to revamp the curriculum for mecha piloting. How are things in the Tokko?" Reiko asked.

"I'm waiting for them to lock me up and tell me it was all part of one of their tests, which I failed," Bishop confessed.

"I didn't know thought police could suffer imposter syndrome."

"It's why I'm so good at sniffing out imposters."

She grinned. "So how did you get into Tokko?"

"What do you mean?"

"In high school, I pictured you as a chef making weird sushi," Reiko explained.

"I made you some of my weird rolls, didn't I?"

"I never knew that fried chicken and tater tots worked so well with sushi rice and wasabi."

"If I remember correctly, the first thing you told me was that it looked awful," Bishop said.

"It did. But it was tasty."

"I have a secret ingredient that helps it blend together," Bishop explained.

"What secret ingredient?"

"I wouldn't be a good Tokko agent if I didn't keep my secrets."

"So you're not going to tell me how you got in?" Reiko asked.

"Let's just say my past service and sacrifice didn't go unnoticed."

Reiko grinned. "Fair enough. I read the reports Colonel Tsukino sent me. You think this Dr. Metzger is trafficking guns?"

Bishop nodded. "I'm hoping we can find proof of it with the shipment at Nakajima Airport."

"Let's go."

"Subway or taxi?"

Reiko shook her head. "Mecha."

BISHOP HAD NEVER BEEN IN A KATAMARI-CLASS MECHA. WHEN HE thought about it, he hadn't been in many of the newer mechas. These were smaller, more agile, and good for skipping traffic. The *Inago* had its wheels out and was zipping through the city on the rails.

Its bridge was smaller than he'd thought it was going to be from the outside. There was just enough space for Reiko's piloting seat, a navigator, and munitions. A door in the face allowed the *Inago* to connect with other mechas, and the emergency locker held two rocket packs. Bishop took the navigator's spot.

"You know how to use the navigation panel?" Reiko asked.

In the rocket pack legions, which were basically aerial infantry, he'd learned the basics of navigation. Everyone had to as an emergency backup in case of injuries to crew members.

He explained as much and added a caveat: "I'm rusty since it's been a few years, but it'll come back to me."

"Which mecha were you assigned to?" Reiko inquired.

"I was part of the Djangos which were deployed out of the *Syren*, piloted by Lieutenant Lina Niijima."

"She was two classes ahead of me, but a damn good pilot. You were in good hands."

"I don't know about that," Bishop replied.

"You didn't like her?"

"Not a matter of like or not. Her priority was to herself, not us."

"Should it have been you?"

Bishop shrugged. "We had different ideas of priorities," he snapped, angrier than he'd intended.

"Sorry, I don't mean to pry."

"No need to be sorry," Bishop said. He got back to the navigation console, trying to recall what did what.

"Don't push that," Reiko said when he was about to click a button.

"What's it do?"

"Self-destruct the mecha."

"Really?"

"With the wrong combination, yes."

Bishop moved his hand away. "You ever fight in this thing?"

"Only once in real combat."

"How'd it go?"

She looked disturbed by the question. "The *Inago* performed well, but there's a lot about her I've learned since then," she finally answered. "If we got into another scrap, we'd do much better."

"I could swear what that really means is 'not well.'"

Reiko laughed. "She's still in one piece and I'm still alive. I can't ask for more."

"True that."

From this height, he could see the skyscrapers of Dallas Tokai jutting like spikes in a toy capital. Life stumbled through its chaotic procession, and downtown had been undergoing a massive change in the infrastructure, a whole upper tier built in the past decade. The outer periphery was becoming more militarized in light of all the conflict in the Quiet Border. Nuclear bunkers were being constructed in major residential areas. The vault complexes were said to be elaborate and quite cushy, depending on the price range you went for.

Big ads with nationalistic slogans were everywhere, starkly painted in contrasting colors to delineate right and wrong. "Love the Emperor with All Your Heart and Mind." "When in Doubt, Report It." "Never Forget Kansas," which went hand in hand with "7.02.1996."

They arrived at Nakajima Airport in less than twenty minutes. There were two Anubis mechas on the periphery. A single Sentry-class mecha was near the rear, though it appeared inactive. After getting permission from security, they parked in the military section and climbed down the ladder to ground level (unlike the bigger mechas, there was no platform elevator on the Katamari in order to save space and energy). Several technicians met them below, asking Reiko if the *Inago* needed any maintenance.

Reiko stayed in her pilot suit as they went through the station, though she did change her shoes to something more comfortable. Bishop changed his z-cloak to a poncho and shorts.

"That's a weird combo," Reiko commented. "You still have thin ankles and oversized calves."

Bishop looked at Reiko, not sure how to reply as he'd never noticed that about himself.

"Just trying to blend in," he finally explained.

"By sticking out?"

Bishop changed to regular slacks and a coat.

"Better?" he asked.

"Don't be so sensitive," she said with a laugh.

An army official met them. "S9," Reiko addressed him. "Thanks for flagging this for us."

"You're the Tokko agent?" S9 asked Bishop, not overtly hostile, but not pleased to see him either. Many in the army considered Tokko the enemy.

"I am," Bishop affirmed. "What'd you find?"

"We found weapons inside a shipment that was supposed to be hundreds of stuffed guinea pigs being sent to a taxidermist."

"Can you show us?" Bishop asked.

"That's why I'm here."

Bishop checked S9's record and saw that he had a distant cousin who'd been arrested by the Tokko last year, interrogated over some statements against the Empire he'd made on a session of the game *Cat Odyssey*. He'd been cleared, but lost his job and became shunned by many of his social contacts in the process. No wonder S9 seemed unhappy.

Bishop dismissed all portical profiles throughout his trek. They were too distracting. There were intermittent reminders over the speakers to "report all suspicious behavior. Vigilance is the key to safety!" They walked past multiple terminals, and Reiko pointed at some of the airport art. "Those paintings are amazing. They're by my favorite artist, Rona L, so vivid and graphic."

Bishop recalled how Reiko had taken him to several art galleries in Kauai, explaining what made each artist unique. "I'll definitely look her up."

"Maybe it's better if thought police refrained from looking into specific artists."

"You have the wrong idea about Tokko."

"They arrested two of my favorite artists last year."

"For what?"

"Art against humanity."

At first, he thought she was joking, but then realized from her intent gesture that she wasn't. He'd have to look it up later. Or maybe Reiko would have preferred he didn't.

They entered a cargo hold. There were rows of crates, medium-sized Labor-class mechas helping move them. S9 led them to four crates filled with hundreds of guinea pigs.

Reiko looked inside, removed the guinea pigs, and loosened a hatch. There were guns. But there were also chips and machinery he could not identify.

"Where's this shipment headed?" Reiko asked S9.

"This was heading to Los Angeles. What is that?"

"This is a KLGOF-9921, an essential component for a mecha BP generator," Reiko replied. "Expensive, and difficult to access for non-military."

That surprised Bishop. "Why would Nazis be sending mecha parts here?"

"Good question," Reiko replied.

"Who checked it in?" Bishop asked S9.

"The manifest says it was a group called the Animal Rights Activists of Atlanta, represented by a Mr. Frank Lenthauser. We haven't detained him yet, per your request, Captain," he said to Reiko. "But we're keeping close tabs on him."

Just by his name, Bishop knew Lenthauser was from the German Americas. After the Pacific War, everyone in the Empire was required to take on a Japanese name to integrate them into the system (though most people had a nickname in their native country's language). In the Reich, people were required by law to keep their original family names to make certain their ethnicity was never mistaken and to keep them separate from the pure Aryans.

"Can you excuse us?" Reiko asked S9.

"If there's any business related to the cargo, I need to be informed."

"Understood," she replied.

S9 was unhappy about leaving, but Reiko insisted.

"What's the next step?" she asked.

"We seize it and send it in for forensics. They'll inform us about the contents. We'll interrogate this Mr. Lenthauser and get the information we need."

"Really?" Reiko questioned dubiously.

"What?"

"I doubt Lenthauser even knows what he's carrying," Reiko said. "I have a different proposal."

"Shoot."

"Take one of the chips for yourself, send it back to Tokko forensics. Let the rest go through. Follow Lenthauser until delivery in Los Angeles. Find whoever is on the other side and pick them up."

He liked the idea, but then thought of what Akiko might say. "I have to report this."

"Go ahead."

"Don't you need to get clearance?" Bishop inquired.

"I have full discretionary authority in this. If your boss says no, I'll manage on my own."

Bishop contacted Akiko and informed him of Reiko's plan.

"What are your thoughts on this?" she asked.

"I think it's worth the risk."

"This is an army plan. Leave it in their hands. Secure as many of the mecha components as you can, then report back to headquarters."

"But, ma'am, I think this is a solid lead. If I could be permitted to just go along—"

"If Metzger is there, the army will get him. If he's not, you'll have wasted your time."

"I really think this is—"

But the communication ended.

"Your masters won't let you go?" Reiko teased him.

"Another mission came up. I've got to investigate," he lied.

Reiko smiled. "So even Tokko have tight leashes."

"Are you enjoying this?"

"I actually am. Tokko usually lord it over everyone."

"I'm still considered a rookie." He looked at the cargo. "You going to be okay by yourself?"

"Who said I'm going by myself?"

They returned to her Katamari mecha. "It was good to see you again, even if it was only a short time," Reiko told him as she began climbing up the ladder.

"You too."

"After this blows over, let's grab a drink. If you're allowed, that is."

"I'm allowed," Bishop said.

After her mecha blasted away, he found himself troubled by something. He couldn't quite place it, but something about S9 bothered him. He placed a flag on S9's portical to monitor his communications, even with his portical off, and notify Bishop if he mentioned Dr. Metzger and 210 flagged terms. He then called the special military transit shuttle and headed back for Tokko's Dallas base with two of the chips.

II.

THE BASE WAS IN A NONDESCRIPT HANGAR NEXT TO AN ABANDONED AIR-field. There was almost nothing to indicate its position as the center of the Japanese secret police in Dallas Tokai. Underneath the airfield, the structure descended almost forty floors. The front door was the principal entrance, though there were five additional entrances that agents could use in a pinch. These were scattered throughout Dallas Tokai in underground tunnels that used the old sewer system.

Bishop entered the tinted doors that were adjacent to the main hangar. The lobby had a massive garden with indoor rivers and bridges which fronted as an imperial shrine in case of unexpected visitors. There were guns hidden next to the grafted plants and a variety of traps that could hold off enemies in case of an attack. It was rumored that the base even had defenses against aerial bombardment with a plasma field, similar to the liquid screenings he had to undergo after every field operation. The four receptionists ignored him, meaning they recognized him. The only time they'd spoken to him was the first time he'd arrived, and that was only to get a fresh fingerprint and retinal scan.

He walked into one of the four elevators and down a floor to the security gate. Unlike the garden above, the bare walls of the access hall were more reflective of Tokko's secretive nature. There was the standard entry for agents through security checks, and then the special entry for those returning from a field operation. He placed the mecha chips inside a separate container for evidence that was briskly taken away. He had to strip naked, fold up all his clothes, and put them through the screener. He himself walked through a curtain of blue liquid that was gelatinous. It checked for foreign organics in his body, detecting chemicals an X-ray or thermal scan could never spot. Once he went through, a heater evaporated the gel as though it had never been there. Since no alarm ensued, he had passed the screening. He dressed himself.

The internals of Tokko HQ were made up of thousands of corridors linking in a serpentine intestine. Agents had access only to what was necessary. Aside from the main cafeteria and training facilities, where all communications were monitored, it was possible to wander the base for hours without bumping into anyone. Everyone was holed away, investigating on their porticals (the internal systems were locked off from the public kikkai network) and collating data from the censors. Lights were tied to motion sensors so that many of the halls were dark until someone triggered the electricity. Unlike the army bases he'd served in, there were no trophies or past awards on display, no indications of what actually took place here. Plain corridors led into more corridors with offices and the occasional debriefing room that could hold groups of agents. Rarely were many assembled at the same time to limit contact. Office assignments were changed regularly, and there were many off-site locations scattered throughout the city, the majority of which only a few knew about.

He stopped by his own office first. It was two floors down in a small room unadorned like every other room. Bishop appreciated it because it gave him privacy, unlike his space in the army, which was an open floor where everyone could watch each other. His glass desk had three porticals on it. His entrance turned on the projectors, which created a visual map flashing in a circle. There were requests for paperwork from fifteen departments, and he knew more would be flooding in once his initial report about the mecha components made the rounds.

He headed to the cafeteria, which had its own staff of twenty-three. None of the cooking staff left the facility without authorization, and all the food was made on the grounds. To maintain the health of the Tokko, they used the freshest products and everything was organic, with little to no chemical supplements. Agents regularly underwent blood checks. In cases of health deficiencies, they were cooked special meals to compensate.

The café could serve several hundred people and was one of the starkest contrasts with the army. There, they served you processed chemicals that masqueraded as food. At Tokko, agents were too valuable to be fed dreck. The tables were spread Western style rather than Japanese, though there were private rooms that had shoji screen doors (with sonic-proof fittings of course). He ordered a spinach salad, no cheese or dressing, with tomatoes and celery on top. He ate quickly, but kept on wondering what bugged him so much about S9.

He met his boss at her office, which was even more bare bones than his. It was a year ago when he'd first met Akiko. His chief on the force had thrown him in the brig, as he'd gone after some Yakuza members despite their protected status with the police. When Akiko came to see him and showed her badge, he believed she was here for his head. When she mentioned recruiting him, he thought she was taunting him.

"You did apply to become a member, didn't you?" Akiko had confirmed.

"I did. But I wasn't expecting for it to be taken seriously."

"Why not?"

"Just in case you weren't aware, my father was executed for treason," Bishop explained. "He committed seppuku after a Kempei agent made a false accusation against him."

Agent Tsukino was unfazed. "I'm aware. I fought behind the scenes to overturn the false conviction."

It was a reply Bishop did not expect as he asked, "You did?"

"I served with your father. He was a mentor to me, so it was the least I could do."

Bishop was surprised, not just that they knew each other but that she would acknowledge it.

"He was exonerated of all wrongdoing," she pointed out.

"Outwardly," Bishop said. "But a lot of people still hold it against me."

"Much of that had to do with the fact that you fought so many of the ones who questioned you," Akiko pointed out.

"What would you do if someone called your father a traitor when he wasn't?"

"You think beating them will solve the problem?"

"No," Bishop replied. "But it makes me feel better."

"He was one of the most ethical officers I ever served with."

"I think that's the first kind thing anyone has ever said about him to me outside of my mother."

"He was grievously wronged," she said. "I would never hold that against you. But if you weren't expecting to get in, why did you bother to apply?"

"Because I hoped it would somehow help me find the agent who got my father killed."

"I see," Akiko replied.

"Do you know the officer who made the false accusation?" Bishop asked.

"I do," Akiko had replied.

"Is she still alive?"

"Why do you ask?"

"Because I've tried for over ten years to find out who it was, but I've never been able to."

"If she were alive, what would you do?" Akiko inquired.

"What do you think? I'd make sure my father got justice."

"If I gave you that information, what would you pay for it?"

"Whatever the price."

Akiko motioned the guard to release him. "Let's go meet her. I want to see what 'justice' means to you."

"Agent Wakana, are you there?" Akiko asked in the present, sitting behind her desk.

"Something about the shipment feels wrong," Bishop said.

"Can you be more specific?"

Bishop thought about it. "The timing is too convenient. And the way the cargo was being smuggled was sloppy."

"Have you considered the possibility it is a decoy intended to distract us from the real cargo?"

"You think it's a fake?"

"That's what I'm relying on you to tell me," she replied. "The initial report on the mecha chips you retrieved indicate they are old parts, intended to look more sophisticated than they are."

"Do they function?"

"Not on contemporary mechas."

Bishop said, "We need to tell Reiko in case there's a trap on the other side."

"The army can handle themselves. Our job is to track the real shipment."

"Where's that?"

"You should be telling me," Akiko said. "Do you have any suggestions on where we might look next?"

Bishop told her about his track on S9.

"Airport personnel should also be closely watched," Akiko said.

"I've already been tracking their past and current communications," Bishop replied. "Back when I was on the police force, the Yakuza bought off a lot of the officials to help them traffic contraband. There might be something worthwhile I can find out from my old contacts."

"Report back to me if you learn anything," Akiko stated.

Bishop bowed and left.

HE HAD CHOSEN TO STAY IN THE TOKKO DORMITORIES, BUT HE HAD A HARD time sleeping in the room. There was the smell of new carpet he couldn't get out of his nose. He got off his bed, did a hundred restless push-ups, took a hot shower, and lay back down. Exhaustion eventually overwhelmed anxiety, and he was able to sleep for six hours. He didn't remember his dreams.

In the morning, he watched his daily morning message from the Tokko that played automatically when he picked up his portical. It showed a series of graphic images of all those murdered the day before by enemies of the Empire, a reminder of how important their work was. There were only eight deaths yesterday, seven at the hands of the Nazis. As in all official Tokko messages, it ended with the symbol and their official motto, "Hand and Eye of the Police."

After Bishop brushed his teeth, he made an appointment with one of his top Yakuza contacts and headed out.

THERE WERE THREE MAJOR BLACK MARKETS IN THE EASTERN PART OF Dallas Tokai. Two were held inside defunct shopping malls. The third, and biggest, was inside the remains of an old American super-church that had been partially converted into the market called the Shichitaka.

The church in its heyday had multiple worship halls, hundreds of classrooms, four reflection centers, dormitories for proselytes, and open spaces that could be used for various religious festivals. It even had an underground facility for the hard-core, members who gave up contact with the outside world to surrender their lives in service of the pastor. All had been replaced by illegal vendors, some from the old Americas, many carrying contraband from the German Americas. There was a whole section devoted to Nazi junk food, from sausage-flavored marshmallows to fried-bear pizza chips. There was an illegal skin rejuvenation center that promised fresh-looking skin using military-grade lasers for patients with radiation damage, even though the treatments usually ended up doing more harm than good. An obnoxious loudmouth was asking people passing by, "Want to lose weight? Buy our robot parasites and you can hit your target weight in less than a month."

Whenever Bishop needed information about stolen goods, particularly items Nazis sought, he knew the Shichitaka was the best place to find it. The city police turned a blind eye to the illegal transactions thanks to copious bribes from the Yakuza, who ruled the place.

To blend in, he was dressed as a member of the Church of Narelle Z, the cultic mecha group who believed mechas were the embodiment of gods on Earth. The members wore silver robes and were known to be fanatically loyal. They also had a sizable branch inside the Shichitaka. His contact, Ichika, met him with the same silver robes on, and they sat in the pews. He handed her a portical with an anonymous credit account filled with yen, as was their usual arrangement.

Her rap sheet showed up on his portical view. Two arrests for assault, eight for beating up Yakuza members. There was also petty theft, burglary, extortion, and several scrolling lists that continued on until he switched them off.

"Been a while, Mr. Wakana," she said. "What brings you back to church?"

"Business."

"Thought you weren't a police officer no more."

"I'm a different kind of police now. How's business going for you?" Bishop asked, staring at the head of the big Sentry-class mecha on the front altar.

"Good. Some lady in East Texarkana wanted bondage baseball cards, so I took a whole set of the Minci edition over, and she paid very well."

Their normal exchange would go on for a bit as they talked about the lay of the land, but time was short and he wanted to get straight to the point. "Are any mecha parts being shipped over here from the Nazis?"

Her eyes narrowed and Bishop could see her become extra alert. "Usually, it's mecha parts being shipped from here to the German Americas," she said.

"That's not what I asked."

She brought her face closer to him. "I don't generally keep track of the cargo. Better for business if I don't. But two days ago, I saw some gigantic crates coming through Nakajima Airport."

"Do you know who's delivering it?"

"Beyond my pay grade, dude."

Bishop handed her another portical. Ichika was going to refuse it until Bishop signaled she take a look. She turned the portical on and whistled. "That's mighty generous. What kind of police are you now?"

"The kind that likes answers to their questions."

"It was the Yamamori clan that was handling it on this side."

Internally, he flinched at the mention of the Yamamori, but outwardly, he showed no expression.

"They're still pissed about what happened," Ichika reminded him.

"I know. You take care of yourself."

"Always do, Mr. Wakana. A few more payments like these, and I'll finally be able to leave this life behind."

Bishop did not reply. He was already heading to confront the Yamamori.

TWENTY YEARS AGO, ONE OF THE STREETS IN DALLAS TOKAI HAD BEEN rebuilt from the ground up to mimic parts of the Gion District from Kyoto. It was a haven for tourists and Yakuza alike. The touristy "maikos," or geishas in training, walked down the streets, thronged by excited travelers who snapped pictures on their porticals. But they were mainly for show, since all vestiges of geishas had long ago disappeared on this side of the Pacific Ocean. The modern-day geishas worked hostess clubs in much ritzier areas in the city, and their dances were much more exploitative. They also came in both genders. Most people never paid attention to the shadows. Bishop noticed the drug-addicted "dancers" shivering in the alleyways over their chemical condition and the "scouts" on the prowl for easy victims to set up for money scams.

The gyoza bar the Yamamori owned was his target. Even from outside, it smelled of pork, chives, and vinegar. As soon as he entered, the identity of the twenty-three patrons were recorded on his portical and collated against Tokko's list of suspected collaborators. The limited space was crowded, locals dropping off for a late-evening beer. They chose from one of twenty gyoza dishes they could order that included ginger, enokidake mushrooms, and green perilla. There was a familiarity between the patrons and two cooks, one of whom was an elderly woman with a bawdy mouth named Masako. Gyozas could be ordered fried, boiled, steamed, and even microwaved.

His target was a lieutenant of the Yamamori clan, Goro. Goro had shaved most of his head and had a red horn of hair he must have used an ungodly amount of gel on to keep upright. He wore a tank top and had animal tattoos all over his arm. He was helping Masako boil gyozas.

"I'm sorry, Officer," Masako said, her face turning cold at his entry. "We don't have any open spaces for the evening."

"I just need to speak with Goro."

"Goro is quite busy with hi—"

Bishop ignored her and approached Goro. Goro immediately grabbed a meat knife and held it up in a menacing manner.

"I should kill you for what you did to Eda!"

Bishop knew the Yamamori clan would never forgive him for the beating he inflicted on their leader's son. "Put the knife down so we can talk like—"

Goro didn't listen and instead tried to attack him. Bishop seized

Goro's left hand, then thrust it into the boiling oil in the deep fryer. Goro let out a scream, his entire arm sizzling. He struggled to break free, but Bishop overpowered him.

"I need to ask you some questions," Bishop said.

The customers were too shocked to protest, staring at them aghast.

Bishop lifted up his badge and said, "Tokko business. Get back to eating."

Goro was still howling when Bishop took his arm out from the oil. Much of his skin had melted, and it was a soggy mess that smelled of fried shrimp and burned flesh.

"When did you join the Tokko?" Masako asked.

Bishop didn't answer her and instead took Goro outside to a side alley.

"I'm sorry about the arm," Bishop apologized, as he genuinely felt bad. But he knew violence was the only thing these gangsters responded to. "But it's still salvageable with regenerative vats. Tell me what I want to know and you can save it. Don't, I'll shoot and you won't even have a stump left. Then I'll take you back inside and do the same to your right arm."

Goro told him everything about the mecha shipments, including the fact that Dr. Metzger would be aboard the plane that was picking the cargo up.

BISHOP TOOK A MILITARY TRANSIT BACK TO NAKAJIMA AIRPORT AND CON-tacted Akiko-san four times. There was no answer on any of his calls. He left a brief message recounting what he'd learned. His portical also had a match on the filters he'd placed on S9's communications, and it relayed an audio message to him that was recorded on an encrypted line.

"Why are you calling me on the portical?" an upset voice asked. Bishop's portical ID could not identify the subject.

"This is an encrypted line," S9 replied.

"You sure?"

"No way anyone can track these messages," S9 stated, unaware the Tokko had already broken the encryption.

"What do you want?"

"I gave the Tokko and army the fake parts you told me to, but once they figure out it's a trap, they'll be back."

"We know. We've already adjusted the plans for it."

"What do you mean?"

"We can talk, but not on a portical."

The communication ended at that point. It was confirmation for what Goro had told him. Bishop checked the time and realized he only had half an hour to intercept the Yakuza.

He called Reiko to warn her, as he felt the stakes were elevated, but her portical was off.

"Reiko. Bishop here," he said. "I've been following up some leads. Just wanted to give you a heads-up that the shipment you're tracking might be a fake. I'm at Nakajima Airport tracking additional mecha parts. I'll contact you again if I have more information."

When he got to the airport, he checked the GLS on his portical for the location Goro had pointed out. He ran as fast as he could, and his badge got him past most security doors. His destination was a private airfield on the south side of the airport. He contacted Akiko again, hoping for backup. He was transferred to an operator.

"Agent Wakana," the operator said. "Agent Tsukino is not available, but she asked me to relay a message. Do not engage with the Yamamori clan. Investigate cautiously, but withdraw at the first sign of danger."

"Tell Agent Tsukino that Dr. Metzger is going to be aboard that plane," Bishop stated, and disconnected.

He stepped out of the terminal, spotted a passenger shuttle. He overrode the controls using his Tokko authorization and drove straight toward the plane.

It wasn't far and Bishop spotted the jumbo cargo plane. There were forklifts and Labor mechas carrying massive crates aboard. Yakuza members with guns were standing guard. Bishop thought again of all the people who'd been killed by Dr. Metzger's experiments. He accelerated, intending on ramming into the plane. His shuttle slammed into four of the Yakuza. But just as it was about to crash into the plane, the shuttle came to an abrupt stop. From behind, a Labor mecha had grabbed the shuttle, preventing it from moving. One of the Yakuza tried to break into the shuttle. Bishop took out his pistol and fired at them. Suddenly there was a strong pounding, and he knew the Labor was attacking from above. The roof came crashing down, and the last thing he heard was S9 yelling, "That's the Tokko agent!"

III.

WHEN BISHOP WOKE, HE WAS ABOARD THE PLANE, TIED SECURELY TO A chair. There were eight Yakuza pointing rifles at his head. Two soldiers wearing swastika armbands were watching him. Nazis.

The plane's engine was a cacophonous buzz that drowned out most other noise. There were four military jeeps in the cargo compartment that smelled of gasoline, a form of fuel the Nazis still used. Multiple stacked crates were filled with contraband, though Bishop could only surmise what was inside. It was cold despite his z-cloak, and everyone present had gloves on. He felt queasy and there was a throbbing pain in his stomach. He didn't know what was causing it, but he took tabs on everyone present. There were two sealed hatches, and the windows had been removed and plugged. The only escape was the cargo doors, but he didn't spot any parachutes. There wasn't much to reassure Bishop of his chances for survival other than the fact that if the Nazis and Yakuza fired their guns inside the cargo hold, they risked depressurizing the plane and killing themselves too.

"He's up."

A blond German scientist approached, boyish, handsome, with square glasses.

Bishop recognized him as his target, Dr. Metzger. Now that he was closer, Bishop saw that the man was in his forties. Half his teeth were gold, and there was an arrogance in his impertinent stance that seemed vexed by everything around him. He had thick lips, and there was a port-wine stain that covered part of his left neck.

"How are you feeling?" Dr. Metzger asked.

"Peachy."

"How much does the Tokko know?"

"We know about your Sincerity Lab," Bishop said.

"My research there concluded and I left it months ago. What do you know about Operation Jiken?"

Bishop calculated what the best approach was. The best method was to keep the conversation going so he could better determine his options. "I have no idea what that is unless it has something to do with the Ulfhednar," Bishop stated honestly.

Dr. Metzger's eyes widened. "What do you know about the Ulfhednar?"

"Only that it has to do with your sick experiments cutting people up."

"I do tend to the sick. Even the Reich Command couldn't understand how important my research was. That's why instead of my own facility, I'm up here trying to earn money to finance my work. But if you're not here for Jiken and you don't know much about the Ulfhednar, why are you here?"

He preferred the blunt approach. "I was sent here to arrest you."

"Arrest me?" Dr. Metzger said. "You flatter me, Agent Wakana.

Perhaps you can tell us how you knew about my whereabouts in the first place?"

Since he'd told the truth before, he hoped a lie would pass muster. "We tracked your encrypted messages."

Metzger smiled condescendingly. "Bring them," he ordered.

Ichika and Goro were brought out and placed on their knees.

Metzger held up a gun that looked like it was made out of plastic and bones. "Bioorganic guns are the way of the future," he said. There was a tube that went through the entire frame of the gun and was filled with a blue liquid.

Ichika looked at Bishop. Her eyes were narrow beads, pulsing with fear. Goro looked resigned to his fate.

"They didn't tell me where you were," Bishop said. "You can check my portical. I'll show you the encryption break."

"It's touching that you care, but they knew better."

Ichika said to him, "I guess we can't ever leave this life."

"I'm sorry," Bishop said to her.

Metzger pulled the trigger twice, one for each victim. Rather than a chemical injection, there was a hissing sound, similar to a steaming plate hitting cold water. The projectiles hit Ichika and Goro in the neck, sizzled, and caused the veins in their faces to bulge, calcify, and increase in weight. Slowly, their cheeks caved in and their foreheads followed. Bishop forced himself to look at the cavity where Ichika's nose and mouth had been. Her skull was dissolving like an icicle in the Mojave.

Metzger pointed the gun at Bishop. "I'll be honest. The Yamamori clan has offered me a whole lot of yen if I deliver you to them alive. What'd you do to them?"

"Yamamori's son liked to torture people to death, and I knew no one on the force would do anything to stop him. So I made sure he could never do it again," Bishop replied.

Metzger clapped. "How brave of you. But I wonder how long

that bravery will last under my scalpel. Is there anything useful you can tell me that's worthwhile enough for me to keep you conscious? Or should we proceed to surgery?"

"Your shoelaces are untied," Bishop said.

"Excuse me?"

"Your shoelaces."

"You're a joker."

"I mean it."

Dr. Metzger looked down and saw that his right shoelace was untied. He signaled one of his underlings to tie it for him.

"You don't even know what awaits, do you?" Metzger said with a contemptuous laugh.

"Your scalpel?"

"A lot worse." Metzger raised his gun again, switched the dial, and asked, "Will you give me the access codes to your portical?"

"Sure," Bishop replied nonchalantly, which surprised Metzger. "But I should warn you, they change them every four hours."

"That's all I need."

The Yakuza guards loosened Bishop's bindings. Dr. Metzger handed him his own portical back. Bishop accessed the portical with his thumbprint. He directed the kikkai search to a private Tokko link and recited, *"Jigoku ni mo shiru bito."* It meant, "Even in hell old acquaintances are welcome."

"9355021351344." He confirmed the auditory password.

The portical's visual sphere changed to his private link with contact details in case he was in trouble. Access meant it would trigger alarms with Tokko, which was the plan. That also meant it would change to a masquerade orbit with false information about a variety of topics that would keep the perpetrator busy until other Tokko agents could track them. He didn't know if that would do him much good up here. Metzger looked at the portical, then at Bishop.

"You really let me in?"

"I did," Bishop replied. It was Tokko protocol to try to appease any captors and avoid torture if possible, since keeping his mind intact meant he could gather more intelligence.

"Access the files Tokko has on me."

Bishop complied and handed it to him.

Metzger seemed disturbed. "This profile photo is terrible. Can it be changed?"

"I'd have to file a request with IT," Bishop answered.

"There's so many inaccuracies here, it makes me look sloppy and inefficient. I was not responsible for the sewer contamination of Detroit," Metzger protested, sounding genuinely offended. "And I had nothing to do with those shitbergs either. Why isn't there anything about the Ulfhednar?"

Bishop was trying to see if there was any chance of escape now that his arms were free when suddenly, there was a huge explosion from the back of the cargo hold. The burst of heat was a warm welcome in the cold. There was a small fire, and part of the floor to the lower compartment had a hole. Bishop wondered what the hell was going on.

He turned to the guard closest to him and punched him in the jaw, felt a reverberation along his elbow. Had to be careful where to hit him in case he hurt his own hand in the process without gloves. As the fist connected and the man spun backward, Bishop felt his opponent's spit hit him on his cheek. A second Nazi tried to slash at him with a machete. Bishop kicked him in the groin, causing him to drop the weapon. He then backhanded him across the face and elbowed him in the nose. There was always something palpably personal striking someone flesh to flesh, and the moment of impact was communication at its most bare. Facial expressions always stuck with him, from the cleave of a flattened nose to the gape of a mouth being struck. Bishop picked up the machete and held it with both hands. Three more Nazis charged toward him. He slashed his machete across one's shoulder, wounding him. The next two he deflected with a kick and a slicing swing at one's leg, causing him to stumble. But then four others came up from behind and grabbed him, forcing him to drop his weapon. They began to punch him repeatedly. This only made Bishop angrier as he wrestled against them, raging and tossing them away.

He heard gunfire. Someone was firing at the Yakuza and Nazis. But who?

He turned and saw Metzger aiming his bioorganic gun at him. He was about to launch himself at the doctor when he felt something sharp prick his cheek. Suddenly it was as though his brain was being sucked into a drain, pain imploding to a single point of suction. Disoriented, he couldn't tell the floor from the ceiling, his fingers from his toes. He blinked and his eyelids weighed a ton, refusing to lift back up again, his corneas interminably long. Darkness was the Earth blinking, or was it the sun taking a bathroom break? Even gods used outhouses, no? He thought he'd fallen to the ground, but became convinced he was dropping from the sky.

WHICH TURNED OUT TO BE HIS PREDICAMENT WHEN HE WAS ABLE TO OPEN his eyes again. There was wind blowing in his face. He was being dragged to the aft cargo door. They were still twenty-nine thousand feet in the air, though the cargo plane was descending in a steep decline.

There was a woman next to him with an oxygen mask covering most of her face, goggles shielding her eyes from turbulence.

"W-who are you?" Bishop asked, not sure why he was still alive. "Where is everyone?"

"They're all dead," the woman answered.

Bishop still wasn't sure how he'd survived and asked, "How am I still alive?"

"I saved you with a counterinjection that reversed the bioweapon."

"T-thank you. Are you Tokko?"

She laughed.

Something about her was familiar.

"Where's Dr. Metzger?"

"He numbers among the dead," she replied.

Bishop spotted Metzger behind them, a knife in his neck.

The large crates he'd seen earlier were all gone now as well, replaced with mounds of dead Nazis and Yakuza. Several women in oxygen masks were removing the remaining cargo.

"You're Bloody Mary," Bishop said, recalling his torture at the hands of the Nazis and how he'd finally escaped. "This is the second time you've saved my life."

"You're a soldier who keeps his secrets, aren't you?"

Did she know what he'd endured for her back at Texarkana? "A soldier who can't keep a secret is no good to anyone," he replied.

"I agree. That's why you alone will escape to tell them."

"Tell them what?"

"That I see through their tricks and their schemes."

"Who?"

"The Sons of War and this foolish trap."

"I don't know who that is, but why would they want to trick you?"

"It's always for power. But they can't stave off the revolution." She looked at Bishop intently. "Do you remember your first kill?"

Bishop remembered the complete mess of a fight that led to his first kill.

"You do," she said. "That's good. Mine was a woman designated as number 489,003. How pathetic to not even deserve a name, just a random number out of hundreds of thousands. She was a Nazi spy working as a receptionist in a pharmaceutical company. I got to her while she was at home, sitting on the toilet. I still remember her expression. Shock, outrage that I was targeting her in the toilet.

I had a gun, but when I saw her, I hesitated. She knocked the gun out of my hand. We wrestled. I eventually used the electric toothbrush on the sink and shoved it down her throat, made sure she choked to death on it."

Bishop was repulsed at the thought, not even sure how that was possible, as it seemed a toothbrush would be too big to fit down someone's throat.

"When I reported back what I'd done," Bloody Mary continued, "my commanding officer reassured me by saying, 'At least she died with clean teeth.'"

Bishop thought of his first kill, a Nazi who'd ambushed him. He'd always believed killing a man would be easy, but it took forever when you used only your own hands. He still remembered the way the Nazi had struggled for life, how he kept on flailing about. Even as the breath was escaping him and his face turned dark red, he kept on fighting.

"You want me to tell them about your first kill?" Bishop asked.

"I want you to tell them it was me that killed all these Nazis and Yakuza." The woman lifted up a rocket pack. "There's your way out."

"What about you?" he asked.

"I'll be fine."

"Thanks for another save," he said.

"Consider it a gift from your acquaintance from hell," she replied, and flung the rocket pack overboard.

Bishop leaped out, searching for the rocket pack, which was already far below him. He angled himself into a dive pose. The clouds were unwelcoming, a forest of cumulonimbi in his way. There wasn't any way to die pleasantly from so far up. If he calculated even slightly wrong and overshot the rocket pack, no matter how much he could try to use air resistance, he'd have no chance.

The layer of clouds thinned as he dropped. His eyes hurt from the air pushing against his pupils. He'd never liked skydiving.

When the army ran drills with parachutes, most of his fellow soldiers were exuberant jumping out of a plane. He dreaded the unnecessary risk to his life. But the experience was invaluable, as it steeled his nerves in the present. They'd practiced scenarios like this, and he reminded himself that he was prepared for a hopeless plummet. His first priority was to relax his muscles, making his whole body limber like a cat so that he wouldn't lose control. Gravity was a current that couldn't be resisted. Using his hips, he was able to adjust his falling slope and control his angle. Being off by even one degree now meant a huge difference a few seconds later.

Bishop flattened his arms against his body, kept himself as straight as possible. He could see the rocket pack getting closer. Below was desert, a desolate plain of sand. The rocket pack had straps that were flapping haphazardly to either side, increasing his ratio for error and giving him a bigger target. He thought of Ichika's imploded face. He had to get back to HQ and report. Bishop extended his arm as the gap decreased. The turbojet cylinders were almost his.

There was a jarring blast behind him that hurtled him off course. It must have been the cargo plane, its demise protracted in a raucous din. He tumbled out of control. He instinctively tried to resist, correct his course through ballasts he didn't have without the ground to press against. His training came back to him; he had to let himself flow and channel the gravity through his bones. He forced a slow breath, counted to five. He fought to relax the strain in his toes and calves, used his hips to arch and ease his fall. Air resistance slowed the descent, and he tilted to the right to align himself with the rocket pack again. *You still have plenty of time*, he assured himself, even though a part of him knew he didn't.

The rocket pack came within reach again. He extended his arm, tried to grab it too quickly, which caused the strap to slip from his finger. He curved his hips again to decrease acceleration just enough for him to get closer to the rocket pack. The strap was within his grasp and he snatched it up, pulling it around his right arm. He had to be careful not to spin out of control as he equipped the rocket. Bishop pulled the left strap over his left arm and buckled the belt around his waist. He hadn't flown a rocket pack in years. But he remembered the switch for releasing the carbon-fiber wings which he could use for gliding. He had his fingers on the valve for the fuel, but didn't want to use it until he was in a better position, especially without a heat-resistant suit—the rocket packs were extremely hot when their engines were being fired.

Ahead, he saw the cargo plane dropping like an asteroid toward the mountain range, a trail of smoke billowing behind it.

He was in control of the wings, and it brought back memories of his service during the Texarkana Fortress Invasion. Bishop's commanding officers determined that rocket pack soldiers were the most efficient way to stem the tide of the Nazis' disposable soldiers charging at them (some of the more cynical soldiers noted it was also one of the cheapest).

Bishop had only one week of training. His superiors mainly wanted to make sure he could handle the G's and that he wasn't afraid of heights. With low-wage workers overseas mass-producing rocket packs, the army was throwing every aerial soldier they could at the front. Survival rates weren't high, and not just because they had no protection from the Nazis firing machine guns at them. The majority of soldiers were killed due to an equipment malfunction. The rocket packs were pieces of junk that could fail at any time.

This one at least felt sturdy and the parts didn't reek. Plus, he wasn't being shot at. He was planning his landing trajectory when a piece of debris from the cargo plane plummeted into his left wing, perforating it. He started spinning, and the force which overtook him made him feel like a dangling marionette. His instincts went back to a time when the same thing had happened to him in combat during Texarkana. *What did I do then?*

Bishop searched for and found the emergency parachute release, which would detach the rockets and allow him to descend safely. He had to level himself before he could release, but he didn't think about egress. Instead, he breathed deeply, closed his eyes, and basked in the idea that even if he died, at least it was an exhilarating death. A few gyrations later, the spinning wasn't as chaotic. He clicked the valve for the rocket pack, which, for a moment, straightened his drop, even if it burned his back. He knew he had to time this perfectly and waited for the spinning to become more subdued. Right when he felt he was curving into a straight descent, he shut off the engine valve, then pressed on the switch to detach the rockets and release the chute. The rockets ejected, and a parachute sprang up out of his back, pulling him upward. The torque in his shoulders caused pain, which was quickly replaced by the serenity that, short of another disaster, he would survive. He checked the sky for any other debris that might damage his parachute, but didn't see anything.

Questions started their inquisition. But he stopped them. He would deal with them once he returned to HQ. For now, he had to pray in gratitude that the gods had granted him another chance at life.

IV.

HE WAS AT THE HOSPITAL IN A REGENERATION VAT FOR HIS WOUNDS. A doctor told him he was going to be okay. One of the nurses asked, "Do you have any immediate family you'd like for us to contact? There wasn't anyone listed."

He thought of his sister-in-law and his niece, but did not want to trouble them. "I'm fine," Bishop replied.

But he didn't feel fine. He was still frazzled by how close he'd been to death.

He remembered that night all those years ago when his family had gotten the call that changed his life. Bishop and his brother were so proud that their father was a general and a war hero. General Wakana had been sent to Los Angeles to deal with the George Washington terrorist threat. Bishop's father even had three mecha under his command when he fought in Vietnam, which made Bishop the envy of all the students at school. But two days before the national holidays, his father had made an emergency call. It was on audio only, as visuals had been denied.

"I only have a few minutes to talk," General Wakana had said. "Where's your mother?"

"She's sleeping," Bishop replied.

"Wake her up. What about your brother?"

"He's staying over at a friend's house. What's going on, Dad?"

"I don't have much time. Get your mother. I need for both of you to hear this."

Their mother joined them.

"Are you still in Los Angeles?" she asked.

"I am. The Kempei officer in charge of the prison was a friend, and he let me make this last phone call. I've been falsely accused of crimes. But in exchange for my life, they won't pursue anything against you and will leave my benefits intact."

"Your life?"

"I've been sentenced to death."

Bishop had felt as though the ground had crumbled underneath him. How could his father, the famous general, be executed?

"For what?" his mother managed to ask.

"They say failure of security under my watch, incompetence, negligence, and a bunch of other crap. It's their excuse to get me out of the way."

"Why?"

"I've had issues with the Kempei since San Diego. One of their agents got upset with the way I handled a recent event. She was the one who brought the false charges against me."

"The army is going to let this go through?"

His father became silent as someone spoke to him. He sighed, then said, "I'm sorry, but I have to go. Bishop."

"Yes, Father."

"Take care of your mother and brother, as I won't be there any-more. Don't let anyone talk down to you. There's a chance they will smear my name. Know that I always acted with integrity and stuck to my convictions, even if it damned me. I won't apologize for being true to what I believed was right. Make sure you act the same way."

"I will."

His mother shook her head. "This is insane. I can't accept this."

"I have to go. I—I'm sorry. For everything."

"No, you can't go. Not like this."

The communication came to an abrupt end.

It was the last time he heard his father's voice. Next thing he knew, reports came out that his father had committed seppuku.

"What's on your mind?" a voice asked him from the present.

Bishop looked up and saw his boss, Akiko. "Ghosts."

She asked, "Dr. Metzger is dead?"

"Unless there's two of them," Bishop replied. He'd filled out a preliminary report, but knew he had to do a more extensive one later.

"Do you know why Bloody Mary chose to attack Dr. Metzger?"

"I don't know. But she seemed to think it was a trap by the Sons of War," Bishop replied.

"Were you able to determine where Bloody Mary went?"

"No idea."

"And the cargo you were tracking was gone when you woke?"

"That's right."

"Do you have any idea what Operation Jiken is?"

"Dr. Metzger mentioned it, but I didn't get specifics," Bishop answered. "Did you find anything useful in the plane?"

Akiko nodded. "The crash and fire had destroyed much, but some of the porticals, including Dr. Metzger's, were functional." She checked her portical again, then asked, "How are you feeling?"

"Reckless and stupid. I should have listened to your warning."

Akiko nodded. "But you resolved the case satisfactorily, and Metzger has been dealt with."

"Not me. Bloody Mary. Thank the Emperor the army sent her or I'd be dead."

"That's actually a matter I want to discuss with you."

Bishop noticed the slight shift in Agent Tsukino's voice, but couldn't identify what it signified. "Sure," he said. "What about it?"

"In your report, you expressed gratitude to the military for sending Bloody Mary to rescue you. But she is not part of the military any longer."

"Then who sent her?"

"I don't know. But we have reason to believe she has gone rogue."

"Bloody Mary couldn't have gone rogue," Bishop said, astounded. "I served with her and she hated the Nazis."

"It is possible that she could be directing her hate toward the Empire as well," Akiko stated. "Captain Reiko Morikawa is outside. She would like to talk."

Bishop was surprised that Reiko was here. "What's she want to talk about?"

"Several things, including some information we retrieved from Metzger's portical."

"What information?"

"We've learned Dr. Metzger received the mecha parts from a Nazi weapons manufacturer with the code name Cossack. Cossack has access to mechas that were destroyed on the German side and has been doing quite a bit of work re-creating our machines for the Nazis. We don't know who Metzger was planning on delivering the parts to, but perhaps Cossack does."

"Where is this Cossack?"

"On the German side of Texarkana. I'll let Captain Morikawa explain further."

Akiko messaged Reiko, who entered. She looked riled up.

"What's up?" Bishop asked.

"I read your report," Reiko said. "Why didn't you fire on Bloody Mary when you had the chance?"

"I didn't have a chance. But why would I fire on her? She was saving my ass from Metzger and the Yakuza, who wanted my ass dead."

"She's a ruthless traitor!" Reiko yelled.

Bishop was confused and looked to Akiko. "I don't know if she's gone rogue, but as far as I'm concerned, she saved me."

"Are you actually defending her?"

"Captain Morikawa," Agent Tsukino called. "Agent Wakana is not up to speed on all that has transpired." To Bishop, "What the captain hasn't told you is that Bloody Mary killed forty-five of our army officers last month and a dozen others in the past two days."

"Are you sure it was her?"

"I was there when she betrayed us," Reiko replied. "I was the only survivor, like you."

"Why would she do that?"

"Because she's turned against us," Reiko answered.

"That doesn't make any sense," Bishop replied. "She's been on our side as long as I was in the army."

"Not anymore. She's a murderer, and you let her go."

"I didn't know I was supposed to take her down. Remember, my job was tracking Metzger."

"Since you were both spared by Bloody Mary," Akiko began,

"and you have your unique history with her, you two should work together to find her."

Bishop shook his head and said to Reiko, "You got beef with her, that's on you. Like I said, she saved my life twice. I owe her."

"Then you're a collaborator and traitor too."

"Let's not be so binary."

"That's fresh coming from a Tokko agent."

Bishop was about to protest, but Akiko cut in. "You have a direct order from the highest echelons of the Tokko to assist Captain Morikawa. Usually, the German Americas are outside of our jurisdiction, but they have made an exception here."

"Why?"

"They believe your past history with her puts you in a position that will be advantageous in her pursuit."

"Why don't you send someone from special forces?" Bishop asked, as that made much more sense.

"We've already tried," Reiko said.

"And?"

"The forces we sent from the Sohei Ghost Legion have gone missing."

Those were the elite groups within the special forces, units that were the best of the best. "If the Sohei Ghost Legion failed, what makes you think we have a chance?"

"This is not about whether you have a chance or not," Akiko interjected. "These are your orders, Agent Wakana. You are to assist Captain Morikawa in apprehending the operative known as Bloody Mary. If you find you cannot peaceably arrest her, you are to execute her."

Bishop chuckled incredulously. "Execute Bloody Mary? I'll be lucky if I survive another meeting with her. This is suicide."

"I didn't realize you were such a coward," Reiko said.

"If I choose not to run into death incarnate, that makes me smart, not a coward."

"Captain Morikawa," Akiko called. "Will you please excuse us?"

Reiko was agitated, but she left.

Bishop stared at Akiko as he thought about the past few days. "This whole thing with Dr. Metzger. It wasn't really about him, was it? Y'all were after Bloody Mary and knew that Dr. Metzger's weapons would get Bloody Mary's interest."

"Not initially. But the case evolved. There is a belief that identifying who Cossack was sending those parts to will help us find Bloody Mary."

Bishop put his hands on his face and rubbed his cheeks. "Bloody Mary's a Nazi killer."

"Are you afraid of her?"

"Of course I'm afraid. But that's not what's holding me back. You know . . ." And the memory of the Nazis torturing him came back to him. "You've read my record. You know what I sacrificed for her . . . When I was up in the plane, Metzger and his goons were going to kill me. She saved my ass and now you're telling me to bring her in. This feels wrong in every way."

Agent Tsukino had an empathetic glint in her eyes, but that vanished and melted into a pained glower. "As a Tokko agent, you already know we must often compromise our personal values for the good of the country."

No matter how Bishop tried to spin it in his head, he couldn't justify going after her. But it's not like he could quit and become a private citizen, since the Tokko or Kempeitai would bust his ass for disobeying orders.

"You all realize I just fell out of a burning plane?"

"You're young."

"Can I have a day to rest up?"

"Our contact has set up a meeting with Cossack tonight at a public location in East Texarkana Fortress."

That meant on the Nazi side. "You want me to leave *now*?"

Agent Tsukino did not reply, meaning that was a yes.

"She called herself my acquaintance from hell."

"Most demons are fallen angels," Akiko noted.

"Angels don't generally leave heaven without a reason," Bishop stated.

"Unless they're forced to do so."

"Do you know why Bloody Mary targeted the officers she killed?"

"I would presume she believes she has just cause," Akiko replied.

"There's more to the story than Reiko's letting us know, isn't there?"

"Of course."

"Anything you'd care to share?" Bishop asked.

"I believe Captain Morikawa will brief you on pertinent information. But I will tell you, the captain is part of an organization that has now taken charge of the country."

"What organization?"

"The Sons of War. They are a group of patriots who believed the country was going in the wrong direction."

"Are you part of it?"

She shook her head. "I've sent you the Tokko file on the Sons of War. There's actually much more to it. But those parts were classified beyond my clearance level."

"What's that mean?"

"It means my warning to you from last time still stands."

Be careful in your dealings with the army, Akiko had told him.

Bishop knew he was pushing it, but he still wanted to make one last protest. "I really don't think I'm the right person for this job."

"I understand your concerns, Agent Wakana. I will assist you where I can. But for now, you have your orders."

He had no choice but to comply. "Yes, ma'am."

"Your father used to have a saying. A friend of a friend is my friend, the friend of my enemy is my enemy, and the enemy of my enemy is my friend. But sometimes, even your friends can be your enemies."

"I don't have any friends," Bishop replied.

"Good," Akiko answered.

BISHOP GOT CHANGED AND MET REIKO OUTSIDE.

"I'm sorry if I was harsh in there. It's been a rough couple of weeks," Reiko said. "I appreciated your warning about the shipment. We'd figured it out by then, but thanks for confirming it."

"Sure. Look, I didn't know Bloody Mary killed our officers. From my perspective, I was about to be killed. Then I woke up in a burning plane. She gave me a rocket pack, so I thought she was helping me out. I couldn't just turn on her and shoot her."

"I thought the Tokko knew everything."

"That's the image they like to present. But I'm not all-knowing," he told her. "So where we heading?"

Reiko turned around. "We have a train to catch. You ever been to a bear fight?"

"A what?"

REIKO MORIKAWA

★ ★ ★

QUIET BORDER

I.

THE KATAMARI MECHA *INAGO* WAS BEING TOWED BY THE *SHINKANSEN* through the Quiet Border from Dallas Tokai to Texarkana Fortress. Reiko Morikawa was inside the bridge with Bishop. Though the Katamari was on autopilot, she made sure to check scans for any issues.

Over at the navigation panel, Bishop was reading a report of his own, and it appeared to be about the Sons of War. Reiko understood the governor's desire to have the Tokko involved, but didn't like it. Even with Bishop, she couldn't tell whether his reluctance to kill Bloody Mary was really out of a sense of obligation or a hidden agenda the Tokko had.

"You going to tell me the real deal, or force me to read this whole report and figure it out on my own?" Bishop suddenly asked Reiko.

"What do you mean, 'real deal'?"

"Who really are the Sons of War?" he asked.

Reiko was not expecting the question, as she assumed Bishop would already know. "They are a group of officials dedicated to protecting the Empire from all its enemies."

"Are you part of the Sons of War?"

"I am."

"Really?" he asked.

"Why do you sound surprised?"

"I just figured, you know, the name 'Sons' and all."

"It's a general term that's not meant to specify gender. They couldn't be called the Children of War. And we choose members irrespective of ethnicity or gender."

"So why did you join them?"

Reiko turned to Bishop, wanting to understand why he was asking. "Because the country needed change, and the Sons of War were the only ones willing to take action," she said, being cautious in what she revealed.

"What kind of action?" Bishop asked.

"After Governor Tamura was killed, we stepped up to make sure the country didn't fall into chaos."

"Why would Bloody Mary want to kill your members?"

"That's what we need to figure out," Reiko replied.

"She thought the Sons of War were trying to trap her on board the cargo plane," Bishop pointed out. "Were they?"

"Not as far as I know. But they could have been."

"Is there anything one of them might have done that pissed her off?" Bishop asked.

"If she has grievances, she hasn't told us about them. But I don't believe there's a valid reason for her to attack."

Bishop shook his head. "I don't think she agrees."

"That's why we have to find her and question her."

"She doesn't strike me as the Q-and-A type."

"Isn't the Tokko's specialty making people talkative?"

"Someone like her won't ever let us take her alive. The Nazis have been after her for as long as I can remember, and they still haven't been able to get her. Besides, she let you live, right? Why didn't you kill her?"

"I tried."

"How'd that go?"

"I'm more prepared now and will do anything to stop her."

"Getting your revenge will take more than preparation," Bishop said.

"This isn't about revenge."

"It's not?"

"No," Reiko disagreed. "It's about stopping a killer."

"Y'all didn't seem to mind as long as it was Nazis she was killing."

Reiko wondered if Bishop really didn't know about Bloody Mary's involvement in the former governor's assassination. If that was the case, it meant the Tokko didn't know the details. Or was he just pretending not to know?

"The only good Nazi is a dead one," Reiko answered.

Bishop said, "They have a similar saying on their side. Just substitute 'Nazi' for a word that's derogatory about us."

"You've been to their side?"

"During Texarkana, we had the Nazis on the run," Bishop said. "It was so bad, lots of them forgot to take their shoes, and we'd find dead soldiers with their shoes missing 'cause the other Nazis were stealing them. If Governor Tamura hadn't stopped us, we would have kept on going."

Reiko heard the rancor in his voice. "I know it was tough for the soldiers."

"Tough, we can handle. The stuff we endured was beyond that. So many of our soldiers were killed. If we'd taken over more and kicked the Nazis off the continent, maybe their sacrifices would have meant something. But it's depressing thinking it was all for nothing, since we gave up half of Texarkana and command wanted to give up the western half too."

"Which branch did you serve in?"

"Army, rocket pack corps."

"For some reason, I thought you served as an army chef."

Bishop laughed. "If only I had, I'd probably be in a different place now."

"Where's that?"

"Still married, but with kids, running a restaurant," he answered, both sarcastic and plaintive.

"Sounds like you long for that life," Reiko said.

"It's stupid to long for a past you can't change."

"Even in high school, you wanted to run a restaurant with your brother, right?"

"I did. But my brother died outside of Texarkana," Bishop said.

"I'm sorry," Reiko said.

"Don't be. Didn't you tell me you wanted to be a mecha designer?"

"I became one," Reiko said.

"Job not for you?"

"Something like that," she replied, remaining intentionally vague.

"Is it a good or bad thing that it's years later and we're both where we were when we were eighteen-year-old kids?"

"Where's that?"

"Lost, not sure where we're going, hunting an elusive someone."

"Who was that elusive someone when we were eighteen?"

"Ourselves," Bishop answered.

Reiko shook her head, not liking the underlying assumption he'd made. "Bloody Mary is nothing like us."

IT WASN'T A LONG RIDE, AND AS THEY GOT CLOSER, REIKO RELAYED HER detach protocol via portical to the *Shinkansen*. They separated a minute later with the station in visual range. Her entry would be through the military gate connected with the USJ's main base. There was a direct road to East Texarkana that all military vehicles had to pass through for necessary authorization.

She was comforted by the familiarity of the controls. Much of it had become instinctual, so that she could adjust the mecha's route without consciously thinking about what she was doing. The gel within the Salamander kept piloting painless. She swerved around some debris by the tracks and checked the weather again.

Governor Yamaoka had been in charge of the armed forces at Texarkana until his promotion. His replacement was General Furuya, a man who was said to have wrestled eighteen Nazi soldiers to their deaths. The general was a loyal member of the Sons of War and had already cleared Reiko's entry.

West Texarkana Fortress stationed over fifty mechas, which was good from a security perspective but a nightmare for logistics. The fortress, having been German until the invasion, wasn't set up to support the maintenance requirements of such a high volume of mechas. That meant equipment was constantly being shipped in. As Reiko made her way through the base, she felt like she'd been here before even though she never had. It was because she'd studied the camp schematics back at Mechtown in Berkeley. Her design sensibilities came back to her as she observed the heavy construction going on for the new mecha facilities. Four massive domes hid several of their top secret prototype mechas. She felt two of them weren't aligned properly to take advantage of the geography and the solar energy they could harvest if they'd planned it slightly better.

Outside of them, multiple Anubis- and Leviathan-class mechas were still undergoing repairs. Jets and tiltrotor aircrafts were arriving and departing. Several officers who recognized the *Inago* sent their cursory greetings. She'd get back to them later.

"How long since you've been back?" Reiko asked Bishop.

"I've visited West Texarkana a few times over the past year, but not the base," Bishop said. "It's grown a lot since I was stationed here. I think almost three times its size. It was just tents and dirt back then."

"You miss it?"

"Miss? I guess you can get fond of even hell if you've been there long enough."

"The camp was that bad?"

"For the longest time, they didn't have bathrooms, and the Nazis had snipers who'd shoot people going to the outhouse in the middle of the night. If you woke up and had to pee, you were risking your life making that trip." Bishop pointed at all the Labor mechas doing construction work and asked, "I thought we were getting ready to withdraw?"

Reiko knew there was no way in the world their forces were going to leave voluntarily, agreement or not, a decision she wholeheartedly supported. "You'd have to ask USJ Command about that."

"You think they'll tell me?"

His question sounded so sincere, she had to look back at him to see if he was serious. "You're the Tokko agent. You tell me."

"I'll send them a portical message to ask."

Reiko noted wryly, "I'm sure they'll tell you their master plan."

"Would they tell you?" he asked.

"Only if they felt it necessary. Everything's on a need-to-know basis."

"I'm digging through Bloody Mary's files, but most of it's classified or doesn't officially exist."

She thought of asking the governor for his assistance. "I might be able to help with that after we get back from Texarkana."

"Ooh, you got that kind of pull?" Bishop asked.

"We'll find out."

They were halfway through the base when Bishop pointed at a mecha unlike any other, massive, bulky, and wielding a fusion sword that was almost the same size as its frame. "Which mecha is that?" he asked.

Reiko recognized it. "It's the *Zombie*, General Furuya's personal mecha."

"You think that sword's big enough?"

"I think in the original design, it was twenty-five percent bigger."

The general's adjutant contacted her with a text message and wrote, "Good luck with the investigation. Notify us if there's any trouble."

"What happens if there *is* trouble?" she replied.

"Return to our side of the border and we'll handle it."

"Thank you," Reiko wrote back, appreciating the support, but understanding its deeper import. As long as they were on the other side of the border, the general could not come to their aid.

They exited the base and went down the road that connected to the Nazi side. As they got closer, the wall loomed above them. The Nazis were building additional layers on top to make it taller. There were multiple prisoners hanging off the side of the wall with hooks in them, still alive, trying their best to ward off flies and ravens.

She'd seen the intelligence reports that the Nazis were working on a new Hitler statue to replace the old one their mechas had smashed. They hoped to make this one even taller, as the original statue had been smashed to pieces by mecha fists.

Three biomechs moved toward them. They were each around ninety meters tall and covered in the regenerative skin that resembled oil being melted in a cauldron.

"No matter how many goddamn times I see them, they always seem uglier," Bishop said.

Reiko checked the biomechs on their scans. They looked different from the ones from Kansas. These had more musculature, as well as more of an anthropomorphic appearance. Ever since the Leviathan classes were able to defeat the biomechs, the Nazis began to incorporate imperial technology. While these biomechs had the tumor-mutated flesh, they also had armor plating on their chests, legs, and arms to better shield them. The swastikas on their armor were colored red.

"This is Captain Reiko Morikawa," she said over the communicator, audio only. The governor's office had arranged authorization through their ambassador, who resided in East Texarkana. Arrangements like this weren't uncommon, but they'd be watched everywhere they went. "I'm sending over proper visa documents for myself and Bishop Wakana."

"Do you have any cargo?"

"Just a box full of paintings."

One of the biomechs stepped closer.

"You okay?" Bishop asked.

"Why?" Reiko asked back.

"You're shaking."

"It's the seat," she replied, doing her best not to follow her instincts and fire.

"Is Bishop Wakana a military officer?" the biomech pilot asked.

"Negative. He is a retired army officer," she lied, providing the cover story they'd arranged for him.

"State the purpose of your visit," the pilot ordered.

"We're going to watch a bear fight with an acquaintance."

"Is that the sole purpose of your visit?" he demanded.

"Yes," she said, even though she was thinking, *And if it's not?*

I've already gotten permission. Get out of my way and stop wasting my time.

"Don't step out of line, especially driving that small garbage collector," the biomech threatened her as he ended the call.

"This garbage collector is good at taking out Nazi trash," Reiko said, though the Nazis couldn't hear her.

As they went through the gate, the biomechs watched them all the way through.

She knew her Katamari wouldn't be able to handle a biomech, but she still would not walk away from a fight if challenged. Reiko thought back to Kansas all those years ago. She couldn't believe she was inside the German Americas.

The initial area around East Texarkana Fortress was mostly in ruins. There were cages, tanks, soldiers, and biomechs she spotted on guard. She spotted two men fighting over a piece of bread. Her auto magnification indicated the bread was rotten with maggots.

"Have you been to East Texarkana before?" Reiko asked.

Bishop shook his head. "We went straight from the base to the battlefield." Bishop looked toward the eastern part of the city. "I've always wondered what Texarkana used to be like when the Americans were in charge."

"It was smaller. The Nazis expanded it, and it grew after it became a border town."

"I mean the actual living conditions."

"Everything was great as long as you were rich," Reiko stated.

The coliseum was not far and was one of the few sites undamaged during the invasion, primarily because General Yamaoka had spared it. Unlike Dallas Tokai, which was full of modern buildings and skyscrapers, East Texarkana looked like a city from antiquity. Houses, farms, and military factories were mostly what she saw.

"Is that all smog?" Bishop asked.

The dense pollution around them appeared to be coming from the factories pumping out gas. "They still use fossil fuels for energy."

"How quaint," Bishop commented. "Who are we meeting here?"

"One of our agents, Rudo. He's arranged a meeting with Cossack. We're hoping she'll be willing to part with information about the buyer."

"In exchange for what?" Bishop asked.

"That's what we'll find out. Since we're only asking her to identify one of our citizens, we hope she'll be amenable at the right price."

"Unless there happens to be Nazis hiding in our country she's delivering them to."

"We'll get the information one way or another," Reiko stated firmly.

Bishop caught the intentness of her voice, but did not probe. Instead, he asked, "Rudo's army intelligence?"

"He is, though he actually used to be part of Tokko," Reiko said.

"Used to be?"

"He was fired."

"For what?" Bishop asked.

"Misuse of intelligence from his portical reports. He was censured and relieved of his duties. The army was all too glad to pick up his tab. He provides the best intel on the Nazis. But he's addicted to gambling. We're keeping a close eye on him in case his need for money gets the better of him and the Nazis tempt him with a bigger pot of cash."

"Thanks for sharing that."

"Sure. Anything about the case you'd care to share?"

"If I do, I'll let you know," Bishop replied.

"Does your portical scan tell you everything about me?" Reiko asked, genuinely curious what her report would say.

"Not everything. Most important government officials and current military are exempt."

"You wouldn't lie to me about that, would you?"

"Why would I lie?" Bishop asked back.

She was going to ask if he was being rhetorical, but thought better of it. "It can tell you about other people?"

"Depends, but yeah."

Reiko had something on her mind. "There's a friend I've been looking for, Daniela Takemi. She's been missing for a few months. Is there any way you could check on her whereabouts?"

Bishop shook his head and stated, "I don't do personal searches unless they're related to the mission."

"Even if you just told me she was okay," Reiko continued, "I'd be fine with that. I've tried asking everywhere, but no one will tell me."

"I can't help you even if I wanted to," Bishop said.

"Because of your Tokko ethics?"

"No, because my portical isn't working. I don't think I have a connection."

Reiko checked her portical too. "That's because your kikkai connection is disrupted."

"We're not that far from the border."

"I know. But Nazis have disruptors everywhere."

They arrived at the coliseum and parked a few kilometers away at the request of security. Reiko emerged from the Salamander, her suit immediately drying. She put on a jacket and cargo pants over the suit, then got her utility belt ready and checked her equipment. The belt had gotten heavier over the years, but she found most of the gear essential. This included upgrades for her portical that could extend scanning range and provide a bright light in dark spots, and a grappling hook she used in case she had to get back into the *Inago* as soon as possible.

"What's all that for?" Bishop asked.

"They're accessories I take with me on all my missions."

"You mean like a toothbrush?"

"Toothbrush along with my blow dryer and lipstick," Reiko sarcastically replied.

"Just asking."

"You armed?"

"Of course." Bishop raised his Nambu heat pistol. "It has an automatic directed energy reload and a smart target interface that'll determine what spot on a target causes most damage and compensate for movement and environmental hazards."

"Nifty. Standard Tokko issue?"

Bishop winked. "Not exactly. What you packing?"

Reiko had a solar-powered laser gun. It had minimal recoil, and the heating ventilation had been vastly improved so that it didn't burn her hands if she fired too many times in quick succession.

Bishop looked impressed. "All the laser guns I've seen were big and bulky. That's pretty damn cool."

They descended from the *Inago*. It was blazing hot outside.

Bishop wiped the sweat off his neck as they waited for a shuttle. "Glad to be back at hell on Earth."

Reiko shook her head. "Hell is a lot hotter."

"You sound like you're talking from experience."

She grinned. "You're welcome to join me on a tour if you'd like."

"I like Earth." Bishop looked up at the coliseum. "They have bear fights back when the Americans ruled this place?"

"It's a Nazi invention."

"How are they?"

"From everything I've read, they're disgusting, decadent, and profligate."

"Are we talking about bear fights or Nazis?" Bishop asked.

"Touché," she replied.

The shuttle arrived and took them to the gigantic coliseum. Inside, there were swastika banners everywhere and the walls were painted a dark red. A majority of the attendees were carrying guns, though most had them holstered. There was even a group of elementary school kids visiting. They all wore bulletproof vests, and their teachers were armed with machine guns. There was a cloakroom that took jackets but also checked in bigger weapons like assault rifles and bazookas. "If there's even a scratch on my darlings, I will hold you personally responsible," one Nazi officer warned the coat-check worker about his pair of Skorpion machine pistols.

Holographic projections of savage bears loomed above them, snarling at spectators.

"It's become the most popular sport in the German Americas," Reiko said. "There's our contact."

A stranger approached. He had a short blond flattop, a golden visor, an oversized fur coat with a massive silver emblem covering his chest, and a diamond-encrusted rifle.

"Rudo at your service," he said with an exaggerated bow. "Those small pistols all you got?"

"Were we supposed to bring bigger guns with us?" Bishop asked back.

"You gotta stay armed in Texarkana everywhere you go," he said with a grin, then gave Bishop a jovial sock. "Nice to see one of my former kind. You new?"

"I am," Bishop answered.

"Good thing about being Tokko is that you're forever off their scan list. That's probably why you're not seeing me on your portical readouts."

"My portical doesn't work here."

"But you heard why I left?"

"I heard why you were fired," Bishop replied.

"All the bastards I blackmailed deserved it."

"That's your version of it. I don't know the details."

Rudo laughed. "Funny words from a Tokko agent." He looked at Reiko. "Either of you ever see a bear fight before?"

They both shook their heads.

Rudo brightened. "You're in for a treat. Gurgeh's fighting tonight. He's never been defeated. Hope you aren't squeamish."

"Why?"

"The fights are brutal. You gotta bet on the matches tonight." Rudo said as he pointed at more of the holographic bears.

Reiko noticed several people staring at her and Bishop. At first, she thought it was a coincidence, but she saw so many odd glances it was making her uncomfortable. Rudo noticed it as well and said, "If people stare at you, don't take it personal. They ain't used to seeing nonwhite people who don't got chains on them."

"Why would nonwhite people be wearing chains?" Bishop asked.

"Because the majority of them are slaves."

"So the Nazis dream of a world full of Aryans. But what happens after their dream comes true?" Bishop asked.

"The same thing that happened in Europe. They go after the poor people next, then the religious, then the eccentric and ideologically 'impure,' till pretty much everyone's a slave. It's not about race. Never been."

One of the slaves bought the wrong type of beer and was getting slapped around by his German overlord, who demanded out loud why he shouldn't be killed on the spot. Not a single German looked in their direction.

Reiko was about to intervene, but Rudo stopped her and shook his head. "You don't want to do that," he said.

"Why not?"

"You'll get the slave killed for sure if you do. But more importantly, you'll be kicked out of the coliseum and deported back to West Texarkana."

"Nazis sure fit their stereotype," Bishop noted.

"They're not stereotypes if they're real," Reiko replied.

The slave was a man of Asian descent, thirties, maybe forties. He had a chain around his neck and took the beating silently. Reiko closed her eyes, took a deep breath. *Remember your mission. This is not the time or place to—*another harsh kick to his chest. "Goddamn Oriental slaves aren't good for anything!" the officer exclaimed.

"How's Akiko doing these days?" Rudo asked Bishop.

"You know each other?"

"We go way back. I've never met anyone so adept at killing. You work with her?"

"She's my boss."

"Boss?" Rudo said, and seemed amused. "Hard to imagine her as a bureaucrat. But good for her. She once killed a dozen terrorists with—um, what's she doing?" he asked, noticing that Reiko was moving toward the Nazi officer.

Reiko pretended to stumble, collided into him, timed it so her arm pushed his face hard against the floor. He was unconscious on impact with the cement.

"Oops, sorry about that," she said, gave the slave a wink, then came back.

Rudo bounced in agitation and whispered angrily, "You want to risk our lives for a slave?"

"Don't worry," Reiko said. "By the time he wakes up, we'll be long gone."

Rudo's face shifted from consternation to incredulous amusement. "You got guts, Captain Morikawa."

"We all do, Rudo. It's just a matter of how much crap we can take before it bursts out."

They went up the escalator and entered through the southern gate. The main arena looked like a sumo ring if the ring were floating on a platform. There were 12,209 people present according to a scrolling text on the portical display that went around the entire coliseum. Gigantic German words were printed on the gates. Bishop asked, "What's that say?"

Reiko translated it: "'Can spiritual ideas be exterminated by the sword?' It's from Hitler's *Mein Kampf*."

"I've never read it," Bishop replied. "I heard it's boring."

"It was part of the curriculum when I studied in Paris for a year," she said. "We were required to read and study all five volumes: *My Struggle*, *My Rise*, *My Triumph*, *My Peace*, and *My Art*."

"Hard to think of Hitler as an artist. Was he any good?"

"There's a whole wing of his art at the Louvre, but members of the French Resistance vandalized all the paintings, so I couldn't see what was underneath."

"The museum didn't clean it up?"

"The curators didn't want to fess up to the security lapse, and all the Nazi officers thought it was what Hitler intended and were too afraid to mention it in case it was."

Bishop laughed and said, "I could swear I've heard this story before."

Their box seats were a floor above the center ring, a private room with eight chairs in total. It gave them a good view of everyone in the crowd, many of whom were drinking beers and acting rowdy. There were some attendees in Nazi uniforms, but most were wearing civilian clothes, mixing red leather, velvet tracksuits, leggings, and sporty hairdos. A group of performers onstage were clad in togas and played trumpets as the bear fights began.

"How'd the bears get so damn big?" Bishop asked.

Rudo explained as he chugged down a beer: "They receive genetic modifications before birth to increase aggression and fighting prowess. The trainers use growth hormones to make them twice as big as their normal size. They hook the bears on to wires from an early age and train them to combat each other in midair. Do you see the device on their foreheads? Those are special neural enhancers hooked in each so that a manager can give them instinctive pushes and adrenaline surges. Savagery is rewarded, cowardice is punished."

The first fight they watched was savage. The bears ripped into each other. Both were at least three meters tall, maybe even more. The way they floated in midair gave it an almost acrobatic feeling, spinning, diving, and attacking. The crowd was lively, screaming at the more deadly exchanges. The match ended when the bear called Bermoiya had its arm cut up like a messy casserole of flesh.

"What do y'all think?" Rudo asked.

"I've never seen anything like this," Bishop replied as the combatants bit each other, one bear cutting out part of the other's shoulder.

"That mean you like it? Feel free to say what you want. I have a nullifier on me so the Nazis can't hear."

"This is animal cruelty," Reiko said. "It's disgusting."

She was repulsed by what the animals were being forced to do, but even more by the audience, who were enraptured by the brutality, gulping down beers and reveling in the event.

"No disagreement here," Rudo said. "Gurgeh's the best. He's won thirty-two matches in a row. They really push it, since it's a frontier town and people get their release here. They'll get more vicious in the later rounds 'cause they let them fight till death and inject them with more drugs to make sure they last longer."

Rudo was right. Meat chunks from the bears started dropping into the audience. The combat was all over the place as the bears swung above the audience. A bloody piece of bear flesh hit Reiko in the face. Rudo handed her a towel and an alcohol wipe. The whole crowd was mesmerized, roaring and screaming with each violent strike.

"So this is how Nazis have fun," Reiko noted, revolted and sickened.

"It's an acquired taste," Rudo stated.

"Not one I hope to acquire," she said.

"Nature is cruel. The Nazis embrace that reality and refuse to shy away."

"This isn't embracing reality. This is amplifying the worst elements and pushing everything to the extreme, then putting it on show for profit," Reiko replied. "Where is Cossack?" she asked, irked by the sight of all the wounded animals.

"She'll be here soon."

"What can you tell us about her?"

"She's one of the wiliest bear trainers in the Reich. One of the richest too. She has her own actual castle and personally funded Dr. Metzger. She's very well connected in the Reich. She won the National Prize for Art and Science three times and an Adlersschild twice for her services to the state—those are huge awards here, handed out at the annual Nuremberg Party Rally. She's also a key member of the Cultural Senate."

"What's the Cultural Senate?" Reiko asked.

"They control the culture here. Art is a big part of the life of the German Americas. The only class of people exempt from taxes in the Reich are artists."

"Did not know that."

"Art is probably the only area where the Nazis allow non-Aryans to excel," Rudo said. "If you want to offer her something, talk art."

"Does Cossack know Metzger's dead?" Reiko inquired.

"It's a good bet she does. But you can ask her," he said as he received a buzz on his communicator. He stood up and explained, "She just arrived. I'll bring her up from the lobby."

He excused himself.

"Enjoying the fights?" Reiko asked Bishop.

"I haven't been paying attention to them. Mostly checking out all the people," Bishop replied.

"Oh?"

"Look at all those skinheads with tattoos of Japanese characters on their heads. That idiot over there misspelled a bunch of words so his tattoo says 'I'm an idiot of honor and sacrifice pee in my toilet.'"

Reiko laughed hard and asked, "You want to tell him, or should I?"

In between rounds, advertisements from the coliseum played on the big display screen, including season tickets for the forthcoming alligator battles, the latest deals on flame-throwing chainsaws, and toy versions of their favorite bear competitors that had detachable limbs. For the elementary school students, there were ads for the latest "kid guns," which were .45 pistols with smaller handles so they could protect themselves from the "Evil Empire" of "Oriental Murderers."

Even their commercials made Reiko feel sick.

"Is there a plan?" Bishop asked Reiko. "Or are you winging it?"

"I've conducted eighteen simulations of our negotiations with Cossack."

"Do any of them end up with us dead?"

"Four of them," Reiko answered.

"Can we try to skip those ones?" Bishop asked.

"Depends on Cossack. I've brought a shipment of art that we know she's very interested in."

"What kind of art?"

"Last year, a dealer out in Sacramento kidnapped four artists and had them literally work to death in an underground studio. He was documenting how starvation and sleep deprivation changed their art. He tried to have it shipped to some Nazi galleries, but we confiscated all of it."

"You'll offer that in exchange?"

Reiko nodded.

"The Nazis even make art deadly," Bishop noted.

"Even without Nazis, art is deadly," Reiko stated bitterly.

"Thought you loved art," Bishop said.

"I did."

"I remember you used to paint mechas all the time in class, and you did that big mural too on the auditorium wall."

"I can't believe you remember that," Reiko said.

"It was a powerful image of the Battle of Berkeley."

Rudo returned with Cossack and her three bodyguards. Cossack had on thick shades and was a wiry woman in her forties of British and Dutch descent, with auburn hair that was straight, and an elaborate mink coat that made it appear as though her head was surrounded by a white bush. Rudo raised a tinted glass wall to cover the balcony so no one could see or hear them from below.

"I've always wanted to meet a member of the Tokko," Cossack stated. "I know why you're here. Tell me what you're offering and we can go from there."

Reiko had been expecting Cossack to ask about Metzger, but jumped ahead with her plan. "A shipment we've confiscated from Relm Bailey."

Cossack showed no emotion, but her fingers began twitching rapidly in excitement. "You have access to them?"

Reiko raised her portical, and it was already set to a grisly painting of two bears savagely eating each other. Another was of a bear cooking another bear on a grill. There was a whole series of bear paintings that looked as though the artist was splattering random patterns on canvas, a bear barely visible as the hues raged at viewers with their clashing color contrasts.

"How can I be sure you'll deliver them?" Cossack inquired.

"How can I be sure your information is worth the exchange?" Reiko asked back.

"Oh, believe me, it's worth it."

"Half the paintings are aboard my mecha. I'll release them to you, but I want the name of the person you were sending the mecha parts to," Reiko said.

"I want the paintings first."

"I think I'd have a hard time leaving the coliseum alive if I reneged," Reiko replied.

Cossack considered it. "Pris Watanabe," she stated.

Reiko was shocked but quickly hid it, not wanting Cossack to see and, as a result, weaken her negotiating position.

It was too late. "Hard to believe, isn't it?" Cossack asked. "One of your best mecha pilots planning a revolt."

"It could be for personal use. She could be building her own mecha."

"Trafficking our contraband parts?" Cossack scoffed. "You can believe that if it helps you sleep better."

Reiko knew she was right. "Did she tell you why?"

"I was curio—"

Suddenly bullets perforated the glass. Reiko jumped onto Bishop, bringing both of them down to the floor. Rudo and Cossack weren't as lucky. The assassin put a dozen bullet holes in both of them before dropping to the ground floor.

"Who the hell was that?" Bishop asked.

Reiko cautiously peeked over the edge of the broken glass. She spotted a male with blue hair and an auburn tunic carrying two assault rifles. He was wearing a Noh mask like the other members of the Sons of War. The sound of gunfire put the whole audience on alert.

"I don't think that was Bloody Mary," Bishop noted.

"You think the Gestapo killed them?" Reiko asked, looking at the bodies.

"We won't know until we grab him."

The assassin fired at the pair of bears who were preparing to fight on the center stage without having been lifted into the air yet. The restraints on one of the bears was destroyed. The bear, called Ripper, seemed uncertain how to handle its sudden freedom. It tentatively tried to step forward. Realizing the restraints were broken, Ripper launched itself at its handlers. Ripper was a feral giant and completely overwhelmed the people closest to it. It jumped at the gawkers in the front row, mauling two teenagers, then biting the face of a man and violently swinging him around. Reiko was surprised that no one in the stadium was leaving. They actually cheered excitedly and thought it was part of the show.

Reiko took out the grappling hook from her belt, wrapped it around one of the chairs.

She asked Bishop, "Can you sit here for a minute?"

"What are you doing?" he asked as he complied.

"Taking a shortcut," she said, then grabbed on to the other end of the rope and leaped down. Bishop clinched to his end, barely holding on. She was able to quickly drop to the lower floor. The assassin was just ahead of her. Reiko raised her pistol and fired at his leg.

He fell but got back up. Reiko figured he must be wearing some type of armor. Even then, the leg must be bruised unless it was artificial. She was going to shoot again, but out of the corner of her eye, she noticed something big sprinting her way. It was Ripper, and it pushed a trio of men into the chairs, hurting them badly.

Reiko jumped out of the aisle, barely avoiding the bear's furious dash. The audience members were slowly realizing Ripper was out of control. People who'd kept their guns holstered began firing at the beast. A shower of bullets fired from both sides of the aisle. Unfortunately, the majority of the gunshots ended up hitting other people who were trying to escape. Those who were wounded screamed out loud. The crowd became more scared of the haphazard gun-shots than they were of the bear as people began sniping at each other in anger over stray bullets.

Reiko searched for the assassin. She saw him running down the aisle for a different exit. People were stampeding out, and with their instincts taking over, it had become a frenzied panic.

Moving in the opposite direction of the human wave was Bishop.

"What took you so long?"

"Guards outside wouldn't let me in. Where's the assassin?"

"Making an exit," she said, pointing in his direction.

They set off in pursuit.

"You think he was waiting for Watanabe's name before he fired, or the timing was just coincidental?" Bishop asked.

If not for the shooting, she would still be reeling from the rev-elation that Pris Watanabe was shipping in mecha parts from the Nazis and possibly working with Bloody Mary. "I don't know. But that'd mean someone leaked our meeting."

"Who, though?"

Reiko couldn't make sense of it. Her attention went to the assas-sin running out into the parking lot. They chased after him, and just as they exited the coliseum, they heard heavy gunfire.

In the middle of the parking lot, a tripedal unmanned ground vehicle (UGV), or TriWalker, was firing at Nazi guards and parked cars. It had the bulk of a tank, two J290 miniguns that fired several thousand rounds per minute, three articulating arms, and three corresponding legs to walk on. The TriWalker was eight meters tall and was shooting at a Nazi armored car along with a group of sol-diers in the parking lot. Behind the UGV, she saw the assassin climb aboard a tiltrotor aircraft. It was an older model with four rotors, while all the markings had been scraped off. There was no way they were going to catch up. But Reiko had another idea. She took out a peripheral for her gun, attached it to her pistol, and aimed at the assassin. She was too far to get a lock and ran forward.

"What are we doing?" Bishop asked as he followed her.

"I need to get closer to that tiltrotor."

"You get any closer and that minigun'll take you out."

"Fortunately, it's focused on the Nazis," Reiko said.

She crouched behind the automobiles and peered carefully over. It was clear. She rushed toward the plane. Bishop followed behind, gun ready. Reiko was able to obtain a lock on the aircraft when she noticed something in her periphery. From her flank, a Nazi soldier was about to attack with his assault rifle. Just before he fired, Bishop yelled, "Get down!"

He fired his pistol at the Nazi's shoulder. The soldier twirled at the impact, firing into the air instead of at Reiko. Bishop pounced on him, stripped away his gun, and knocked him out.

"Thanks for the save," Reiko said.

"I owed you."

Reiko turned back to the assassin's aircraft, which was taking off.

"Cover me," she said.

She climbed on top of the car. A Nazi who saw her was about to fire at her, but Bishop picked him off, shooting him through the chest. Reiko compensated her aim for speed and wind, then pressed the trigger. The tracker hit its target in the air.

"Reiko! Watch out!" Bishop shouted.

The TriWalker had finished mopping up the Nazi soldiers and turned its attention to them. Reiko jumped down from the car just in time for the minigun to puncture holes through the car instead of her. Reiko tried to see if any more Nazis were coming. The armored car was destroyed, and all the soldiers appeared to be killed. They were pinned at their location, and the UGV began walking their way.

"You tracking it?" Bishop asked, pointing to the sky as the aircraft flew past them.

Reiko nodded. The tracker was lodged on the hull of the vehicle and would be difficult to detect without a thorough search. It'd relay a signal to the GLS that'd pipe back its location to her portical.

The TriWalker was getting closer. She sent a "come here" signal to the *Inago* on a tethered channel that she knew would circumvent the kikkai disruptors.

"What are our chances of surviving this?" Bishop asked.

"The *Inago* has never failed me."

"Hope today isn't the day that changes."

"It won't be."

Reiko checked the distance of the *Inago* versus the rate at which the TriWalker was getting closer. She sped up the *Inago* to its fastest speed, but it was going to be tight.

Bishop said, "I'm going to try distracting it."

"How?"

"By playing hide-and-seek." Bishop put the hoodie over his head, and his body became a reflection of his environment so that he was nearly impossible to spot.

The UGV stopped firing for a few seconds as it looked for them. Bishop used that chance to run to the next car. Reiko watched her portical to check the *Inago*'s proximity. It was still two minutes away. She could hear the TriWalker's footsteps getting louder and louder. Just then, there was a blast as something fired at its head. It must have been Bishop.

The TriWalker rotated around and began walking in his direction.

Reiko amplified the strength on her laser gun to fire at a car on the other side, causing it to explode. For a moment, the TriWalker became confused and turned its attention to the new blast, trying to identify its source. That's when Bishop pummeled it with more rays from the opposite end. Again, the TriWalker moved to investigate before unleashing bullets.

They were both pinned in place.

But these distractions gave them the minute they needed for the *Inago* to arrive. The TriWalker began barraging the mecha with its gun as soon as it was within visual range. But the *Inago* was too strong for it, the bullets barely making a dent on its armor with the plasma shield up. Reiko had a first-person view of the mecha via her lens and moved so that it would close in on the UGV. Using her shield in conjunction with her fists, she punched the walker, immediately destroying its main section. The TriWalker tried to set off missiles, but the *Inago* used its magnetic gun to delay its ejection, and the missile blew up in place. The TriWalker exploded, and its remaining legs fell over to the side. The final move by her mecha was a heavy stomp to make sure the TriWalker's legs couldn't take any autonomous actions.

Bishop ran toward Reiko and said, "I'm sorry I ever doubted."

"Don't be. That was close."

Reiko and Bishop ascended the ladder that dropped from the *Inago*'s bridge and got into their seats, strapping themselves in. She checked her scans. The assassin was long gone. But Nazi forces were heading toward the coliseum.

Reiko drove to the border as fast as she could. With all the chaos back at the coliseum, she knew it'd distract authorities enough for them to make their getaway. According to her scans, security forces had surrounded the arena. No one chased her yet. At full speed, very few craft could keep up with a Katamari anyway. But as they arrived at the border gate, two biomechs approached. These weren't the bipedal ones she'd seen earlier. Both biomechs had six arms and a massive Githu-Nafoi cannon protruding out of their chests. They also had horns over their heads and a bright red bony structure jutting out of their shoulders like epaulets. The armor with the swastikas covered vulnerable spots.

"This is Captain Morikawa. I'm returning back to West Texarkana," she relayed her audio message.

The massive twin monsters came menacingly close. "Captain Morikawa," the pilot replied. "I'm Gryz of the Lashiec. Eight of our citizens were assassinated, including one at the bear fight you attended." Eight? What were they talking about? There was only Cossack. "We request your assistance in this matter."

"You can send a message to the embassy. I'm in a hurry to get back right now."

"Captain, we need you to get out of the mecha and return with us for questioning," the pilot insisted.

"Questioning of what?"

"Surely you can see that you're not in a position of strength. Don't force us to take a regrettable course of action."

Reiko grinned. "I'm not getting out of the *Inago*, and I'm not returning with you anywhere."

"You don't fully understand your situation. We will annihi—"

She ended the communication and sped past them. The initial acceleration caught them off guard. She hopped through the gate and entered Texarkana's demilitarized zone. Several cannons from the wall fired at her. An unlucky shell hit her mecha's hip and caused a disruption in the wiring. The joint stiffened and slowed her by half. She toggled the automatic repair articulation module to try to fix the issue. They started their process, but initial prognostics indicated she needed to replace the part for a full recovery. She limped toward the other side.

The biomechs were faster than she'd expected for their size and caught up to her. The first biomech lunged at the *Inago*, breaking its shoulder and causing the *Inago* to spin in place. The biomech's cancerous skin looked like it was morphing and eating itself at the same time, a disturbing ooze that was in disruptive turmoil. Reiko got out her magnet gun and tried to repel the biomech via its armored plating. But the biomech was too dense, and she couldn't push it back. It moved its way through the magnetic force and came straight at her.

"Hold your seat!" Reiko ordered Bishop.

"Why?"

Reiko hit the emergency drop so that the bridge would descend from the head down into the stomach. They did it just as the biomech battered the *Inago*'s head, causing a big chunk of it to cave in. The monster struck again and this time decapitated the mecha's head off. Emergency alarms rang, which Reiko immediately shut down. Their space was much tighter, and auxiliary controls had remained above. She used boosters on her boots to make distance between the two. Reiko had an idea.

She lifted the *Inago*'s separated head with the magnet gun. Just as the biomech tried to attack again, she used the head like a cannonball to lambaste the biomech. This pushed the biomech to the side. It wasn't enough to defeat the Nazi. But that wasn't her goal. What she wanted was to give them space to make a few more meters to their half of the border. It worked. The biomech took a few steps back before lunging forward again. She triggered the plasma shield which temporarily repelled the biomech. Reiko sped quickly toward West Texarkana. The biomech renewed its pursuit.

"It's still chasing," Bishop said.

"Any suggestions on how to avoid getting killed?"

"Invite them to watch a bear fight together."

"What do you think this is?"

The biomech caught up to her and lunged at the *Inago*. The *Inago* hit the boosters and barely avoided the biomech. But the other Nazi monster was about to smash into her and knock out her main systems. Suddenly, a massive sword blocked its attack. Behind them, the Zombie, commanded by General Furuya, had come to the rescue. The mecha, with its bright emerald armor and its enormous blade, stood at equal height with the biomech.

"Thank you, General," Reiko said.

The Zombie kicked the biomech, then sliced its head off in one quick swoop. The Nazi monstrosity dropped to its knees and fell over, causing the ground to shake. The other biomech raised its arms, preparing to attack.

General Furuya sent a public message, "Nazi biomech. You might not know me, but you've heard of my mecha. I make zombies out of Nazis. I'll only warn you once. You're trespassing. Withdraw immediately, or I will destroy you and add you to my collection."

The Zombie raised its sword with both arms. The blade was as big as the mecha, and its shadow pierced right between the biomech's two halves. The Zombie held its pose, waiting for the right moment to strike. The biomech hesitated.

It was clear to Reiko that no matter what the Nazi did, the fate of the battle was already determined.

They sped ahead.

"Okay, that was awesome," Bishop said. "How did it get here so fast?"

"The Zombie is known for its speed."

"And its big goddamn sword," Bishop laughed. "Y'all don't mess around."

"Only things Nazis respond to is might."

"And bear art."

"You feel bad for Cossack?"

"No. But I do feel bad for Rudo. We left his body over there."

"The army'll work it out with the embassy."

"Yeah, but he used to be Tokko."

She plugged her portical into the *Inago* and brought up the map on her holographic display. The tracking signal for the assassin flashed on.

"Where's he heading?" Bishop asked.

"West."

"To Dallas?"

"I don't know. We'll have to wait and see."

"I hate waiting and seeing," Bishop said.

"So do I," Reiko replied.

Behind them, the second biomech fell, headless.

IT WAS PAINFUL FOR REIKO TO SEE HER MECHA SO BADLY DAMAGED. THE *Inago*'s head would need replacing, and the legs needed an overhaul. The technician in charge tried to assure her by saying, "I've seen a lot worse."

"How long will you need?"

"Depends on appropriations and supplies. Could be a week. Could be a month. There's custom parts needed for the *Inago* that we don't have here."

Since the Katamari classes were still a rare model and equipment for them wasn't as readily available, it made sense. From her production experience, it was actually more cost-effective to have plentiful spare parts than to build new mechas, since that meant damaged machines could be fixed. The Nazi's obsession with building more tanks rather than providing sufficient replacement parts almost ended up costing them the victory in their invasion of the old Soviet Union decades ago (their tanks were breaking down in the wintry snow and the terrible road conditions). If the Imperial forces hadn't attacked from the east, who knows how the war might have gone?

Mechas broke down as well, though terrain wasn't as big an impediment. Their breakdowns had to do with their sheer complexity. She remembered the time a pigeon accidentally squeezed into one of the *Inago*'s ventilation shafts and blew out multiple fuses, causing the left arm to become paralyzed. It took a technician four days to fix it, and she shadowed him the entire time so she could learn how to do it too.

A lieutenant approached them and said, "Captain. The assistant mayor wants to talk to you ASAP."

Reiko had never met the assistant mayor. "Let's go."

"WHAT THE HELL DID YOU DO OUT THERE?" DEMANDED THE ASSISTANT mayor of West Texarkana Fortress, Giichi Kubo. He was a tall male of Irish-Scottish descent who had served in the army.

"We were watching a bear fight when someone shot at us," Reiko replied.

"They killed our host," Bishop added.

"According to the German ambassador, eight political targets were killed, including Gauleiter Goring's nephew and two Nazi generals. The Gauleiter is furious. The embassy has sent multiple remonstrations and demanded justice. I'll ask again: What were you doing out there?"

So the biomech pilot hadn't been deceiving them about the other assassinations. "We weren't involved," Reiko stated, more confused now than before.

"The Nazis are blaming you two."

"It's an unfortunate coincidence," Reiko replied, flustered because she knew how bad the optics appeared.

"Unfortunate coincidence that someone from the army and Tokko entered Nazi territory and eight important figures were subsequently assassinated under suspicious circumstances? Then said officers attacked two of their biomechs when they requested clarification?"

"I know it looks bad, but we didn't kill those people."

"Then who was it?" Kubo demanded.

"We don't know."

Kubo did not look happy with Reiko's answer. "Do you know how hard we've worked at a compromise with the Nazis?"

"I can guess, sir."

"No, you can't. I have to deal with their racist crap every day. If the military wishes to carry out operations against the Nazis, they have to include us in their plans. The intricacies of politics in the Quiet Border go beyond mechas and biomechs. The boring stuff you don't want to deal with, like trade, tariffs, resource management, and road construction, are the kinds of things that ultimately win wars. When mavericks like you and this Tokko agent go off on an operation without informing us, it puts us in a precarious situation."

"I'm very sorry, sir," Reiko said, even though she wasn't. "But like I said, we weren't involved."

"Your official brief said you were going to meet with the army operative Rudo, conduct a meeting with a Nazi baroness named Cossack, then return."

"Look, we weren't expecting Cossack to get assassinated," Bishop angrily stated. "We nearly got our asses handed to us, goddamn bullet storms over my head. Stop treating us like we're the criminals here."

"You might as well be! If a war starts over your actions—"

"We'll beat the crap out of them," Bishop snarled. "But we didn't do anything. If I killed some Nazis, I wouldn't be pussyfooting around it. Don't take no Nazi's word over mine."

Assistant Mayor Kubo sighed. "Even if what you say is true, the trick is convincing the Nazis."

"I'm sure the Gestapo was monitoring our movements. They'll know where we went and how long we were there," Reiko said.

"Let's hope, captain. The governor wants to see you right away. You're to take the first plane back to Los Angeles."

Reiko was taken aback by the order. "I'll leave right now."

"Please ask the governor to keep us informed next time he plans something like this."

"What about the situation here?"

"Hopefully, the Nazis won't do anything rash."

"If they do?"

The assistant mayor looked toward the border. "We'll have a world war with the Nazis on our hands."

WORLD WAR NAZI WAS APPEALING TO REIKO, AND SHE WOULD HAVE LOVED to have wiped the Nazis off the face of the planet. She arranged to take a military transport back to Los Angeles and met Bishop outside the terminal.

"I'm sorry I lost my cool in there. Too much crap happened today, and I couldn't take his attitude," Bishop said.

"Don't apologize. I was pretty pissed too."

"You did a good job restraining yourself."

"I mostly tuned out everything he said," Reiko confessed.

"I need to learn that trick," Bishop said.

"It gets tricky in important meetings 'cause sometimes they say something useful that you need to hear."

"How can you tell what you need to tune out?"

"Depends on how much I want to punch the speaker."

Bishop grinned. "You going to be okay with the governor?"

It was the worst of all possible combinations, a political, military, and social defeat. "I don't know. What are you going to do next?"

"I hope I can go to Los Angeles, find Pris Watanabe, and take her in for questioning," Bishop answered. "But I have to check with my boss. Did your tracker tell you where the assassin went?"

"I lost the trace after they entered Dallas. I have the GLS piped into my portical, so if I get within a hundred kilometers of them, it'll alert me."

Bishop went to a private room to make a few calls. The gates opened, and the transport was ready for passengers. Bishop returned.

"You get permission to come on this plane?" Reiko asked Bishop.

"I gotta stop by base first and give a full report," Bishop replied. "But I'll be there tonight."

She gave him a playful thumbs-up and said, "Call me as soon as you get to Los Angeles."

Bishop shuffled awkwardly.

"Something wrong?" Reiko asked.

"I looked up your friend Daniela Takemi," Bishop replied. "She was imprisoned a few months ago."

Reiko was stunned. "Why?"

"She was charged with treason," Bishop replied.

"Treason? Where is she now?"

"She went missing three months ago."

Reiko looked down at the ground, trying to understand how this could be possible. Was it Daniela that had betrayed them to Bloody Mary?

She looked back up at Bishop and said, "Thank you for telling me."

Bishop avoided her eyes. "Usually when they go missing like this, it's not a good sign," he said. "But she just came back up on a Tokko report earlier today."

"What'd the report say?"

"She was spotted in Los Angeles earlier in the day, but she vanished before our agents could get to her."

"Where in L.A. was she?"

"Downtown. I'll send you the information."

Aboard the plane, there was a show playing in front of her seat about the great exploits and feats of General Yamaoka. She closed her eyes as the plane took off, but the blackness that confronted her reminded her of the past and that summer when she'd returned home from Berkeley.

Her parents liked to sculpt in their free time, and they'd done some human studies based on photographs. Unfortunately, one of their images bore an uncanny resemblance to a notorious German officer who had killed many of the empire's citizens. Her parents weren't even aware of it, but they posted images of their respective sculptures on SOCIAL. It was a portical orbit that people used to post personal thoughts, photos, and silly links from the kikkai. They didn't have many followers. But a friend "socialized" by sharing the image, and that's when one of their friends with a much bigger following noticed the resemblance. They shared it, but included an additional note mocking the image and accusing her parents of glorifying the Nazis. Within minutes, it had begun to spread across SOCIAL. Condemnation came pouring down on them. By the time her parents realized what had happened, it was too late, even though they tried to delete the images. Death threats, angry accusations, and calls for them to get fired from their jobs were bombarding them. "Nazi lover!" was the most common note. Strangers tracked down their private information and broadcast it to the public. Even their friends began to ignore them.

Her parents argued that whole night. She remembered the way her dad had become so pale. Her mother had put up a tougher front, saying, "Forget them. It'll blow over."

"It was your idea to post these! We should never have shared them."

"It's just a sculpture. We didn't do anything wrong!"

They tried to defend themselves by posting the original image they had based the sculpture on, but that only aroused more ire. Why didn't they just fess up to it and apologize? In this precarious time, they should have known better than to sculpt such a sensitive subject.

They got death threats, hate mail, and the most vulgar language possible describing the violent things they wished upon their family. Reiko couldn't help herself from going onto SOCIAL and seeing the witch hunt happen live on her feed. Only it wasn't some random person the kikkai had turned against. It was her own parents. In the afternoon, matters took on a more sinister turn when there was a knock at their door. Two agents from the Tokko had come to investigate.

She rapidly blinked, the memory of it infuriating her.

Her father was the most devastated. He lost his job, his friends, and his dream of becoming a sculptor. No one gave him any more opportunities, even after he was cleared of all wrongdoing. One wrong share on SOCIAL had destroyed him. Her mother had been more resilient, or tried to be. But it was hard to get hired when the very first thing that came up on kikkai searches was the false accusations against them of secretly harboring Nazi sympathies. Even when her parents showed documentation that they'd been cleared of all wrongdoing, the accusation alone became a blemish they couldn't overcome.

Reiko was angry at the arts, but she was even more angry at the kind of world where kikkai mobs were standing by, ready to destroy anyone just for kicks. Art had never been free, but now, it had become a noose that anyone could hang themselves with. The idea that a work of art could be weaponized against the creator, the same way those artists held captive by Relm Bailey had been destroyed, scared her.

The only person that stood by her the whole time had been Daniela. While many of Reiko's friends became distant after what happened to her parents, Daniela didn't care and was angry on her behalf. One time when some cadets made verbal jabs at Reiko, Daniela got in their face and told them, "Don't talk trash when you're not even a quarter of the pilot she is."

As she read over the report Bishop had forwarded, Reiko couldn't help but wonder what Daniela was doing in Los Angeles and what her presence portended.

II.

NORMALLY WHEN REIKO VISITED THE CAPITAL, SHE WAS IN AWE OF ITS grand architecture. L.A. was the biggest city in the country since their victory in the Pacific War. The metropolis was the epitome of modernity with its field of skyscrapers. The freeway was rife with cars speeding home like electric ants after a day's work. A large gate surrounded the cluster of skyscrapers and buildings that represented the central hub for Los Angeles. Inside, there were parks that were integrated at the ground level into the high-rises, bridges and small lakes forming a natural contrast to the imperial monuments that towered above. The whole area was bustling with activity; people rushing to their jobs, parents strolling with their children, the occasional police officer lending a hand.

But as Reiko looked out of her taxi window, she felt less awe and more dread. Each of the skyscrapers had massive displays on the side, projecting important government officials. It was Governor Yamaoka's turn, and as he spoke, captions in Japanese indicated he was being honored for all his years of service. He had been invited to Tokyo for a special session with the Emperor. Footage of his feats were interspersed with ads for the latest portical games. The governor, dressed in a fancy kimono, exuded confidence and sagacity.

Blimps with commercials for the trendy "simulation personalities" were showing off portical experiences that could re-create any personage in virtual form. A popular band of three women called the Phantasy Nocturne was going to perform an anti-Nazi concert the following week at the Bishamonten Amphitheater. There were drones shaped like electric crows that soared through the skies with miniaturized Vulcan guns, the eyes and ears of the internal security force that was also fed to the Tokko. The new Pangolin-class mechas that were replacing the Sentry ones were in position, equipped with the shotgun ice and electric shields that made them defensive bulwarks.

Reiko arrived in the reception area of the governor's office. There was a line of several hundred people waiting outside.

"Who are they?" she asked a security guard.

"People who want something from the governor."

Governor Yamaoka had twelve assistants, each from a different jurisdiction in the city. The inner sanctum had piles and piles of gifts people had sent him just this week. Yamaoka's military assistant said, "The governor is still in a meeting. He'll be with you when it ends."

Thirty minutes passed, then an hour. Still, the governor had not come to see her. She thought about all that had transpired so far and read the portical report about General Pris Watanabe. Watanabe was a decorated war hero who was also one of the Empire's best pilots. But Reiko also recalled that her father had been arrested earlier in the year. Is that why she had betrayed him? And who was the assassin who had killed Cossack after she'd revealed that Watanabe was the one who'd ordered the mecha parts? What was the intent behind all those Nazi deaths?

An alert popped up on her portical. She opened it up and saw that the tracking signal indicated the assassin's aircraft was not far away—only about forty kilometers. She was surprised and checked her portical records for information about its destination. It was an abandoned government lot that hadn't been in use for over a decade. She was going to dig further when one of Governor Yamaoka's assistants informed her, "He'll be available shortly."

The assistant was a man in his twenties who had a carefully constructed coiffure of many curls, like a sea of fractals.

"Thank you," Reiko replied.

"What you did out there was a disgrace," the assistant stated.

"Excuse me?"

"You heard me."

"What do you think I should have done?"

"Capture the assassin, not start a war. You're lucky the governor was so generous. I can't believe you even had the gall to show up."

His insolence was too much for her. "I risked my life out there. What the hell have you done behind this desk?"

"The generals were furious with you and insisted the governor sack you for your incompetence, especially as you got their operative killed! He defended you even though you didn't deserve it! You put him in a compromising position!"

So officers in the army blamed her for what happened, even though it wasn't her fault. Reiko felt crushed.

The assistant's phone rang. He picked up, then informed Reiko, "The governor will see you now."

Reiko entered the office, fully expecting her career to be over. She bowed. "I'm sorry, sir," she apologized.

"For what?" Governor Yamaoka inquired, which caught her off guard.

"For messing up the situation. You sent me out to work together with the Tokko to investigate Bloody Mary, but I haven't had much luck tracking her down."

Yamaoka waved her off, which was another unexpected reaction. "Nothing ever goes as planned. Otherwise, desk clerks would win wars with their paper strategies."

"Your assistant told me the generals asked you to fire me," Reiko bluntly told him.

"He told you that?" Yamaoka asked, clearly displeased. "I apologize for his bad manners."

"I'll accept any punishment and resign if you'd like."

"Do you want to quit?"

"No, sir."

"The generals are on edge. Every little thing, understandably, concerns them. I've calmed them down. We know your past service and what you sacrificed. If you can, please forget my assistant's words."

"But, sir—"

"Did you kill the army operative Rudo?"

"No, sir."

"Did you assassinate those eight German targets?"

"No, sir."

"Those were circumstances out of your hands. We'll work to figure out what happened and move on accordingly."

Reiko was genuinely grateful. "Thank you, sir."

"Let's get to what you've learned so far. Are you closer to determining Bloody Mary's whereabouts?" the governor asked.

"No, sir," she replied. "But there's a chance one of our own is working with her."

"A traitor?"

"Yes, sir. General Pris Watanabe."

Governor Yamaoka's brows raised. "That's a shame if it's true."

"Our contact with the Nazis, Cossack, indicated Watanabe has been illegally shipping mecha parts from the Nazis."

"What for?"

"We believe Bloody Mary and General Watanabe are preparing an attack of some kind using mechas."

Yamaoka looked disappointed. "As you may have heard, her father was executed for treason."

"Yes, sir. If you'll recall, I was trying to bring up his treatment to you before," Reiko said, recollecting the first time they'd met.

"It was a deeply troubling case. Though there was overwhelming evidence of his crimes, I wanted to spare him because of his past service. I considered him a mentor. But we took an oath to put country over anything else, so I approved his execution. I spoke with Pris at length, and I was grateful for her understanding. I had believed she'd put loyalty to country over family. Where is she now?"

"The Tokko agent I was with is going to try to find her and question her," Reiko replied.

"I see. I will speak to the Tokko and make sure they don't employ their usual methods."

Reiko was nervous about her next question, knowing it could get her into trouble. But she had to ask. "Speaking of prisoners, sir. Do you remember Daniela Takemi, a member of the Sons of War?"

"Of course. You two were the only survivors of Bloody Mary's attack," the governor replied, no hint of hostility in his voice, which she took as a good sign.

"Do you know what happened to her?"

"As far as I knew, she was questioned about the incident and released," Governor Yamaoka said. "Why?"

"I was informed she was put into prison and went missing. Earlier today, the Tokko spotted her in downtown Los Angeles, but she went missing again before they could get to her."

Yamaoka gave no visible reaction and said, "That's news to me. I'll have someone look into it. Now what about those eight Nazis that were killed?" he asked, changing the topic. "Was that Bloody Mary's handiwork?"

"I don't believe it was her, sir," Reiko replied, surprised he was trying to avoid getting into details about Daniela. Was there something he was trying to hide?

"What do you mean?"

"I believe the assassin was a third party," Reiko stated.

"Any idea who that might be?"

"We'll figure that out soon."

"I actually would like for you to leave Bloody Mary and Watanabe to the Tokko."

Did this mean she was being removed from the mission? "Respectfully, sir. I would like to pursue this and believe it's important that we do so, sir," Reiko said.

"I know you do, and I agree it's important. But for the time being, the most effective use of your time would be back at Berkeley Academy. You don't need me to tell you that there's a lot at stake over the next few weeks." The governor stood up and walked over to the globe. "If word got out that Bloody Mary and General Watanabe were trying to start an insurrection, Tokyo Command could use the incident to forcibly wrest control away from us."

"That would not be good," she said.

"No, it wouldn't."

There was a deeper import to his words. If Tokyo Command did try to seize control, what would Yamaoka's reaction be? "If you need me to go to Berkeley, I will."

"Thank you, Captain. The—"

There was a tremor that felt like a minor earthquake. It passed and she wondered if her anger was making her shake. "The situation is precarious, and in regard to this matter—" He was cut off by his portical ring. He tried to ignore it, but it kept on ringing. "I'm sorry, this is an emergency line. I have to take this," he said.

She felt a vibration and noticed that someone was trying to contact her on her portical. She ignored the call. But then she saw multiple messages from friends.

WHERE ARE YOU?
ARE YOU OKAY?

She was puzzled, then looked over at the governor. His expression was grim as he disconnected from his portical.

"Did something happen, sir?" she asked.

"There's been a bombing at the Alvarado Sento," he said.

That was the bathhouse just down the road from them. Was the quake earlier from the bomb blast?

"Do we know who it was, sir?" she asked.

For a second, she saw something like confusion flit across the governor's face. "We don't have any information yet. But I was scheduled to be there right now if it hadn't been for this meeting."

Was *he* the target?

Could it have been the Nazis? Would they retaliate this fast? Possibly. But a lurking part of her suspected Bloody Mary.

The governor turned on the big portical display on the wall. There was footage from the bombing, which was just a hundred meters away.

"We've just received this recording from someone calling herself Bloody Mary who has taken responsibility for the attack," the broadcaster said, confirming Reiko's instincts.

On the screen, the captain of the Sohei was shown. He was shaved bald and had bruises all over his face. His right eye was a mound of flesh that remained closed. He was trembling.

"I am Captain Albert Yokoyama of the Sohei Ghost Legion Delta," he said weakly, which made Reiko cringe, as everyone knew the Sohei were the elite of the elite. "I was part of an illegal mission to assassinate Bloody Mary. We were wrong and what we did was ignomon-mi-minious." He struggled with the word *ignominious* and Reiko wondered what was done to break him down like this. "For our crimes, we—we—we were pu . . . punish-punished. The . . . Delta has been defeated. We deserved failure for attacking a . . . attacking a patriot." Reiko looked over at the governor. His expression was grim.

"Not a patriot," a digitized voice said. "Who am I?"

"Bloody Mary."

"Why were you sent to kill me?"

"I don't know."

"You obeyed your orders without knowing the reason why?"

Captain Yokoyama looked afraid to reply. "I—I think so."

"And worse, you failed."

Someone stuck a knife into his shoulder and another into the opposite side. The Sohei captain did his best to control his pain. But the knives were plunging too deep.

The camera raised up toward someone wearing a surgical mask that had been stained red. "I am Bloody Mary. I've killed more people in the name of the Empire than anyone in the Empire. But no longer. You sent your loyal hounds at me, but they can't help you. I hold every citizen responsible. Many of you believe you're innocent. But there are no civilian bystande—" The footage cut out. It was jarring, but Reiko realized the censors had stepped in and cut Bloody Mary off. Fortunately, Governor Yamaoka had the authority to get the full, uncensored version.

In it, Bloody Mary declared, "In every empire, every citizen is responsible for the actions of their military. Even if they ignore what goes on, do you think you can reap the rewards of what your soldiers do but not suffer the consequences? Your silence makes you culpable. Your taxes finance their weapons. Your social pleasures justify their atrocities. The Empire has waged war all over the world, causing untold harm to people. And now I'll make sure every single one of you knows what it's like to feel the terrors of war, unsafe within your own walls. If you don't want to take part, you can flee Los Angeles, as I will make no distinction between civilian and military personnel. All are guilty in my eyes. Today's bombing is only a warning. Starting tomorrow, the real war begins."

The footage turned back to the captain as more knives entered his body.

Yamaoka cursed. Reiko could not believe the Sohei had fallen so easily and felt a chill. She reminded herself this was a ploy straight out of the terror playbook. Don't just attack. Exploit it, make it symbolic, broadcast it publicly, and wage psychological warfare on the target. The suddenness of the attack must have caught even the censors off guard, since they hadn't made adjustments until after the first minute played.

"Sir, I understand Berkeley may need me, but I'd like to request permission again to continue this search," Reiko said. "I can do so without authorization as long as you give your tacit permission."

The governor looked at the captain. "Have you heard what happened to my family?"

Reiko, like many others, had heard the tragic story and seen the footage from the airport. "They were killed by American terrorists."

"It was my two brothers, younger sister, and my parents, who were visiting for the holidays. We were all assured that the terrorists weren't a threat. I didn't even think it a possibility that my family would be in any danger, which is why I invited them here. When the terrorist destroyed the plane before takeoff, I couldn't believe it. How had our leaders failed us so badly? I thought I could effect change through my own actions. In the Irvine Trap, I was so resolute in vanquishing terrorism, I took it to what many considered an inhuman extreme. I was willing to do anything I could to contribute to the safety of the nation, even if many had to suffer. And then

Kansas happened and I knew I could no longer leave the safety and defense of our country in the hands of others. We took action against Governor Tamura, not just because he was a traitor but because we felt it would make our society safer. I remembered my family anytime I doubted myself."

"We all did what we thought was best," Reiko stated. "And I'd like to continue doing so."

The governor saw the conviction in her eyes. She saw something like wavering resolve in his. He'd been more shaken up by this than she had been. "Be discreet," he said. "If there's anything I can do to assist through unofficial channels, let me know."

Reiko recalled Bishop's earlier request. "There is some classified information about Bloody Mary that would be helpful to have access to."

"Tell my assistant what you need."

"And Daniela Takemi?" Reiko asked.

"As I said, I'll have someone look into it."

Just then, several soldiers entered the door.

"Governor," a major said. "We need to take you to a safe location."

They hastily escorted him out.

Reiko called Bishop.

He smiled in relief to see her. "You okay?"

"I'm fine. You've been watching the news?" she asked.

"A little. I just landed in Los Angeles."

"You see that footage from Bloody Mary? I can't believe she got the Sohei so easily," Reiko said.

"I can," Bishop replied, having seen multiple times how deadly she could be. "I'll meet you at the bathhouse. Tokko agents are already at the Sento, and I'm reviewing footage from the external cameras."

"I can get you the info you wanted earlier," she said.

"You mean about Bloody Mary?"

Reiko nodded.

"I'll send you the list of files I'm looking for," Bishop said.

A minute later, she got a list of files.

She asked for the classified info on Bloody Mary from the civilian assistant who'd challenged her earlier. His eyes were full of contempt, but he complied.

She rode the elevator downstairs and raced for the Sento.

THE ALVARADO SENTO WAS MORE THAN A PUBLIC BATH. THE EIGHT-STORY building entertained thousands of guests every day and had been built in the early seventies. Two generals who'd come out from Asia had wanted a bathhouse similar to the massive social structures that were so prevalent there and suggested one in downtown Los Angeles for government officials. The bottom four floors held the baths. The top floor had a private club with a gymnasium, shooting range, pool hall, and conference center. There was a rooftop swimming pool that converted into a discotheque on the weekends. Twelve different restaurants were spread throughout, run by top chefs from Kyoto, Osaka, and Hokkaido. Reiko loved the latter's *ishikari-nabe* (their salmon miso stew was the best) and *kani-ryori*; the long-limbed crabs from Wakkanai were some of the tastiest. It was common for members of the government of all age ranges to congregate at the Sento and relax according to their various needs.

Now there was a gaping hole through the middle of the building, the eastern front decimated. Ash was still raining down, and it smelled of chlorine and smoke. Body parts were everywhere, and emergency workers were doing their best to find survivors. Four S&R mechas were helping to prevent structural collapse and spraying several thousand tons of water from their arms, which had turned into water cannons. She knew they worked in conjunction with the

Cerberus canine robots that were about the size of a *shiba inu* and designed to enter zones like this to track down survivors. She'd trained using one in the past. But the injured weren't only on the inside. Many of the pedestrians who'd been passing by had been badly hurt by the explosion and the resulting debris. Crushed cars along the street looked like mechas had stepped on them.

She counted over a hundred bodies being taken away on covered medical stretchers. The army had blocked off everyone but the emergency rescue workers.

Reiko's portical rang. It was Bishop.

"You there?" he asked.

"I am."

"Got some news for you. I was looking at some of the footage, and there was a positive ID on your friend Daniela."

Reiko's eyes went to the Sento. "She was inside?"

"She may have left before the explosion, but at some point today, she did go in."

Reiko thanked him and hung up. She ran toward the Sento, where security stopped her. "Sorry, ma'am, no one's allowed in."

She saw one of the Cerberus dogs rushing into the fire.

"Who's operating that Cerberus?" Reiko demanded of the security guard.

The guard pointed her in the direction of an S&R mecha, the *Hyuga Uzuki*.

Reiko sprinted toward it and climbed up the ladder to the bridge. A lieutenant in a sooty uniform with disheveled hair said, "You can't be up here."

"I'm Captain Reiko Morikawa, and I need to use one of your Cerberuses."

"Reiko Morikawa?" he said, and it was clear he recognized her name. "You're one of the Sons of War."

"Correct. You are?"

"I'm Hotaka Inoue, adjutant to General Kondo."

Reiko did not know the general personally, but she was aware he had been part of the Sons of War.

"Was he inside?"

Inoue's lips tightened. "He was . . ." The lieutenant looked back at the burning Sento.

"As a fellow Son of War, I need to borrow a Cerberus and find someone inside."

"Three of our Cerberus operators were killed in the blast, so we definitely need some help."

Beneath the bridge was a control deck where Cerberus operators worked at one of eight stations arranged in an octagon. Five were occupied. Reiko grabbed one of the empty seats. The controls were somewhat similar to Reiko's own mecha, though without the healing properties of the Salamander. She was given goggles which provided a first-person visual feedback of the dog and even olfactory feedback to check for poison and gas levels for humans. The controller had a joystick she could maneuver and button mapping for jumps, rolls, and other maneuvers. She hadn't used controls like this since before Kansas and didn't know how her hands would respond. The initial driving went smoothly. The tricky part was that the environment was in constant flux. The Cerberus used a sonar and thermal scan to create a more accurate layout of the Sento, which gave her real-time feedback. She passed by a dozen corpses which already had tags from the five other operators so that emergency workers would be aware of them and the S&R mechas would include them in their overall planning. She found a profile of Daniela Takemi on the network, which she changed into a signal that would detect her physical characteristics. Reiko did a scan for Daniela's signal and left it on. Its range was limited, which meant she had to search everywhere.

Lieutenant Inoue, who was patched into another Cerberus, relayed a request by emergency workers inside the Sento asking if Reiko could aid them. She met them two floors up, jumping through a fiery hall to get there. As she did, she looked at the swarming conflagration, alive, growing, gorging without any real center. There was something eerily beautiful in its flow as it greedily destroyed everything in its path. Part of the floor was missing, and the emergency workers warned her that the rest could go at any time. She cautiously navigated the room, making sure the rest of the floor wouldn't cave in. A segment of it did, but the Cerberus leaped to safety. There were three men in army uniforms on the opposite end, trapped by the heavy fire. Reiko activated the Cerberus's sonic fire extinguisher, which used sound waves to separate the oxygen from the burning materials and put out the fire. There was a wide gap in the floor that wasn't humanly crossable. The Cerberus had a portable ladder that came out of its spine. Reiko laid it down so that the soldiers could cross, which they did. The emergency workers were able to guide them out. She escorted them, knowing the fire in the hall was fierce. Her sonic extinguisher once again helped them to get safely through. However, no Daniela on the scans.

As Reiko continued her aid, she checked the database for General Kondo. Wherever he was, that was where the Sons of War had met. There was a good chance Daniela may have been close by as well. His body had been found three floors up in a conference room. Based on the initial scans, that had been where the destruction was most severe, meaning it was also most likely where the bomb had gone off. That indicated the Sons of War were the primary targets. All these people had been killed just to get to them. She pushed her Cerberus to search more hastily. They were able to find four additional survivors, whom she assisted in getting through the fire.

"Captain Morikawa. How are you holding up?" the lieutenant asked.

Even without the aid of the Salamander system, which had the regenerative fluids to help her hands, she was able to manage. "I'm fine," she answered, checking that there wasn't any tingling sensation. She pinpointed what seemed like a faint signal for a human. It was coming from the kitchen. She went to its location.

Two cooking assistants had been badly burned and were lying on the ground. Their heartbeats were very slight. She was afraid that moving them could cause them more damage.

"Can I get some help here?" she asked.

But before anyone could arrive, the ceiling began to collapse. Reiko pushed one of the assistants close to the other and placed the Cerberus's body on top of them, hoping she could shield them. As more of the ceiling caved in, she lost her connection to her Cerberus and felt something like a charge go through her head. Her eyes became blurry and she felt a momentary dizziness. Her Cerberus had most likely been destroyed. She took off her goggles, hopped to the next station, and was about to run back to their aid.

"What are you doing?" Lieutenant Inoue asked.

"Going to help."

"You need to take a short break after forcible separation from a Cerberus. You might get nerve damage."

"I'm fine," Reiko replied, even though she was still feeling dizzy. "Let me check up on them. It'll only take a minute."

She dived back into a new Cerberus and ran back toward the kitchen. It was completely destroyed. The thermal map, which was hard to read thanks to the fire, barely differentiated the humans and her previous Cerberus from the environment. The precision laser in its mouth could shoot through most building material, so she triggered a sonic ruler to determine the depth of the debris. She fired the laser to try to break through without hurting those underneath.

"Captain," the lieutenant called.

"What?"

"The structural integrity of the building is failing. I'm ordering all Cerberuses out."

"Just give me a minute."

"Captain."

"Just one minute!"

The laser weakened the big slab on top of her previous Cerberus. She used the dog's front legs to remove it completely, finding her previous Cerberus. Its top had been flattened, but it had protected the humans underneath. She pushed the Cerberus aside, found the two humans. They were still conscious, but an initial diagnostic indicated they had broken bones. Reiko heard rumbling and felt the ground shake. She spoke through the speaker in the canine's mouth: "The ceiling's about to fall. Let's go!"

The woman did her best to get up. The man underneath could not stand without dropping to his knees. His feet and hands had been shattered. "Get him on top of the Cerberus," Reiko ordered. "C'mon, hurry!"

Reiko activated the stretcher mode from the Cerberus's back, which caused a panel to open, the compressed stretcher expanding above its torso. The Cerberus could only safely carry one human, which was the male. They began making their way out. The Sento was collapsing. Reiko navigated out of the kitchen, made her way down a hall. Fires were blazing, and she triggered the sonic extinguishers. But it was hard to aim freely with the man on the Cerberus's back. She did her best to hit the bigger concentrations of fire and plowed through. They got to the stairs, where several workers were evacuating, which was fortunate. The emergency workers grabbed the stretcher (which she detached) and helped the woman out.

Reiko did one last scan for Daniela. No match. But there was a faint life sign coming from two floors away. She raced there. On the way, she saw over a dozen people who'd been killed in the blast. Reiko wondered if they even knew what hit them or if, for those within the blast radius, it was a mercifully quick death. Halfway to reaching her target, the heartbeat ended. Whoever it was she had been hoping to find had died. No one else was showing up in her vicinity. She continued to search for Daniela, but the instability of the Sento caused a major part of it to implode, crushing her Cerberus.

She took off her gear and rushed outside. Maybe Daniela had escaped earlier? Reiko saw three teenagers being carried out on a stretcher, badly hurt. Two officers were sitting in pain, nails that had blasted out from the building stuck in their faces. Reiko's eyes turned wet as she saw more corpses being carried out. She blinked repeatedly to suppress the tears. The chaos and frenzied odors reminded her of the Kansas Massacre. Years and hundreds of kilometers away, destruction still smelled the same.

BISHOP WAKANA

★ ★ ★

DALLAS TOKAI

I.

BISHOP DROVE TO MEET HIS BOSS AT THE SHIRER AUGMENTATION CLINIC.
There were over a dozen patients in the lobby. There wasn't anyone
as good as Dr. Shirer with artificial body parts in the city. According to Bishop's portical, the two sisters across from him had both
lost legs fighting Nazis. A man whose neck had been replaced had
broken circuitry that kept his head shaking. A family had brought
their electric sheep to address defects in their artificial legs.

A nurse came out and led Bishop to the doctor's office, where
Akiko's arms were being tuned. Her left arm was exposed, and there
were three separate panels open. Dr. Shirer checked all the connections and had her spin her wrist in a full circle, rotating up, then
down. Part of her arm had been replaced, and Bishop saw burn
marks on the old pieces. The doctor injected fluids that helped cir-
culation, which he tested by bending the fingers until they touched
her palm. Once he finished, Akiko closed everything back up.

Bishop had heard rumors that her right arm had a special weapon inside it. From the outer surface, it looked like a normal hand, complete with skin grafts and finger articulation that made it indistinguishable from a real one.

"All good?" Akiko asked.

"All good for now," Dr. Shirer replied. "Be better next time if you can avoid a gunfight."

Akiko exited the office and gestured for Bishop to follow.

"Gunfight?" Bishop asked.

"A dispute that went awry," Akiko replied, but did not elaborate.

They went to a closet filled with bottles. She moved aside eighteen in a specific pattern, and a door in the back opened up. They went through and entered the elevator for Tokko Outpost 6102, which began to descend.

"I wasn't sure if I'd see you alive again," she said.

"We had lots of help," Bishop said.

"I didn't think you two beat both biomechs by yourselves. Did you also assassinate eight political targets in the process?"

"That wasn't us."

"Why don't you tell me your version of what transpired?"

Bishop tried to summarize everything that happened on his and Reiko's trip to Texarkana, from the assassination of Cossack to the fight with the biomechs.

"Do you know the identity of the assassin?"

"No. But if you saw my report, General Pris Watanabe was supposed to be the recipient of the cargo Dr. Metzger was shipping."

"How do you know that's accurate?" Akiko asked.

"Ma'am?"

"What if Cossack was lying and trying to get us to arrest an innocent soldier?"

Bishop knew Akiko was testing him. "I considered that, which is why I've been attempting to track General Watanabe's whereabouts and listen in on her communications. There was nothing on her main accounts, but she had three burner accounts she used to contact the Nazis. They were encrypted with a cipher, so I've asked cryptanalysis to look into cracking it."

"Have you read Yasu's report about Dr. Metzger's portical?"

"No, ma'am. But it was next on my to-do list once I reported in with you."

The elevator stopped, and they emerged into a massive underground hangar. An enormous mecha leg was being taken apart by dozens of Tokko scientists.

"What's this?" Bishop asked.

"This leg was going to be shipped from Ida Train Station to the south of Los Angeles in Long Beach. Fortunately, one of our informants tipped us off. Interrogation of the crew has revealed multiple parts have already been shipped to Long Beach."

"What for?"

"That's what we need to figure out. We've collected information from Kempei agents near the Quiet Border who've reported three mecha graveyards have been ransacked."

"Is that where older mechas and their radioactive BPGs are discarded?"

"It is. They tend to be less guarded than the Arizona Junkyards and the ruins of San Diego, and less documented too. We don't know what parts they retrieved, other than by determining what is missing from the graveyards."

"So someone is assembling mechas."

Akiko nodded. "That's a safe assumption. Initial reports concluded it was excavators selling parts within the Quiet Border to Americans wanting to improve their Chimeras. With our new intelligence, we believe otherwise. Our interrogators will get us more information as soon as they can."

"That leg looks familiar," Bishop said.

"Our agents have concluded it's a stolen backup part for a mecha driven by a pilot you may be familiar with. Lina Niijima."

Bishop bristled at the mention. "How's she involved?"

"Her personal mecha, *Syren*, has gone missing. So has she. She was last spotted in the Quiet Border in one of the mecha grave-yards."

"I never heard anything about this."

"The corps is doing their best to hide this fact. Two other pilots are also missing."

"Pris Watanabe is one of them?" Bishop asked.

"Yes."

"It's hard for me to believe Niijima would be working with Bloody Mary. I don't like her, but I know she's one of the most dedicated pilots in the corps."

"I'm aware of your history with her," Akiko replied. "But my prognosis about her sense of loyalty would be different from yours."

"You think she could join the terrorists?"

"I assume your conclusion is that she couldn't," Akiko said.

"You have facts I don't?"

"If traitors were easy to spot, we'd be without a job."

"I never thought smart traitors equaled job security."

"Her husband and their entire family were executed by Gover-nor Yamaoka."

"What was the reason?"

"They were accused of treason since they worked with Governor Tamura," Akiko replied.

"Were they guilty?"

"They wouldn't be dead otherwise, would they?"

"My father's dead, and he was innocent."

"You are correct," Akiko acknowledged. "Your father tried to bring about change to the Empire in what he felt was the honorable path, but he was punished for his integrity. There are many who have sacrificed themselves to right wrongs that were unfixable to begin with."

Bishop recalled how after their very first meeting, Akiko had taken him to see the Kempeitai agent who had falsely accused his father. The two had flown south to the Mexican Confederation of Japan, heading for a ranch just outside of Monterrey.

"Her name is Tiffany Kaneko," Akiko said as she showed him the portical files with the official charges Kaneko had filed against his father.

"Is she still part of the Kempeitai?" Bishop asked once he'd read it over.

"She left eighteen years ago."

"If something were to happen to her, would there be repercussions?"

"Do you really care about the repercussions?"

Bishop thought again about his father, trying to make his voice strong despite knowing it was to be his last time talking with his family. "No."

They approached the main building. It was a resting place for senior citizens and those unable to take care of themselves. Many were in wheelchairs or had to rely on mechanical parts to move. Nurses were helping a majority of the patients. There was no sign indicating what type of facility it was, but Bishop guessed it was for veterans and military personnel based on all the paraphernalia on the walls. An administrator approached them. Akiko showed her badge and ordered, "Take us to Tiffany Kaneko."

The administrator nodded, then glanced at their guns. "Should we prepare a medical team?"

Akiko looked at Bishop and said, "We'll see."

Bishop suspected that something would be wrong with the Kempeitai agent. The closer he got, the angrier he became as he recalled the life his family had to live after their father's death. He could endure the scorn and mockery from the other students. But knowing his father died because of false charges made him furious.

When they met Tiffany, she was a comely woman with long blond hair in her forties. She was working on her garden and got up to greet them. "You have guests," the administrator told her.

"It's good to have guests!" Tiffany exclaimed. "You look familiar. Do I know you?" she asked Akiko.

"We were friends once."

"Ah. My apologies. My memory isn't what it used to be."

"What's that mean?" Bishop demanded.

"I don't remember much about my past. The doctors have told me I suffered a degenerative brain disease after a terrorist attack."

"So you're saying you don't remember how you killed my father?"

"Killed your father?" Tiffany asked in genuine shock. "What are you talking about?"

"You had my father killed!"

"I have no idea what you're talking about."

Bishop turned to Akiko and asked, "Is she telling the truth?"

"I'm afraid so. A terrorist group called the NARA launched a biological attack that inflicted serious brain damage to most of their targets. Those who weren't killed suffered heavy brain damage and memory loss."

Bishop glowered at Tiffany. "It doesn't matter if she doesn't remember. She's still guilty."

He took the gun out of his holster and aimed it straight at Tiffany Kaneko. Tiffany looked horrified, fell to the ground, and began weeping.

"I don't know what you're talking about. I swear, I didn't do anything," she sobbed.

Bishop looked at Akiko. "You're sure it's her?"

"I'm sure."

Bishop's anger focused on Kaneko. He wanted to shoot despite her tears and the snot dripping from her nose. He'd never killed anyone this close up and definitely never someone who was unarmed. But this was for his family. He kept on thinking about his mother, who could never come to terms with the way her husband had died.

Bishop just wanted to be certain about her identity. He looked at his portical file of Tiffany, then back at her. The photo was of a younger woman, but there was no doubt they were the same person.

Should he shoot? She clearly had no memory of it. But did that make her less culpable? His hand began to shake. Don't be weak! he yelled internally. Seeing her so helpless made him waver.

But he thought about his brother and his mother, and his rage came back to him.

He fired twice into Tiffany's forehead.

Strangely, no bullets came out.

Bishop thought something was wrong with his gun. But Tiffany got up and took off the latex face mask she'd worn. The administrator helped "Tiffany" remove the rest of her makeup. Akiko put her hand on Bishop's shoulder. "I had the bullets removed."

"This was a test?" Bishop asked, stunned.

"It was. I'll be honest. Many of my superiors did not think you'd make a good agent based on the demerits you received on the police force. But I told them those are trivial, since you have a stronger will than any other prospect I've seen. Now we've confirmed it."

"I don't understand. Who is that lady?" Bishop asked.

"One of our agents."

"You were toying with me?"

"I was testing your will," Akiko replied. "I wanted to see if you'd carry out your vengeance despite a morally conflicted situation. Most people waver in their purpose and then relent, which is not something that members of Tokko can do. You fired despite knowing she did not know what happened in the past."

"*Doesn't that make me a bad guy?*" Bishop asked, conflicted by the notion when presented in these ethical terms.

"*What do you think Tokko are?*" Akiko asked.

"*What about the real Tiffany Kaneko?*"

"*I killed her twenty years ago to avenge your father under these same circumstances.*"

Bishop looked at Akiko, shocked. "*She'd lost her memory?*"

Akiko nodded.

"*Did you have second thoughts?*" Bishop asked.

"*Maybe,*" Akiko said in a way that hinted at more conflict.

"*Thank you, Akiko-san.*"

"*For?*"

"*For avenging my father,*" Bishop said.

"*I did what I had to, and I can see you'd do the same. Welcome to the Tokko.*"

"So what are people supposed to do?" Bishop asked Akiko in the present.

"That's a question for the politicians, not us."

"Leaving our fates in their hands seems like a recipe for suffering."

Akiko put her metallic hand on Bishop's shoulder and gently said, "Careful. The line between using empathy to capture our targets and actually harboring treasonous thoughts is a blurry one."

"Understood, ma'am . . . Who's the third missing pilot?"

"Her name is Daniela Takemi," Akiko replied.

The mention of the name surprised Bishop, which Akiko noticed.

"You know her?" she inquired.

Bishop explained how Reiko was looking for her and she'd been seen earlier in Los Angeles. "This can't all be a coincidence."

"You think Captain Morikawa is involved with the disappearance of the pilots?"

"No," Bishop stated.

"You're sure she wasn't misleading you?"

"I'm positive," Bishop stated.

"You trust her that much?" Akiko asked.

"Not her. My instincts. She's the one who brought up Daniela's disappearance. And I've had her communications monitored for suspicious activity."

"Anything?"

"No."

Akiko appeared to accept his conclusion. "I've had agents looking for all three pilots. We haven't had much luck," Akiko conceded.

Somehow, this was all connected to the Sons of War, but he was missing the link.

A Tokko agent approached Akiko and reported to her in Spanish. Bishop didn't understand, but Akiko replied back with complete fluency. Bishop did know a few phrases and thought he heard something about calling someone, but he couldn't make sense of the rest.

The agent saluted and left.

"Go see Yasu first," Akiko ordered. "He has an update about Metzger's research. Then I want you to follow up with the Yamamori family and figure out who handled the shipping of the parts and how they were contacted."

"What about Long Beach?"

"I'll follow up on that personally."

He bowed and left.

BISHOP FOUND YASU IN THE WESTERN WING OF THE OUTPOST. THE SEC-tion resembled a hospital. There were multiple stasis tubes with people inside, and many had strange protrusions growing all over them.

"What is this?"

"The Mota Biolab, my private research facility," Yasu said.

"Who are these people?"

"These are subjects exposed to Nazi biological weapons along the Quiet Border. I was able to get to them before they'd been killed and arrest the state of the viral decay so I could study them here."

"There's so many."

"Not as many as I'd like. But that's not what I want to show you."

Yasu took Bishop to a table where there was a detached arm. He clicked a part of the flesh, and it opened up. Inside were chemicals and wires.

"What is that?"

"An Ulfhednar," Yasu answered. "The word is German. They were old Norse champions who were part of Odin's elite forces, kind of like berserkers. They were said to be shapeshifters, which fits."

"Fits what?"

"They're humans with bioengineered limbs that have highly explosive chemicals inside."

"What do the chemicals do?"

"It makes them human suicide bombers. They can avoid detection on regular scans since their arms look like regular body parts unless someone knows exactly what they're looking for. The people carrying the Ulfhednar parts might not even know they have the explosives wired inside of them."

"How's that possible?"

"Say it was stored inside a fake lung or somewhere in the intestines. A person could be carrying the explosives and not know, since their bodily functions would be the same. They'd be walking along and *boom!* They're dead and they've killed everyone around them."

"That's scary."

"And fascinating. Hold on. Lift up your arms."

"Why?"

"Let me check you."

Bishop raised his arms. Yasu used the sensor on his portical and checked Bishop from toe to head. "You're not an Ulfhednar. But I want a live subject so I can see how Metzger tricked the body into accepting the fake parts."

Bishop did not think Yasu would catch the irony in his voice, but said, "If I find one, I'll send it your way."

"I'm glad you're so cooperative. We want you to head to Long Beach and search for a Stanley Sugimoto. His name was on the receiving end of the mecha parts. We have contacts there who are looking for him as we speak. If any of them find him, they will notify you."

"But Akiko-san just told me to stay here and follow up with the Yamamori family."

"Check your portical for new orders."

Bishop did and saw that Yasu was right. The assistant director of the Tokko had personally sent him the order to pursue Stanley Sugimoto and capture any Ulfhednar he came across. Bishop was surprised, as he'd never heard from the Tokko's assistant director before. Why was he contacting him instead of Akiko? Did they know something that went even beyond her clearance level?

"There's eighteen of them out there, according to Metzger's lab," Yasu excitedly informed him.

Bishop thought he heard wrong. "Did you just say there's eighteen Ulfhednar out there?"

"Yep."

"Where are they?"

"No idea. But Dr. Metzger was trying to sell them to at least thirty different clients," Yasu replied. "He had some Ulfhednar on board the cargo plane Bloody Mary seized. One of them was killed by Bloody Mary, which is how I connected everything."

"So Bloody Mary has them now?"

"Probably," Yasu replied.

Bishop understood now why the mission was urgent enough to warrant the assistant director's attention. "Is there any good news?" he asked.

"What was the bad news?" Yasu asked back, and his total sincerity worried Bishop, even if he knew it was just Yasu being Yasu.

BISHOP'S FLIGHT TO LOS ANGELES WAS FAST. BEFORE HE EVEN HIT THE ground, he received several emergency messages that were sent to all Tokko agents. He felt an anxious knot in his stomach that got worse as he read the report. There'd been a bombing at the Alvarado Sento. Summaries and footage from the scene played. He had a difficult time watching Captain Yokoyama of the Sohei under duress. Even though there was no confirmation, Bishop was certain it had been an Ulfhednar that had caused the blast.

He received a call from Reiko and agreed to meet her at the Sento. The Tokko had a car ready for him, and he input his destination so the car could automatically drive him.

It was a thirty-minute drive from the airport. He noticed his sister-in-law had called back, so he dialed her.

"Hi, Maia. Are you doing okay?"

Video of her face replaced the front window. "I've been better. What's going on with the bombing?"

"I can't talk about it, but I'm in L.A."

"Can you come by?" she asked.

"Later in the week," he replied. "For now, I'd strongly advise you to avoid public places."

"What about this Bloody Mary that was threatening everyone?"

"We're investigating," Bishop said.

"Are we in danger?"

"If you are, I'll send someone to help. How's Lena?"

Lena came on the screen and waved.

"Lena!" Bishop said with a smile. "I saw your music video."

"How was it?"

"Really good. I'll be by soon, but I have some work to take care of."

"You're coming to the concert?" she asked happily.

"I hope to."

"After the concert, can we go back to the ice-skating rink? I want their shaved ice cream."

"If you'd like," Bishop told her. He was going to say more but noticed he had several new emergency reports demanding his attention. He wanted to ignore them but knew the Tokko monitored his portical usage. "I've got to get going, but stay indoors for the next day or two and I'll see you soon."

Maia came back on. "Before you hang up, I need to talk to you about something."

"What is it?"

"Lena's been acting up in school."

"How?"

"She's been telling everyone she's going to join the Tokko and investigate them," Maia said.

The image of his young niece acting as a Tokko agent brought a chuckle, though Maia did not seem pleased. "I'll talk to her and let her know it's no joking matter," he assured her.

"I hope you can get through to her," Maia said. "She's as stubborn as her father was."

The call ended. Bishop had seen how stubborn his niece could be. As a baby, if she didn't like certain foods, she refused to eat and cried until she got what she wanted, which was usually what the adults were eating. "You're spoiling her," his brother complained lightheartedly.

"Life is too short for bad food," Bishop had replied jokingly as he mashed up food for his niece (his brother was one to talk, since he was always sneaking bites of ice cream for Lena!).

Bishop focused on the report on his portical. The casualties from Alvarado numbered in the hundreds, and they were still finding bodies. Emergency services had spent the entire evening trying to put out the fire.

He flipped the orbit to photos from his past. Saw the one of himself and his ex-wife on a trip with his late brother, Maia, and Lena when she was just a baby. He marveled at how fast she grew every time he went to see her, from being completely dependent to crawling, standing on her own, then walking. He still remembered the first time she'd yelled "Uncle Bishop!" and feeling strange to be called "uncle."

Bishop met Reiko near the Alvarado Sento as two new emergency mechas arrived to assist with the fire. They gazed at the bomb site, both at a loss for words.

"The Tokko screwed up," Bishop finally said.

"Why do you say that?"

"Because we didn't catch Bloody Mary before she did this."

"This wasn't on you," Reiko said.

"This is the Tokko's job, right? Track all internal threats. Some of our agents are so busy tracking petty thought crimes, they let the big one go by."

"Petty thought crimes can lead to serious thought crimes," Reiko said.

"Don't tell me the company line. Nazis have officially denied the bombing," Bishop said. "They've even passed on their condolences. But our forces on the Quiet Border are on high alert."

"They should be. The Nazis are the ones who'll gain most from this."

"They're not the only ones. Were you able to find Daniela?" Bishop asked.

"No."

"She might have left."

"I hope so," Reiko answered.

"Where's the governor right now?" Bishop asked.

"He's in hiding. But I don't know how much good that'll do since even the Sohei got wiped out by Bloody Mary."

Bishop knew Bloody Mary was deadly, but the ease with which she'd dispatched the Sohei, the elite of the elite, was disconcerting. "You think Bloody Mary has someone on the governor's team?"

"Could be. The Alvarado Sento had tight security. It's not like just anyone can get inside. And the Sons of War were the target," Reiko revealed.

"How do you know?"

She explained about General Kondo.

"I've asked for security footage from inside the Sento," Bishop said. "It'll take them a few hours to extract it if it survived. We're trying to get a log on everyone who was there."

"Whoever did it had to have known when and where the Sons of War members were meeting."

Bishop looked at one of the S&R mechas as it elongated its arms to spray water at a new fire that had broken out. He told Reiko about the Ulfhednar.

Reiko looked at the charred remains of the Sento. "Do you think an Ulfhednar was involved here?"

"I do. We'll have to wait to get the forensics report for Yasu to confirm it."

"So it's a good bet Bloody Mary has more of these Ulfhednar and a whole bunch of mecha too," Reiko said as she began connecting the dots. "Do you know what the public's reaction was to Bloody Mary's threat?"

"According to my feeds from infrastructure and transportation, people are fleeing the city. Fortunately, traffic should be going away from Long Beach, which is my destination."

"Why Long Beach?"

Bishop explained about Stanley Sugimoto.

"I'm coming with you," she said.

"Would love your help."

"There's something else."

"What?" Bishop asked.

"The tracker I put on the assassin's tiltrotor is only forty kilometers away."

Bishop checked Reiko's portical and it pointed east, the opposite direction from Long Beach. Cossack's assassin was nearby.

"They're from Los Angeles?" Bishop asked.

"Looks like it."

"Which do you want to do first?"

"You're under orders for Sugimoto, right?"

Bishop nodded. "The contacts I was given are still on the lookout for Sugimoto, but they'll let me know as soon as they spot him." He could feel something was off in Reiko's stiff, almost deadpan tone. "Where exactly did the assassin land?"

"According to official maps, it's abandoned government property."

"You don't think it is?"

"I don't know. I've tried asking, but I've been told there isn't anything out there."

"You don't believe them?"

"If it wasn't only forty kilometers away, I might have."

"Do you mind if I try finding out?" Bishop asked.

"You can do that?"

"I can try," Bishop replied.

Reiko relayed the tracking coordinates to Bishop's portical. Bishop forwarded them to the Tokko operators, who'd in turn investigate. To his surprise, he received a call from Akiko-san almost immediately.

"Are you in Los Angeles?" she asked.

"I am. I received new orders to follow up in Long Beach with a Stanley Sugimoto."

"I see. Why are you asking about these coordinates?" Akiko asked over the portical.

"The assassin's getaway aircraft landed there."

"It's a secret training station for the Sohei," Akiko replied. "I'd advise you to stay away. I'll have agents from the Los Angeles office investigate. I'll be arriving in Los Angeles shortly as well."

"Thank you, Akiko-san. One other thing. My niece is in the city."

"I'll send agents to take her to safety."

"Thank you, Akiko-san."

He hung up and told Reiko that it was a Sohei training station.

"What the hell?" was Reiko's reaction.

"Does that mean the Sohei executed those eight political targets?" Bishop asked, confused as to why their own special forces would be involved.

Reiko did not answer.

"Who's controlling the Sohei?" Bishop asked.

Reiko again hesitated to answer. Bishop figured it out himself.

"It's Governor Yamaoka and the Sons of War, isn't it?" he asked.

"Yes."

"But that makes no sense," Bishop said. "If the Sons of War deliberately sent special forces to kill Nazis, that'd be a direct provocation for war."

"Maybe that's what they want," she said.

"Then why send them while we were there unless—" and he connected the dots. "Your Sons of War wanted to blame us."

"It's hard for me to believe. There's other explanations for this," Reiko stated.

"Like what?" Bishop asked, dubious.

"Like the Sohei acted on their own, or they had another agenda, or it's not even the Sohei. We can't assume anything until we get the facts, but we can only be in so many places at once."

"What reason would the Sohei have to act independently without orders?"

Reiko mulled on the question. "I don't know. But we shouldn't jump to conclusions."

Bishop nodded. "My boss will follow up. We can focus on tracking down Sugimoto and, through him, Watanabe and Bloody Mary."

Reiko nodded without much conviction. Bishop recognized that despite her strong front, doubt had crept in.

He empathized with her, and even though they were short on time, he felt a short break was necessary for them to recharge. "When's the last time you ate?" he asked.

"I'm not hungry."

"I'm starving. Let's just get something quick. Do you know anything good nearby?"

"We can grab a burger to go."

"I don't eat meat, so anything else?" Bishop replied.

"Really? I remember we went to Shanghai for burgers, didn't we?" Reiko checked with him.

"I used to eat meat then."

"What converted you to the dark side?"

There was a part of Bishop's life he never spoke about. But he understood what Reiko was going through and thought it might be helpful to share. "During Texarkana, I was captured by the Nazis thanks to shitty commands from my superiors."

"I read about it in your profile."

"The Nazis tortured me, burned me. Even now, whenever I smell meat getting cooked, I feel nauseous."

"I'm sorry," Reiko said.

"I'm sorry for bringing it up. But whenever I think about those officers who sent me, I get pissed off."

"I'd be too," she replied.

There was an uncomfortable silence which Bishop broke by asking, "Do you know any good noodle places?"

"I do. But don't you feel bad for plants? They're conscious too."

"Do you feel bad?"

"Horrible. C'mon, I know just the place."

Unlike downtown, large areas of West Los Angeles were flat in comparison. Miracle Mile and Beverly Hills were booming commercial and residential strips, though Rodeo Drive was a street full of shops selling cheap wares made overseas. The rest of the way to the restaurant was filled in by phalanxes of apartment buildings sprawling down La Brea, Wilshire, and Fairfax.

The noodle shop Reiko wanted to go to was one street over from them on La Cienega, which was home to restaurant row.

"This place has the best *Ise udon*. Their noodles are perfectly thick and chewy, and their black sauce is exquisite," Reiko said, hoping good food would help make both of them feel better.

"I don't know," Bishop replied dubiously. "There's only a few places in Ise-Shima that do it right. I'm very skeptical about *Ise udon* outside of the main island."

"There's a really good tiger blowfish restaurant right next door if you're feeling a little more daring."

"I'll give the *udon* a try."

"You're making me nervous."

Bishop chuckled. "Don't be."

The inside of the restaurant was smoky and damp. The inner chamber had a bright red light, and the lack of an air conditioner was making both of them sweat. But the smell of the *udon* conquered all hesitation.

The space where they could sit was tight, and Reiko ordered the *Ise udon*.

When it arrived, Reiko watched Bishop's reaction. He took a bite, was about to say something when a call came.

"I'll be back."

He stepped outside.

Yasu went on a long diatribe about how frustrated he was with the agent who'd collected the samples from the Alvarado Sento. "'Terrible amateur' would be a compliment for his incompetence," Yasu complained.

"Were you able to determine what caused the explosion?" Bishop asked.

"It's an Ulfhednar," Yasu said, and gave him more details, including that about a meeting between the suspect and Reiko's friend Daniela Takemi.

Bishop was perturbed by the rest of the call.

"I'm heading to the Nakahara Unity to investigate further," Yasu said. "After you find Sugimoto, stop by."

Bishop came back inside, ready to tell Reiko about it. But she stopped him and said, "Finish the food first and we'll talk outside."

He worked on his food.

"Were you always left-handed?" Bishop asked Reiko as he noticed her eating with her left hand. "Or ambidextrous?"

"Why do you ask?"

"It's a weird thing, but I always remember what hand people use to eat," Bishop said. "You always ate my sushi with your right hand."

"I used to be right-handed until Kansas."

"What's that mean?"

"You didn't know?" Bishop shook his head. Reiko held up her right arm. "I was badly hurt during the Kansas Massacre. I couldn't use my arm for a year. They gave me augments to fix it and replaced the joints with artificial limbs to give it better articulation. But after that, no one would give me a job designing mechas anymore because they were afraid I'd get hurt and not be able to work. The only people willing to give me a second chance were the Sons of War."

"Generous of them."

"More than generous," she said. "They didn't just want to bring change to the old regime—they wanted to create opportunities for those who'd never had any. They implemented a Salamander system in my mecha so that I could use my arms to pilot again. They did things like that for all their members."

"I can see why you joined them."

"The job was part of it. The biggest reason was to avenge Kansas," Reiko said.

"What do you mean, 'avenge Kansas'?" Bishop asked, confused.

"I mean in a general sense," she said, trying to cover up.

He was going to press, but thought better of it. *Later*, he told himself.

They made their exit after paying via porticals.

"So?" Reiko inquired.

"It was an Ulfhednar, and they found out his identity," Bishop said.

"I mean the *udon*."

"Better than I was expecting," he answered, though he didn't sound enthusiastic.

Reiko gave him a playful tap. "My bad for trying to take a chef to a restaurant."

"I liked it."

"Are you being condescending?"

"Never," Bishop protested.

"Good, 'cause then I'd have to punch you," she said, swinging around her augmented arm. "So who was it?"

"My Tokko contact, Yasu, says the Ulfhednar's name was Juro

Takahashi. A lieutenant in the army. I knew him. We actually served together. He was part of the rocket pack legions too. Do you know if he was a member of the Sons of War?"

"I don't know for sure because I don't know who he is, but I can find out," Reiko replied.

"Your friend Daniela was spotted meeting with Takahashi. We don't know what they said, but she covered her face with a veil, which was why external cameras didn't initially pick her up. We have no idea where she went after that, but she did leave the Sento."

"So she's involved with the explosion?" Reiko asked in surprise.

"It looks like it. We're still trying to get more information."

"Were you close to Takahashi?" Reiko asked about the Ulfhednar.

"Not close," Bishop replied. "But we went for drinks a few times. He was tough. But I don't know how Metzger could have gotten hold of him or if Takahashi even knew he was an Ulfhednar . . ."

"You don't think he knew?"

Bishop nodded. "It's possible. Any of us could be Ulfhednar, and we wouldn't know it until we were dead."

ONCE THEY GOT IN THEIR CAR, HE CHECKED HIS PORTICAL, BUT NO ONE had spotted Sugimoto yet. As they drove south on the 405 Freeway toward Long Beach, they saw that the opposite direction heading north was full of cars.

"Good luck getting anywhere," Bishop said their way.

"The army set up a periphery?" Reiko asked, aware of standard protocol in a bombing of this nature.

"It's for anyone leaving the city, to make sure Bloody Mary isn't with them."

"I don't think she'd try to escape."

"Neither do I. But they have to be sure."

Reiko saw Bishop yawn and checked the time. "If your sources haven't found Sugimoto, we should get some shut-eye."

Bishop acknowledged, "That's a good idea."

"There's a capsule hotel near Long Beach I like," Reiko suggested.

"Capsule hotels make me feel like I'm inside a casket."

"You don't like a sneak preview of death?"

"I've already had too many sneak peeks," Bishop replied.

A few miles from Long Beach, they grabbed a motel with two beds. It was already midnight.

He slept on the left bed, Reiko on the right. Bishop kept on thinking about the Sento and all the dead inside. Consciousness and unconsciousness blended together, and his memories of the bathhouse took on a life of their own. Somehow, the Sento wasn't destroyed yet. People were congregating, talking about trivialities. He was on his rocket pack, yelling at the people inside, warning them of what was to come. But no one could hear him. Instead, Nazis were coming for him again, and they ripped off his rocket pack and began to pull his flesh off his body. He heard a rumble, the ground shaking, someone screaming. He woke to his own screams. Reiko was pushing him.

"Bishop!" she yelled. "It's just a dream."

"W-where am I?" he asked, confused by his surroundings.

"Motel," she replied.

He rubbed his eyes, relieved it was only a dream. He lay back down, but couldn't go back to sleep. He was still perturbed by the fleeting imagery from his dream. He turned left, then right, trying to find a comfortable position, knowing it was futile. He hated the way his dreams exposed him to his own vulnerabilities.

A minute later, Reiko asked, "You sleeping?"

"No," he answered.

"What were you dreaming about?" she asked.

"Flying. Goddamn Texarkana's affecting my subconscious. What is it with the Nazis?"

"You mean why are they insane murderers bent on destroying and torturing humanity in the worst ways possible?"

"Yeah."

"I don't know," Reiko replied.

"When we captured some of them, we asked them why they were so cruel. They looked shell-shocked, confused themselves about what they were doing. They were in denial about everything."

"You think Bloody Mary would have the same reaction?"

"I have no idea."

"You will after we capture her."

Bishop scoffed at the assumption. "I'll be lucky just to survive this. I get the feeling this all ain't gonna end well."

Reiko found his fatalism unsettling. "Then why are you even coming?"

"I'm under orders. Isn't that why you're doing this?"

"I . . . I was actually ordered off this mission."

"What?"

Reiko explained Governor Yamaoka's decision and her plea to get back on the case.

"I think you're out of your mind," Bishop stated.

She laughed. "I don't disagree with you. What would you be doing if you weren't here?"

"Playing with my niece," Bishop replied.

"How old is she?"

"Seven. She lives in Culver City with her mom. She got in trouble for going around saying she was part of the Tokko and investigating other kids."

"I'm sure the other kids were thrilled."

"Yeah . . . What would you be doing?" Bishop asked.

"Building noncombat mechas," Reiko replied. "I know mechas

are mostly used for fighting, but they weren't always meant to be war machines. I want to build the kind that can explore the depths of the oceans or be deployed in space."

"That'd be cool."

"It'd be a dream come true," Reiko said. "You get a chance to look through the files you asked for?"

"I did. Thanks for that. They had a lot of information about her missions—she's assassinated hundreds of people. But I couldn't find what I was looking for."

"What's that?"

"Her real name."

It was something Reiko hadn't thought about.

"It wasn't in her files, and there's nothing about her past," Bishop said. "The first mention of her was one of her missions as a tactical operative in Manhattan."

"What was she doing there?"

"She assassinated a defector who was feeding the Nazis classified information," Bishop replied. "She used a hot steam iron to kill him."

"Is there anything that isn't a weapon to her?"

"I bet she could kill us using paper clips."

"What else was on there?" Reiko asked.

But she heard light breathing and no other response. Bishop had fallen back asleep. She turned over to the side and nodded off.

It was 4:00 a.m. when Reiko felt a nudge. Bishop said, "I just got a call. One of our sources spotted Sugimoto at the Eden Food Emporium. Need a caffeine boost?"

"I'll manage."

THE EDEN RESEMBLED A NIGHTCLUB MORE THAN A PLACE TO EAT. THERE were bright flashing signs and large holographic projections of dancers in front of the main entry. Inside, Bishop was expecting a rambunctious environment, but it was eerily quiet. The host, a young man who called himself Vapor, bowed. "We're always honored to have guests from Tokko," he said, aware of who Bishop was even though they hadn't identified themselves.

"We're looking for a Stanley Sugimoto," Bishop said.

"I'm sorry, but I don't know the names of any of our clients," Vapor said. He'd dyed his hair white and even wore white contact lenses.

Bishop grasped Vapor's bow tie and began to tidy it. "You think I don't know about your little electric donkey business on the side?" he asked, reading Vapor's Tokko report on his portical. "Does your boss know how you steal all the leftovers and give them to your biomanufactured pets? Listen to your own advice, shut up, and lead the way to Sugimoto."

Vapor looked shocked and scared, but did his best to maintain his resolve. "I'm sorry, but I really don't know any of the names of the clients here. Confidentiality is very important. As for the food, it would have been thrown out anyway."

Bishop didn't think violence would be effective with so many security guards around, so he checked Vapor's personal messages and communications.

"I can see you've been careful," Bishop said, "but I don't think your boss would be happy about the relationship you're having with his—"

"I just remembered Sugimoto-san," Vapor quickly said before Bishop could complete his sentence. "I believe I can lead you to him. You know our rules?"

"What rules?" Reiko asked.

"The club is very strict about our rule that no one is allowed to speak inside. You can express yourself in any other way you'd like."

"What if we need to ask questions?" Bishop demanded.

"You can write them to each other, use sign language, or lip-read. If at any time we hear you speaking, we will be forced to ask you to leave."

Bishop looked at Reiko, who nodded.

The host slid open a thick steel gate and led them through, closing it behind them to ensure silence. They removed their shoes and gave them to one of the waiters, who took them away. The corridors were covered with *ukiyo-e* art from the prestigious artist Kilgore depicting a thousand different manifestations of plankton. The only noise Bishop could hear was their footsteps and the stream of water from an artificial waterfall. Everyone in their way was a mime, using hand motions and their bodies to communicate. "What is—" Bishop began, when the host confronted him with an index finger to his mouth, sternly warning him to shut up.

The first chamber had a line of beautifully dressed men and women who bowed to them as they entered. The clients were dressed in all sorts of uniforms: janitors, book firemen, solar sailors, construction workers, maids, and more. Bishop was amused by the men in skimpy cheerleader uniforms and the women dressed in German astronaut suits. There were doors all along the walls, more hallways, multiple stairs leading to rooms he couldn't see. The club felt like a labyrinth filled with people from all avenues of life talking to each other in sign language. In theory, the event would get more graphic as the evening progressed, caressing, groping, and kissing as permitted (consent was marked through portical agreements and strictly enforced by the guards).

Bishop wondered what it would be like to spend a whole evening with strangers, using only his body to communicate. The array of food being served included the rare Matsutake mushrooms, *toro* platters, Wagyu beef slices with truffles, caviar on top of special soufflés, the nigiri including mackerel and tuna, and the delicate carpaccio.

They walked through three of these halls before arriving at a room with four people who were dressed in animal costumes. The host indicated this was their destination.

Bishop checked the IDs of the people around them on his portical. "Sugimoto isn't here," Bishop said out loud.

Vapor was outraged, as were the four women in kangaroo suits who were flustered and making all sorts of gesticulations.

"Where is he?" Bishop demanded angrily, not caring.

Vapor pointed south.

Approaching them with a drink was a man adorned in jewelry—three gold necklaces and five platinum rings—over his raccoon suit. He had colored the area around his eyes black like a raccoon, and his nasolabial folds were accented by his thin lips.

"Hello, Stanley Sugimoto," Bishop said.

"You're not supposed to talk in here!" Sugimoto snapped.

"Then we can talk somewhere else," Bishop stated.

"Who are you?" Sugimoto demanded.

"I'm Bishop Wakana of the Tokko."

Sugimoto's annoyed expression changed to that of forced compliance at the mention of Tokko. "What do you want?"

"We had a question about your cargo."

"If you're here about those mutant super alligators, you can have them back. They killed too many of the spectators and ain't worth a quarter of what I paid for them."

"We're not here about your mutant super alligators," Bishop said. The Tokko file on Sugimoto covered his extensive belongings and businesses. He'd become rich when he'd accidentally stumbled on a method of androgenesis where fish could use the eggs of other fish to clone themselves. Sugimoto became affluent thanks to sushi vendors who were willing to pay ridiculous amounts of money, since he could re-create very tasty tuna on demand. Since then, he'd dabbled in everything from ball-bearing factories to cabarets and burlesque shows. He'd been sued multiple times for endangering lives in his businesses. But the charges, along with his accusers, often vanished under mysterious circumstances. "Where's a room we can speak in?"

Sugimoto pointed to the host and said, "Ask him."

They were led to a room filled with hundreds of display screens with mimes making expressive gestures. Everywhere Bishop looked, there was a clownish representation of human emotion. He activated the audio nullifier, which created a field around them, blocking off noise and preventing anyone from listening in.

"This is about the crabs, isn't it?" Sugimoto conjectured. "The bioengineers told us they would be bigger and tastier with their changes, but they didn't warn us about the poisonous claws. I've compensated the families of the dead chefs generously."

"We're here about the mecha parts you've been shipping."

"Mecha parts? I don't have any government contracts," Sugimoto said, doing a convincing job of looking surprised.

Reiko stepped closer. "Are you in contact with Pris Watanabe or Bloody Mary?"

"You mean the drink?"

"Don't play dumb."

"How do you play dumb?"

Bishop got annoyed by Sugimoto's defiant expression and moved menacingly toward him. "The whole point of this club is that you can't speak, right? But it's voluntary. Don't force me to make it permanent for you."

"I don't know any Bloody Mary or Watanbe," he stated, mispronouncing Watanabe's name. "You have to bring up any questions about cargo with my managers. I don't handle the day-to-day. I hire people for that. But if you let me check my portical—" he said as he reached into his pocket. He took out a pistol and fired at them.

Reiko raised her right arm, and the bullet bounced off her prosthetic arm.

Sugimoto bolted out.

"Are you okay?" Bishop asked Reiko, seeing blood.

"I'm fine," she replied. "I'm seeing a different side of you tonight."

"Work face," Bishop replied.

"I'd hate to be on the other side of that."

"Me too."

"What if we tried something different?"

"What'd you have in mind?" Bishop asked.

"Let me tag him," Reiko said. "Let him lead us to Watanabe and Bloody Mary directly."

"*If* he leads us to them."

"He will," Reiko confidently assured him.

Bishop nodded his agreement.

They chased Sugimoto as he went through several doors.

"It's weird running without shoes," Bishop said.

"We gotta go back and get them afterward," Reiko replied.

They followed Sugimoto into a massive ballroom. There were hundreds of people dancing together, most in pairs. They all wore strange masks, swaying in unison even though there was no music. The mood of their expression changed based on the angle. Divine anger, apathetic amusement, and wild lust were carved into the cypress, natural pigments coloring their facades with the illusion of human sentiment. Even though they didn't speak out loud, their bodies intimated any emotions that mattered. At the center of a circle column above the rest was a singer, her face covered by a mask. She wasn't actually singing, though she was pretending to in her white gown that made her resemble a swan.

"Where is Stanley Sugimoto?" Reiko yelled.

But no one responded.

Bishop started to rip off their masks, ignoring their muted protests. Reiko did the same. "I know you're here," Bishop called. A few people struggled to keep their masks on. One tried to punch Bishop, but received a fist back into his chest. Bishop removed his mask and was disappointed to see that it wasn't Sugimoto. He raised his gun into the air, about to fire.

"He went that way!" the singer shouted in exasperation, pointing to the opposite corner. She wanted them gone.

Reiko and Bishop pushed people aside in their pursuit and saw Sugimoto running through another door.

This led into the kitchen, where several chefs carted bowls of pork miso ramen that smelled very good. Squid was being fried, and sushi was being meticulously crafted. Bishop spotted a tank full of crabs, stacked up so they had no place to go other than to await their end. They were twice as big as normal crabs, and he wondered if these were the ones with the poisonous claws.

Sugimoto was no longer wearing a raccoon suit but in his underwear, the tattoo of a dragon chomping on a man covering his chest. He was aiming his gun at Bishop. Reiko fired her pistol, and the tracer hit him in the right ankle, causing him to stumble and drop his gun.

"You shot me! I can't believe you shot me."

"You'll live," Reiko said.

Sugimoto fired multiple times their way, hitting one of the chefs in the chest.

Bishop sprinted toward the chef and pulled him behind the kitchen counter for cover. The rest of the staff were huddling there as well. Reiko fired at Sugimoto, but all her remaining shots just barely missed, making them very convincing. Her marksmanship was incredible, Bishop noted.

Sugimoto bolted out the kitchen's back door.

THEY GOT THEIR SHOES BACK AND STEPPED OUTSIDE OF THE CLUB. FORTY local police officers confronted them with guns.

"This is a huge police presence," Reiko said.

"Lot of politicians spend time here," Bishop explained. "Lot of money being thrown around that the police want to protect."

"Place any weapons you have on the ground and put your hands in the air or we will shoot," their commander ordered over the speakers.

"What should we do?" Reiko asked Bishop.

Bishop grinned. "I'm Bishop Wakana of the Tokko. Back off before I arrest every single one of you!" he barked at them, raising his badge.

At the mention of Tokko, they did just that, some even bowing in apology. Bishop knew everything about the police officers from the Tokko files on his portical; the bribes they'd taken, charges of excessive violence, and even the illicit relationships some of them had with prisoners.

"No wonder your niece wants to be a Tokko agent," Reiko commented.

"That's not a good thing," Bishop said.

"You don't want your niece to take after you?"

Bishop thought again about Texarkana. "Never," he answered.

REIKO MORIKAWA

★ ★ ★

LONG BEACH

I.

SUGIMOTO'S TRACER INDICATED HE HAD DRIVEN TO LONG BEACH.

Long Beach was a port bazaar, stinking of salt water, seaweed, fried tempura at the nightstands, oil used by cargo boats, and the rusticated metals of automated mechas that had been in the water too long. Bright neon signs stained the building fronts, offering anything imaginable in purchasable doses. Even though it was early in the morning, the streets were full of shoppers, partiers, and drunks looking for a companion among those as lonely as they were.

The Long Beach Fish Market was one of the busiest places to be in the early morning. Thousands of people were coming and going. There were a dozen or so buyers who were hastily carrying large tuna and swordfish on wooden pushcarts. Mechas that were only six meters tall and had a crew of three were carrying crates full of seafood. The floors were wet from being hosed down, and fresh fish were being cut by band saws and electric knives.

A forklift truck honked at them. Bishop and Reiko got out of the way, and a stream of motorbikes followed the vehicle.

"He's nearby," Reiko said about Sugimoto.

Bishop and Reiko entered the tuna auction area. There were crates everywhere and enormous tuna lining the floors. The genetically modified tuna were four times the size of their natural counterparts.

"You know a lot about the auctions?" Reiko asked.

"Enough to get by. The main auction was over an hour ago, but this is a cleanup round for the smaller vendors who can't afford the best fish," Bishop said. "Purists insist the engineered fish don't taste as good as the ones grown in the wild—those go for premium prices, especially the fish shipped in from the Tsugaru Straits just off of Hokkaido, as they're more creamy with rich fatty meat. Theoretically, the cloned ones are the exact same, only at a tenth of the price."

"Are they?"

"I honestly can't tell the difference."

"You think one day they'll clone all of us and only keep the 'best' around?" Reiko asked.

"As soon as humanly possible, and add in a docile gene to keep us tidy and subservient."

Bishop pointed to the quick finger movements of the purchasers and explained the intricacies of tuna auctioning.

Reiko marveled at his knowledge and said, "It's not too late for you to become a sushi chef."

"It wouldn't feel the same without my brother," Bishop said. "All the real tuna are sold. Now it's clone time."

They spotted Sugimoto limping around the cloned fish.

"He seems in a rush," Bishop noted.

"Why?"

"He's not examining any of the tuna."

"They're all clones. What's the point?" Reiko wondered.

"It's part of the ceremony and ritual," he said, miffed.

Reiko found his irritation amusing. "Sorry he didn't respect the ritual of the cloned tuna."

"Not cool."

Sugimoto left the fish market and walked briskly toward the docks. He went through several fenced areas, which Reiko and Bishop furtively climbed over. There were mountains of containers, organized into a maze that was confusing to navigate. There were mobile container cranes on rails that could access most of the quay. Labor mechas were outfitted with special equipment to help with the big loads.

Reiko and Bishop spotted guards with concealed weapons, which struck Reiko as highly unusual. They were trying to look like civilians, not military personnel. "Who owns this area?"

"The government," Bishop replied. "Those two guards are ex-navy, but they're not employed by the port authority."

"Who do they work for?"

"My records don't show. Last official spotting is Bangkok two months ago, where they were working as private contractors."

Reiko motioned Bishop away from the gates and toward the stacked container crates. She took out the grappling hook on her utility belt and attached it to her pistol. The hook had a magnet that could clinch on to any metallic surface. She aimed, let the portical calculate the distance up to the tenth crate, and fired. It took a few seconds for the hook to secure itself, and she tugged on the rope to be sure it wasn't loose. She climbed up the rope first, using her feet against the crates to make it a fast ascent. Bishop followed behind. They didn't see any guards on top.

Reiko gestured toward the waterfront and said, "Sugimoto isn't far."

They moved on top of the container crates, using the grappling hook as necessary. It wasn't long before they arrived at an open space next to the pier. They dropped to their stomachs, as the Labor mechas were tall enough to spot them. Though she couldn't see Sugimoto, she could see four super tankers that were weighed down in the water by heavy cargo. A Labor was removing a massive cargo box from a ship's deck and carrying it toward one of the five bulk storage warehouses along the waterfront. Reiko espied several women in working clothes who were giving orders as though they were part of a military regiment. "We have to figure out what's in the cargo," Reiko said.

"They're all ex-military," Bishop pointed out, then tapped his portical. "Kikkai connection is bad. There might be a disruptor, as it's really slow. Hold on." It took a minute for him to get the answers to his search. "Sixty-four of the ninety-two people working down there are ex–mecha corps. The rest are navy."

"Mecha corps?" Reiko looked back at the cargo boxes. "Can you see cargo manifests on your portical?"

"They haven't been registered. But it's a good bet they're mecha parts."

Reiko recognized the oversized containers as similar to the ones they received when she worked at Mechtown. "You're right. They're assembling mechas here," she said.

Bishop was reading something on his scans. "Nineteen of those present are mecha engineers."

"How many are pilots?"

It took another thirty seconds before he could find out. "The eight driving the Labors are certified to drive them, but they're not military. I'm only spotting three official military pilots."

"What are their names?"

"Lina Niijima, Pris Watanabe, and your friend Daniela Takemi," Bishop replied.

"Daniela Takemi?!" Reiko startled. "Are you sure it's her?"

"Yep."

"There's no mistake?"

"No mistake. She must have come here after leaving the Alvarado Sento."

Reiko was troubled by Daniela's connection to the bombing. Reiko thought of her last conversation with her right before Bloody Mary attacked. Was Daniela really the one who'd betrayed them? "Is there any chance this whole thing is military related, like a secret operation our forces are carrying out?" Reiko asked, wanting to confirm that it wasn't official business they were mixing up with something more insidious. She had a hard time accepting Daniela could have betrayed them.

"I wondered that too. But if it's a covert op, usually my feed will go blank on them with a 'classified' notification. I'm not seeing that. I've also messaged my boss, Akiko-san, to check if they're aware of anything going on here, but I'm seriously doubtful."

"Did she reply yet?"

"The message just barely got out."

"They're three of the best pilots we have," Reiko stated.

"I can see that," Bishop said as he read his portical. "Their list of awards and commendations is ridiculously long. I've read up on them before, but now that I'm seeing this list, it's incredible."

Even if Reiko had the *Inago*, she could not fight against them and expect to win. The idea of fighting against her friend Daniela bothered her more than anything else. "If those are mecha parts, then I need to get the basic measurements and see the way the helmets are shaped," Reiko said. "I might be able to guess what type of mecha they're constructing and what their aim might be."

"You want to get closer?" Bishop inquired.

"We have to so I can do a visual check. How snug is that z-cloak?"

"It can expand."

"It has camo mode, right?" she asked, remembering him using it at East Texarkana against the TriWalker.

"It does," Bishop warily answered. "Why?"

Reiko made sure her gun was ready. "Let me under."

Bishop switched to saggy mode, which stretched out the entire cloak. Reiko came in underneath, and it felt like she was under a small tent that reached down to their feet. The cloak was one-sided as well, so she could look outward and see everything around her. "Put on your hoodie and let's go."

The two of them slowly walked toward the storage building. With the hoodie on and the camo doing an effective job of refracting light, no one at ground level spotted them. They were too preoccupied handling their business anyway. Reiko saw the inner tubing of a mecha being carried over by a gigantic forklift truck. There was something about its coating that looked different. Rather than go to the containers that were close to the warehouse, they went around to the backside, where there was minimal security.

"Any ideas how to get down?" Bishop asked.

Reiko took her grappling hook, fired into the top of the container, then threw the rope over the side.

"I'll go first," she said, and came out from under the z-cloak, held the rope, and dropped down, occasionally grabbing the rope to soften her fall.

Bishop's descent was much slower, as he carefully lowered himself on the rope, never once letting go.

When he finally reached the bottom, Reiko looked at Bishop with her brows raised, and he in turn reacted with a defensive, "What?"

There was a soldier guarding the door, but he was distracted reading his portical. "I got this," Bishop mouthed to her.

He snuck up on the guard, stealthily using the crates to come up from behind. Reiko aimed with her pistol on tranquilizer mode, just in case. Right as Bishop was about to grab the guard, he stepped on a piece of plastic trash. The guard turned around. The two stared at each other in surprise. Before either could react, Reiko fired at the guy's chest. The tranquilizer dart perforated his armor, but it would still take a few seconds before it could do its work. Bishop punched the guy as hard as he could, knocking him to the ground. He was about to follow up with another punch, but the guard was already unconscious.

"Thanks for the assist," he said.

"I knew you'd have it all under control," Reiko said with a teasing smile.

Bishop picked the guard up by his arms and dragged him away from the door. "He's heavier than he looks," he said.

"He might have artificial parts," Reiko suggested. "Most soldiers are getting supplements to improve their strength. Help me take off his uniform."

The uniform was big for her, but it had an autofit function which made it automatically match her size. He was a hairy man, and the clothing smelled like he hadn't washed in weeks. Reiko did her best to ignore the odor. Bishop hid the guard inside one of the lockers and swiped his portical to connect with his own.

"Anything fun?" Reiko asked.

"Not much, but there are two encrypted communications with another mecha officer in Los Angeles discussing the patrol routes for their defense force."

"Does he explain why they need the patrol routes?"

"No. But that would spoil the mystery."

"I like spoilers," Reiko said.

Inside the warehouse, Reiko saw the first of the mechas. Only its upper half was assembled, and they were still getting the legs out. She did not recognize its head as it was some new type, based possibly on the Leviathan class, though with far sharper contours. She did notice a distinctive type of wiring for the BPG, which, theoretically, could give it much more energy. She had to check the armaments, even if they were in a separate compartment. There were so many questions she had. Most of the ground crew were too busy on the mecha's construction to notice her in uniform and Bishop in his z-cloak.

"What kind of mecha is it?" Bishop asked.

"I've never seen this type."

"Can you tell if it's a combat model?"

"I think so. Based on the helmet, you can tell what kind of bridge they have and if it's designed to withstand bombardment."

"Is it?"

"It's titanium and there's all sorts of sensors on the helmet. It looks like it has a bridge crew of five, which is small but not abnormal for military." Something was bothering her. "The hatches and conduits on the armor look different from anything I've seen before."

"In what way?"

"It's almost like they're designed to have a fluid field around them, but I'm not sure how that would work," Reiko said, wanting to get even closer. It had anatomical features like a rib cage and clavicles, rather than the samurai-styled armor most mechas had been designed after.

Suddenly she remembered Bloody Mary's words: *I'll make sure every single one of you knows what it's like to feel the terrors of war, unsafe within your own walls. If you don't want to take part, you can flee Los Angeles, as I will make no distinction between civilian and military personnel. All are guilty in my eyes. Today's bombing is only a warning. Starting tomorrow, the real war begins.*

"I think they're going to attack Los Angeles," Reiko said.

"Which part?"

"I mean the whole city."

Bishop stiffened. "If that thing attacked Los Angeles, how much trouble would the city be in?"

"Hard to say without checking its weapon systems," she said. "But with those three piloting, they'd cause a hell of a lot of destruction."

"I got to get a message out to my sister-in-law and niece."

"Go ahead," Reiko said.

Bishop tried to send a message and ended up cursing. "I'm not getting any reception on my portical."

Reiko pointed up at a Labor that was inactive. "Are you thinking what I'm thinking?"

"What are you thinking?" Bishop asked.

"We can't let them assemble these mechas, and that's our way of stopping them," Reiko said.

"I think we're thinking the same thing."

Reiko stared back up at the Labor. "What about getting help?"

"We can get help after we kick some ass," Bishop said.

"I can get behind that."

"Will the Labor even work?" Bishop inquired.

"No reason it shouldn't."

They approached the Labor. It was an older model and had seen its share of rough times. The upper chest contained the BPG and an engineering nook for maintenance crews of two. Labors in general looked like construction equipment if they were anthropomorphic. She climbed up the ladder on its front and entered the bridge in its head. If there was a security lock in place, it would be over before it began. Fortunately, there was only a kikkai restraint which was intended to prevent access. Reiko had dealt with these at Berkeley in a manner that annoyed all her colleagues. She just reset the entire program so that it'd go to its default factory settings and lose any additions or changes others had made. She preferred that anyway, as other users would switch up the controls and adjust camera settings and limb articulation sensitivity so that it was like driving something alien.

Power came into the bridge as the BPG started to warm up. It was an older-styled bridge without the usual augmented controls. Instead, there was a seat full of buttons and handles to drive the mecha. Reiko checked the diagnostics to see if there was anything faulty in the machinery. There was some circuitry that needed maintenance and the left arm wasn't working properly, which would explain why it wasn't currently being used. But she'd be able to make it function by rerouting the energy through the chest widget and the alternate clavicle conduits, which were mainly put in place in case the main lines failed. The Labor took two minutes to warm up, but she did a test articulation, rotating it forward, then up and down. The arms were functioning as expected. She checked the interface again and saw the Labor was called the *Nagumo*. It was sturdy and sufficient for their objective.

"What should I do?" Bishop, who had followed behind her, asked.

"Get on the communicator and try to get a message out to call for the cavalry," Reiko replied. "And contact your sister-in-law too."

Labor mechas had interchangeable arms, which meant they were able to swap out a standard-issue hand with a magnet, crane, and power drill as well. The drill was on the *Nagumo*'s right hand, and its left hand was still in its normal state.

Reiko looked at the nearly assembled mecha and hesitated, not because she had any scruples about her mission but because she hated destroying a mecha, especially one that looked so elegant.

"You getting anything?" Reiko asked Bishop.

"I've sent out a few emergency bursts. There won't be any reception, but it should have gone out."

"What about your sister-in-law?"

Bishop shook his head. "Nothing yet."

"Strap yourself in."

Reiko stepped forward. The Labor mecha was heavier than she was used to on the *Inago* and it took a minute to calibrate herself.

Her motion caught the attention of the crew members on the ground. Reiko knew she didn't have much time. She moved toward the unassembled mecha and smashed its head, then its chest, pounding it with its fists. As it hadn't been fully stitched together, the arm dropped onto the ground. Another strong punch caused the torso to cave in, the wiring sundering apart. The mechanisms supporting the mecha broke apart and it began to topple backward, crashing into the containers behind it. She took the drill in her arm and drove it into its head, destroying the bridge. When she began drilling its chest, a gelatinous substance that reminded her of the biomechs' skin seeped out. The goo reacted to her drill, suddenly becoming hard. Her drill snapped in half. She tried using her fist to penetrate, but her fingers ended up getting dented.

"I think," Reiko began, "this mecha we broke incorporates bio-mech technology."

"Huh?"

"Take the best of our mechas and combine it with the best of a Nazi biomech. You'd have something indestructible." She pondered its implications. "Our forces won't stand a chance. We have to destroy the others."

The *Nagumo* stood up. Even with a half-broken drill and weak hands, Reiko felt they should be able to cause damage to the other unassembled mechas. But as she emerged from the warehouse, a mecha approached her. Unlike the one she'd destroyed, she recognized Pris Watanabe's mecha: the *Sygma*.

"I've seen that mecha before," Bishop said. "That's General Watanabe."

The general's mecha, *Sygma*, was colored a bloody red that looked eerily impervious to attack. Its helmet had elephantine features, with tusks that curled toward its face. The chest plate appeared to be made out of titanium rib cages, and all the limbs were bulky in size. The knuckles and shoulder pads had spikes on them, and there were special blades on its forearm for attacking. The *Sygma* wielded a massive chainsaw it had to hold with both arms, while its fusion sword was sheathed. Reiko also knew it had a trunk blade that emerged from its retracting proboscis to attack enemies that got too close.

"You think you can defeat her?" Bishop asked.

"No," Reiko answered immediately. "But maybe we can ask her to let us go."

"You think she would?"

"Let me try."

Reiko pinged the *Sygma* on audio only. Pris Watanabe showed up on her communicator.

"I'm suffering a malfunction with the Labor's controls," Reiko lied. "I've lost control of it. Possible viral infection. Please help."

There was no answer. Instead, the *Sygma* directed its chainsaw straight at Reiko, slicing off the *Nagumo*'s arms. It whirled around, stuck a chainsaw through the Labor's engine so they could not escape, then put the saw to their head, which Watanabe used smoothly to decapitate them. It was like a dance, only Reiko was the victim. She held on to her seat, and Bishop was strapped in too. The drop came quickly as they crashed into the floor, safety foam filling the bridge to try to cushion the damage. Neither of them could move. Reiko looked over at Bishop, who looked back. He didn't say anything, but she could see he was sending a message with his hands. They didn't have long, as someone burned a hole into the side of the mecha head, and several soldiers rushed in with guns pointed at them. Reiko and Bishop unstrapped themselves and followed the soldiers outside.

Two figures emerged from the *Sygma*'s kneepad, where they took a ladder down. Reiko recognized one as Pris Watanabe, the ethnically Japanese pilot who'd shaved all her hair, including her lashes and brows. Next to her was a woman who matched the height and build of Bloody Mary but wore a white pilot mask and white leather.

"Reiko Morikawa?" Pris asked.

"General Watanabe," Reiko said back.

"It's been several years since Mechtown."

"Yes, ma'am."

"Why did you destroy our mecha?"

"I should be asking what you're doing assembling these mechas," Reiko defiantly demanded.

"Do you know the true story of what happened to the late governor Daigo Tamura?"

"What true story?"

"About his assassination," Pris asked.

"He was assassinated by terrori—" Bishop began.

"Shut your mouth before I rip out your tongue," Pris warned, unsheathing her sword and pressing it against Bishop's neck, causing a line of blood to form. "As I was asking, do you know what happened to the late governor?"

Reiko looked over at Bishop and saw the confusion in his face. "I do," she admitted.

"Then you know this entire government is illegitimate," Pris said. "Do you know what Governor Yamaoka did to his enemies? To all of Governor Tamura's henchmen?"

"Whatever their fate, they deserved it. He betrayed us to the Nazis."

"I have no love for the late governor, and I don't condemn the reasoning behind his assassination. But Governor Yamaoka put my mother and father inside pig cages and dropped them alive into the ocean, along with a hundred other officials."

"Th-that's not true," Reiko said.

"I accepted their deaths as a loyal citizen of the Empire and because I believed the deception behind Governor Tamura's death. But I was told my parents were given poison and a painless death. If they had betrayed us to the Nazis, I had to abide by the decision. But now I understand that this wasn't about collusion. This was about maintaining power," Pris said.

"Who's power?"

"Governor Yamaoka, of course," General Watanabe said. "We believe tradition makes us strong when it's just a leash meant to bring us to our knees." Pris pointed at Bloody Mary. "She told me the truth. I won't be under the yoke of the Sons of War any longer. If you know what's best, you should join us."

Reiko thought about the night of the assassination again. Then of the corpses at the Alvarado Sento. "My condolences for your parents. I had no idea. But I could never join a terrorist group who'd harm innocent civilians to make a point."

Pris nodded. "You don't even see the invisible chains that leash you."

She raised her sword, about to cut their heads off, starting with Bishop.

"Not him," Bloody Mary said as she approached them.

"We can't leave him alive," the general stated.

"We can if it serves our purpose," Bloody Mary replied. To Reiko and Bishop, she said, "You two make for an odd couple. I wondered if you'd come to thank me for sparing your lives."

"You killed hundreds of people at the Sento!" Reiko yelled.

"One murder is the same as a thousand. Your delusion is that you believe there's such a thing as an innocent civilian." Bloody Mary stiffened straight up and said in a manner mocking speech-makers, "We're going to commit tremendous atrocities to make our country great again! How tragic it is that you choose to close your eyes to wanton violence in exchange for—what is it? The freedom to waste your time?"

"An assassin with a social message," Reiko muttered. "How original. Why don't you spare the rest of us and share your grievances on SOCIAL like everyone else?"

Bloody Mary laughed.

"Watch the way you speak to her!" Pris yelled, kicking Reiko.

"It's okay," Bloody Mary said. "I do have a SOCIAL account, and every once in a while, I do post a kill or two. But interacting through fake avatars on the kikkai doesn't compare with directly seeing the way my actions affect people."

"You mean your victims," Reiko said, sensing the joy in her tone. Bloody Mary was genuinely giddy, but it wasn't because of their conversation.

The whole situation thrilled her.

"You like to stand on your high moral ground," Bloody Mary said. "But you're not even aware of your part in nearly starting a war."

"What war?"

"In Texarkana, eight political figures were assassinated. Governor Yamaoka tried to blame me, but I had no part in it. Yamaoka wants a war with the Nazis, and he was going to blame you two for it."

Reiko wanted to shout back in denial. But she couldn't—at least not with conviction.

"You knew?" Bloody Mary inquired amusedly. "And yet you still choose to remain loyal. Can't you tell your feet from your hands?"

"How did you find us?" Pris Watanabe asked him.

"The Tokko know all about this place," Bishop lied.

Bloody Mary sighed. "Leave it to a man to botch everything. Bring Sugimoto here."

The soldiers dragged Stanley Sugimoto to them. He was wearing a thick belt that had a tuna gaff, ruler, and flashlight.

"You had followers," Bloody Mary stated with a neutral voice, referring to Bishop and Reiko.

"I'm sorry," he said. "I just needed to step out and check the tuna. That lady shot me in the leg."

Bloody Mary inspected his knee, then took the tuna gaff from his belt. She pointed the sharp hook end at Sugimoto and slammed it straight into his leg, causing Sugimoto to scream. He cursed her and shouted numerous expletives.

"So this is how you found us," Bloody Mary said to Reiko, having destroyed the tag. "What's the point of having eyes if you can't see the obvious?" Bloody Mary took out the gaff and this time struck Sugimoto in his right eye, causing it to burst. Bloody Mary took the gaff back out and thrust it into his forehead multiple times until he died.

The soldiers surrounded Bishop and Reiko, ready to fire, but Bloody Mary stopped them.

"But they destroyed the *Speer*," Pris protested. "If you let them live, they'll report back on us."

"That's the point," Bloody Mary replied. "I want the public to know what they know, and what better way than to send them to cyber purgatory."

"What's cyber purgatory?" Reiko asked.

"You'll find out."

"At least tell us why you're doing all of this," Reiko said, motioning to the mechas that signified their impending attack.

"You still don't understand?" Watanabe asked Reiko. "We've both taken part in many battles, but what was it all for? The glory of men. I thought Governor Tamura's death would make a difference. But Yamaoka isn't any different."

"If you gave Governor Yamaoka a chance . . ."

"We did," Watanabe replied firmly.

"Do you mind if I ask a question too?" Bishop asked.

Bloody Mary shook her head. "The time for questions is over."

"How come she got to ask a question?"

"One question equals one limb," Bloody Mary said to Bishop. "Which would you like to lose?"

Bishop became quiet.

Bloody Mary and General Watanabe went back to their red mecha, the *Sygma*.

"Don't tell me you were going to ask her name," Reiko said.

"How'd you know?"

"Because you're an idiot."

"Guilty," Bishop said. And as they looked at each other, she felt deeply sad realizing this might be the end for both of them. "If we survive this, I'll have to take you to Ise-Shima for some really good *Ise udon*."

"So you didn't like the one we had last night?" she asked.

"It was decent for Los Angeles. But my dad used to take me to the best places when we traveled to the main island."

The soldiers injected both of them with needles, and Reiko felt everything become disoriented.

II.

REIKO WOKE AND FOUND HERSELF HOOKED TO AN IV. NEXT TO HER WAS A woman whose body was wrapped in bandages. There was a liver placed in a glass jar full of liquid by her side. Several limbs were frozen inside a glass case, and the whole area smelled of liquid septic treatment and isopropyl alcohol. The ground wasn't very hygienic, splatters of blood and human tissue littering the area. They were in a warehouse, and Reiko's arms refused to listen to her brain's request to move. She tried lifting her legs to stand, but they too remained unresponsive.

"Ah, you're finally up," a man in a surgical mask said. He was holding a blood-drenched organ which he placed on the table. "I have a few questions for you, more for confirmation than anything else. If you answer truthfully, the experience will be as pain-free as we can manage. You can't talk right now, so if you can just blink once for yes, twice for no, that will make this much easier to manage. First off, are you a blood type A?"

Reiko wanted to ask which hospital she was in, but she blinked twice.

"Very good. You're not a type A, and I mainly wanted to make sure you understood me. Now I know you're very confused about what's going on. You don't need to worry. The less you think, the better it'll be. Does your family have any history of diseases that our doctors have not been able to handle?"

Reiko blinked twice again.

"Excellent. You're doing really well. This is going to be a tougher question, as we weren't able to access your personnel files on this, which were all marked classified. Do you work for the government? Don't answer that one, because I already know you do. The one I really want to know is, were any organs in your body replaced?"

Reiko tried to remember, but her memory was a haze.

"It's okay," a nurse next to the doctor said. "I'm reading your parental history. It seems they were accused of committing treason and speaking in favor of the Nazis. Is this true?"

Reiko shook her head angrily. *They were cleared of all wrongdoing!* she wanted to scream.

"She's still dry," the doctor, who had serpent scales on his coat, said. "Give her some more, on me."

The nurse placed something on Reiko's head. She felt something sharp stab her temples and electric pulses surge through her body.

Were these organ and body harvesters? She'd trained for this kind of situation, hadn't she? She tried to remember how she was supposed to get out of it.

The doctor brought out a sharp blade that was glowing red. They fastened her arms to a table so they were perpendicular to her body.

"I like your artificial arm," the doctor said. "I see quite a bit of scarring where it meets the shoulder. Where'd you injure this? Don't worry. You should be able to talk now."

"W-what—what are you doing?"

"We're recording your emotions, your memories, your feelings while I conduct my operation," the doctor said. "You can try to resist, or not. The most important aspect is to be authentic so the Cyber Bubble will record it and relay it to audiences. But even if you pretend otherwise, it'll be part of the recording."

"O-operation? Cyber Bubble?"

"I'll be cutting your arm and replacing it with hers," he said, pointing to the woman lying next to him. "She's shown a special type of proclivity with mutations in chromosomes that—"

Memories were being triggered in her mind, like it was a store selling glimpses of her past. It was a mashing of mysteries and her parents were very understanding, encouraging her to follow her passions rather than chase after a letter on a piece of paper. *Grades don't matter*, they'd said to her. *Only do what you love.*

A mecha emerged from the ground in the shape of her mother, who then split into two parts, one morphing into her father. Her father did a kabuki dance on one foot and the two jumped on a big chicken that flew up into the air. Other virulent chickens yelled at the two of them, doing their best to bring them down. The whole planet became filled with their angry squawks.

"Don't listen to them!" she begged her parents. "Don't listen to any of them!"

But everything disappeared and there was someone walking her way. At first, it looked like a biomech miniaturized to the size of a human. It held an enormous ax that it could barely hold up. She tried to withdraw, but her legs were encased inside cement blocks. Reiko panicked, hitting the blocks with her fists, doing what she could to try to escape. As the figure got closer, she prepared for the worst. The screech of the ax as it hit the ground vexed her. It was actually Bloody Mary, not a biomech. Bloody Mary was covered in blood from her face mask to her boots and Reiko braced herself for an attack. Blood was darker than in portical films, not that bright red but a darker hue that soaked into her organic suit. But Bloody Mary didn't see her, walking past her. Behind them were hundreds of people, helplessly fallen on the ground. Reiko tried to yell at them, "Run! You have to run!"

Bloody Mary took her massive ax and swung it. The people turned into wisps of gas, evaporating at the blow.

"Please stop!" she pleaded. "Please!"

Bloody Mary did not listen, decimating the phantom spirits mercilessly. They did not scream as they were killed. They had no voices, and even when they opened their mouths, their vocal cords were muted. Inside their mouths, their teeth had rotted off and their uvulas were tarred black with oil. At the center of the crowd were her parents. They'd landed from their flying chicken. Bloody Mary was heading straight toward them. Reiko tried to warn them, begging them to escape.

Suddenly Bloody Mary and all the people vanished. Reiko saw the ceiling, which had mouse and elephant patterns on it. She looked over and saw the doctor operating on a woman. Had she been hallucinating? No, it must be the chemical defenses within her body.

When Reiko had the procedure to get the artificial arm installed, she'd also asked to have chemical boosters implanted that would automatically counteract foreign substances beyond a certain threshold. It had been a recommended process for military officers, but many had objected on grounds it could cause mental diseases despite scientific evidence proving otherwise. As Reiko's consciousness came back to her, she was glad she'd ignored the critics and gotten the upgrade. But she knew if she didn't do something immediately, she was going to lose consciousness and get stuck in this Cyber Bubble dream until she was— What was their end goal? How far did they take these Cyber Bubble experiences? The doctor was working on the other woman, sawing from the sound of the female screaming and the jarring noise of the blade on bone. Were they not using anesthetics? Were there people actually paying to directly experience a painful surgical procedure?

The thought angered her, and energy pumped through her body. There were restraints on her, but if she could activate the knife missile and use it to free herself, she might have a chance. She noticed there was music playing on the radio, a violinist racing against seeming chaos in a frenetic aural clash with an orchestra. Reiko began her struggle toward freedom.

★

THE
REVOLUTION
OF THE
BLOODY MECHAS

BISHOP WAKANA

★ ★ ★

LONG BEACH

I.

BISHOP HATED SLEEP; HE NEVER KNEW WHERE HIS SUBCONSCIOUS WOULD force him. Even after Bloody Mary's soldiers injected him with hallucinogens, he resisted sleep as long as he could.

"Where is Bloody Mary?" he heard someone from his past echo.

He looked up and saw swastikas that were made of human bones. "I don't know."

"What is your name?" the Nazi officer asked. His hair was on fire and his skin was semitranslucent, so Bishop could see the skull underneath.

"Bishop Wakana," he'd replied.

"What is your role in the army?"

"I'm—I'm a surveyor of crops."

"Are you lying, Bishop Wakana?"

"N-no. I'm a surveyor," he confirmed.

"Good. There's nothing I hate more than a liar."

The Nazis whipped him. They beat him. They pulled out his teeth one by one. They put wires on his eyes to keep them open. They kept on asking, "What's your mission? Where's Bloody Mary?"

Except these weren't Nazis above him. It was a doctor and his nurse, their faces covered by sanitary masks. They weren't looking for Bloody Mary anymore. Bloody Mary was the one who had brought them here.

His vision blurred again and he saw black blobs moving all over the ceiling. They were amorphous gatherings of slime that were waiting for him to get weak and vulnerable so they could mutate him into a blob too. Bishop gritted his teeth and saw a claw reaching out for his neck, trying to throttle the breath out of him. He closed his eyes and after he reopened them, the claw was gone. Water was dripping down the walls, colored a sickly green that was acidic. He wanted to vomit, and nausea was making him dizzy. An earthquake wracked the floor, and the whole room was spinning. The tiles were heads of all the corpses he'd buried. He closed his eyes, ignored their accusatory expressions. The Nazis were going to take him away again, laughing at him after what they'd subjected him to.

"Just tell us where Bloody Mary is going," they'd told him.

But that was the past, when he'd sworn, "I don't know. They never told us anything about her."

The Nazis put Bishop in a room that spun ever so slowly. Every time he lay down, they accelerated the spinning sensation to put him in a constant state of dizziness. Whenever he opened his eyes, the Nazis decelerated again, and he couldn't tell if the speed changes were part of his delusion. Somehow, the chemicals they'd injected him with were dredging that all back up.

How long had the Nazis tortured him? He remembered the mosquito room, where they'd isolated him in the complete dark. He couldn't see anything, but he heard the mosquitoes buzzing in his ear. They were all over his body and within a few hours, every part of him was itching. Since he was chained up, he couldn't scratch his body. It was worse knowing he was being sucked dry. How many mosquitoes did it require to drain a human of all his blood? He should have been more worried about what diseases the Nazis infected them with. He wished there was some way he could kill the mosquitoes. Anytime he was about to doze off, they buzzed in his ear. How long were they going to leave him inside with the mosquitoes?

"Where's Bloody Mary?" someone asked again.

Why did they keep on asking him that? Whatever mission she'd been on, it was completed by now, wasn't it?

He was itchy all over, and the thought of these tiny insects feasting on his blood made him angrier and angrier. Why didn't he just tell them where Bloody Mary was going? It would be so easy.

"Do you want kids?" the Nazi asked.

"I haven't thought about it."

"You've never thought about kids?"

"Never," Bishop lied.

"You should. I can tell that death doesn't faze you," the Nazi said, glancing at all of Bishop's wounds and broken bones. "What about your future?"

"What about my future?"

"If you don't comply, we will sterilize you. Then what would your wife think?"

How did they know about her? "I don't have a wife," he tried to lie.

"You told us you were married."

"No, I didn't."

"Are you lying to me? I told you I hated liars. You told us how much your wife wanted children."

Had he really told them about his family, their plans for at least three kids? He didn't remember what he'd said, what he hadn't. But it was true. For Bishop, having lost his father at a young age, he wanted to have the family he never had as a kid. The Nazis brought the sterilizing gun and gave him a choice.

"What are you doing?" Bishop demanded.

"Where is Bloody Mary?"

Bishop looked desperately at the gun. They'd already taken everything away from him personally. Now they were taking away his chance to have children. The Nazi saw the helplessness in his eyes.

"Last chance. Are you really willing to give up everything you cherish and hold dear for Bloody Mary?"

He was about to tell them everything he knew, anything he could to clutch on to the dream that he'd eventually be able to escape and have kids with his wife. It took all his strength to remind himself that even if he did give Bloody Mary up, the Nazis would still kill him. He spat in the Nazi's face, defying them at his most vulnerable. The sterilizer was barely noticeable. There was a luminescent gleam and heat emanating from the faceted prod. It was over in a minute.

"I salute you for sacrificing everything to keep your secret," the Nazi had said with a begrudging hint of respect. "You can no longer have children."

They beat him badly that night. He didn't care then because he'd lost the one thing that had kept him going for much of his life. He cared even less now that the doctor was pumping him with chemicals that transformed his subconscious projections into a torturous reality. He was jumping through time and it was his wife, Felicia, angrily accusing him of sabotaging their future.

"They said you had a choice," she said.

"Who told you?"

"Who cares who told me? Did you?"

Bishop had a hard time meeting his wife's angry glower. "I did," he confessed.

"Why didn't you just tell them what they wanted to know?" she'd demanded. "Everyone else did."

"How can you say that to me?" he asked furiously. "Do you know what they did to me? I couldn't let them win after all the ways they tortured and humiliated me!"

"You could have for your family."

Family. Bishop thought again about his father, killed for . . . for what?

Felicia had a temper. So did he. Their yelling matches went all night. Security guards in their apartment came by a dozen times, told them the neighbors were complaining.

"Even with the veteran benefits, we're barely making ends meet!" Felicia yelled. "I don't want to live in this studio forever. You can't walk outside without fear of getting mugged, the toilets always get clogged, they turn off hot water all the time, and the elevator breaks every other week. It's hard for me to climb up fourteen floors on my bad knee!"

"I don't want to go back to the police force."

"Why didn't you want to go back?" a voice asked. But it wasn't his ex-wife. It sounded like Reiko.

"Because I hated being around dead bodies all the time."

There were so many corpses during the Texarkana attack. Up above in the mecha called the *Syren*, everything looked like toy figures. Even in his rocket pack, it appeared to Bishop as though humans were ants in combat.

"You're doing well," the doctor said. But he wasn't the Nazi physician. "Your Cyber Bubble is getting the highest traffic on the site for the past three hours. That's superb. People are looking through your past and it's abnormally lucid. I've never seen past dives that are this vivid without some type of augmentation or memory recorder."

"Which past?" Bishop asked.

"In the Nazi camp. They want to see all the details. Your memory is blocking out the faces for some reason, which is okay, but if you can recall specifics, that'll be great because audiences love a rivalry. All the arguments with your wife are helping too. Adds real drama and stakes to the situation. But what exactly is it you were protecting? If you saved a grand reveal for everyone, I think that could really spice up ratings to the point where sponsors will send ad money your way. I'm not guaranteeing your freedom—that's out of the question. But with sponsors, we could mix up the memories and potentially upgrade you to full-fledged 'Author' status. That means you'd get a variety of experiences and genres people will pay to watch. I can also give you something a little more . . . pleasing, depending on your preferences."

Sponsors? Bishop thought again about Felicia, wanting all the things he could never provide her. It was basic stuff, but they couldn't afford a home of their own. Not with prices skyrocketing in the capital city, Los Angeles. The police force job he'd been offered was in Dallas Tokai, but he didn't want to take it, which infuriated Felicia. "Housing is cheaper there," she said. "MEZ Enterprises has houses on sale that have a progressive development factor of five at affordable rates."

But it was too close to the Quiet Border for him to feel comfortable. He didn't want to go and became upset with himself because he couldn't do what was best for his family.

"Why didn't you just tell the Nazis what they wanted to know?" Felicia demanded again.

He pondered that decision all the time. Why hadn't he just betrayed Bloody Mary's location? The other soldiers did, and the ones who survived weren't punished by USJ authorities.

The Nazis tied his limbs in four opposing directions with a motorcycle at each end, a modernized quartering. "They'll begin to pull and once they go, there's no way to stop until your arms and legs get pulled out from your body!"

They had lists of executions they'd been improving on, from scaphism to dismemberment, all of which his interrogators meticulously described. "We have the medical technology to kill you, then bring you back to life and kill you all over again. Your whole life will be a thousand deaths," they warned him.

What was death? he wondered. Was it a physical end, or was there a spiritual one too? Would he be reincarnated as a ghost, wandering the planet, burning with a desire for vengeance? Or did life cease when its physical form was ended?

Beyond the Nazi interrogators, he noticed shadowy figures watching him. There were endless numbers of them, no faces, and barely discernible bodies. He could feel their eyes. It wasn't just his physical self they were watching. Their sight was somehow boring in on his brain as they studied his emotions. He wished there was a divider between him and them, but he was tied on a metal frame, and the skin on his back was turning ashen from the volts.

He was surprised to see Reiko approach him. "Wh-what are you doing here?" he asked her. "You have to get out of here!"

"None of this is real," she said as she began to loosen his straps.

"What are you talking about?"

"This is part of a Cyber Bubble, the unregulated and illegal side of it from the looks of it. I changed the preferences so you can see everyone who's watching in avatar form. You're plugged in, but if I disconnect now with the way they've hooked into your brain, you'd suffer a bubble psychosis and have really bad mental damage. If you wake up naturally from it, you should be okay."

"I don't understand. This is all fake?"

"This is a rescue, Bishop. Wake up."

Rescue? That's what they'd told him in the past. The Nazis staged fake rescues, sent in fake soldiers from his rocket pack unit to try to trick him into thinking he'd gotten out. "Did your mission succeed? Did Bloody Mary reach her target?" they asked.

He replied, "What mission? Who was Bloody Mary supposed to target?"

"You need to tell us," the Nazi soldiers masquerading as Bishop's own said to him.

"I don't know anything!" he'd yelled.

When he finally did get out, the sight of couples with their kids made him bitter. He hated hanging out with friends who only talked about their newborns. He hated when they sent him their pictures and videos, bragging about the dumbest things. Oh, look, my kid is petting a dog for the first time! Hey hey, my son is dressed up in this cute mecha pilot costume. Whenever he saw his wife look longingly at other couples with their kids, it made him angrier and meaner.

"I don't know where she is," he often said to himself in the shower, making Felicia ask who he was talking about.

"That's already over," someone said to him. It was Reiko again. "These are just bad memories getting all jumbled up."

"It's not over!" Bishop yelled. "I don't know where Bloody Mary is. Stop asking me!"

"I don't care where she is!" Reiko yelled back, releasing him from the charged torture bed.

"Then what do you want from me?"

"Give me your hand."

"Why?"

"So we can leave together."

She looked so much like Reiko. Was it really her? Or had they dug out his memory of her and projected it to deceive him? They knew about Felicia. Why not Reiko? She extended her hand out for him to grab.

She looked so real. Would it cause any harm to follow? When he touched her hand, he felt himself being drawn somewhere else.

Suddenly he was on a street he didn't recognize. Looming above them was a massive biomech. The biomech was taller than the ones they'd fought outside Texarkana, reaching all the way to the stars. Was that even physically possible? It was terrifying to behold.

"Wh-where are we?" he asked, and saw Reiko cowering in a doorway. He went to reassure her, but there was a shield of energy around her, preventing him from getting close. The biomech above was destroying everything in its wake. Bishop was more confused than scared.

"Reiko," he said. "Are these your memories from Kansas?"

At the word *Kansas*, she looked up at him and they zipped somewhere else. It looked like a room, and everything was messy. Reiko was in pain, unable to move her arm. There were artificial augments that had replaced most of her arm, but she was crying because it hurt so much.

"What's wrong?" Bishop asked.

"My arm. I can't use my arm anymore."

"Why not?"

"The attack. Nerve damage. The—"

But the whole environment changed again, and this time they were inside a laboratory or workplace. Bishop did not recognize it. There were many cubicles and offices where mecha parts were being designed. Reiko was by herself and somehow, he could read her thoughts. She was afraid because her arm hurt so much. All the designers around her were very talented, churning out new mecha designs around the clock. She couldn't because of the chronic pain she suffered after the Kansas attack. She noticed she was getting fewer assignments, as she kept on missing deadlines. Her colleagues were walking around with big shining crowns on their heads. Bishop stared at Reiko's arm and it appeared to be made out of sticks.

"I don't belong here," she said. "I just wanted to make cool mechas. But it's too much for me . . ."

Without any notice, they were inside another room. There were mecha toys scattered all over the ground. A young girl was playing war with them by herself. She made exploding sounds as they fought each other. Was this a younger Reiko? Bishop looked around the room. On the walls were news printouts of popular mecha battles, art from their films, and mecha statues of varying sizes. Suddenly they zipped ahead many years and Reiko was older. She was still playing with her mecha toys, but the walls were covered with new mecha paintings Reiko herself had done. They were stunning and looked like something out of an animated portical show.

There was a ring on their front door. Reiko grabbed two of her favorite mecha toys and went outside her room. At their front door were two men. They took out their badges and Bishop realized they were Tokko. What were they doing there?

"No no no!" Reiko yelled as she ran down the steps. "Don't go with them," she pleaded to her parents.

Did the Tokko arrest her parents? He saw them put bags over their heads, cuff them, and inject them with drugs to pacify their minds.

Suddenly they were back at Bishop's torture camp. The black shadows were watching more greedily.

"This is not about me," Reiko said. "This is about you."

"What about me?" Bishop asked.

"All of this is over. It was over years ago."

"Not for me," he replied, but he wondered more about her past and what those Tokko agents had come to her house for.

"Do you realize this is just a Cyber Bubble?"

Bishop looked again at all the shadowy figures. "I think I do."

"Good. Let's burst it. Just come with me this way."

But as she was walking away, he swore there was something unusual in her gait. It seemed stiffer than normal, as though she had a replacement leg. One of the Nazi officers who'd interrogated him had an artificial leg. She loved demeaning him, hanging him up on chains, whipping him, and asking how much he could endure. Was this woman even Reiko? Or was she an imposter, pretending to be her so she could get the truth from him.

"Bishop! Where are you going?"

"Stay away from me!" he warned her.

"Bishop."

"I don't know where Bloody Mary is. I don't know who you are."

"You idiot!" she yelled. "This was years ago. They're exploiting your memories to entertain themselves. Stop falling for it!"

Bishop thought again of the thought police coming for her parents. He had to know more about her past. He followed along through a bright door.

WHEN BISHOP WOKE BACK UP, HE WAS RELIEVED TO SEE REIKO, NOT Nazis.

"W-where am I?"

"In reality," Reiko replied,

Bishop remembered the biomech and the Tokko coming to her house. He wondered if those had been her actual memories, but she avoided his eyes. "I've already given you something to counteract their drugs. I'm also going to give you a shot of steroids to give you a boost and help clear out your system. You need to drink lots of water."

Before he could object, she stuck a huge needle inside his arm, injected, and pulled out. She handed him a bottled water and ordered, "Drink this all down."

He did, and tried not to think about everything he'd experienced. It had felt so real, and he shuddered as he thought of the memories he'd fought hard to suppress. Despite all his efforts, he'd betrayed himself emotionally, and this in front of anonymous strangers on a Cyber Bubble. A part of him still missed Felicia. *Missed* wasn't the right word. Was there a word for the kind of regret a person could have even though they knew there was nothing they could have done differently?

"Where's Bloody Mary?" he asked, looking around. They were inside a motel room.

"They're attacking Los Angeles right now."

"What do you mean, 'they're attacking'?"

"Bloody Mary, General Watanabe, Daniela, and another mecha are in full-out attack mode."

"Is the situation bad?" he asked, thinking immediately of his niece.

"It's devastating," Reiko replied. "They began their attack four hours ago and have wreaked catastrophic destruction on the city. Casualties are high."

Bishop had to find a way to reach his niece and get her and her mother to safety. But his head was throbbing and he felt disoriented. "How did—how did you find me?"

"You were a room away from me."

"I thought I saw a doctor and a nurse."

"I took care of them," Reiko said grimly.

From the vicious glint in her eyes, Bishop understood her meaning. Reiko handed him his portical and gun. "I found these next to you."

He grabbed both and turned on his portical. The feed connected again to his eye lens, but there was no connection with the kikkai, so nothing else showed up. He called Lena and Maia multiple times, but the call did not get through.

"I'm not getting any reception," he said.

"The whole kikkai network is down. I've been trying to reach out for help," Reiko said. "But I haven't been able to contact anyone yet. I do know there's a mecha station nearby because I visited it a few years ago. They should have a combat mecha there."

"What are we waiting for?"

"You," Reiko replied.

Bishop frowned abashedly. "I'm ready."

"Can you walk?" she asked.

"I think so."

Bishop tried to stand, but stumbled. The effects of the drug made him nauseous. He sat for a minute, drank more water. The steroids were kicking in, giving him extra strength. It took a few more tries, but he was able to steady himself. He swung his feet around, rotated his head, and flexed his fingers. "Anything to eat?" he asked.

She tossed him a bag of wasabi chocolate chips. He took a bite, and though it wasn't that good, he was starving. He chomped the whole thing down.

"Feel better?" Reiko asked.

"I'm not sure."

"Need a few minutes?"

Bishop shook his head. "Let's go," he said.

They exited the room.

In the lobby, the motel clerk had a wild-eyed expression and warned, "It's not safe outside."

"We'll manage," Reiko said, returning the key card.

They navigated around the makeshift barricade the clerk had set up. As soon as they exited the motel, Bishop smelled smoke and his eyes became itchy. A man ran across the street with his clothes torn up. "Hey!" Bishop yelled at him. But he ran ahead, oblivious to anyone.

Aside from him, the streets were abandoned. It was eerie that no cars were present either.

"It's four kilometers from here," Reiko said, and they hurried their pace.

"That whole whatever it was . . . I'm glad it's over," Bishop said, still having a hard time grasping it'd been a Cyber Bubble. "Thanks for, uh, rescuing me."

"Sure. It'll still be a day or two before you're fully clear. But I got all that junk out of you."

"How did you escape?"

"I have a chemical defense system," she replied.

"That should be required for all Tokko agents." He rubbed his head. "I never knew this was how Cyber Bubble experiences got made," Bishop said. "Did I say anything weird to you?"

"You kept on calling me Felicia."

"Sorry . . . that's . . . that's my ex-wife."

"I figured."

"You saw my bubble?"

She hesitated, and by that, he already knew the answer.

"After the Nazis sterilized me," he said, "they tortured me for another week . . . I was unconscious when they rescued me."

"Our soldiers?"

Bishop shook his head. "Bloody Mary."

"Bloody Mary saved you?"

"Hard to believe, right?"

"You never betrayed her."

"No," Bishop said. "Not out of courage or anything like that. It was just because I was so pissed off at the Nazis for what they were doing to me. It was the only thing that kept me going. It took me months of recovery. Our doctors had to regenerate my body because the Nazis tore out so many of my muscles and tendons. It took me half a year just to walk naturally. Felicia waited for me. But my brain . . . I was totally messed up in the head and couldn't tell anymore what was real and what wasn't. I . . . I couldn't do that to her . . . She thought I just needed to get a job, join the police, and fight through it. But I insisted she leave and made her life miserable until she accepted."

"Why?" Reiko asked.

"It was her dream to have a family. As long as she stayed with me, it'd be a reminder to both of us of what happened and what we couldn't have. I couldn't put her through that."

"Even if she was willing to sacrifice it?"

He blinked, thinking back on how they'd yell at each other until their voices were hoarse and both were too tired to say another word, continuing only out of stupid spite. "I don't know."

They arrived at the mecha station. Like many mecha stations, there was a dome and a larger underground structure. The dome had been badly damaged, and four of the security mechas within had been smashed.

"Anyone here?" Reiko yelled.

But there was no answer.

They climbed over the debris and entered the inner chambers. They saw eight corpses, soldiers who had been killed at their panels by the blast. Reiko's eyes narrowed.

"They probably didn't know what hit them," she said.

Bishop rushed to a walled communicator and tried calling his niece and sister-in-law. But he only got static.

"Bishop!" Reiko called.

A woman in uniform limped toward them with a gun. "Who are you?" she demanded. Her ranking indicated she was a major, and half of her body was covered in blood. She used a splint for her right leg to keep it steady.

"I'm Captain Reiko Morikawa, army," Reiko replied. "You were stationed here?"

The woman nodded. "I am. What's the security code for the week?"

"Terra's enigma is not an illusion but the blazing soul of Gaia." She lowered her gun. "Who are you?" she asked Bishop.

"Bishop Wakana of the Tokko. And you?"

"Nori Onishi," she stated. "I'm in charge of this station."

"I don't know if you still remember me, Major Onishi," Reiko said. "I visited the base a few years ago to review the Hazard mechas for the city's fortification."

Major Onishi was ethnically African Japanese, a black officer with lots of medals on her uniform. "I thought you looked familiar. I remember your design suggestions for our Hazard-class mechas, Captain," Major Onishi said. "We integrated the armor and generator changes in your proposal. They made a big difference."

Reiko was flattered the major had recognized her. "That's kind of you to say. What happened here?"

"General Watanabe and two accompanying mechas attacked us without warning. We didn't know she'd gone rogue until she blasted the place to bits. I'm lucky only my leg got hurt. They've disrupted the kikkai, at least in this area, so I can't send messages out on normal channels, but I have been trying to send OWL reconnaissance drones out to try to warn other stations."

"Any luck reaching anyone?"

"Three other stations, but they'd already been attacked. They said strangers infiltrated their building and blew themselves up."

"Those would be Ulfhednar," Bishop said.

"What's that?"

Bishop explained about them and their involvement at the Alvarado Sento.

Nori was irate. "That's information Tokko could have shared earlier with the rest of the armed forces."

Bishop was about to defend himself, tell her they'd just learned about it, but then thought better of it. "You're right," he conceded.

"It was an evolving situation, but we should have sent a warning out."

"Are there more out there?"

"I haven't been able to reach anyone in the Tokko," Bishop replied. "So I have no idea."

"Do you have any combat mechas available here?" Reiko asked.

"Why?"

"So we can try to do something about General Watanabe's mechas."

"I have a prototype I've been using," Nori said. "If I had a good leg, I'd pilot it myself. I can show you."

Reiko had to help Major Onishi to the elevator, which they took twenty floors belowground. Underneath the dome was a cavernous depot for mechas.

The mecha they saw was bigger than the *Inago* but had similar features, including a magnetic gun. Its armor was arrayed to make it mobile and dexterous, and its angular features made it resemble a work of samurai art rather than the typical mecha knights.

"It looks like a taller Katamari," Reiko said.

"You're familiar with the Katamari?" Nori asked.

"I've piloted one for a year now."

"This is an evolution of the Katamari class, bringing it up in size and strength," Nori said. "Unfortunately, the batteries for the magnet gun were damaged during the attack. But the rest is intact. Say hello to the *Kamakiri*."

"Hello," Reiko said.

The *Kamakiri* was almost 75 percent bigger than the *Inago*, and Bishop could see how excited Reiko was.

They took a lift located at the *Kamakiri*'s foot all the way up to the bridge. Bishop noted the electrical motors for the auxiliary tech driving the hoists, steering gears, and exhaust pumps. They entered the bridge in the middle of the head. Lights were triggered by motion sensors, and the path lit the way in.

The circular bridge normally held a crew of seven. The walls were transparent, giving them a fully open three-sixty view of their surroundings. Portical panels were minimalistic, as most of the controls were hooked into AR visuals that popped up for the user. Reiko went to the pilot's seat. Bishop helped Nori to the munitions seat. He himself took a seat at communications.

"You were trying to reach someone earlier?" Nori asked him.

"My niece and sister-in-law. They're out in Culver City."

"I haven't had any luck either," Nori said. "I keep telling myself Watanabe wouldn't target my brother's veterinary hospital. But I can't get hold of him."

"I hope he's okay," Bishop said.

"Will the *Kamakiri* run without a crew?" Reiko asked Nori.

"It'll be difficult, but I'm rerouting most of the other functions to me so you can just focus on the piloting." She turned to Bishop. "You good at more than just reading people's minds?"

"I've served aboard a mecha before."

"Get over to navigation," Nori ordered. "I've rerouted communications there too. I just turned on the help mode for you."

"What's that?"

"It treats you like you're a first-time navigator and spells things out for you."

"I could use a help mode for life right now."

"So could we all."

Nori brought up the deployment interface. "The normal exit is destroyed. But there's an alternate route we can take whenever you're ready."

"Do you have access to the mecha database and pilot preferences?" Reiko inquired.

"You want yours uploaded to the controls," Nori surmised.

"That would make things a helluva lot easier."

Bishop looked at his navigation panel. There were three rectangular displays. One showed a real-time map of their surroundings. The second had various measurements—for the weather, ground integrity, geographical bumps, and more. The third and final had a split screen, with cameras attached to both feet. The "helper" module informed him he could switch any of the panels around and customize fonts, adjust screen size, and map automatic calls to controls as he wanted. He could point his finger at any menu and get a pop-up describing its functions. He'd trained for this when he was fighting at Texarkana, so it slowly came back to him.

"Hot damn!" Reiko exclaimed giddily to Nori. "You got all the preferences to match the *Inago*."

"Everything got through?" Nori asked.

"It did. Even some of the obscure changes I made to the default settings are here. Thank you."

"Don't mention it."

The *Kamakiri* was hooked to magnetic rails, where it moved down the tunnel to a wall. From there, it ascended straight up. A fake building was its exit, and the glass facade of the building opened up.

"Take some time to get used to the bigger size and strength," Nori cautioned Reiko.

Reiko started moving, swinging her fusion sword around, playing with her Skaria magnetic gun even though it had no power.

"This is amazing," Reiko commented as she practiced a few punches.

"I have a question, and you've got to be completely honest with me," Nori said.

"Of course."

"How much experience do you have in mecha-to-mecha combat?" Nori asked.

"Compared to Niijima, Takemi, and Watanabe, minimal," Reiko replied. "Are you concerned?"

"Of course," Nori said. "We have to stop them, and I have to plan accordingly."

"What should we do now?"

"Let's head east," Nori said. "I'm spotting several mechas dueling eighteen kilometers from here."

Bishop inspected the navigation panels as they warned him of obstacles, specifically civilian cars, two of which Reiko stepped on despite the big red X's and alert beeps noting that they should be avoided.

Nori sent out several more OWL drones, which was a convenient way for officers in command to keep an eye on the field, as they had extremely sophisticated reconnaissance equipment. She had their visual feeds tied directly to her panel at munitions.

Bishop hoped he wouldn't screw up at navigation and tried to learn what each menu item did.

Reiko attached the *Kamakiri* to the rails on both sides of the road and moved ahead at full speed.

II.

"HOW MUCH DO WE KNOW ABOUT THEIR SIDE?" BISHOP ASKED.

"Based on information I received before kikkai connections were disrupted, they have three mechas: the *Sygma*, *Stryder*, and *Syren*," Nori explained. "They struck multiple mecha stations and wiped them out. Reinforcements are being sent from outside of Los Angeles, but I'm not aware of their status. Since most of our airfields were badly damaged, rapid aerial deployment will be difficult. I've sent an emergency signal to a pilot in Catalina who's especially suited for these kinds of operations. But I don't know if he'll respond. Until we hear otherwise, we're on our own."

"That doesn't sound too promising."

"We don't have many other options. We need to act quickly to minimize civilian damage before it gets worse."

"What do you mean, 'civilian damage'?" Bishop asked.

Nori pointed ahead of them to three apartment buildings that were on fire.

"Their mechas are attacking civilian targets," Nori said.

Bishop was stunned. Los Angeles looked like a war zone. Big chunks of the city had been destroyed, and burning skyscrapers were all over the place. The thermal scans on the navigation panel indicated that the casualties numbered in the thousands.

Bishop spotted a man jumping out of a building from fifty floors up, dropping to his death in order to avoid being burned alive. He focused his scans on the building and detected four people on the thirty-second floor, unable to escape. He relayed the information to Reiko. Before he'd even explained anything, Reiko moved toward the survivors, who were stranded helplessly on their balcony, a fire about to swallow them. Reiko stretched out the *Kamakiri*'s hands. It was a couple with two kids. They moved onto the mecha's hands. They waved joyfully toward the mecha, especially their young daughter. Reiko carefully placed them on the ground. The parents and son ran toward safety. The young girl looked up at them and kept on waving.

Bishop tried not to think about his niece.

"This should be the jurisdiction of the 120th and 367th," Reiko said, aghast.

"It should be," Nori replied. "But I'm not getting any of their signals. Do you see anything, Agent Wakana?"

"No, ma'am. And you can just call me Bishop. I do see a mecha coming our way. Nav says it's a Perseus class," Bishop said, reading off the nav panel.

"Why's it heading our way?" Reiko asked. "Is it hostile?"

"I don't think so. None of its weapons are armed."

"That's the *Albatross Goney*," Nori said, recognizing the mecha. "I have friends on board."

"Send them a message," Reiko said to Bishop, who opened up the mecha-to-mecha communications. "*Albatross Goney*, this is Captain Reiko Morikawa. Have you engaged the *Sygma* or seen it?"

Bishop sent the message, but there was no response.

The *Albatross Goney* appeared as though its armor had been breached. Its arms were destroyed, and its helmet was bashed in. There were life signs within, and it was clear it had power, but they refused to reply. All that came back was static as it walked past them.

"Their communications are busted, or they just don't wanna talk to us," Bishop concluded.

"According to my OWL, there's activity within, and readings indicate crew members are active inside," Nori told them.

Bishop saw it too on his thermal scans. It was eerie that this mecha, which looked like it was in working condition, was walking quietly without saying anything back. What had spooked it so badly? According to nav history, it'd been built at the Dallas Mecha Yards six years ago, received an upgrade at Bakersfield recently as part of the corps modernization effort. Only four Perseuses had been constructed with their experimental Andromeda Engine and Joppa Launcher, which attempted to harness sound and water as a weapon.

"Another mecha is coming up. Signs indicate that's the *Machi*," Bishop said. "But they're moving away from the battlefield too."

"Any ideas why?" Reiko asked.

"They took heavy damage," Bishop said. "It could be they're withdrawing for repairs. I've contacted them five times, but they're not answering."

"Are their communicators broken?"

"I don't think so. But the signals are all mixed up."

"What's that mean?"

Bishop checked again. "They have more damage internally than on their external armor. Maybe they had mechanical failure? But I'm not seeing anything wrong with the BPG, and the armor hasn't been breached anywhere. There's definitely issues originating on the bridge, including damage that seems to have originated from gunfire . . . There's a chance it might have been caused by the crew members." Bishop, who was always thinking about the angles, followed his own conjecture to its logical conclusion based on some of the public crew personnel records he'd accessed. "I think there was a mutiny on board."

"Mutiny aboard one of our mechas?" Reiko looked disturbed. "That's hard to believe."

"I believe it," Nori said. "Battle changes people. Be on guard."

Reiko kept her weapons locked on the *Machi*. The *Machi*, which should have detected the weapons lock, ignored them and continued walking in the opposite direction like a ghost mecha, adrift without any concerns.

"You ever seen anything like this before?" Bishop asked Reiko as the *Machi* moved farther away.

"Not like this," Reiko replied.

Only a few hundred meters forward, they came across a new mecha.

"That's the *Jeroboam*," Bishop said.

The Guardian-class mecha had seen better days. Its arms were torn off and its torso had smoke fuming from it. The buildings around them were burning.

"They must have fought one of the mechas," Reiko assumed. "Ask them if they know which direction it was heading."

"I'm contacting them now," Bishop replied. A minute passed, then another. "Their communicator doesn't seem to be working. I'm receiving text communications from a Major Miura."

"What does the major say?"

"He says the mecha's porticals have been infected by a viral attack from the *Syren* and they've lost control of the *Jeroboam*. They don't want to call us directly in case our porticals get infected too."

"Do they know where the *Syren* currently is?"

Bishop asked them but there was no response. "I think they're still trying to get their bearings. Only eight of their crew survived."

Bishop could see from his nav readout that the *Jeroboam* had started with a crew of twenty-two. It'd been stationed at Texarkana, but suffered from major malfunctions in its inner circuitry that limited its tour of duty. After being retrofitted, it was stationed in Los Angeles. There was one official complaint filed about one of its officers, though his identity was sealed. It accused him of fervid religious proclivities and a deranged belief that he could predict the future since he could communicate with celestial kamis.

"Major Miura refuses to tell us where the *Syren* went," Bishop finally said.

"Why not?" Reiko demanded.

"He's warning us to stay away from the *Syren*. He says they're too powerful and can't be beaten."

"Can't be beaten?"

"He believes . . . he believes they're evil spirits, and humans have no chance of stopping them."

"Bishop," Nori called. "Can you ask them more about the virus? Is the *Syren* using kikkai attacks to disrupt mecha controls?"

He sent the question. "No response. But that's a safe bet."

Nori stated, "We need to prepare for a kikkai virus."

"How do we do that?" Reiko asked.

"I'm going to come up with some options. But if our pilots are losing control of their own mechas, it's no wonder they're so spooked."

Ahead of them was the tourist site called the Destiny Tower, based off Paris's Eiffel Tower but twice as tall. Close to it was the

Jungfrau, another mecha attempting to incorporate the German biomech's armor-regenerating technology. Bishop saw on the nav profile that it was a Hercules class, designed for combat and built at Long Beach. Eight of these were built and deployed in the California Province in the past year, though their inefficient use of their BPGs put seven of them out of commission. The *Jungfrau* was the only Hercules class left, but its crew had seen a fair share of personnel turmoil over the past few years, command changing multiple times due to political issues that remained classified to him. It appeared to be an emaciated version of a standard mecha, its vents and open tubes widespread, like oversized skin pores.

"Are they damaged?" Reiko asked.

Nori shook her head. "I think they're having mechanical issues."

Bishop wondered if they'd act similar to the other mechas and avoid them.

"They're sending us an urgent message," Bishop said, dispelling his earlier notion.

"Let's hear it."

"We're short on Bradlium particles. We ran out of energy for the regenerative skin on the way. Can you spare a core or two?" their captain asked.

Reiko was about to reply in the affirmative, but Nori stopped her.

"What are you doing?" Nori asked.

"We can send them one of our spares."

"We need every core we have," she stated firmly.

"But they need our help," Reiko said.

"I know it's harsh, but even with another core, they won't be able to fight. That extra core could mean life and death for us."

Bishop agreed with Nori. Reiko deliberated for a minute, before nodding her consent to Bishop. He messaged them, "We don't have any cores to spare."

"Please, give us just a little siphon," they replied.

Bishop ended the communication.

The *Jungfrau* began moving west.

"Where they going?" Reiko inquired.

"I don't know." As the *Jungfrau* faded from view, Bishop asked Reiko, "What is going on with these mechas? They're not acting like the crews I've fought with."

"It's because the best of the corps is stationed along the Quiet Border," Reiko answered. "The ones here have never dealt with anything like Bloody Mary."

"Crews are being called in," Nori said. "But it takes time, since we can't leave the border vulnerable to attack."

"You mean just in time for Bloody Mary to completely destroy Los Angeles?" Bishop asked.

Reiko was upset. "We still haven't learned since the Kansas Massacre," she said. "We have to be ready for *anything*."

"I thought there were three mechas on Bloody Mary's side," Bishop said.

"That's right," Nori said.

"Why am I spotting eight mechas attacking a government building?"

Nori stood up and limped over to Bishop's navigation readings. "Those should be ours," she said.

"That's what I thought too."

On the visual feed, they could see eight Anubis-class mechas attacking.

"Either they defected, or those mechas were stolen. That's the 367th, half of the Downtown Los Angeles Defense," Nori said. "Without them, downtown is vulnerable."

Bishop didn't need the portical scan to recognize the building. It was a Tokko base, outwardly known as the Office of Moral Thought Protection, that housed government censors. There were five other censor centers spread throughout Los Angeles, each focusing on a different medium. But this one's role was to watch the way people played games and extrapolate moral irregularities based on their decisions. Much of the information was studied by the Tokko, who in turn would follow up with gamers displaying suspicious tendencies. The Anubises had destroyed half of this building.

Three of the Anubis-class mechas noticed the *Kamakiri* and turned toward them.

"What should I do?" Reiko asked.

"Fight them," Nori replied.

They engaged the three Anubises. Reiko raised her fusion sword, which was gleaming purple. The Anubises approached with their combined twelve arms. Nori waited for them to get close and stood motionless.

"Should we put up our defenses?" Bishop asked.

"Not yet," Reiko replied as she waited for them to strike.

Just as they did, Reiko did a swirling attack that caught the forward Anubis off guard. Her swing slashed off two of its hands and left behind a wiry end that was full of sparks. She was amazed at how easily the sword cut through the Anubis. Reiko grabbed the electrically pulsating limb of the Anubis, then directed it back at itself, causing it to get inundated by its own volts. She then used the shocked Anubis as a shield against the other two, swiping at them with her sword whenever they tried to get around. She parried the two other mechas with her sword, then lopped off the arms of both.

"Thought you said your mecha-to-mecha combat was minimal," Nori said.

"It was. But that sword," Reiko said excitedly. Since that battle against the Anubis last year, she'd been practicing against them in simulations. She was relieved to see the training had paid off.

"It's the new Raiden Fusion sword model with the plasma cutter and hafnium to ionize gas and make mecha parts easier to slice up."

"I thought it was still in the prototype phase," Reiko said.

"It is," Nori replied. "We've been testing it for Mechtown."

"In live combat?"

"Yep."

Reiko kicked the third Anubis into the ruins of Tokko base. It fell back, flattening the lobby and adjacent offices.

The five Anubises began firing shells at the *Kamakiri*. Reiko took out a mecha-sized rifle, the Suigetsu GRL-40, and charged at them. Rapid fire ensued, Reiko shooting each as fast as she could. The *Kamakiri* used boosters in her legs to move even faster, deflecting the enemy shells with her sword. The plasma field acted as a shield against projectiles, and Reiko timed her rifle shots to match the strikes from the Anubises' multiple limbs. Any time an arm flung itself at them, a bullet would knock it back. Bishop felt like he blinked and two of the enemy mechas were cut in half. The remaining three stepped backward, cautious that this lone mecha had already destroyed five of them.

"Send the octopus mechas a message, will ya?" Reiko requested, feeling confident. Her body was pumping with adrenaline, a kind she'd never felt in the simulations. "Power down and surrender."

Bishop relayed the message. Only one of the mechas lowered its arms, shutting down the entire unit. The two others tried to attack. Reiko stepped forward, swinging at one's chest in a swift arc. This sliced up its chest plate and exposed its BPG, which was humming in a steady throb. Reiko spun around and used the back of her fist to crush the generator, bringing the mecha to its knees. The second Anubis tried to punch her. Reiko used rear thrusters to move swiftly out of the way, causing the Anubis's arms to go through its companion rather than the metal mantis. Reiko took the opportunity to lop off all its outstretched arms, then fired her rifle straight at its head. Both Anubises were out of commission.

"Nicely done," Nori said.

Reiko nodded nonchalantly, even though inwardly, she was jubilant.

"Call the one who surrendered and ask them if they know which way the three mechas headed," Reiko ordered.

Bishop did and said, "Forwarding the reply."

On the display portical, a young man appeared. "Thank the Emperor you came. The other Anubis pilots forced me to go along with them and threatened to kill me if I didn't. I had no choice. Forgive me."

"You have information about where I can find the other mechas?" Reiko asked.

"They're specifically targeting the censor stations and anything that might block a communication their leader wants to send."

"What kind of communication?"

"I don't know."

"Which way did the mechas head?" Reiko asked.

"Toward downtown."

"You better come with us," Reiko ordered.

"Yes, ma'am."

The *Niwatori* flanked their side. It was only a short trek before they came across the mecha called the *Endersby*. Its pilot was a Major Samuel Saito, who had only limited military action, since he'd served mostly in urban settings.

He was fighting another mecha which Bishop recognized, the *Syren*. It was under the command of Lina Niijima—Bloody Mary's cohort from earlier and the pilot of the mecha Bishop had ridden at the time of his capture by the Nazis.

Bishop recalled that Niijima had been decorated with numerous medals for her piloting. She'd graduated from Kyoto University, second in her class, and had served as a pilot throughout Asia. She had only one official reprimand. In her time in Moscow, a Nazi officer made racially offensive comments about her (something along the lines that all "Asians" are more or less "Oriental idiots" and "brute degenerates"). She single-handedly beat him and his gang of bodyguards. Her mecha was painted a dark red, with heavy armoring that made her wider than the *Kamakiri*. It was slower than Reiko's mecha but also bulkier, meaning it had more force.

There was armor plating on its back, sturdy, rectangular, and nearly impervious to all known weapons, which was appropriate considering it was an Armadillo class. Only four of these had been built, since the construction of its back was so expensive. Once it rolled into a defensive position, it could withstand most bombardments short of atomics. The arms had special armored sleeves that gave them a menacing bulk.

"That arm," Reiko said, looking carefully. "Can you do a closer scan?"

"What am I looking for?" Nori asked.

"That mechanism on her arm looks like a prototype weapon that was in development a few years back."

"I'm not detecting any unusual energy readings."

"Just keep an eye on it."

Bishop knew that Niijima had used the *Syren* in sixteen different battles and had emerged victorious each time. There were gauntlet knives in both hands that were charged by electric fields. Niijima's mecha wielded a scimitar, and its curved blade gleamed crimson from the blipping lights on its giant arm.

Bishop's memory of Niijima was very different from the official record. He'd been one of twenty-five Djangos, rocket pack soldiers in the 29th Squadron, named after their commanding officer. Rocket pack failure rates were high, and despite all the psychological and adaptive emotional therapy they'd received prebattle, most of them still felt nervous. No one wanted the new emotion plugs either—even though they purportedly regulated hormonal levels and promised to keep all soldiers cool, eleven of the soldiers who got them ended up going into a vegetative state a day after their installation.

Bishop remembered the mission at Texarkana Fortress when he was captured. It was an abnormally hot day, and he had to drink multiple bottles of water to keep hydrated. The suits they wore to protect themselves from the rocket fuel worsened the intense heat. Then again, everything at Texarkana felt like it was on fire. The Djangos carried out careful inspections of each other's suits. If anything got loose or was misplaced and dangling in the wrong place, they could burn to death from their own rocket packs. His nose was still sore from the new booster shot they'd been given deep up their nostrils. It was supposed to protect them against the biological weapons the Nazis were using.

Captain Niijima informed them over the speakers, "We're almost at the drop-off zone. Heavy enemy fire detected, though no biomechs in the area for now."

Sergeant Django explained that their task was to pick off soldiers planting mines and damaging terrain that would affect the mecha's traversal. The Nazis had set all sorts of traps in the hopes of hampering mecha mobility. But this cover story was just in case they were being listened to. Their real objective was to protect the woman sitting by herself in the corner. She was wearing a mobile armor suit. Bishop had never seen one so advanced. Neither had the other members. It was like she was wearing a miniaturized mecha with an arsenal that could take down a tank battalion. The mobile armor had the latest chameleon refractory system installed, which had tech similar to z-cloaks and allowed her to blend in with its environment. It was currently off, so it was like staring at a samurai suit made of mirrors.

She was going to eject at the same time they were. Their mission was to defend her until she could infiltrate the opposing side.

When someone asked, "What's her mission?" the response they got from the sergeant was, "You want to volunteer for it? 'Cause she got it a hundred times worse than your sorry asses."

Anyone else who got curious was told to shut up. None of them knew who she was, what her objective was, or even where she was going. Everyone knew her nickname, though. "Bloody Mary."

"She's the best goddamn Nazi killer we got," their sergeant informed them.

She didn't speak to them. Even when they asked her questions, she didn't reply.

There were all sorts of impossible rumors about her. Someone said she fought eight hundred eighty-eight Nazi soldiers by herself and killed each of them, sharpening her blade on their necks to make sure it was kept fresh with human blood. Someone even heard a rumor she fought a biomech and single-handedly took it down. That was too ludicrous for even the most reverent to swallow.

The moment they got to their deployment zone, they were locked into a launcher which essentially ejected them from a mechanical sling. Bishop looked down and saw artillery units firing at them. The *Syren* stomped most of them, taking out the rest with laser beams from its chest plate.

Bloody Mary ejected to the ground at the same time they were thrust into the air. Her mobile suit had wheels which made her as fast as any of them. She was racing toward the front like a robotic skater zipping through the battlefield. She triggered the chameleon tech and vanished. Bishop did his best to protect her from any opposing infantry. A few Nazi motorcycles headed her way, driven by human pilots who were genetically fused with the vehicular parts. That was meant to give them full synchronicity with their bikes, but it also subjected them to pain if the motorcycle itself got damaged. Bishop picked them off using his "smart" bullets, which, after being targeted, automatically compensated for environmental conditions and made sure not to miss. He did not know if Bloody Mary noticed his aid, and she gave no acknowledgment if she did. It wasn't just him assisting her. The twenty-four other Djangos were doing their best to ensure that her path was clear, even if they had no idea where she was going.

Rocket packs all stank of diffused Bradlium, but the stench of a biomech was unmistakable, originating from the cellular decay and the cancerous shells that gave them their rotten odor. Unlike the bipedal biomechs they'd encountered before, a new one marched toward them. This biomech had eight legs and looked like a spider with a human body extruding from its top, spliced together in genetic chicanery. Its limbs were covered by structures that looked like black bok-choy leaves and masses of cabbages sprouting from its tumorous skin. It didn't have a human face but a monstrous one, with fangs and bulbous protrusions that resembled spider eyes. The biomech's tongue was lashing out at rocket pack soldiers, slapping them out of the air. It was brutally efficient and its size dwarfed their own mecha. The thrashing noise from its regenerative skin made Bishop feel queasy. At least with the previous biomechs he'd confronted, they had an idea of its attack patterns. This one was very different. It used its legs to crush soldiers and vehicles on the ground. Bishop had no idea about its range, its weapons, or its capabilities. He learned quickly, as it pounced on his fellow soldiers. The Djangos fired at the biomech, sniping at it to try to debilitate it. The biomech released a swarm of gnats in response.

Through the communicators, he heard a dozen of his compatriots being perforated by the gnats who flew inside their throats and blew hundreds of holes from within. Their lifeless bodies dropped from the sky like rag dolls. One of the rocket pack soldiers used her parachute to try to escape, but the insectoid drones ripped holes inside her chute, causing her to drop like a stone.

Bishop and the other members of the rocket pack corp searched for Niijima's mecha, hailed it several times, and hoped it would back them up. But when Bishop tried to track the *Syren* down, he couldn't find it.

"*Syren*, we're under attack. This is a new type of biomech," Bishop called. "*Syren? Syren?*" But there was no reply, and a visual search revealed that the *Syren* was heading away from their direction.

This meant they had no mecha support. Why had the *Syren* abandoned them? If it had been ordered away, standard protocol was that they should have at least been notified.

Bishop searched for Bloody Mary. He couldn't see her, but he assumed she was ahead of them and had safely navigated past the spider biomech, which was now between them. Even if they wanted to aid her, they couldn't.

Could he escape back to the *Syren*? But there was no way he could out-fly the gnats. Bishop saw another one of his compatriots get destroyed and decided he was going to wreak as much damage as possible before dying. He turned toward the biomech and readied his rocket pack to explode on impact. Suddenly he thought of Felicia. He hesitated just long enough for two gnats to spot him and fly his way. Bishop tried to avoid them, but they were too fast and destroyed his left rocket, causing him to spin as he began a downward trajectory. He tried to regain control, tried to access his portical to trigger the parachute. But the damage was too severe and as he continued his plummet, he prayed Bloody Mary succeeded in whatever mission it was that would cost him his life. He thought of Felicia again and wished he could talk to her one last time. He lost consciousness as soon as he hit the ground.

When he woke up, he was in Nazi shackles.

What made him most angry was that after he'd been rescued, he learned Niijima had left them to help another squadron deal with their own biomech. She was decorated for bravery in the battle, as she had taken down two biomechs by herself. But her duty had been to the Djangos. And they'd been left to die. He was the only survivor! Her primary responsibility was to have protected them. He tried to protest, filed a complaint, but the brass told him to keep his mouth shut. Niijima was a war hero. He, while brave, had just been a prisoner and a grunt at that. He was in no place to complain.

Bishop felt wronged and had little admiration for Niijima.

The *Endersby* had an enormous artillery gun and was firing rapidly. But Niijima's mecha was impervious to the shells, moving forward through the bullet storm before it sliced off the *Endersby*'s arm. Niijima used her gauntlet knife to puncture the *Endersby*'s shoulder, then cut downward, fracturing its body. A liquid began pouring out.

"Is that fuel?" Reiko asked.

Bishop checked navigation and was surprised by the chemical analysis. "It's beer."

"Beer?"

Bishop saw from the security records on the *Endersby* that the pilot had been reprimanded four times for swapping out backup generators for barrels of beer. The pilot had defended himself, saying most of their work was guard duty in peacetime, so the crew got bored and needed to pass the time with a good brew. Although Bishop couldn't check the alcohol levels in the crew, he wouldn't have been surprised if most of them had been intoxicated when the attack had commenced. It embarrassed him that crews like this were defending Los Angeles, while on the other side, Niijima's only reprimand had been for beating up Nazis.

"She's cutting all the circuits connecting the upper half of the body to the BPG," Reiko said to Bishop. That meant no juice for the upper half. "He's toast."

Niijima used her boot to stomp on the *Endersby*'s right knee. The entire leg buckled backward, and the mecha began to fall. But

Niijima grabbed the *Endersby*, not allowing it to drop. Instead, she pummeled its face, crushing its facial features and showing no mercy.

Reiko fired several warning shots her way.

"Send them a hello from me," Reiko said. "Tell 'em if they don't stop, I'll attack."

Bishop sent the message. "They're responding," he said.

Lina Niijima showed up on the display, head and brow shaved, ethnically a mix of Thai and Czech according to the family history, and muscular like most pilots. Another image popped up of Major Samuel Saito of the *Endersby*. He was also Eurasian and hairless like all pilots, but in contrast to Niijima, had a potbelly and was sweating profusely.

"What is the meaning of attacking us without pr-provocation!" Saito said, slurring his words.

Niijima ignored him and said to the *Kamakiri*, "Reiko Morikawa. You survived."

"Whatever your cause, killing civilians is wrong," Reiko said.

Niijima smirked, amused by her response. "When Governor Yamaoka murders tens of thousands of civilians, he's called a war hero and promoted. When we do it, we're called terrorists. The double standard is the true madness. I didn't even realize how entrenched I was until Bloody Mary broke us out of our chains."

Saito appeared to have a hard time focusing and keeping his balance. Several crew members were behind him, trying to keep him steady. Bishop made a mental note to make sure to have Saito removed from his position if they survived.

"I won't waste my time trying to convince a drunk," Niijima stated on a public channel. "But to all the others on board, my fight isn't with you. I'm fighting *for* all of you against this illegitimate government. Your old mechas stand no chance against the *Syren*.

Force your pilots to stand down and we can avoid unnecessary conflict."

"You might have the best motivation in the world," Reiko replied. "But killing so many people to make a point . . . I'll never be a part of it."

"But you were willing to be a part of Yamaoka's revolution? He killed even more people," Niijima said.

"For a noble cause."

"Fighting for your freedom isn't noble?"

"You call this freedom?" Reiko demanded, pointing to the devastation around them.

"Freedom isn't cheap. But if you insist on your ways, you can die aboard that heap of junk."

"The *Kamakiri* isn't junk," Reiko said, immediately defending her mecha, offended.

"What do you want me to do?" the *Endersby*'s pilot asked Reiko.

"Stay out of the way unless you want your other arm chopped off."

The communication ended and the *Endersby* withdrew. Reiko looked at Bishop and Nori. "If either of you has second thoughts, it's cool. Just let me know now before I kick the *Syren*'s ass."

"We're in this together," Nori replied.

"No second thoughts from me. She betrayed my entire corps," Bishop said.

"You served with Niijima before?" Nori asked.

"Yes, ma'am. She doesn't give a damn about anyone other than herself."

The *Syren* attacked their accompanying Anubis first and, within ten seconds, spliced it up into a hundred parts. The *Niwatori* crumbled to the ground. Bishop messaged the pilot, but there was no response.

"Any life signals?" Reiko asked Bishop about the *Niwatori*.

"Hard to tell right now," he replied.

The *Syren* turned toward the *Kamakiri* and attacked with its scimitar. Reiko took out her fusion sword and swung it quickly at Niijima. The *Syren* parried with its scimitar, but the blade was quick and slashed a segment in its palm. Whenever the *Syren* tried to get close, Reiko forced it back with her sword, meticulously cutting apart its circuitry. But just as Reiko began to step in, the *Syren* raised its forearm and a cannon popped out. She began firing at a rapid pace. At this close proximity, the shells had a deadly impact, blowing off two of the *Kamakiri*'s fingers and causing the sword to drop. Reiko picked her blade back up, but then her mecha's arms stopped functioning.

Bishop looked over at the arms, which were still in a fighting pose, just frozen there. He noticed the hands appeared to be covered by some type of insect swarm.

"Why aren't my arms working?" Reiko demanded as she moved the *Kamakiri* away from the *Syren*.

Nori got up and moved toward Bishop's panel. "Those insects. They're some kind of parasite."

"Put it on my screen."

Nori relayed the command.

Reiko zoomed in on the metallic parasites and said, "Dammit, I was right. This is the Legion."

"Legion? I thought they couldn't get it to work," Nori questioned.

"Wait, what's Legion?" Bishop wanted to know.

"It was part of a secret project at Mechtown to fend off a mecha attack," Reiko answered. "It's made up of thousands of tiny micro-sized robots that'll latch on to its target and digest its metallic parts. They can self-fabricate, so if you kill a bunch of them but there's even one left, it'll reproduce. Nori's right, though. It was still in development when I was there, and they were having problems getting it to work under restraints because the AI was uncontrollable."

"How do you stop them?"

Reiko didn't know. Nori examined the scans again. "We might be able to create a really strong charged shot from the BPG if we direct the energy into a wave and disable the parasites," Nori suggested.

"What's that mean?"

"Use the energy from the generator and aim it at the parasites to make them inoperative."

"Can you do it?" Reiko asked.

"I'll try," Nori said. "But I have to go down to the engine room."

"But your leg—"

"Will manage," Nori said. "If I screw up, it could end up destroying the entire mecha."

"Is there a Plan B?" Bishop asked.

"No," Nori replied.

Reiko asked, "How long do you need to set it up?"

"Normally, twenty minutes," Nori said. "But I know we don't have that. Use an echo and burn as much time as you can," Nori urged Reiko before climbing down the ladder despite her bad leg.

The *Kamakiri* began running the other way and launched an "echo" drone, which would fly in a haphazard pattern and bounce any communications from the *Kamakiri* to the *Syren*. The net effect would be that if the *Syren* tried to find the source of Reiko's messages, it would target the echo rather than the mecha itself.

Scornful laughter rang over the communicator. "You have less honor than a dog," Niijima taunted them.

"Why do you have to make fun of dogs?" Reiko asked her.

"I'm not disrespecting dogs. I'm talking about you," Niijima replied.

"I like dogs. I used to have a corgi, and there isn't any shame being compared to a dog. I love them. Plus, they don't take cheap shots like you just did."

"When the old Americans first arrived in the main island of Japan, they brought superior ships and weaponry and forced their will on the government," Niijima said. "The Americans proudly proclaimed it 'gunboat diplomacy.'"

"So what?"

"Was it unfair that the—"

Bishop realized Reiko was trying to distract her but also prevent her from moving on to other targets. At the same time, as the echo was flying rapidly away from them and bouncing communications, if Niijima was tracing the signal, she'd chase the fake and not them. They moved toward a series of skyscrapers that were still under construction.

Much of their mecha's forearm was covered with the Legion. The insects were getting noticeably faster.

"How's it going down there?" Reiko asked Nori.

"I need a few more minutes," Nori replied.

"So do those bugs."

The *Syren* somehow found them. "You think this is a child's game, using an echo on me?" Niijima asked.

She attacked with her scimitar. Reiko, who couldn't use her arm, barely dodged the strike by using the mecha's skates and firing boosters in reverse to push them backward. The *Syren* pursued, about to swing at them. Reiko got in a perfectly timed kick to the *Syren*'s torso, causing her to stumble. The *Kamakiri* immediately fired shots from her stomach cannons, but it wasn't at the *Syren*. Instead, they were bombs that created big smoky pillars in order to obfuscate the view. Reiko used her skates to create more distance between the two mechas.

"How much longer?" Reiko inquired.

"Just give me another minute," Nori answered. "Are we in a safe position in case the mecha loses power?"

"We will be."

Cars underneath were getting destroyed, but Reiko ignored the destruction of civilian property and found a series of apartments that were shaped like a pentagon with only one way in. These too were under construction, and there were no people inside. Reiko crouched in the central courtyard, hoping to stay out of sight. More importantly, Bishop realized that the *Syren* had only one direction in which it could approach them, so there wouldn't be any sneak attacks from the rear.

"I think I got the pulse ready and focused in the direction of the Legion on our arm," Nori said. "But if there's instability and it goes outside of its range—"

"We'll manage somehow. Just pull the string!" Reiko shouted.

The entire mecha shut down and the three-sixty view in the bridge vanished. They were enveloped in total darkness. Bishop wondered how long the shutdown would last and whether the pulse would work. Would the *Syren* find them before then?

Auxiliary power returned first, dousing them in a saturated red light. It was as though the world were painted red. Bishop remembered hearing that people used to dream in black and white before they added color to portical shows, causing their monochromatic reveries to go fully colored. He wondered how a world predominantly red would change their perspective on things as simple as dreams and bloodshed.

Bishop heard the hum of the BPG a few seconds before energy began streaming through the mecha again. The visual panels began to brighten and the view screen followed. There was no *Syren* in sight.

The arm was moving again, which relieved Reiko. All of the Legion robots were dropping dead like gnats, falling from the mecha's fist. Reiko was eager to get back to the fight. But when she tried to walk, she found the *Kamakiri*'s legs were immobile.

"Um. My legs aren't moving," Reiko informed Nori.

"One of the circuits to the leg kinematics lost its wiring," Nori replied. "I'm on them, but it'll only be a short-term measure."

"I live minute to minute."

"If we need to replace the kinematic system, it could be a while," Nori told Reiko, "which I know we don't have."

"At least you got the gnats off. I can fight *Syren* with just my hands if we need to."

It was fortunate Reiko had cover behind the pentagonal apartment structure.

"Any people inside?" Reiko asked.

"Nothing on thermal sensors," Bishop replied.

Reiko fired the rear grapplers on the *Kamakiri* at the buildings as a way of stabilizing the mecha and using the structure as support.

"Slick," Bishop commented.

"Thanks. I saw someone use this method in a mecha tournament a while back."

Bishop could see from his portical reading that the construction of the condominiums was supposed to finish in three months. Half the units had already been sold at an absurdly high rate. These were homes for the elite, spacious and luxurious, the kind he'd dreamed of one day owning for the family he never had.

A loud rumbling noise came from their flank. The apartment began crumbling. The *Syren* wasn't going to approach them from the obvious opening. It was breaking apart the building and attacking them from the right. Although the *Kamakiri*'s legs weren't working, Reiko used its arms to lift itself up to its feet, then rotate to face the impending strike.

"When can I get my legs back?" Reiko asked Nori via communicator.

"They won't need a rehaul, but I have to swap out the articulation modules on the hips. I just need a few more minutes."

"In a few minutes, the only thing left will *be* the legs."

Even without energy, the legs were able to bend and the autostabilizers built within were keeping them steady. But time felt too tight, and Bishop wished there was something he could do.

Maybe there was.

"You have a rocket pack in here?" he asked.

Reiko looked back at him. "I don't know."

"Major Onishi. Are there rocket packs aboard?" he asked over the communicator.

"We have emergency packs. Why?" she asked.

"Thinking of using one. Maybe I can distract them."

"It's in the aft exit in the eighteenth vertebra."

"Thank you," Bishop said, and looked to Reiko. "Mind if I try something?"

"Just don't die on me."

"Wish that were up to me."

Bishop climbed down the ladder to the hallway in the upper chest. While mechas outwardly looked very different, the inner workings were usually based on a template they tried to keep similar so that crews could easily be exchanged. Bishop walked to the aft toward the spinal nodules, where lights triggered by sensors showed the way. He climbed down the pole to the rear bay, which housed four escape pods and eight rocket packs. Each had carbon-fiber wings and Bradlium burning engines. He got into a heat-resistant suit and helmet to shield him from the exhaust and grabbed the rocket. Bishop could see they'd performed upgrades to make them more user-friendly and heat-resistant. He checked the parachute several times to make sure it was in working condition. The rifle was a Hazard SG-01, which packed a nice punch without being too heavy, making it the weapon of choice for flight. The standard-issue Suzuki boots had magnetizing capabilities as well as wheels.

He opened the escape hatch in the spine. Across from him was the condominium, floors built, but no walls to seal them off. He made sure everything was in working order. Bishop jumped out and onto the scaffolding, which connected to the floor with its steel frame. It was all mild steel, which construction Taro bots were reinforcing with boards and spray coatings of fire protection. Two approached him and asked, "Human, do you need anything?"

Bishop had a momentary flashback to the first time his father had taken him to a military base under construction in Saigon. There too had been Taro bots with their automata AI and their super-personable behavior. His father was going to have the biggest office in the building and was telling Bishop about their upcoming operations in Vietnam. Even though Bishop was very young, he'd been so proud.

Bishop ignored the bots and ran to the opposite side of the building, readying his rocket pack. The whole process became instinctual, and without him even being aware of how he did it, he was in the air. Muscle memory was still as active as ever as he prepared to harry the *Syren*.

"You hear me?" Reiko said to him over a communicator he could hear in his helmet.

"I do. Got any suggestions on how I might slow the *Syren* down?"

"Anything you do will most likely get you shot."

"I know."

"Then why are you out there?"

Bishop thought again about his torture at the hands of the Nazis. "Mosquito tactics," he answered.

While he'd ridden the rocket pack when he was escaping from Metzger's inferno, that had been more of a mad dash to save his life. Now, flying up here again, it felt like the old days but better, since his back was better protected against the heat with a shield that extended the nozzles past the tail of the pack. Also, the controls seemed much tighter, with the rotating grips for the yaw and the general throttle responding better than the junk packs he'd ridden in Texarkana. The Bradlium gave him sixty minutes of flight. He was much higher in the air than the mecha and could see more of the devastation Bloody Mary had caused. He forced himself to focus on the *Syren* and not worry about his niece. He doubted there were any weak points that would cause significant damage to a mecha. His main hope was to annoy and delay it. As he flew, he saw the armadillo plates on the back of the *Syren*, making it almost invincible against rear attacks. It was smashing away at the building and would be on Reiko soon.

Bishop took a deep breath. This could be the end of him. But he had to try something to distract Niijima. Most mechas had cameras that were nearly impervious to explosives. But they could be visually impaired. Fortunately, his pack had a full armament, including an oil hose meant to annoy opponents. If he could get in close to the *Syren*'s faceplate and spray oil at it, then it'd be forced to change to its sensors. That could annoy the *Syren* enough to focus its attention on him and buy the *Kamakiri* the few minutes it'd need to recover its legs. The key to survival, for both him and mosquitoes, was aggressiveness. Don't hesitate, don't dawdle. Aim for the target and take the plunge. His hope was that with all the Taro bots around, he would barely register on their sensors. He flew toward the *Syren* and flipped the nozzles to hovering mode. He wouldn't be able to get directly in front of the *Syren*, but if he could lower the hose and shoot, he hoped it would murk up their camera. He spotted the visual sensors on the faceplate and flew above the *Syren*, waited for it to swipe down at the building so its arms were below. Slowly, he descended to the front of the mecha and fired the hose. The oil sprayed out, but completely missed. He tried using his rifle instead, but the sensors were resistant to gunfire. At the same time, he'd gotten the *Syren*'s attention. It turned its helmet guns at him. A second before it fired, he flew straight up into the air, accelerating as fast as he could. A torrent of bullets destroyed a string of construction bots instead of him.

So much for that plan.

"Reiko," Bishop called with another idea. "Can you link my portical with the *Syren* on a private channel?"

"Right now?" she asked.

"If possible."

"Hold on a second," she said, muttering, "I need two more arms." A few seconds later, "I don't know if she'll reply, but I've connected you."

"Captain Niijima of the *Syren*," he called. "This is Bishop Wakana. I once served with you during the Texarkana Campaigns." There was no answer. "I was one of the rocket pack soldiers you abandoned to die. Everyone in my squadron was killed except for me. I was taken captive by the Nazis. We looked everywhere for you. We—"

"What can I do for you, Bishop Wakana?" Captain Niijima asked via portical, her mecha ceasing its blind attack.

He was taken aback that she'd replied. "I—I wanted to talk."

"I figured that. The brazenness of your actions has piqued my curiosity. But surely you didn't try shooting my sensors just so we could chat about the past."

"I want to know why you abandoned us."

"I don't recall abandoning you. Are you certain you haven't mistaken me for someone else?" she challenged him.

He felt anger well up inside him. Was she trying to deny responsibility? "I'm certain of it. Your one duty was to protect us. Our duty was to protect Bloody Mary. You forget where you met your new leader, Bloody Mary? She was part of the mission at Texarkana!"

"You're one of the Djangos," she stated.

She remembered. "I was," Bishop affirmed.

"I do recall that mission. I also remember that I was not allowed to inform you of the true nature of our mission."

"What do you mean, 'true nature'?" Bishop asked.

"You've never thought to ask that yourself?"

"We were told it was to protect Bloody Mary."

"From what? She didn't need your help," Niijima answered.

Bishop maneuvered above the *Syren*, careful not to get too close. "Then why were we sent?"

"Isn't it obvious? You were meant to be sacrificed."

"Explain what you mean."

"I was ordered to drop you off and leave the battlefield. The plan was for as many of you as possible to be taken prisoner."

Bishop almost lost control of his rocket pack, but steadied himself. "What the hell's that supposed to mean?"

"It was part of some secret op. I asked my commanding officer, but he wouldn't tell me anything. I don't think *he* even knew."

"That's impossible. They—they told us it was a vital mission. Bloody Mary had to infiltrate the other side."

"Which she would have done with or without your help. If I'm correct, she had a mobile suit on her. Why would she need your assistance?"

Bishop could not believe it. All the official commendations, the words of praise from his superiors, and it had never even been intended for him to make it out alive. Was she lying? Was she trying to get under his skin? All those years of suffering had been . . . been for what?

"I understand your emotions right now," Niijima said. "I experienced it myself when I found out certain truths about our country."

"What truths?"

"I was no fan of Governor Tamura. But after he was killed, Governor Yamaoka sent my family to Shayol. My father's only crime was that he tried to protect some of the political and military leaders that had been targeted by the Sons of War," Niijima said.

Bishop had heard of Shayol, the Nazi hell the governor had seized and then refit as his own punishment for those who opposed him. It was a genetically manipulated biosphere which induced rapidly mutating cancer via radiation guns. The group of biomolecular scientists known as the "cattle guard" ran Shayol like it was a playground for their medical experimentation.

"When my husband objected to my family's imprisonment, his superiors warned him to back off. He refused, and got sent to Shayol too. They would have sent me as well, but they 'needed' my mecha piloting skills so I could help them hunt down more political criminals. I spent my whole life training to be a mecha pilot so I could defend our country, not be an executioner for a power-hungry cabal."

"Executing enemies is our job," Bishop retorted.

"You would call groups of terrified politicians scared they said the wrong thing 'enemies'? It's not the job I signed up for. Soldiers kill their enemies in combat. Executioners murder weaponless targets at the orders of their government. Ignorance can only be bliss if you block your ears to all the terrors happening right outside. I can't. I will spare you for now because I understand you're driven by a state of ignorance. Even the glint of a pearl can make a pig shine. But if you try anything again, I'll blast you out of the skies."

The *Syren* went back to destroying what was left of the building.

Bishop knew he should do more to distract the *Syren*, take aim and blow up his rocket pack in a collision that would be massive if he could trigger the Bradlium. But he was too stunned to make sense of what he should or shouldn't do. The governor's true killer was the least of his concerns. Was Niijima speaking the truth about Texarkana? Had his superiors really intended for him to be captured?

"Did you hear what Niijima said?" Bishop asked Reiko.

"I did."

"Do you know if there's any truth to what she's talking about?"

"I don't. But I can help you find out more if we survive. For now, stay clear of the fight."

"Not like I have a choice," he said.

"If I need anything, can I still count on you?" Reiko asked.

"Depends on what you need."

"I might need some catering. Last rites and all."

"What would your last meal request be?" Bishop asked.

"Pork and chive dumplings, Sichuan spicy fish, and kimchi fried rice with SPAM. You?"

"Right now, fried armadillo," Bishop replied, which made Reiko laugh. "I've never eaten a mecha before, but we could toast it on my rocket pack."

Bishop flew to the east wing of the building to watch the battle. Reiko didn't shut her channel and he could hear intra-communications within the bridge.

"Good news," he heard Nori say. "Legs are functioning."

"Just in time," Reiko said.

The *Syren* broke through the building and rushed toward the *Kamakiri*, swinging its scimitar. Reiko was able to lift the *Kamakiri*'s arm to block with her sword. The *Syren* raised its arms again, preparing to fire the Legion shell. Reiko readied her blade and aimed carefully. The *Syren* fired one of her Legion shells. Reiko anticipated the attack and hit the *kote tegai* as it triggered, causing the trajectory to shift upward. The shell flew into the building, and the Legion began devouring the steel frame. Taro bots confusedly confronted the Legion.

Reiko threw another knife quickly. It pierced the *Syren*'s forearm, but missed the Legion cannon. "Dammit dammit dammit," Reiko muttered before firing at the knife with her Suigetsu GRL-40, making contact. The knife exploded, rupturing the *Syren*'s arm. "Got ya!" she yelled, though the arm still appeared to be functioning, as she was able to swing it back.

Reiko rushed the *Syren*, swinging hard as she said, "Let's dance."

Their swords locked. The *Kamakiri* punched the *Syren* in the side of its chest, causing it to tumble back. The *Kamakiri* tried to thrust its sword into the *Syren*'s neck, but the *Syren* deflected the blade with its own, hurtling a fist back with its other arm. The *Kamakiri* took the blow in its cheek and stumbled into the building.

"Not with moves like that," Niijima said.

Reiko chuckled, getting quickly back up. "Nice punch," she said.

Bishop watched as the two battled back and forth. Every time it looked like either side had the advantage, the other would reverse the move and the titanic struggle continued on. Everything around them was shaking. Reiko got a series of blows in, puncturing the wires in the other's arm. The hand appeared to go limp. Reiko was about to pierce through the *Syren*'s stomach. The *Syren* put its arms in front of it and curled up, like an armadillo. The armored plating was too strong, and when Reiko tried to hit it, she was repulsed by a defensive charge. *Kamakiri* struck it harder, but that only caused an even stronger deflection.

"Sorry to cut the dance short," Niijima said.

"I thought we were just getting to the fun part," Reiko replied.

Farther away from them, the Legion was having a battle of their own against the construction bots.

"Bishop," Nori called.

"What's up?"

"We're in trouble."

"Why?" Bishop asked.

"I've been analyzing the *Syren*. When the *Syren* transitions into its defensive armadillo mode, the plating absorbs the kinetic energy and will fling it back at any attacker with equal force. It's basically impossible to attack right now, and it can stay in this mode until it can make full repairs. We can't allow that."

"What can we do?"

"You up for a delivery?" Nori asked.

"Sure, as long as it's not pizza."

"I need to access your portical and put a disruptive system on it."

"What'll it do?" Bishop wanted to know.

"It'll reprogram the Legion so that I can activate them from inside the *Syren*."

"You want them to eat the *Syren* from the inside out?" Bishop figured.

"Exactly."

"Why can't you send the program directly to the *Syren*?" Bishop asked.

"Niijima's mecha is closed off to external porticals. You'll have to directly connect to it," Nori explained.

"Um. How do I do that?"

"That's the tricky part. In the head, there's an access port for maintenance. If you can directly connect your portical to it, I can take care of the rest."

"You want me to land on the *Syren* and plug my portical into its head?"

"Let's put your rocket pack skills to the test."

He granted Nori access to his portical and turned in the direction of the *Syren*. While the mecha was in its defensive, and stationary, mode, it might be possible to land safely. But all it would take was one stray bullet to kill him. Landing directly on its head would probably get their attention. If he could time his landing so that it would occur exactly when the *Kamakiri* next struck, then ride the rest of the way up, he might be able to mask himself better. He checked the Suzuki boots. The magnet seemed functional, as did the wheels. But was he pushing his luck too much for a single day?

What do I have to lose? he asked himself. The sober answer came to him: *My life.*

"How long does the program need to completely download after I'm plugged in?" Bishop asked, not wavering in the face of mortality.

"Thirty seconds," Nori said.

"Sounds easy," Bishop commented sarcastically.

"I'll let Reiko know. Ready?"

"Not really. But I have a plan I want to explain to both of you."

Bishop explained what he wanted to do.

Reiko answered, "Good luck, rocket man. When do you want to do this?"

"Now."

Reiko immediately went in for another attack. Bishop watched the trajectory of the *Kamakiri*'s attack, gauged the flight path he should take, and waited. Just as Reiko struck the *Syren*'s plating, the counter-jolt pushed the *Kamakiri* back. Bishop confirmed the brunt of the shock had been absorbed by Reiko, then used a burst thrust to land almost exactly where the sword had hit. He engaged his wheels and magnet to align himself as soon as he hit its armor. He fired the rockets so he could skate all the way up the *Syren*. It was a trick some of the Djangos had taught him, the best way to get back on board a mecha, as the launch doors were so small. The armadillo plates were smooth and easy to skate on, and unless someone was visually looking at the exterior of the mecha, it would be hard to register him on scans.

The *Syren* was huge, even in its curled state, and there was something serene about skating on its metallic planes. Bishop reached the *Syren*'s head, turned off the jet pack, and disengaged the wheels. He clambered toward its apex, looking for the panel with the portical connection.

"You get there yet?" Nori asked.

"I'm looking for it."

"Permission to look through your portical sensors."

"Go ahead."

"I should be able to spot the access port with thermals," she replied. "There, toward the back of its head."

Nori helped him spot it on his portical and he was on his way toward it when the *Syren* shook. There was heavy movement as it stood, and Bishop realized it was coming out of its defensive pose. He was about to turn the magnets on in his boots via the control, but the force from its rise was too sudden and hurtled him back. Just as he was about to go into a free fall, he toggled the magnets on his boots. They snapped him to the surface of the *Syren*'s head, though he was perpendicular to it.

"You okay?" Nori inquired.

"I'm not sure," Bishop replied.

"You weren't able to plug in?"

"Not yet. But don't worry about me. Just do your thing against the *Syren*."

The *Syren* and *Kamakiri* began another round of sword attacks. Bishop noticed the *Syren* had fixed the rupture in its armored sleeves and, while not at full force, seemed to have recovered during its curled state. The two mechas attacked each other relentlessly, the sword blows and parries making the entire surroundings shake. This time, the impact of blade hitting opposing blade was too strong for him, and even the magnets were having a hard time keeping him attached. Bishop was cautious about moving his boot off the surface.

"I don't know if I can get there," he conceded.

"Disengage, then," Nori said. "We'll try something else."

Bishop felt it would be a waste to leave now. If only there was a brief reprieve in the combat.

Something caught Bishop's attention. He looked over to where the Legion had been fired into the construction Taro bots. Robot corpses were piling up at breakneck speed. Since self-fabrication allowed both sides to reproduce infinitely, it was getting huge. Their private battle was just as brutal, if not more so, than the fight between the two opposing mechas. One side, represented strangely enough by Reiko and the Taro bots, was the status quo, while the other, blazing chaotically forward through Niijima and the Legion, wanted to destroy everything in its wake.

The *Kamakiri* jabbed with the sword, piercing the *Syren*'s shoulder. It withdrew and jabbed again, spiking its sword through the *Syren*'s right chest. "You're not getting out of this!" Reiko declared. It seemed like the battle was going to be decided when the *Syren* clutched the hand holding the sword, refusing to let it go, leaving itself impaled.

"Don't intend to," Niijima replied.

The *Syren* raised its other arm and prepared a new Legion shell with the two of them locked.

"You fire that now and we both get infected!" Reiko yelled to her.

"You think I expected to survive the day?" Niijima asked.

"A dance isn't supposed to end with both dancers dying."

"Welcome to my ball of death."

Bishop had only one option he could think of that could get him into place. He had to time this carefully. He heated up his jet pack. He triggered the rockets as he simultaneously switched the magnets to wheel mode. It thrust him upward, but he was able to control the throttle of the rocket so that he could ride along the curve of the head instead of straight up into the air. He cut the jet pack off when he got to the spot Nori had marked, toggling the magnets again. The panel was just three meters away. He stomped toward it and tried to open it. The panel was stuck tight. Bishop bent down, pulled on it again, heaving with both hands. It came loose and he pulled it out. There was a console with several plugs. Bishop inserted his portical and contacted Nori just as the Legion was warmed and ready.

"How much more time do you need?" Bishop asked.

"I'm connecting to their internal kikkai right now. Why are you still attached?"

"My portical."

"I'll get you a new one! Get off!"

Bishop complied, turning on his rocket pack and flying away.

"Did we get her?" he asked.

"It's going to be close," Nori replied.

He watched from midair as the *Syren* tried to fire the Legion. If Niijima succeeded, it was over for both of them. Instead, a small explosion took place in its armored sleeve. Then another in its elbow. Its fingers went limp and it released the *Kamakiri*.

"Reiko! Disengage from her!" Nori ordered.

Reiko let go of the Raiden Fusion sword as the Legion began to swarm all over the *Syren*.

"You let the bugs out of the cage?" Reiko asked.

"Didn't want to hog them all for ourselves," Nori replied.

From within the *Syren*'s arm, they could see the armor rupturing and thousands of the parasites cannibalizing the entire arm.

"Can they do the same pulse thing you did to get rid of them?" Reiko checked with Nori.

"They might. But at the pace their Legion is going, I don't know if they'll be able to salvage anything," Nori replied. To Bishop, she said, "Get back in here. I'll open up the exit on the shoulder pad."

Bishop saw the opening and flew in. After he landed, he threw off his rocket pack, struggled his way out of his suit, and then climbed back up to the bridge.

"Nice flying," Reiko said.

"Glad the major's plan worked."

Niijima came up on the visual display. Her bridge was on fire.

"Good fight," Reiko said. "I got the upper hand this time, but I'll admit, I had a little luck on my side. We can do a rematch some other day. Raise your white flag so we can continue this later."

"You know that's not possible."

"Don't be hardheaded. You don't have to die today."

"You think I don't know what'll happen to me if I surrender?" Niijima asked, shaking her head. "I won't dishonor the cause with any discussion of this. But I would like to say one thing to the soldier called Bishop Wakana. I won't apologize for my actions. I own up to my choice, as I believed it was for the greater good . . . But belief and good intentions don't excuse actions that cause great harm. I hope you find your peace."

The *Syren* took its sword and impaled itself in the neck, causing the BPG to overload. Its head, and the entire bridge crew aboard, exploded.

Reiko sighed, put her hands together, and did a short bow. "It's a strange world where everyone is convinced they're doing good even though all they do is cause each other a lot of pain."

Bishop was torn by Niijima's decision. He knew if the Tokko got her into an interrogation room, she would have wished for death anyway. Even if by some miracle the Tokko took it easy on her, she'd killed too many people to escape public execution or imprisonment in Shayol, which was the fate of most political prisoners under Yamaoka.

What would he have done in her place?

They moved back toward the *Endersby*.

Captain Samuel Saito hailed them. "I didn't think you stood a chance. Congratulations. That was spectacular."

"There isn't anything spectacular about seeing another mecha pilot go down," Reiko replied coldly.

"It is when that pilot's trying to take your head," Saito said, trying to be lighthearted. "I'd invite you over for a beer, but I think you got other things on your mind."

Reiko nodded. "That's right. Need a hand?"

The *Endersby*, whose left arm was missing, replied, "You have a dark sense of humor, friend."

"You think this is funny?!" Bishop roared.

"Didn't say it was," Saito replied.

"You're getting drunk on duty while the whole city burns. What the hell's wrong with you? Haven't you got any sense of shame?"

"Bloody Mary can't be stopped," Saito said.

"You don't deserve to pilot a mecha."

"Be careful of your tone with a higher-ranking officer, navigator."

Bishop snorted in disbelief. "I'm a Tokko agent, Samuel Saito," he said. It took Saito a second to realize what Bishop had said, and there was an immediate change in the coloration of his face when he did. "Watch yourself," Bishop warned.

He ended the communication and looked over at the *Syren*, which was a heap of metallic bones on fire.

"What an asshole," Reiko commented.

"I can't believe that guy's supposed to be on our side."

Nori messaged them from below: "The *Kamakiri*'s arm needs a replacement. The temporary articulation fixes I put in place won't hold, at least not in another fight. And your armament supplies are low too."

"What can we do?"

"We need to head to the Culver City Umegra Mecha Station."

"A mecha station survived?" Reiko asked.

"It's a civilian station, so it wasn't one of their targets. I've sent one of my OWLs to confirm and have communicated with their chief engineer. They'll have a new arm and leg replacement ready for you."

They changed course for Culver City.

Bishop said, "After we get to Culver City, I may have to separate with you to find my niece."

"I understand," Reiko replied.

"All this time, I was so angry at Niijima, thinking she'd betrayed me at Texarkana. I should have known better. You saw what I suffered in my Cyber Bubble. If that was all for nothing . . ."

"You can't take everything she says as truth."

"Why would she lie?"

"We *were* fighting," Reiko points out.

Bishop lowered his head. "I almost wish she hadn't told me."

"Sometimes stuff happens, and there isn't any reason for it," Reiko said. "Doesn't make us stronger, wiser, or better. It just sucks. I hate that fact. But we have to be able to move on or it can consume us with so much anger to the point where we no longer even care what happens to the people around us."

"Too late," Bishop says.

"Not for your niece."

Bishop took a deep breath. "The only thing that's keeping me going is finding my niece."

"We'll find her," Reiko assured him.

Bishop watched the city falling to ruins before his very eyes and felt rage through every muscle of his body. *They're alive*, he said to himself to try to calm his nerves. *They're alive.*

REIKO MORIKAWA

★ ★ ★

CULVER CITY

I.

REIKO THOUGHT OF TAIKO CITY AND THE NIGHT SHE WAS SENT TO ASSAS-
sinate Governor Tamura. Her decision then was coming back to
haunt her with a bloody fury. How had things turned out so badly?
Wasn't Tamura's assassination supposed to be the beginning of a
new era?

She looked over at Bishop, who was at communications, still trying
to get a signal through to his family. She could not imagine what must
be going through his mind after Niijima's revelation. Reiko was scared
of what truths of her own she'd find the further she went, especially
when it came time to confront her old friend Daniela Takemi.

Bishop groaned in pain.

"Something wrong?"

"I'm just suddenly feeling very weak," Bishop said. "I think maybe
the painkillers are fading. You got another dose?"

"I do," she replied, and directed him to the medical cabinet.

Nori plotted the route to the Umegra Station using her OWLs so they could avoid any combat zones.

Nineteen kilometers northwest of where they'd defeated Nii-jima, they came across five Labor mechas that'd been cut up like pineapple slices. They'd been working on an infrastructure project, building out a new highway extension by adding two lanes. Now there was a gaping crack in the highway and a pile of destroyed cars. The Labors were sending out SOSs, requesting aid. Reiko plowed ahead, knowing there was a chance they were being used as bait by the enemy. Even if these were genuine pleas for help, there wasn't much they could do in their condition.

Eight minutes later, they got to Inglewood and changed course to move north. Inglewood had been spared the devastation of the other parts of Los Angeles. The advertisements were still playing on the massive buildings and shopping areas even though there were no patrons. Chez Haluna, the most famous chef in the world, was broadcasting announcements about her latest food journey to the Underwater Ice Fortress in the South Pole. The Natalia Cervera exhibit, a showcase of space war machines reconstructed out of clay letters, was opening next month. The Sowards Pop Music Festival was starting up again, with the best singers from all over the Empire coming for a week of festivities.

A surprising sight awaited Reiko. Three Labor mechas were still working on the construction of the expansion wing for the Gakushi Shopping Arcade, acting like it was business as usual. The shopping arcade was a complex designed to attract students from the nearby Shinji Maki University, which was famous for its architectural mar-vel of a gigantic monkey-shaped central building.

"What are y'all doing?" Reiko asked.

"We're doing our jobs," the Labor pilot replied. "Who are you?"

"Captain Reiko Morikawa. You didn't notice Los Angeles is under attack?"

"Attack? Since when?"

"The whole city is being destroyed," Reiko informed them.

"We didn't notice. We're on a tight deadline, and if we don't finish our part by the end of the week, we'll be without jobs."

"I'm strongly advising you to power down and step away from your labors."

"Respectfully, Captain, our jobs are on the line here."

"Your jobs will be the least of your worries if you're dead. There's an attack on every mecha in the city."

But they ignored her and continued working.

The *Kamakiri* moved on.

Culver City was home to one of the biggest portical entertainment studios in the Empire and seemed like an amusement park. There were massive holograms with famous portical performers, from James Leyton playing *Jesus Christ, Shinto Superstar* to famous director Coco's most recent project, *Fish Mecha Intertwining Final Ganymede Love Tears Saga XIV Pt. III*, which was considered a masterpiece of art and comedy. There were a bunch of exotic cat statues from the popular artist K. Yi all along the streets. The Umegra Station was within sight. It was the main hub for nonmilitary mechas in the western part of Los Angeles. Fortunately, the facility was also able to upgrade, replace, and retrofit military craft.

Reiko messaged them. "This is Captain Reiko Morikawa. I've been told you have replacement parts for the *Kamakiri*."

"This is Masami Higuchi, chief engineer for the Umegra Station," a man replied, chewing on a big cigar. "I've gotten the requisitions order from Major Onishi, and the arm and leg were in transit." He took out his cigar and spat on the ground. "But it's been chaos out there. I've already lost four shipments. The transport with your parts sent a distress signal and I never heard from 'em again."

"Do you know where they were?"

"Last communication we got from them was eight kilometers

east of here." He put the cigar back in his mouth and spoke through a small sliver on the right side of his lips. "I think the transport pilots didn't get enough sleep or were smoking something funny. Drivers said they were attacked by a ghost mecha that disappeared whenever they got close."

"Disappeared?" Reiko wondered. "I'll go check it out."

"Your arm is broken," Nori pointed out.

"The other is working fine. Plus, we don't have many other options."

Nori relented but cautioned, "Don't take unnecessary risks."

"I never do," Reiko replied. She looked to Bishop. "If you gotta get going, I understand."

"After you're fully repaired," Bishop replied.

"I appreciate it. But we might get damaged or worse on the way out."

"I'm not leaving you like this," Bishop said. "I know there's not much I can do, but my rocket pack might come in handy."

Reiko appreciated his sense of duty. "More than handy," she replied.

They drove east and saw squadrons of police cars and local security transports that had been decimated. The streets were mostly empty, as people either were in hiding or had moved as far away as they could.

A massive mecha was squatting on the ground with smoke coming out of it. "Friend or foe?" Reiko asked Bishop.

"I think friend. They're hailing us."

"I'm Major Rachel Takamaki of the *Hakucho*." Its pilot greeted them first. "I'm glad you're here."

Reiko knew Major Rachel Takamaki by reputation. She was one of the most decorated mecha pilots Reiko knew of and a key part of the defense force of Los Angeles. She was a veteran with over forty mecha engagements during the past two decades, serving with distinction at Texarkana Fortress, San Diego, Vietnam, Afghanistan, Burma, and Wichita. Her mecha, the *Hakucho*, was an upgraded Leviathan-class vehicle, silvery, with slick curves and special stealth armor designed to withstand the attack of a biomech. The M91s with their bayonet laser blades were the scourge of Nazis in their recent conflicts.

"I'm Captain Morikawa," Reiko said. The *Hakucho* had several deep cuts in it, both hands missing. Reiko wasn't sure if it could even stand. "What happened here?"

"The mecha called the *Stryder* happened," Major Takamaki answered. Rachel Takamaki was in her midforties and a very muscular woman, with arms that Reiko swore were twice the size of her own. Of mixed Russian and Chinese descent, she was the same height as Reiko, though she was bulkier. She was wearing her lightweight flexible exoskeleton, gloves, goggles, and adhesive helmet. She had dark green eyes and, like many mecha pilots going to combat, had black war paint over the upper part of her face. "Its pilot, Daniela Takemi, has an accelerator module."

Even though Reiko knew Daniela was with Bloody Mary, a part of her had hoped they wouldn't have to face each other. Now that she knew her next opponent would have to be her old friend, she had a hard time hiding her anxiety. "Those are the special modules that allow mechas to fight at supersonic speeds in close-quarter combat, right?" Reiko asked.

"Right. Most pilots couldn't handle its use because it's too fast to control. Takemi is the only pilot in the corps that has been able to use it effectively."

"The energy it'd require for constant supersonic motion would be high, wouldn't it?" Reiko asked.

"That's why it has two BPGs," Nori replied.

"I don't think battles last that long either," Takamaki said. "Ours was over in less than a minute. I could barely see what hit me."

"Which way did the *Stryder* leave?" Reiko asked.

"I'm sorry to say my scans were destroyed. I don't know where it is now. It's my fault. I thought I could take the *Stryder* by myself, but I was wrong. That Skaria Type-19 magnet gun you have on you would make a world of difference."

"What do you mean?" Reiko asked.

"You can counteract her speed with the use of the magnet gun. It would slow her down enough that you could actually fight her. I'd heard rumors of the accelerator module's development, but I'd never fought a mecha that was using it."

"Unfortunately, the Skaria isn't powered," Reiko said.

"Then you have no chance."

"Don't worry about that," Nori immediately said. "We'll get it fixed at Umegra."

So she has a plan in mind, Reiko realized.

Bishop said to Reiko, "The nav sensors say that four of our mechas are fighting a mecha just east of here."

"Could that be the *Stryder*?" Nori inquired.

Reiko hoped not, while at the same time wanting to see Daniela again.

"Most likely," Major Takamaki replied. "You're not thinking of giving chase, are you?"

"We have to investigate because repair parts for my mecha have gone missing," Reiko said. "What about you? Can you get up?"

"My mecha's legs are dysfunctional," Major Takamaki said with a frustration that was unaccustomed to helplessness. "She knew exactly where to attack to make the *Hakucho* immobile. Even if I wanted to, I can't help you. I'm sorry."

"It's all right," Reiko said. "Will you be okay?"

"There's a shelter nearby I can stay at."

The *Kamakiri* moved east toward a series of commercial buildings that were eight stories tall. Four Guardian-class mechas were arrayed against a single mecha that Reiko immediately recognized as the one that had saved her the night of Governor Tamura's assassination. Its horns, beetle-like face, and twin boomerangs belonged to Daniela Takemi's *Stryder*.

Reiko's eyes tightened as she watched Daniela dismantle the first Guardian. The scary part was that her movements were so fast, Reiko couldn't see them. She did spot the two transport mechas carrying the replacement parts for the *Kamakiri*. They were essentially flatbeds with four legs, designed to carry huge loads. Reiko hailed them and a gruff pilot replied, "Our rails are blocked and the only way around is through that killer mecha."

Bishop said, "There's two destroyed mechas blocking their path."

"Any survivors aboard?"

Bishop checked and replied, "None according to the scans. But, um, I think we're going to need to deal with the *Stryder* first," he said.

It wasn't that the *Stryder*'s victory had ever been in doubt. But Reiko couldn't believe she'd already defeated all four of the mechas in the time since Reiko had turned around to talk to the transport pilots.

Removing the mecha remains blocking the transports would have to wait.

The *Stryder* turned its attention toward them and raised her boomerangs in front of her.

Reiko took a deep breath. "This is Captain Reiko Morikawa of the *Kamakiri*. I've been looking for you for the past year."

Daniela Takemi was the same age as Reiko. Her brows and head were shaved. She was tall, of mixed Italian and Spanish descent, with strong cheeks accentuated by slashes of paint. Her mouthpiece was transparent, but it regulated temperature and sped up her interactivity with the *Stryder*. She had on a black pilot suit with additional armored accoutrements to help her interface. There was other complex machinery equipped to her that Reiko did not recognize, almost spring-like in nature, as though to compensate for abrupt movement. Was this for the acceleration module?

"Have you now?" Daniela asked.

"I didn't know where you were," Reiko said.

"Are you here as friend or foe?"

Reiko paused to think about her answer. "Foe, but it doesn't have to be that way."

"I agree."

"We can still avoid this if you throw down your weapons and walk away."

"What happened to Niijima?" Daniela asked.

"She's dead," Reiko replied.

"You killed her?"

"We defeated her in battle. She killed herself."

There was no hiding the pain that shot through Daniela's eyes.

"She died with honor," Daniela said.

"I know I can't dissuade you. But we should be fighting side by side against the true evil, the Nazis. They're the ones who benefit most from our fighting."

"I assure you that after we triumph, we'll deal with the Nazi threat accordingly. But before we begin, I must warn you. I have a mecha which has far superior technology to yours. I urge you to withdraw."

"You know I can't do that," Reiko replied.

"No, I figured you could not."

The *Stryder* charged at the *Kamakiri*, and Takemi used her long boomerangs as blades to attack viciously. Reiko, who could only use one arm, deflected carefully, meeting every strike before it could pierce her. She attempted a few parries, but was blocked each time. Reiko could sense Daniela was holding back.

Nori said, "Captain, I'm going to detach our arm."

"Why?" Reiko asked.

"Trust me on this," Nori said, and made changes from her munitions console to override engineering.

All of a sudden the *Kamakiri*'s bad arm fell out of its shoulder socket and crashed with a loud bang. Reiko was about to protest to Major Onishi when the *Stryder* took a step back.

"Your mecha is severely damaged," Daniela said to Reiko. "What happened to your arm?"

"It was infected by Niijima. But I don't need pity points. If I lose, that's on me."

"I presume that the arm and leg from the transport is for you?" Daniela asked.

"It would have been," Reiko replied.

"This would not be a fair battle. Make your fixes, then come find me again. We will fight in earnest then."

The *Stryder* turned away from them and moved east.

"Wasn't expecting that," Bishop said.

Reiko was not surprised. "During the mecha tournaments way back when we were at Berkeley, her first opponent was a cadet who was inferior in skill level and could barely get his mecha to stand up. Daniela avoided all his attacks but refused to deliver a final blow. She believed it was dishonorable to hurt a weaker opponent. When she was threatened with disqualification by the Imperial Judge, she accepted her loss without protest."

"I remember that," Nori said.

"Then you knew she would back off?" Reiko asked.

"I hoped," Nori replied.

"If she hadn't?"

"Our arm was barely functional, so it was a risk worth taking."

Reiko thought again about their time at Berkeley. They were neighbors in the dormitories. Daniela cooked all her food, making bento boxes every day with gyozas, tofu soup, *nashis*, and whatever was part of her regimen for the week. Reiko, who hated cooking, always ate out, going either to the dormitory café (where she quickly got disgusted with the buffet slop), or for a slice of her favorite Neo-Kobe pizza at Snatcher Slices. Daniela occasionally cooked for her, trying to convince her it was healthier than eating out.

"But I like my food decadent," Reiko protested.

Reiko remembered sleepless nights talking about their favorite class at Berkeley—Professor Kojima's lectures on existence and social politics in the modern world, with all his brilliant nuances that shed light on subjects they only thought they knew. The two used to debate different topics all night long, sometimes getting heated as they insisted on their points and interpretations. Daniela was a passionate debater but always fair, willing to concede when her arguments were weak. She liked to probe for ways to take advantage, wanting to thoroughly understand a subject before venturing in.

"Why are you licking your lips?" Bishop asked Reiko in the present.

"Was I?" Reiko asked back.

"Your eyes had this distant glaze, like they were a thousand kilometers away."

"How far is Berkeley again?"

Bishop laughed.

Reiko removed the mecha remains blocking the transports, and they headed back to the Umegra Station.

II.

THE CULVER CITY UMEGRA MECHA STATION WAS HOME TO SOME OF THE most colorful mechas Reiko had ever seen. They were designed for custom use by patrons during special events that needed the bombast of the big machines. Umegra also provided mecha rentals for portical films, as the military did not loan out their own mechas. Reiko spotted a re-created Fox-class mecha, the original legendary warriors who were the subject of a new cinematic series. She also spotted the Boktai-class mechas that harnessed solar energy to wield deadly beams and were the focus of a popular show she really enjoyed.

Umegra would have appeared to be a gigantic pit from the air, descending hundreds of meters to where the different mechas were stored on concentric layers.

Just as they were about to enter, a new mecha moved toward them. It was bulky and covered in thick armor, a mecha samurai with two fusion swords. Its bearings read *Harinezumi II*. Reiko raised her sword with her remaining arm, ready to fight.

Nori said, "You can stand down."

"You know them?" Reiko asked.

"It's the backup I requested."

A man with long hair covering his face appeared on the display screen. His mouth was covered by food scraps. "Sorry I'm late. I had to pick up some chorizo hot dogs with pineapple juice from the market. You ever try these?" he asked, opening his mouth wide and showing all the chewed-up food inside.

"You never change, do you?" Nori said with a bright smile.

"What's there to change?"

"Who are you?" Reiko asked.

"You can call me K," he replied. "What the hell happened to the city? Actually, don't tell me. Whose ass do you want me to kick, Nori?"

"We'll talk more down at Umegra."

"Sure. Long as they have sausages. Y'all like sausages?"

Bishop answered, "I tend to avoid processed food."

"What's 'processed' food mean?" K asked.

"It means any food loaded with chemicals and processed to make it taste like it's one thing when it's actually another."

"I hear you on purity, man. That's why I like sausages without all the fancy toppings. But this chorizo is nice, and so are the wasabi hot dogs. You ever have those? They'll make you tear up. I gotta drink chocolate milk with 'em or my butt's on fire and I gotta use the bathroom ten times in an hour."

"That sounds very unhealthy."

"Everything will kill you at one time or another, man. Even worrying about it'll kill you from stress. So just don't think about it."

Reiko parked at a designated spot. The *Kamakiri*'s faceplate opened up, and they waited for the crew to raise up a platform they could take down to the surface.

Reiko asked Bishop, "What are you going to do now?"

"Grab one of those rocket packs, and fly to Maia and Lena's apartment."

"Why don't we take a mecha?" Reiko suggested. "I'll see if they have one we can borrow."

"You gotta stay here," Bishop said.

"You can use my help."

"The city depends on you."

Nori, who was checking the munitions console behind them, interjected, "Give me the address and I'll dispatch a drone right now."

"You sure?"

Nori nodded. Bishop relayed their information and photos. Nori dispatched one of the drones. The platform arrived, and three crew members came on board. Bishop and Reiko descended by themselves.

"You have a tough fight ahead of you," Bishop noted.

"I'm not looking forward to it."

"Why do you think Daniela joined Bloody Mary?"

"I intend on asking her and finding out directly," Reiko said. "You going to be okay?"

"Probably not," Bishop said. "But to hell with it."

Chief Engineer Higuchi met them on the ground. "Where's Major Onishi?"

"On the bridge," Reiko replied.

"I've got the adjustment to the Skaria she requested and the Melluso augment for the BPG, which should give your Skaria a big energy boost."

She hadn't been aware of either upgrade. "How long to hook it up?"

"Two hours."

Reiko noticed a stunning mural on the wall of crab mechas fighting a biomech, depicted in graphic detail.

"That's incredible," she said.

"It's an original Ryuji. Paid a goddamn fortune for it, but it's worth every yen." Higuchi moved the cigar around in his mouth. "Is it true Bloody Mary's forces have a ghost mecha?"

"Not as far as I know. Why do you ask?"

"Everyone's been talking about it. My crew is convinced she has a supernatural monster mecha on her side."

"It's not supernatural," Reiko assured him. "Their mecha has access to technology that makes it super fast. Make sure you spread that. I don't want people getting spooked."

Higuchi went to direct the crew that was replacing the *Kamakiri*'s arm.

"Million bucks you'll be hearing about ghost mechas for years on end now," Bishop said.

"Bloody Mary likes to play up the psychological warfare," Reiko noted.

"She's good at it. I think that's why she lets some of us live."

"Why's that?"

"So we can spread the terror for her."

"Someone somewhere must know more about Bloody Mary's past," Reiko said.

"According to those files you gave me, she's been at this for more than forty years."

"Forty years? How old would that make her?"

"I don't know. But all of her commanding officers are dead. Some, by accident, and others from natural causes," Bishop replied.

"Natural causes sounds unlikely."

"All the information related to them was sealed."

"So not only are they dead, but someone is covering up for her," Reiko said in disbelief.

"It's hard to believe secrets can still exist in our age," Bishop said.

"Why's that?"

"Everyone is just a set of numbers that the government has access to. Humanity lies in the interpretation of those numbers."

"So you're saying your real job is interpreter?"

Bishop shook his head. "I have a filter that boils people down to whether they're treasonous or not."

"How do you draw the line between a patriot who wants drastic change for the good of the empire, and a genuine traitor?"

"Usually, my superiors make that call."

"Have they ever been wrong?"

Bishop paused to think about it. "Yes," he regretted to admit.

"That's scary. What happens if you disagree with your superiors?"

Bishop shrugged. "Technically, I can't disagree or else my ass gets put on the filtered list too." He looked up at the mecha arm being moved into the empty socket. "The *Stryder* moves like a ghost. It'll be hard to do anything against its acceleration module."

"A mecha is only as good as its pilot. Doesn't matter the weaponry, the armaments. A good pilot will find a way to overcome."

"Tell that to the ancient soldiers with spears battling fighter jets," Bishop said.

"Or the rocket pack soldier who helped us take down a mecha," Reiko retorted.

"You're surprisingly optimistic."

"Only so I can hide the fatalist inside me," she replied back, and watched as the crews attached the arm. "I don't want to fight Daniela."

"Then don't," Bishop said.

"What do you mean?"

"Don't do anything you don't feel comfortable with."

"But I *have* to face her," Reiko said.

"Why?" Bishop asked.

"To protect the city."

"Leave it to someone else."

"There's no other pilots."

"They'll find some," Bishop said. "Only do this if you want to."

"That's not the way it works in the military," Reiko replied.

"That's what I thought too. Look what happened to me at Texarkana."

"Aren't you supposed to be making sure I always stay in line with orthodoxy?"

"We're in a revolution," Bishop said. "Orthodoxy is changing by the minute."

The pilot called K approached them and asked, "Where's Nori?"

"Here," Nori said as she descended the platform.

"Where's your regular crew?" K asked her.

Nori's face darkened. "General Pris Watanabe attacked us without warning."

"They're all dead?" K asked, shocked.

Nori nodded.

"Sorry to hear that," K said. "They were a good crew."

"The best."

"Your leg okay?"

"Got busted up. I'm going to take a dip in a rejuvenation vat." To Bishop, she said, "Your niece and her mother are safely registered at the Futaba Underground Shelter."

"Then they're okay?"

"It appears so," Nori replied. "The opposing mechas stayed clear of the shelter. It's not far if you want to visit."

"I do."

"I'm coming with you," Reiko said.

Bishop was about to object, but Nori said, "If you can return within the next ninety minutes, that would be ideal. Also, I believe Major Takamaki is there. Please bring her back with you."

"I can do that."

Nori looked at K. "Can you give them a lift?"

"Why me?" K asked back. "I'm not a taxi."

"To ensure the safety of Captain Morikawa and Major Takamaki, both of whom will be essential to our next battle."

"Fine."

"What about me?" Bishop muttered.

"You too," Nori said with a laugh.

K TOOK THEM TO THE LIVING SPACE IN THE SHOE OF HIS MECHA, WHERE there were benches, tables, and a mini-fridge. There were also two samurai swords and a shotgun attached to the wall. Now that they saw K up close, they could see he was in his late thirties. Wiry, he had a pale face, mischievous eyes, and an unkempt beard. He controlled the *Harinezumi II* remotely from his portical while he took out a pack of sausages from the fridge.

"Want some?" he asked Bishop and Reiko.

Bishop politely declined, though Reiko accepted and took a chomp.

"Not bad," she said. "Got anything to drink with this?"

"Prune juice and cranberry juice," K replied. "I left the pineapple juice in the bridge, but you can help yourself to what's there."

Reiko went to the fridge and grabbed some.

"Bishop, you really should try these," Reiko suggested.

"I'll pass," Bishop replied. "So are you part of the mecha corps?"

"Aw hells no," K answered.

"How do you have your own mecha?"

"I built the *Harinezumi II*," K replied. "Took me a few years, but everything about her is perfect."

"Wait, what?" Reiko asked. "You don't mean by yourself?"

"Yep."

"That's impossible."

"It just takes a little longer, but it's very possible."

"How do *you* know Nori?" Bishop asked.

"We fought together a few times."

"When?"

"Here and there." He took a big bite out of his sausage. "Why you ask so many questions?"

"I'm just curious."

"How do *you* know Nori?" K asked back.

Bishop explained how they'd just met and the battle that took place earlier, as well as what he knew about Bloody Mary and her revolution.

"Bloody Mary? Operation Jiken? Ulfhednar?" he scoffed. "I step away for a couple years and it's the same bullshit with weirder names and people still killing each other over weirder bullshit. Glad I got front-row seats to the show."

"You think this is entertaining?"

"Can't say yet 'cuz I haven't seen the action, but I wouldn't be here otherwise," K said nonchalantly.

The Futaba Shelter was not far from where they'd engaged

Daniela Takemi. It'd been designed to provide protection against a nuclear attack and housed two thousand people. "You coming?" Bishop asked.

"Have fun," K said, opting to wait in the shoe while Reiko and Bishop went inside the shelter.

They were greeted by the head facilitator, a Dr. Furutani, who was relieved to see them.

"Is the situation contained yet?" he eagerly asked.

Behind him, they saw a group of wounded police officers and soldiers. Many had bandages on them and were in tremendous pain.

"Not yet," Reiko replied. "How many people do you have here?"

"We're at max capacity, but only have a staff of fourteen," Dr. Furutani replied. "So it's been chaotic. There's over three hundred and eighty-nine wounded, but we're short on medical supplies, especially painkillers. We need to get them to Mitsuyasu Sakai Hospital," which was the big hospital named after the famous playwright. "But we have no way of getting them over without some serious help. Do you have any ideas on how to transport them?"

"Not at the moment," Reiko replied just as one of the soldiers started screaming in agony.

"I'm actually here to see a Maia and Lena Wakana," Bishop stated.

Dr. Furutani appeared confused. "Why?"

"They're my sister-in-law and niece," Bishop replied.

Dr. Furutani checked his portical. "They're logged in here. We'll announce them on the speakers."

A minute later, an automated voice said over the speakers, "Will Maia and Lena Wakana please come up to the top floor?"

"We're also looking for Major Rachel Takamaki," Reiko added.

"You're not here to help us?" Dr. Furutani asked, his tone changing from welcoming to irritated.

"We'll send help later. But—"

Before she could finish, the doctor snorted, "I don't have time for this," and departed.

The injuries of the people within varied, from those with heavy bruising and blood loss to victims who'd lost body parts and were in critical condition. One of the portical charts on the wall indicated there were ninety-two body bags.

"Is there anything we can do to help here?" Bishop asked Reiko.

"We'll have to ask Major Onishi," Reiko replied. "But there's over a hundred shelters in Los Angeles and they're probably all packed."

"So basically, nothing aside from stopping Bloody Mary before she destroys the city?"

"Pretty much."

A young girl appeared ahead of them. Her face was covered in soot, and her hair was disheveled. She looked scared until she saw Bishop. Her frown turned into a wide smile and she ran toward her uncle, jumping into his arms. He spun her around and was so happy to see her well and alive. She started crying and yelled, "Uncle Bishop! I knew you'd come! I told Mom you were coming!"

Bishop held her tightly and said, "I'm sorry I took so long. Don't cry." He rubbed her tears away, but she couldn't stop sobbing.

"It was sooo scary," she said. "A mecha was destroying all the buildings around us and it was so fast. I saw a family get stepped on. A girl was running across the street and a car fell on her. None of the police mechas could beat it."

"We're going to beat it," Bishop promised her.

"Why are they attacking us?" Lena asked Bishop.

"Because they're evil."

"But aren't mechas supposed to be on our side?"

"These aren't," Bishop explained. "They've betrayed us."

"Why?"

Reiko saw Bishop struggle to give an answer and empathized. Even though she was decades older than his niece, they both were asking the same question.

Lena's mom, Maia, was behind her. She was distraught and had a cast around her arm.

"Are you okay?" Bishop asked her.

"No, I'm not okay," she angrily snapped. "Isn't your job supposed to be to stop this kind of thing from ever happening?"

"We tried. How did you get here?"

"Some Tokko agents came and brought us here and told us we'd be safe," Maia replied. Bishop was extremely grateful to Akiko-san. "Is it over yet?" Maia asked.

"Not yet," Bishop admitted.

"Those mechas are still out there?" Maia questioned.

"They are."

"What are you doing here, then?"

"I wanted to make sure you two were okay first."

"We've survived this far without you. We'll manage fine," Maia said in a rude tone. "You need to get out there and do your job."

Reiko did not like her tone or how hostile she was being. "He just put his life on the line to defeat one of the mechas," Reiko defended him.

"And who are you?" Maia snapped in irritation.

"Captain Reiko Morikawa and I—" she began.

But Bishop raised his hand. "She's right," he said. "I should get out there and try to stop them. Let's go back to Umegra."

"We need to grab Major Takamaki first."

Reiko went to try to flag down a staff member. She noticed Bishop talking to Lena about food, doing his best to comfort her further. "I want mango pizza, but no anchovies this time," Lena said.

"But I thought your little turtles loved anchovies," Bishop replied.

"Turtles don't eat pizza," Lena said, and giggled.

Reiko found someone to page the major. Major Takamaki came up to meet them ten minutes later.

Reiko explained Nori's request, and the major agreed to help, exiting out to K's mecha.

"Let's go," Reiko said to Bishop.

"You're leaving?" Lena said.

"I have to."

"I'm going too," Lena said firmly.

"Honey, it's not safe out there," Maia said. "Let your uncle—"

"I'm going!" Lena yelled.

"But—"

"I don't want to just stay here. I can help! I'm a Tokko agent in training. I can protect people from evil mechas."

Bishop smiled and said, "I know you can, and I want your help. But the people here need your help too, which is why I'm going to make you an honorary soldier for today. Okay?"

"There's no such thing as an honorary soldier. You're just trying to get me to stay," Lena precociously stated.

Bishop nodded. "You're right. But things are dangerous out there, and I can't protect your mom *and* the city. That's why you need to be here with her."

"Who's going to protect you?" Lena asked pleadingly.

"I will," Reiko assured her.

"You promise?" Lena asked.

Reiko was about to give Lena her promise, but Maia cut in. "Soldiers never keep their promises. C'mon, Lena." Despite Lena's protests, Maia lifted her up and carried her away.

Reiko noticed the pained expression on Bishop's face.

They exited the shelter.

"Nice sister-in-law you have," Reiko commented as they got outside.

"She's had it hard," Bishop said. "Don't blame her. She was widowed shortly into their marriage. Raising a kid by yourself is tough."

"She doesn't have to treat you that way."

Bishop shook his head. "I promised I'd keep my brother safe. I told Maia I'd make sure he came back in one piece. The night I had to tell them that he—he didn't make it was one of the toughest in my life."

Reiko looked over at Bishop. "I'm sorry."

"Don't be. They're the only family I have left," Bishop said.

Reiko had no surviving family members. The closest thing to family she had were the Sons of War, and her closest connection to the Sons was the person she was going to have to face in combat soon.

They got to the mecha's shoe, where the major was eating a sausage with K.

BY THE TIME THEY RETURNED TO UMEGRA, THE REPAIRS ON THE *KAMAKIRI* were completed. Reiko went aboard the bridge and performed a series of calisthenics for the mecha, stress-testing the arm's strength to make sure the new parts were functional. Normally, this kind of testing would go on for at least a full month before deployment. But they didn't have that kind of time, so they went through the quick version. The upgrade to the *Kamakiri* was also implemented and the Skaria magnet gun was working, able to magnetize four times more weight than the *Inago*.

"How do the controls feel?" Chief Engineer Higuchi asked.

"Good," Reiko answered.

"Try out the Skaria. It has modular parts for energy boosts, so I added a bunch. Your Major Onishi put me in contact with one of the engineers up in Berkeley, Nobusue-san. He confirmed your mecha should be able to handle the Skaria without major difficulties."

Captain Morikawa asked if they could test it one last time.

"You worried it's going to break?" Bishop asked from navigation.

"Mechas are fine-tuned machines, where even a small imbalance can have a colossal impact during battle," Reiko replied. "I've seen mechas break down over the wrong type of screw in an arm joint."

"Don't let me stop you."

THIRTY MINUTES LATER, SHE WAS READY TO FIGHT. THREE OTHER MECHAS met her. The *Harinezumi II* was piloted by K. The new mechas were piloted by Major Takamaki and Major Onishi. They were Bayonetta class from the looks of it, designed primarily for combat.

"They're older, sold by the military to Umegra ten years ago. But with a couple custom upgrades, they'll hold up in combat," Nori said.

"Is your leg okay?" Reiko asked her.

"I've been injected with painkillers and steroids and spent the last hour and a half in a rejuvenation vat. My mobility is limited, but I'm going to do my best."

Takamaki's mecha was designated the *Slave III*, while Onishi's was the *Valkyrie*.

Between the four of them, Nori began explaining the plan to defeat the *Stryder*.

"It's a good strategy," Reiko said. But she had to ask, "Is this fair?"

"What do you mean?" Nori asked back.

"I mean the four of us teaming up against her," Reiko stated.

"If it were up to me, it'd be ten of us against her."

"But—"

"Captain, I understand your reservations, especially after her generous act to you. But, respectfully speaking, this isn't a sport. We're fighting to protect the people of Los Angeles. Being fair is the last thing on my mind. If it'll allay your concerns, her acceleration module puts her at a massive advantage. There's a chance even the four of us won't be enough against her."

"I must agree with Major Onishi," Major Takamaki said. "She has a disproportionate advantage. Teaming up is the wise thing to do."

"You have a super magnet gun!" K suddenly exclaimed to Reiko. "So you can swing other mechas around? Now it makes sense why your mecha is bottom heavy and you have all that density in the legs for balance and anchor supports in the heels. Nori! Can I get a magnet gun too?"

"The *Harinezumi II* doesn't have the proper gear to power and energize the Skaria," Nori replied.

"I mean afterward. Would love one of those, and I can adjust the mass in the legs to compensate. Be really nifty for me to harvest old mechas with a magnet gun."

"Let's talk after the battle's over."

Nori went over the plan again, tried to think up contingencies in case things didn't go as designed.

"You all know what you have to do. Get into positions so we can commence."

"Operation have a name?" K asked.

"Why don't you do us the honors?" Nori asked.

"How about Operation Snail's Ass?" K suggested.

"Is that an appropriate name?" Major Takamaki asked.

"Sure, considering we're trying to slow the *Stryder* down to a snail's speed," K answered.

"It makes sense," Bishop said. "It's the perfect description."

"See, dude agrees. I like you."

Reiko would normally have been amused, but the situation was too somber for that.

About fifty meters from them, she saw two Anubis-class mechas being prepared for deployment. They were 40 percent smaller than the regular Anubis mechas. These duplicates didn't have anywhere near the same armament, since they were stand-ins used for portical films. She saw the crews loading the imposter Anubises with explosives.

Nori stated, "Let's commence Operation Snail's Ass. I'm relaying scan data from another OWL directly to all three of you. It spotted the *Stryder* four kilometers west of here. When you arrive, engage the *Stryder*, but remember not to attempt to destroy it, since it'll most likely be in a populated area and I want to minimize the impact to the civilian populace. There are still many areas that haven't been fully evacuated, and we need to do our best to protect them from harm if possible. I'm sending you the best path to Kodama Lake in Echo Park on your GLS." Reiko saw the path charted out on the geographic location services. "Get the *Stryder* into the lake."

Her primary objective was to work with K to engage the *Stryder* and draw her to Kodama Lake. Retreating without appearing to retreat was easier said than done, as it was hard enough just defending herself normally. How to draw Takemi out? The only way Reiko could think of was to keep her distance.

"Ground terrain looks good," Bishop said from the navigation panel. "Aside from all the property damage."

Reiko checked the energy distribution. So far, the Melluso augments were working as expected and there wasn't any excess drain. The roads were uneven and many of the rails were damaged. A navigator would normally plot out the best way to traverse this and save on the BPG, but she knew Bishop was still learning.

"You ready for this?" Bishop asked her.

"The closest we've had to a mecha revolution like this is the Stanifer Gambit, and even then, that was a military base."

"What about the Ceridwen Uprising?"

"That was bad," Reiko said. "But that was eighteen of our mechas starting up their own kingdom in South Mexico, not an attack in one of our major cities."

"A lot of people died trying to suppress the revolt."

"That's every war."

The *Stryder* was in the business district on Wilshire Boulevard and Western Avenue. There were skyscrapers all along the streets. The *Stryder* had destroyed the circular Censor Office which oversaw the thought protection of portical traffic in the vicinity.

They found Daniela Takemi a few kilometers away. Reiko still held up hope there was an alternative to fighting and contacted her. "You're back," Daniela noted.

"We are . . . Is there any way we can avoid this fight?"

"Surrender and walk away."

"That's impossible," Reiko replied.

"Why would you expect otherwise from me?"

"I wasn't. At least tell me why you've betrayed the Sons of War."

"I never swore loyalty to *them*. My loyalty is to the country," she snapped with a ferocity that took Reiko aback. "Are you ready?" she asked.

Reiko, whose mecha was fully charged, raised her sword. "I am. Thank you."

"You don't need to thank me," Daniela said. "I see you've brought a friend with you. It doesn't matter. I must warn you; time is relative to perception. The Flash Division developed steroids to manipulate the way we comprehend and experience time. Once I understood that a second can seem like an hour and vice versa with the mind, I could control the speed of all engagements."

The *Stryder* moved toward the *Harinezumi II*, but from Reiko's vantage point, it seemed to warp from one spot to the next. Suddenly the *Stryder* was in front of the *Kamakiri*, getting ready to attack the *Harinezumi II* with its boomerang. Reiko activated the magnet gun to repel the *Stryder*, which pushed it back. But then the

Stryder vanished again and reappeared at their right flank. Reiko triggered her boosters just in time to avoid the *Stryder*. It swung, then vanished and appeared at the *Harinezumi II*'s side, attacking again. It was unnerving how fast it moved.

Reiko rushed toward the other mecha and struck. The *Stryder* blocked the series of blade swings, but just as the two prepared to volley again, Daniela ignored K and chased after the *Kamakiri*. It was safe to assume her priority was to destroy the Skaria, which was the smart thing to do.

"K, she's after my Skaria," Reiko said.

"Figured that. Lock her in place so I can fight her."

Reiko got the Skaria aimed and ready, triggering the magnet when she thought she had the *Stryder* in view. The *Stryder* vanished again, reappearing several meters outside of the Skaria's range. Reiko swung the magnetic gun over and tried to fire again, but the *Stryder* took cover behind a building so that the magnet tugged on an automobile, pulling it into the air. Reiko released the car, which crashed down onto a bus stand. The *Harinezumi II* attacked the *Stryder*, or at least tried to. Daniela evaded and Reiko's sword struck the side of the Sousuke Saeki Commercial Center, taking out three floors.

The *Stryder* was fast, and it was only thanks to Reiko's magnet shots that it couldn't maintain a concentrated attack against Reiko.

"Any ideas where the acceleration module is located?" Bishop asked.

"That's something you should be helping me figure out," Reiko replied.

"I've tried searching for any unusual readings on the sensors for the *Stryder*, but I'm not getting anything."

"Have you checked for spikes of energy in the armor whenever she uses the accelerator?" Reiko asked.

"How do I check that?"

It was not the question she wanted to hear.

"Toggle the energy sensors with the motion ones. You can have them overlay each other," Reiko explained.

"Let me try it now," Bishop replied.

The *Stryder* pounced on them, getting a strike into its arm. It would have lopped it off, but Bishop saw an emergency notification suggesting he activate the directional plasma shield. He did so and it repulsed the boomerang. The *Stryder* paused, trying to assess the strength and durability of the shield.

"Nice," Reiko commented to Bishop.

"Wait, I actually did something useful?"

"You did."

Bishop did a fist pump, which made Reiko laugh.

Reiko attacked from the rear, forcing the *Stryder* to spin to deflect.

This seemed as natural a chance as she'd get to retreat toward Echo Park. She used her skates and the boosters on her chest plate to push her backward. K fired both his cannons, but the *Stryder* evaded. The resulting property damage was bad.

"Oops," she heard K mutter.

The *Harinezumi II* took steps to retreat as well, and they pushed their speed.

Bishop said to Reiko, "I still don't see any energy levels on the *Stryder* that stand out as abnormal."

"Keep on checking."

The *Stryder* caught up to them and attacked the *Harinezumi II* first. K did his best to deflect her strikes, but the *Stryder* was too agile and the *Harinezumi II* took a couple blows to her armor. Fortunately, the armor held, but K was flung back into a five-story market structure that collapsed under his weight. While K tried to get to his feet, the *Stryder* turned its attention in Reiko's direction. Reiko hit the boosters to try to speed up, but was no match in speed for the *Stryder*. The *Kamakiri* couldn't maneuver out of the way and was too close to the *Stryder* to activate the Skaria. The captain expected to be cut up like all of Daniela's previous prey.

To her surprise, the *Stryder* hesitated, holding the boomerangs up, but not striking.

"What's going on?" Bishop asked.

"I don't know," Reiko replied.

"I did notice an unusual energy spike when she was moving."

"Where?"

Before Bishop could answer, Daniela asked over the communicators, "I was like you at first, willing to do everything for the Sons of War. But I learned my lesson."

Reiko triggered the boosters on her legs that gave them enough space for her to fire the Skaria and repel the *Stryder*. The *Stryder* was going to come straight back at them when the two fake Anubis mechas moved to confront the *Stryder*. Even if they had been real ones, they stood little chance against her speed. Being props, they had none. The *Stryder*'s sword slashes were so fast, the cut marks on the Anubises were glowing from the heat.

"I'm seeing the spikes again," Bishop said. "They're coming from right above the belly whenever she uses the accelerators."

"Good catch. You get all of that?" Reiko asked Nori.

"I just did. Please disengage and move to the lake," Major Onishi reminded her.

Reiko gave a thumbs-up to Bishop, who in turn beamed with pride.

She sped toward the lake. As she did, she saw both Anubises get sliced up in a boomerang tornado. She saw ejection pods fire at the last minute, the crew safely getting away. Reiko knew Takemi well enough to know she wouldn't attack the pods. That was when both of the Anubises used the self-destruct mechanism and exploded. The *Stryder*'s arm was incinerated, and its body armor took heavy damage.

The *Kamakiri* reached Kodama Lake. Reiko looked over at Bishop, who confirmed that the ground under the lake could support their weight. They moved toward its center, which was not very deep, only reaching the level of the *Kamakiri*'s ankle. Reiko understood what Nori was planning. Water would affect speed and also leave a wake wherever the *Stryder* moved, allowing them to potentially see her movements. But would the *Stryder* step into the trap?

All they could do was wait and see.

"I heard this lake is haunted," Bishop said. "Lot of suicides and accidents here."

"This is a terrible time to tell me this."

"Just saying, if something happens to us, at least we'll have company."

There were lotuses all over the lake, and a massive bird sanctuary. Many of the birds took flight as Reiko approached.

At the edge of the lake, *Stryder* was facing them. The burned carcasses of the two Anubises lay underneath her. Takemi wasn't moving forward; she was scanning the surroundings, suspicious that it was a trap.

"If you have something specific in mind, this would be a good time to let us know," Reiko said to Major Onishi.

"Just wait," Onishi replied.

A minute later, heavy gunfire started pounding the *Stryder*. It was the two mechas piloted by Onishi and Takamaki, *Valkyrie* and *Slave III*, attacking from the other side. Their firing pattern was in a wide net that made it impossible to avoid, with their dual gunshots distributed in a tightly choreographed bullet ballet. The *Stryder* was able to avoid and deflect some of the gunfire, but Daniela's mecha would be destroyed if it remained where it was. The *Stryder* was forced into the lake.

"Captain Morikawa. Please magnetize the *Stryder*," Major Onishi ordered. "K. Please destroy the acceleration module, which is located on the right chest. Bishop can send you the exact spot."

Since they were in the park, there weren't many other targets for Reiko aside from the *Stryder*. The *Stryder* approached warily, but had no choice except to move forward since Nori and Takamaki were still firing on her.

Reiko triggered her Skaria just as the *Stryder* was within distance. The electromagnet locked on and prevented the *Stryder* from freely withdrawing. K sprinted toward her and attacked. Reiko made careful modifications to the aim to make sure it didn't affect the *Harinezumi II*. It was tricky and she knew an automated target would make mistakes, conflating the two, so she kept the lock on manual mode.

"I'm going to pull her toward the middle of the lake," Reiko said.

Every time the *Stryder* tried to utilize its acceleration module, there was a slight blur caused by the magnetic forces that prevented her from fully engaging it. Since its left arm was damaged, it couldn't block with it either. K stabbed the exact location of the acceleration module, destroying it. The *Stryder* was at normal speed again.

"Please withdraw now!" Nori ordered both of them.

K pulled away, but Reiko didn't move. "Hold on, Major," she said, despite knowing that the plan was for the four of them to surround the *Stryder* and fire on her.

"Captain, please follow orders," Nori said.

"You can court-martial me later if you want, but let me talk to her."

"Captain," Nori called again.

Bishop cut out her voice. "Do what you got to," he said to Reiko.

Daniela appeared on the display screen. Her bridge had lost main power and her mecha was on auxiliary lights.

"That was a well-executed maneuver. I applaud whoever designed it," Daniela said over a public channel so that anyone could listen.

But Reiko wasn't in the mood to talk tactics. "Why did you join Bloody Mary?" she instead wanted to know. "She stands against everything the Sons of War were about."

"The Sons of War tortured me and were going to execute me," Daniela replied.

Reiko flinched. "Th-that's impossible."

"After Bloody Mary attacked them, they said I betrayed them to her. They tortured me for a month to try to extract a confession."

Reiko remembered the governor's ambiguous answer when she'd asked about Daniela.

"General Watanabe rescued me from my isolation chamber," Daniela said. "That was the second time she'd saved me."

"When was the first?"

"When I was a teenager living near the Quiet Border."

"You never told me that."

"The Nazis carried out a sneak attack and razed our whole city. We asked for support, but everyone turned us down except for one person."

"Who?"

"Pris Watanabe in a mecha sent by an official with the name of Daigo Tamura," Daniela said.

"As in the late governor, Daigo Tamura?"

"The same. He was in charge of a garrison in the Quiet Border because it was a key point of trade. He was the only one who came to our rescue. All it took was Watanabe-san's one mecha to scare off the Nazis. I know that Tamura's main intent was to protect the trade routes. But all I cared about was that he'd sent the mecha that had saved our lives when no one else did. My parents were killed in the attack, so Watanabe-san took me on as her ward and taught me everything about piloting. Her father was so kind to me and treated me like his granddaughter."

Reiko remembered the night they saw him get beaten, and she felt ashamed for stopping Daniela from trying to protect him. "I never knew."

"I have no delusions about Tamura. He's the reason Kansas happened, and that's why I didn't hesitate to join the Sons of War. But after Bloody Mary turned on them, Governor Yamaoka assumed I was the one who'd betrayed them because of my connection to Governor Tamura."

"Was it the governor himself, or one of his underlings?"

"Of course it was the governor. Nothing happens without his personal approval."

"Then what he said about General Watanabe's father—"

"Was a lie."

"So you didn't help Bloody Mary that night?"

"Are you really questioning me?" Daniela snapped.

"No."

"It wasn't me. But they blamed me." Daniela's face became grave. "My legs are artificial because of what they did to me."

"Wha—"

"They fed my legs to dogs while I was awake," she replied. "Anytime I fainted, my torturers woke me back up again to make sure I felt it. No matter how much I pleaded with the Sons to kill me, they refused."

Reiko felt like puking.

"You ask me why I betrayed the Sons of War. I'll ask you why they betrayed me first," Daniela said with an anger Reiko had never witnessed in her old friend. "We are going to kill Governor Yamaoka and then do something no one else can."

"What?"

"A total reset."

"What's that mean?"

"You'll see."

Reiko knew that Daniela would never surrender. She instead asked, "Does your mecha have an escape pod?"

"Why?" Daniela asked back.

"This wouldn't be a fair fight in your condition," Reiko said, echoing Daniela's own words from earlier back to her. "Evacuate your mecha and we'll fight again another day."

"You think I would flee battle?"

"No. But you could accept repayment of a debt for letting me go earlier."

"Do your superiors approve?"

"Let me deal with them."

Daniela smiled. "I appreciate the sentiment. But for soldiers, there's only life and death in battle. I assume the plan is you back off and your compatriots continue their bullet volley?"

"That's their plan, but I won't let them. We'll—" She paused, as though not saying that they'd fight would mean they didn't have to.

"I'm glad. If I'm going to lose, I want it to be at your hands."

Reiko shook her head, hoping there was some way to delay her further.

"General Watanabe and Bloody Mary will reveal the truth about the Sons of War soon," Daniela said. "Then you can figure out if you're on the right side."

"Please use the escape pod," Reiko pleaded.

Daniela smiled. "I'm glad we had the chance to talk. At least you know the truth about what happened to me. Let's finish this."

The *Stryder* charged the *Kamakiri*. They engaged in hand-to-hand combat, grabbing each other in a jujitsu-style fight. Reiko mixed in a variety of uppercuts, jabs, and elbows. The *Stryder* was able to match many of the fists, though Takemi was at a disadvantage with one arm inactive. But she was unrelentingly fierce in her defense. Reiko was driven by rage at what she'd heard and got faster, almost as though she had an acceleration module of her own. A fist of hers got through Takemi's defense. Then another. Finally, Reiko was able to get her in a hold, place her foot slightly behind her, then use gravity and her boosters to push the *Stryder* into the lake.

But Reiko couldn't deliver the killing blow.

Instead, she felt tears in her eyes as she thought of Daniela being tortured by the Sons of War. *How could I be such a fool not to know?* Reiko raged at herself.

"It's not too late," she said to Daniela. "Please, you can escape."

The *Stryder* raised its boomerangs, about to attack the *Kamakiri*. Reiko had no choice but to plunge her sword into the *Stryder*'s BPG. She quickly withdrew the blade and saw that it resulted in a power overload. Sparks raced through the armor. The *Stryder* was weaker than Reiko had realized. She withdrew just as Daniela's mecha exploded, killing her and her crew.

Reiko Morikawa clenched her fists and bit down with her jaw.

"Reiko," Bishop called.

But she was crying and couldn't hear anything.

Reiko stared at the burning remains of the *Stryder* and felt angrier with the Sons of War than she was with Bloody Mary. What truth was Bloody Mary going to reveal?

"Reiko," Bishop gently called again. "Major Onishi wants a status update."

Reiko wiped away her tears. "Put her on."

Nori showed up on the display screen. Reiko was ready to explode if the major even gave her the hint of censure. But she didn't. "I know that was difficult," Nori instead said. "Thank you. I'm sending coordinates for General Watanabe's last known location as of an hour ago. Unfortunately for us, the general spotted and destroyed the drone I sent, and I haven't been able to find her since.

I understand if you don't want to join us, but your help would be indispensable. If you do come, please proceed cautiously."

K sent Reiko a private call. "I heard what you two said. Bummer that happened," he said. "War stinks worse than a pig's arse."

Reiko looked again at the remains of the *Stryder*. "I've never smelled a pig's arse," she said to K.

K replied, "They have some in Catalina. Let me know if you ever want to try."

The communication ended.

Bishop got up from his nav console and approached her.

"Maybe we're all stupid for following orders to the death," she said.

"Maybe."

"Would you describe what I'm thinking as faulty ideology?"

"No," Bishop answered. "I would call it being mournful."

"And if I want to destroy the Sons of War?" she asked.

"We'll deal with them after Bloody Mary," Bishop said.

"What if—"

Bishop stopped her. "No matter what wrong the Sons of War did, it doesn't justify all the killing and destruction Bloody Mary has carried out today," he said.

Reiko tried hard not to think about Daniela. "I guess you're right."

Bishop lowered his head. "There's no right or wrong here. If it wasn't for my niece, I'd be out of here too."

Reiko thought again about what Daniela had said. *General Watanabe and Bloody Mary will reveal the truth about the Sons of War soon. Then you can figure out if you're on the right side.* What was their ultimate aim? Even if they claimed that the Sons of War had killed Governor Tamura, who would believe them, especially since it was Bloody Mary who had committed the actual act? Besides, anything they sent out would immediately get censored . . . But would it anymore? Reiko remembered that multiple censor stations had already been destroyed. With them out of the way, that meant less chances to filter any message Bloody Mary could send out.

Message.

"Hey, Bishop. If I wanted to send out a message to the entire Empire, what would be the best way?"

"The Empire?"

"Yep. Everywhere."

Bishop tapped the console with his fingers. "You'd probably send it from the Naoya Nakahara Broadcast Unity."

"Why there?"

"It's the biggest communications hub in the country and basically connects to all the portical links throughout the Empire. The primary Tokko base is also located underneath the Unity, so all orbits, media, and information get funneled through there."

"Where's that at?"

"In Hollywood. Why?"

"I think that's where they're heading."

Reiko contacted the others and told her what she was thinking.

"No revolution would be complete without a wacky creed," K commented.

"I'm sending an OWL to the Nakahara Unity," Major Onishi said. "Major Takamaki and I will continue to the coordinates where General Watanabe was last spotted. You and K cautiously approach the Nakahara Unity. If you see the *Sygma*, withdraw without engaging."

"Why's that?" Reiko asked.

"This will be a very different kind of fight. The *Sygma* is designed as a battler and can withstand a lot more firepower than the *Stryder*. All four of us need to coordinate if we want any chance at defeating her, but I can't devise a plan until I know where she will be."

"What is that weird chewing sound?" Major Takamaki inquired.

"Oh, sorry, that's me," K said. "I got these new salmon chowder sausages at Umegra that I can't get enough of. They're perfect with prune juice and strawberry jam."

They changed their course and headed for the Nakahara Unity.

III.

"I'M GETTING A REPORT OF A DAMAGED MECHA COMING UP," BISHOP SAID. "It's a mecha called the *Yorokobi*."

The *Yorokobi* was in a shambles, unable to stand, lying on the ground with arms, legs, and head removed. Its broken torso resembled a coffin, armor seared a crispy black.

"Are there any survivors?" Reiko asked.

"I think so."

"Send them a message. 'This is Captain Reiko Morikawa. Do you require any assistance?'"

Bishop relayed the message.

A Lieutenant Tso replied back, though only on audio. "Is that you, Reiko?" the male voice asked.

"Who are you?"

"I was in your class at Berkeley. I fought you during the second round of the tournament."

"I remember. But you took time off, didn't you?"

"I did." Lieutenant Tso laughed to himself. "How ironic to meet you here. I was so upset at the way you beat me back then, I questioned whether I should have even been a cadet and took two years off before returning. It drove me to become a better pilot. I became obsessed with my training and I watched every clip I could of your fights, from Berkeley to your engagement at Wichita Station against Major Tommy Stella and Colonel Sabrina Tenteromano. You were amazing."

"Thank you," Reiko said, not having expected this kind of praise. "What happened here?"

"The *Sygma*."

"You fought General Watanabe?"

"I did. She was too powerful. I tried everything I could to fight her, but it was useless. I couldn't land a single blow on her. She has a trunk blade and chainsaw that I swear felt like I was fighting a thousand arms. The worst part was the way she taunted me."

"The general?"

"Bloody Mary. She knew everything about me, my military records, even my personal history." Reiko could hear him snort through his nose, wiping away his snot, his voice hoarse from yelling.

"Get a grip on yourself," Bishop said.

"Everyone on board is dead except for me. And it's only a matter of time for me."

"What do you mean?"

"I have a piece of metal through my body. I've lost too much blood. I don't have much time left."

Reiko said, "Don't be weak. Medics will come and patch you up. You'll heal and you'll keep on getting better."

"Not this time . . . I was just thinking back to the tournament. If I'd have quit then, I wouldn't be here and my crew would be alive."

"Just relax. Tso? You there? Tso?"

But there was no reply from the *Yorokobi*.

"Is he dead?" Reiko asked.

No one else answered, so Bishop said, "The scans indicate he's stopped breathing."

She sighed.

How many more have to die today?

AS THEY GOT CLOSER TO THE NAKAHARA UNITY, BISHOP SUDDENLY stood up.

"Something happen?" Reiko asked.

"My portical is working again," Bishop said. "All kikkai functions are back."

"The engineers must have restored them," Reiko concluded.

Shortly afterward, a communication came in from an unidentified source, though it was on an official military channel.

"What should I do?" Bishop asked.

"Accept it."

An elderly male who was ranked colonel appeared on their portical display. He had square glasses, big front teeth, and deep wrinkles under his eyes.

"Hi. Who are you?" Reiko asked.

"That's what I should be asking you. You are?"

"I'm Captain Reiko Morikawa from the governor's office."

"I'm Colonel Iiboshi from Los Angeles Command. Under whose authorization are you driving the *Kamakiri*?"

"Major Onishi."

"She did not have the authority to give you the *Kamakiri*. I'm taking over for her now."

"What's that mean?" Reiko asked.

"The major has done a good job so far, but I have far more experience when it comes to urban conflict."

"Then where've you been this whole time?" Reiko wanted to know.

A flash of irritation crossed Iiboshi's face. "Doing my best to get to the command post from my home."

"You mean you were at home slacking off while Major Onishi helped us defeat two of the three mechas," Bishop stated.

"Who are you?" the colonel asked.

"I'm Bishop Wakana of the Tokko."

"We appreciate Tokko officers helping during this conflict, but hope they'll respect jurisdiction and leave personnel decisions to the mecha corps," Colonel Iiboshi stated.

"I have to concur with Agent Wakana. Major Onishi has been

doing a great job while you were away, sir," Reiko stated in an uncompromising voice. "Let her finish the battle."

"Well, *Captain*," he said in a tone meant to put her in her place. "I appreciate your opinion and, considering your limited knowledge of the current state of the corps, understand your sentiment. But it's time for the professionals to take over. What are your current orders?"

Reiko balked at his tone, but knew better than to object publicly. "To stop General Watanabe."

"Belay that order," Iiboshi said. "For now, remain on standby and I'll issue new orders if needed."

"But—"

"Have you heard the news about the governor?" the colonel inquired.

"What news?"

"He's gone missing. I'd suggest you turn your attention to finding the governor."

The communication ended.

"Nice guy, that colonel," Bishop said.

"I hope he knows what he's doing," she replied, then thought of what the colonel had said about the governor. Based on what Daniela had said, she could only come to one conclusion. "I think Bloody Mary has the governor."

"That would make sense," Bishop said. "Bloody Mary has a flair for theatricality."

"She could execute him publicly," Reiko suggested.

"We should hurry to the Nakahara Unity."

"What about the colonel's orders?" Reiko asked.

Bishop stuck his middle finger at the display screen.

On cue, another call came in from Iiboshi.

"Captain Morikawa," Colonel Iiboshi said. "Major Onishi just told me your Skaria gun has been helpful in the previous battle."

"I'd hope so, sir."

"We are commencing our operation to take down the *Sygma*. I want you to assist."

"Yes, sir. How can I help?"

"I want you on standby to tow the *Sygma* using the magnet gun after she is destroyed," the colonel said.

Reiko thought she heard wrong. "Sorry, sir. Do you mean you want my help during the battle?"

"No, I mean after my Diadochi defeat the *Sygma*, I want you to tow it to the Burbank Airfield."

The Diadochi were a group of eight mechas permanently stationed in the Quiet Border whose specialty was combating enemy mechas. "The Diadochi are here?"

"I've had them flown in. They'll be handling the situation going forward. I'm sending you coordinates where I want you to wait."

"Yes, sir. Will you be there in person?"

He shook his head. "I'm at Los Angeles HQ, overseeing the whole city."

The communication ended.

"Did I hear correctly that he wants to use you as a towing service?" Bishop asked.

"You get used to dealing with jerks like him," Captain Morikawa said.

"I hope not."

The coordinates the colonel had sent were near the Nakahara Unity.

By the time they arrived, the *Sygma* was already facing off against the eight mechas of the Diadochi. The *Sygma* was the mecha that resembled a massive mammoth with tusks and shielded ears. It was twice the size of its opposing mechas, and the ground shook every time it took a step. It lifted its arm, and multiple panels began shifting and transforming into a gigantic chainsaw at its arm. But this was an even bigger one than the one she'd used before on Reiko's Labor mecha. There were multiple blades covering it and an enormous cannon on both sides. Its piercingly red armor had a mesmerizing effect. No wonder survivors had become superstitious about it.

Reiko was familiar with the Diadochi. They were a motley assembly of eight mechas, each specially painted to be distinct from the other. Colonel Iiboshi was a fan of ancient history and made the designation of *Diadochi* based on the generals who followed Alexander the Great and fought each other to carve out their places in the empire after his death. He'd even named the individual mechas after the leaders of the Diadochi Wars. That meant rather than the traditional samurai appearance of most mechas, these resembled the old Macedonian and Greek soldiers, with cuirasses, greaves, and Argive circular shields. Their armaments were spears with xyston shafts and machaira short swords. They had helmets with nasal plates and flaring rims that made it look like their faces were angry. Their accessories went far to individualize them. They moved and fought in a style very different from the mecha samurais and were a scourge to Nazis and rebels throughout the world. They had done away with their BPGs and upgraded to an experimental energy source, the Pfau Quark Generator (PQG), developed by the renowned scientist Dr. Junichi Murata. It was less costly than mining asteroids and could be fused at much higher capacities using a particle accelerator down in the Mexican Confederation of Japan.

Just as the eight Diadochi were about to surround and attack the *Sygma*, two of the mechas in the rear, the *Craterus* and *Antipater*, turned against the other six. They attacked two of the Diadochi from the back and stabbed them in the conduits to their PQGs.

"What's going on there?" Colonel Iiboshi demanded, flustered.

The *Sygma* struck from the front, using her blades to eviscerate the *Ptolemy*. Captain Morikawa saw the way Watanabe used her chainsaw in conjunction with the blades on her trunk and understood what Lieutenant Tso had meant when he'd said he felt like he was being attacked by a thousand arms. The entire front of the *Ptolemy* was shredded apart, its internal circuitry exposed. The *Sygma* smashed the bridge with her fist, then cut the tube that connected the head to the stomach, preventing any type of escape. Meanwhile, the *Craterus* and *Antipater* forced the *Perdiccas* and *Arrhidaeus* to their knees.

"Is there a malfunction on the *Arrhidaeus* and *Menander*?" the colonel asked in agitation.

"There is no malfunction," General Watanabe said.

"Who is this?" Colonel Iiboshi yelled.

"You have so much faith in your machines of war," Pris Watanabe said. "But you failed to realize that mechas are nothing without their pilots."

"What are you talking about?"

"Two of the Diadochi are members of our cause," Watanabe replied.

"There are traitors in the Diadochi?"

"Not traitors. Revolutionaries who know better than to follow an old fart who wouldn't recognize greatness if it crashed down on his head."

The colonel refused to accept this. "Captain Onitsuka. Please respond. Captain Onitsuka!" he ordered.

"Captain Onitsuka has joined us," Watanabe said.

"That's impossible."

"No, it's not," Captain Onitsuka of the *Craterus* replied. "We are honored to stand by General Watanabe in this revolution."

"You won't get away with this," Colonel Iiboshi stated.

"I already have," the general stated. "Your Diadochi were compromised long ago. Even those who are on your side know you're a fool concerned only with your personal glory."

General Watanabe turned her attention to the remaining three

Diadochi. "You can surrender or die. I'd prefer not to kill more mecha crews today."

The pilot of one of the remaining Diadochi, *Cassander*, dutifully responded, "We would rather die than surrender to traitors."

"I applaud your sentiment, even if it is misplaced."

Watanabe swung her chainsaw into the *Cassander*'s neck, causing sparks to vomit out. Her trunk blade pierced straight into its chest, causing a rupture in the PQG. It wasn't much of a battle, as the *Cassander* was almost immediately drained of its energy. Watanabe was familiar with the structure of the Diadochi, including all their weaknesses—the traitors had betrayed their structural secrets. The *Craterus* and *Antipater* were going to engage the last two Diadochi. But Watanabe waved them off. She wanted them for herself.

Just then, a new mecha arrived. It was the *Slave III*, Major Takamaki's mecha. Major Takamaki took out her laser blades. The two remaining Diadochi readied their spears. They lunged at the *Sygma*, but General Watanabe cut both weapons in half using her trunk blade. Her chainsaw tore into the stomach of one, and she used cannons in her legs to eviscerate the other. The trunk blade moved like it had a life of its own, snaking, slithering, and lashing its two targets. With incisive slashes to the PQG, an energy leak caused both Diadochi to lose mobility. They fell flat on their faces.

"Major Takamaki," General Watanabe said. "Your son served me during Texarkana. He was a good soldier. I would hate to bereave him of his mother. Back down."

"My son always spoke highly of you. I'll be sad to tell him of your betrayal."

The *Slave III* attacked with blades in both arms. Takamaki was fast, matching the *Sygma* in speed and strength. When the trunk blade attacked from below, Takamaki was able to deflect the blow, spin around, and get a slash in.

"You're as good as I've heard," Watanabe said. "But it's clear the mecha you're using isn't your own. I'll give you one last chance to back down."

"Traitors always like to hide their doubts with too much talk," Takamaki replied.

Takamaki continued her furious attack, striking rapidly with dual wielded blades. The *Sygma* dutifully blocked the strikes, taking several steps back. The exchange went on for several minutes, and it almost seemed like Takamaki had the advantage. Then, suddenly, there was a quick deflection by the *Sygma*, followed by a rapid thrust of the chainsaw that sundered off the *Slave III*'s right wrist. Takamaki attacked using her left arm, but Watanabe was expecting it and her trunk blade was there to meet the strike. There was another flurry of movements, and the chainsaw penetrated Takamaki's defenses. Watanabe plunged the chainsaw into the *Slave III*'s BP generator.

"Are there any last words you'd like me to convey to your son?" Watanabe asked.

"Don't you dare speak of my so—" Takamaki was saying when her mecha exploded.

Watanabe emerged from the smoke victorious.

"Colonel Idiocy," Watanabe said, intentionally mispronouncing his name. "Instead of sending your soldiers to fight for you, why don't you come and fight for yourself?"

"You will pay for this!" the colonel screamed.

"Gladly, with credit from your account. Report back to your superiors about the fantastic job you've done botching everything."

"Watanabe. I'll personally see to it that you are executed in a—"

Reiko wasn't sure what to do now. She knew if she went up against Watanabe alone in her *Kamakiri*, she'd be destroyed like the Diadochi that were lying on the ground. It wasn't like she had anyone to contact either. She tried sending a message to Major Onishi and K. But there was no response. Had Colonel Iiboshi sent them elsewhere?

Reiko tried to think up other options. Using her Skaria, she might be able to control one of the Diadochi. But with the second one right there and the *Sygma* by its side, that was a suicide attack that wouldn't end well.

"You're wondering what you should do," General Watanabe said to her over the communicators. "You know you have no chance. But honor dictates you fight to your death."

"Are you a mind reader too, General?" Reiko replied.

"What's your name, soldier?"

"You forget me already? It's Captain Reiko Morikawa."

"Captain Morikawa. I'm impressed that you were able to escape captivity," Watanabe stated. "Were you part of the group that helped defeat Niijima and Takemi?"

"It's a waste that both had to die today," Reiko replied as confirmation.

"Why a waste? They died honorably, fighting for the cause they believed in. A soldier couldn't ask for more."

"They were more than soldiers."

"A soldier is someone willing to lay down their life for their beliefs. There is no greater calling."

"Wars are stupid and pointless, and so are the people who die fighting in them."

"But aren't you part of the Sons of War?"

"So what?"

"Don't you know what your boss is after?"

"I don't know the details, but it doesn't justify you exacting revenge on the people of Los Angeles."

"This is not about revenge," Pris answered. "The death of my parents helped me to understand that the entire country has to fall in the embers of a truth it doesn't want to face. And we've succeeded in our hope. Check your portical."

"For what?"

"For the truth."

Reiko looked at Bishop, who in turn quickly put the portical connection onto the bridge's display screen. All of the orbits had been hijacked by a message from the Nakahara Unity. Since the censor stations had been destroyed, whatever Bloody Mary would send out would go unfiltered.

Bloody Mary was regaled in full samurai armor. Not the ancient kind, but a modernized polyfiber suit with the *haramaki-do*, *uma-obi* with tassels, *nodowa* protecting the neck, the *hachi* helmet, and a faceplate blocking everything but her eyes.

"How are you enjoying the revolution?" Bloody Mary asked. "I realize many of you didn't see my full message yesterday because of the censors. Very annoying, aren't they? Thanks to them, you missed the whole point of the revolution that's taking place. Contrary to everything the media bots are telling you, this isn't random terrorist violence. The military you trust has given me the code name of Bloody Mary because I'm one of your top assassins. Last year, members of a group called the Sons of War ordered me to assassinate Governor Daigo Tamura."

Reiko cringed when she heard Bloody Mary implicate the Sons of War. What would the public's reaction be? Reiko found some comfort in the idea that the public would be skeptical of taking the word of a terrorist over those in authority, especially when said terrorist was attacking them indiscriminately.

"They told me Governor Tamura was a Nazi collaborator," Bloody Mary continued, "and that the decision had come down from the main island after long deliberation. I obeyed my orders and killed him. But too many things didn't add up, and I felt haunted by the decision," Bloody Mary said in a sanctimoniously somber tone that made it obvious she was being sarcastic. "So I looked into it more and learned Governor Yamaoka carried out this act on his own, without orders from Tokyo. Why is that, Governor?"

The camera panned to the governor, who was dressed in ancient samurai armor. His face was heavily bruised.

"It's because I wanted to become the shogun of America," Yamaoka weakly stated.

"All hail the shogun!" Bloody Mary yelled. "Tell them your plan."

"I killed Governor Tamura so I could seize power for myself, then take the seat of a shogun like my hero, Ieyasu, and declare the Americas independent of the Empire," Yamaoka said weakly, a broken man barely staying conscious.

"Thank you, Shogun," Bloody Mary said. "I said before, there are no innocents in war. I am no exception. You shouldn't trust me any more than any of your leaders. That's why in case there's doubt, I've released all the confidential files the secret police have on everyone, including Governor Yamaoka. His personal correspondence, his portical feed, and film recordings of the night of the assassination are included, packaged specially by your friendly Tokko. For too long, there have been secrets. I've revealed every file on every citizen so that there's nothing more to hide. You can hear Yamaoka's own personal words and thoughts on Tamura's assassination, as well as the private meetings of the Sons of War when they prepared for a revolt against the Empire."

Reiko could not believe Bloody Mary had revealed everything in this way. She didn't know what was in those files, but the fact that the Tokko knew about Tamura's assassination and did nothing about it was surprising as well. It could very well be that those higher up the chain in the Tokko were members of the Sons of War.

"Since Yamaoka was going to do it anyway, I'll declare that we are no longer under the control of the Empire," Bloody Mary continued. "We are fully independent. We are the true America. The German Americas will be my next target. For anyone who's concerned about the future, don't be. The Nazis will fall at our hands. They have more to fear than you. But in order to be victorious, we had to liberate ourselves first."

Bloody Mary continued: "I'll be frank. I don't trust sheep to do a warrior's job. That's why I've just triggered twelve bombs at Pearl Harbor. Whether you like it or not, the Empire will attempt to invade. It's up to everyone here to fight, or be killed," Bloody Mary stated. She then took out a sword and asked the governor, "Any last words, Shogun?"

"I don't apologize for what I did. It was for the country, and I would do it again if I had the chance."

Governor Yamaoka lowered his head and accepted his fate.

"How dishonorable that even to the end, you try to sugarcoat your ambition," Bloody Mary said, then decapitated him with one swing of the sword.

The message ended.

Reiko could not believe what she'd just seen. Was the governor really dead? It seemed like a show. She scrambled to see what information had been released by Bloody Mary. Text correspondence, recordings, documents, and even notes from meetings of the Sons of War were publicly available. Comments dismissive of Tokyo Command were prevalent, and it became immediately clear that sedition was Yamaoka's intent. The Sons of War were completely exposed. She typed her own name into the filters. All her private messages, communications, and records were there. There were even reports about her, including a frank, but harsh, transcript of an assessment on her value and whether she should be invited to be part of the Sons of War. Five people rejected her and referred to her physical disabilities in a demeaning way. Several others objected, mentioning the Salamander and her previous experience, which would make her invaluable. She felt bittersweet to learn that Daniela had been one of her most vigorous advocates and had agreed to be the one to try to recruit her.

She turned to the comments in the orbits. It was still early, but there was outrage piling up against Governor Yamaoka.

"Punish Yamaoka, not us!"

"He should be the one to be executed."

"Kill all the Sons of War!"

It hadn't taken long for people to see direct evidence that the Sons of War had assassinated the governor. Even if they survived this battle, her life as she knew it was over. She would be arrested for sure and interrogated. She thought of her parents. Would she suffer what they had? No, it would be much worse. Their crime was a stupid work of art. Hers was participation in the assassination of the former governor. The main island would send a task force to mete out punishment in a manner which would discourage this kind of thing from happening ever again.

The public's comments on portical orbits against the Sons of War and Yamaoka were getting nastier and nastier.

"You have a choice to make," Watanabe said to Reiko. "Join with us and fight the Empire and the Nazis, or be punished for your part in the conspiracy to assassinate Governor Daigo Tamura."

Reiko had no idea what to do. She was stunned by the revelation and equally stunned that Bloody Mary had succeeded in her goal.

"What should we do?" Reiko privately asked Bishop.

Bishop looked like he'd been punched in the face. "I have no idea. But becoming a shogun? Damn. That's old school."

Reiko vacillated, unsure what the right thing to do was. But she knew she could not fight General Watanabe.

She was relieved when a communication came in for her and she spotted an OWL drone high up in the air. "Captain Morikawa. How are you holding up?" Major Onishi asked, K by her side.

"Been better," Reiko said. "Major Takamaki is dead."

"It's unfortunate Colonel Iiboshi's plan was not successful."

"Did you see Bloody Mary's message?"

"I did."

"Your thoughts?"

"I can't comment on the governor's actions," Nori said. "Whatever he may have done, he's paid the price for his acts with his life. But unless you have an objection, I'll take over with General Watanabe from here."

"Ma'am?"

"This is a score I have to settle," the major stated firmly.

"Do you want my assistance?" Reiko asked.

"Not for this one."

Onishi's mecha, the *Valkyrie*, stepped ahead of Reiko.

"What you want me to do?" K asked Nori.

"Handle those Diadochi for me."

"Consider them shreds of cheddar cheese."

Nori and K approached Pris, Onitsuka, and the remaining Diadochi.

"Who are you supposed to be?" General Watanabe inquired.

"I'm Major Onishi."

"Major. I've seen enough death today to last a lifetime. Our revolution has succeeded. Why waste your life when we've already proven that Governor Yamaoka was the ultimate traitor?"

"You talk like you're acting with honorable motives. But you killed eighty-six of my compatriots in a sneak attack earlier today, pretending to be on our side. The only reason I survived was because my second-in-command took the brunt of the blast for me."

"That's cowardly by every standard," K added.

"Who are you?" the general demanded.

"Who he is doesn't matter," Nori cut in. "This is between us."

General Watanabe sighed. "I understand and will honor your request."

The *Valkyrie* and the *Sygma* engaged in direct combat. Nori's sword clashed at blinding speed with Pris's chainsaw. Arcs of metal struck each other. Nori matched Watanabe in skill, and it was impressive for Reiko to see such swordsmanship. The *Sygma*'s trunk attachment was as fast as a third arm, trying its best to expose the *Valkryie*'s vulnerabilities. This fight was on another level from anything Reiko had seen before.

The Diadochi moved to assist the *Sygma*, but K was there to meet them.

"Naughty naughty," K said. "Just curious. Why y'all betray your own peeps?"

"Because General Watanabe saved me too many times to count," Captain Onitsuka of the *Craterus* replied. "I'd follow her to Yomi and back if she asked it."

"Kind of a dramatic thing to ask someone, ain't it? *Follow me to Yomi and back!*"

"You think this is a joke?"

"Nah, more like a really intense portical show," K answered. "Except better, since I'm in the middle of it."

"The corps has treated its pilots terribly. As long as they're useful, they're good to them, but the moment they can't pilot, even if it's due to injuries sustained in combat, they're thrown out like trash."

"I know. They pulled the same shit on my mom. That's why I left the corps."

"Then you understand why I'm against them. If you knew what they did to the pilots of the Gnostic Colossi . . ."

"Honestly, don't know, don't care," K replied, then paused to gargle a drink. "You all the bad guys for attacking innocent people. Don't expect your villain's speech to convince me."

"You take us lightly, but you'll pay for your insolence."

"I don't have that much money," K replied as he engaged the *Craterus* and *Antipater*.

K's fighting style was very unusual, Reiko noted. It was loose, with no methodical stance. Instead, it was almost liquid-like as he flowed into battle with attacks that were blindingly fast. Reiko swore she recognized it from somewhere, but she couldn't quite place it.

"Hey, Reiko," Bishop called.

"What's up?"

"Unless we have something to do here, would you mind heading for the Nakahara Unity? My forensics partner, Yasu, is holed up there. Says there's a lot of dead agents and he needs help getting out."

"Bloody Mary's still there?"

"I think so, but I just saw his message and I haven't been able to get ahold of him to confirm."

As the two mecha battles in front of them intensified, Reiko wished she could help and take part somehow. But she knew it wasn't her place. She thought again of Governor Yamaoka's execution. Would that be her fate as well? She shuddered because she had no idea.

BISHOP WAKANA

★ ★ ★

HOLLYWOOD

I.

A PART OF BISHOP WAS EAGER TO GET TO THE NAKAHARA UNITY AND confront Bloody Mary. Another part dreaded it.

"Have you been to the Nakahara Unity?" Reiko asked as they arrived in the *Kamakiri*.

"Only once. Two agents showed me the fancy media center. It was as big as a concert hall."

"What's the whole place for?"

"The main mission at the Unity is regulating communications throughout the country," Bishop said. "Tokko's official term is 'Archetype Construction.'"

"That sounds fancy."

"The Tokko think of society as a series of stories and symbols the people believe in, giving them reasons to follow the rules. Without it, there's only physical force, which won't last long, since the populace always outnumbers those in actual power. The broader symbols are what keep people under control and preserve order," Bishop said. "In the old Americas, the construction of these social beliefs was in the hands of religious institutions. In the Empire, the Tokko took charge of creating and controlling these social archetypes. We supplanted God's role as thought police and created kikkai orbits like SOCIAL."

"I didn't realize the Tokko had a hand in all that."

"Information needs a sieve. Complete, unfiltered freedom would be too daunting and overwhelming. The essential element is to foster the illusion of freedom without actually giving it. People are willing to accept just about anything if you can give them the illusion of choic—"

Bishop's voice trailed off. Reiko looked over and saw that his face was pale and he had to steady himself against the console. "Bishop?" she called.

He took a deep breath and remembered a case that took place shortly after the death of Governor Tamura. Akiko-san and he had been ordered to arrest a group of businessmen who'd been selling military secrets to the Nazis. The businessmen were rounded up in their homes and driven to a Tokko interrogation hall. Eight of them were lined up, blindfolded. Four wore pajamas, two were naked, and the remaining two were in their boxer shorts. Three of them had sullied their pants, and one of them was openly weeping. Tokko agents had guns in their hands, ready to fire.

"I know you've been selling personnel information on our mecha pilots to the Nazis," Akiko said. "The first person to tell me all your contacts, what information you sold, and who else is collaborating with you will survive. Everyone else will be executed. Do I have a volunteer?"

"We didn't sell secrets to the Nazis!" a man screamed.

"We hate the goddamn Nazis!"

Bishop was disgusted by the traitors and looked at his portical to see who was who. But as he read over the charges, something caught his attention. They were the messages these eight had allegedly sent with military information to the Nazis. But they were navy secrets, schematics which they had no access to, not the mecha corps profiles they'd been charged with. Did that mean there was someone in the navy who had betrayed them? But the messages themselves indicated it was mecha pilot profiles they were relaying, not architectural layouts for their underwater bases or their Kraken-class battle submarines.

Bishop went to Akiko and whispered in her ear, "Can we talk?"

She nodded and they went to an adjacent room. Bishop explained the discrepancy.

Akiko replied, "I told data systems to fix that. I see they haven't gotten to it."

"Wait, you knew about this?" Bishop asked.

"Of course," Akiko replied. "It was a sloppy job by the Kempeitai."

"Why?"

"These eight incurred the wrath of a minister who wants to take over their businesses. The Kempei were told to find a reasonable excuse to have them removed. We've come in to mop up."

"So they're innocent?"

"Of this charge, yes."

"And you're okay with this?" Bishop asked, stunned that Akiko already knew.

"I'm not okay with this," she said. "But with a new regime in charge, this is part of our duty."

"You were hiding the truth from me?"

"I was trying to protect you."

"But these are innocent people. We should be hunting down real traitors."

"I brought all of this to the attention of my superiors already," Akiko said. "They have insisted I follow orders."

"What about all the stuff on the news Governor Yamaoka was saying about forgiveness and reconciliation?"

"My assessment of the veracity of a case is separate from my orders," Akiko replied.

"What if we disobey the orders?"

"Then some other Tokko agent will carry out the orders instead."

"But this is wrong."

Akiko looked at Bishop and said, "Do you remember the writers we arrested last weekend?"

Bishop's eyes tightened. "Of course. Don't tell me they were innocent."

"They did write articles questioning Governor Yamaoka. Our original orders were that they be executed. I was able to convince our superiors that execution was too extreme," Akiko said.

"Cutting off their hands wasn't extreme?" Bishop demanded.

"They can get artificial hands," Akiko stated. "These eight businessmen might not be guilty of the crime they're being executed for, but they've been trafficking weapons for some time now. Weapons that were used against our troops. We have to know where and when to fight our battles."

"If your idea of protecting people is to cut off their hands, that's madness."

Akiko had a look of sadness in her eyes that took Bishop aback. "You're right. But we are all snails on the razor's edge, trying in our little ways to dull the pain for ourselves and, if we're fortunate, others as well."

"I don't know what that means," Bishop said.

"It means whether we carry out our orders or not, those eight will be executed. If we put ourselves in a position where even if we do evil things, we can help alleviate evils for people who really need it, that's better than nothing."

"There's got to be a better way," Bishop said.

"Not as long as you're part of the Tokko," Akiko replied.

"Bishop!" Reiko yelled.

He snapped out of it, looked at Reiko, and said, "I had a dizzy spell for a second there. I think I need some rest."

"You're still recovering from being under the Cyber Bubble for so long. If you want to take a short nap, I can wait."

"Yeah, let me take a nap while Bloody Mary burns the city down," Bishop replied. "I'll manage, but thank you."

It was evening, so lights were on all over the Unity, with spotlights pointed up in the air in an emblematic show of authority. Police cars had been stationed in front of the Nakahara Unity, but those that hadn't already been destroyed were abandoned. Bishop didn't know how five security armored personnel carriers got stacked on top of each other, but suspected it had something to do with the *Sygma*.

"You don't have to come down," Bishop said.

"I absolutely need to come," Reiko replied.

"What if we need the *Kamakiri*?"

"Since our porticals are working again, I can control the *Kamakiri* remotely."

They descended to ground level and entered the Unity.

The central lobby had an indoor river and gardens surrounding it. Holographic bees and flowers welcomed them. Normally, there would be guards, sensors, and other precautionary measures that would alert security. But nobody greeted them. Inside the river, they saw a hill of dead bodies. Bishop counted over thirty corpses, all members of the Tokko. He shut his eyes, trying his best not to explode in anger.

At the reception desk, there were four slumped corpses.

Bishop lifted the head of one of the receptionists. He was a young man who'd started working at the Unity several years ago.

"You know him?" Reiko asked. As she looked closer, she saw that there was something about him that seemed plastic.

"Not personally," Bishop replied, then put his fingers inside the receptionist's eyes.

"What are you doing?" Reiko asked, perturbed that Bishop was digging inside the receptionist's eye socket.

Bishop pulled the eyeball out. Connected to the sclera was a viscous clump of electric wires and red-tinted oil. "He—he's artificial?" she asked.

Bishop nodded and connected a wire protruding from the sclera to his portical. "We need to see what he saw." On his display screen, visuals appeared of the moments before the receptionist's death. A masked woman with giant swords was thronged by an entourage of nineteen soldiers.

The receptionist stated, "Welcome to the Tokko. You need the proper authorization to be present, and at the current time, I don't see your identification. Could you please—"

Functions ceased at the last image of Bloody Mary thrusting a blade into his forehead.

"Not much help there," Bishop said. He contacted Yasu again and asked, "Where are you?"

But there was no answer.

Bishop was wondering what steps to take next when eight strangers approached them, brandishing electric prods and katanas. They wore body armor that augmented their natural abilities, making them stronger and providing protection against regular bullets. To Bishop's surprise, the porticals indicated they were members of the special forces group Sohei.

"What the hell do you think you're doing coming in here?" one of the men snarled.

"We're conducting an investigation," Reiko replied. "You are?"

"We're with Bloody Mary."

"Where is she at the moment?"

"None of your goddamn business."

"You think you can come to our base and talk to us so disrespectfully?" Bishop snapped.

"What if we do?"

As answer, Reiko removed four pieces from her artificial arm that became aerial knife missiles and hovered next to her.

"Did not know you had that," Bishop said, then realized his reaction was reflected in the disconcerted expressions of the soldiers across from them.

"I added these after Bloody Mary's attack," Reiko replied. "Custom Skaffens."

The goons raised their katanas and guns. Reiko directed the knife missiles at them. They were fast, deadly, and fired armor-piercing smart bullets. Three targets got shot in the leg, blowing out their knees. The bullets from the other guns disabled four, taking out chunks of their shoulders and arms. The last, and bulkiest, Reiko left for Bishop. But Bishop swore he recognized the man.

"Where do I know you from?" he asked.

"You don't."

Bishop charged him, about to punch him. He instead got a kick to his face and fell back. Bishop returned to his feet and exchanged blows with the thug. Reiko lifted one of the injured, pointed a knife missile at his thigh, and asked, "How important is walking to you?" as she began interrogating him.

Someone once said you got to know who a person really was if you fought them. But in Bishop's experience, that meant everyone was more or less the same: desperate, dumb, and eager to survive. They bled the same, spat the same, cried the same, even pissed their pants the same. More experienced fighters could last longer, but there was always someone bigger and better to get the best of them. Contrary to films and games, there was nothing ennobling about combat. Even the most skilled warriors made mistakes. One punch landing in the wrong spot could shatter their knuckles, ending the match. His adversary had training, and Bishop anticipated his up-percut, blocking it and landing his palm on his face. His opponent had a good mix of strength and agility. Just as they were about to exchange fists again, Bishop remembered where he'd seen him.

"You're Albert Yokoyama, the Sohei agent Bloody Mary cap-tured," Bishop said, sure the facial features matched the man who'd appeared bloody and beaten on the video. Except he had none of the bruising Bishop had seen earlier.

Yokoyama charged fiercely but dropped to the floor, legs busted open by Reiko's knife missile.

"I was about to take him," Bishop protested.

"You were taking too long," she replied. "Don't pout." Reiko pointed four missile knives at Yokoyama and ordered, "Start ex-plaining why the Sohei are working for Bloody Mary."

"Because she speaks the truth no one else dares."

"That's why you put on that show for the porticals?"

"I'd do anything to protect the country."

"Where's Bloody Mary now?" Bishop asked.

Yokoyama remained silent.

"According to him," Reiko said, pointing to the soldier she'd questioned, "Bloody Mary is somewhere called the Portopia Kikkai Cathedral."

"That's one of the four main stages in the Unity." Bishop checked his portical. "It should be on the eighteenth floor."

"What do you want to do with Yokoyama?"

Bishop punched him hard in the face, knocking him out cold.

They took the elevator up to the eighteenth floor.

"There's something very unusual going on here," Bishop said. "No matter how good Bloody Mary is, there's no way she could know how to access a Tokko station with so much ease."

"You forgot all the dead people in the lobby?"

"There's security codes and fail-safes designed to prevent infiltration, even by special forces," Bishop replied. "Someone had to have betrayed us."

"Obviously she's persuasive, since she convinced the Sohei to join her," Reiko stated.

"Did you learn anything else from that Sohei soldier you interrogated downstairs?"

"Governor Yamaoka was the one who ordered them to assassinate Cossack. But Bloody Mary already had them on their side, and they eliminated those political targets as a favor to Marshal Lanser."

"*The* Marshal Lanser who's second-in-command of the German Americas?"

"It looks like he wants a revolution of his own."

Bishop felt like he was stepping into something way beyond his grasp. "This is getting too complicated for me," he said.

"We'll get through it."

The elevator came to a stop, and they ran down two hallways that were filled with wall-sized posters of celebrities before they reached the PKC. It was built like a church with an altar to the entertainment gods, display screens built into the walls similar to stained glass. There were bright lights, high ceilings, and a religious atmosphere about the multimedia cathedral.

Nine bodies were strung upside down near the altar. They were lifeless Tokko agents. Bishop felt his blood chill. Their bodies almost didn't look real. But the smell of death was unmistakable. Any one of them could have easily been him. Their names were the only thing that showed up on his portical, as rank, biography, and case records were classified. The tenth victim was alive, shivering, blood crusted on his face, a butterfly tattoo on his shoulder.

It was Yasu.

"What happened here?" Bishop asked him.

"B-Bloody Mary killed the others after she got what sh-she—she w-wanted. But s-s-she left me alive to tell everyone a message," Yasu said, trembling.

"What's that?"

"The—the—the United States of J-J-Japan is dead," he said as he shivered in fear. Bishop noticed Yasu had puncture marks over his arm and at least four teeth were missing. He'd never seen his forensics partner look so scared.

"Did she say anything else?"

Yasu choked up and stuttered, "S-s-she a-asked if—if I remembered my fi-first kill."

"Did you?"

"Y-y-yes."

Reiko eyed Bishop. The two held Yasu so he didn't fall headfirst to the ground, and Reiko directed her missile knife to cut the rope his feet were hanging from.

"We—we tried, but we couldn't stop her from s-s-sending that m-message," Yasu stuttered.

"Don't think about that. Do you know if Akiko-san is safe?"

"I—I haven't s-seen her. She—she was supposed to—to come here. I don't think s-she m-made it."

He'd have to check up on his boss later.

"Where is Bloody Mary now?"

"I—I think she w-went upstairs to the he-helipad."

Bishop looked at Reiko and said, "Let's go."

"W-wait," Yasu said. "There's—there's something you need to know."

"What?"

"I—I'm sorry. I—I—I . . . I lied to you."

"About?"

"You—you're an Ulfhednar . . . D-Dr. Metzger put it in your bo-body when you were un-unconscious."

"But you told me—"

"I—I lied so I could—could research you a-and t-t-track you—your body ch-chemistry."

"So my body is a bomb?" Bishop demanded. He remembered that after Metzger had taken him captive, he'd woken up and felt something was wrong with his stomach.

"It is. Your body is especially s-suited for it."

"Why?"

"During—during Texarkana . . . you were the only survivor of Operation 4891."

"How do you know about Texarkana?" Bishop demanded.

"I—I was—was in-involved. The—the army needed intelligence about N-Nazi movement east of Tex-x-xarkana. But all our s-s-spies were c-caught and killed. We didn't-didn't know what was going on in the Nazzzzi underground base a-and we needed to know if—if—if they were p-p-preparing biological and—and—and chemical w-w-weapons."

"Isn't that why you sent Bloody Mary?"

"She—she was a d-decoy. The a-a-army w-w-worked with us to outfit several hundred of our soldiersss with portical engrams in their b-b-brains."

"What's that?"

"Y-you got a booster shot up your nose before your mission, r-right?"

Bishop recalled how painful the vaccination had been. "They told us that was to protect us against Nazi biological weapons."

"That was a lie . . . Those w-w-were artificial engrams w-with portical receptors that lodged themselves in your b-b-brain and recorded your s-s-sensations, from s-s-smells to sounds and sights."

Their objective clicked for Bishop. "They were sending us in as reconnaissance."

"E-e-everything you s-s-saw, heard, smelled, and felt would be recorded. E-e-even if you didn't survive, the d-d-data in the engramssss w-would."

They were dangled out there as fodder to soak in whatever they could. Their combined memories would form an image the Tokko, or Army Intelligence, could use for their battle plans. "So it didn't matter if we defended Bloody Mary or not?"

"No. The only—only reason you w-w-were sent w-w-was for intelligence."

"Did Akiko-san know this?"

"No. S-she wasn't involved at all. S-she wasn't c-c-cons-sidered re-reliable."

"Why's that?"

"Her p-p-past record . . . She c-c-cared tooooo much a-about protecting people. De-defied orders too many t-t-times."

Bishop took a deep breath.

"How do I trigger the bomb?" he asked. He wanted to know all his options.

"T-trigger?"

"Set it off. How do I do it myself?" Bishop demanded. If a battle with Bloody Mary didn't go the way he wanted, he had to ensure there was a way to stop her.

Yasu held up his portical.

"P-p-press that a-a-activation button and it'll go off."

Bishop snatched the portical and headed back for the elevator.

"Bishop!" Reiko called. "Bishop!"

"You can't come with me," he said.

"What are you talking about?"

"I have to stop Bloody Mary no matter what," he said. "Get back to the *Kamakiri*."

"You go up there alone, you have no chance."

"Even if we go together, we won't stand a chance."

"So you're going to blow yourself up?" Reiko asked incredulously.

"If that's the only way to stop her," Bishop insisted.

"That's not the only way. We can do this if we work together."

"I don't even know whose side you're on!"

"I'm on your side."

"Stop treating me like an idiot! I know you were part of the group to assassinate Governor Tamura!" Bishop yelled. "It was all over those portical reports Bloody Mary released."

Reiko did not waver from meeting his gaze. "I was part of the group in Seattle that *tried* to assassinate him. And I don't apologize for it. Tamura was a terrible human being, collaborating with the Nazis, exploiting his position to get wealth for himself and his family at the expense of all the citizens. I'm not the traitor here. It's all the people who stood by and did nothing as he destroyed everything dear in our country. But we failed because Tamura's security force already expected us."

"Then how did they—"

"Bloody Mary got him."

"Bloody Mary?"

"She killed the governor. Then a few months later, she started killing the Sons of War," Reiko explained. "Don't blow yourself up."

"I don't want to, but I might have no choice," Bishop said.

"What about your niece?"

"This is for my niece. I have to stop Bloody Mary from putting anyone in harm's way ever again."

"I understand. But I'm not letting you go up alone."

"You realize if I blow up—"

"I'm not afraid of dying," Reiko said. "If she's still up there, let's stop her together."

Bishop did not want to put Reiko's life in danger. But he could tell she would not budge on her stance. Time was too precious to fight with her down here. And maybe she was right. Maybe together, they had a chance.

"This is really risky," Bishop told her.

"I wouldn't be here otherwise."

They got aboard the elevator to the helipad.

Bishop checked his pistol again. Reiko readied her missile knives.

"I grew up without a father and hated it," Bishop said. "I've wondered what would have happened if my dad had swallowed his honor and chosen his life instead. Lena had a hard time after her dad died, and I tried to fill the gap a little. I don't want to leave her now."

"We're going to get through this alive, okay?"

He looked pensively toward the door.

"There's so much I wish I could tell her. I wonder if my dad thought the same thing before his end," Bishop said, and thought again about the night his father had called to tell them he was going to be executed.

"Shut up about the end," Reiko ordered.

They arrived at the top floor.

Outside on the roof, they spotted Bloody Mary by herself, dressed in the modern samurai armor they'd seen in her message. She was watching the mechas battle. K's *Harinezumi II* had already defeated Onitsuka and his fellow Diadochi, both their mechas lying in smoky heaps.

Nori's *Valkyrie* was battling the *Sygma*. Both of them had been severely damaged. Both of them were missing parts from their armor, and the *Sygma*'s trunk had been chopped off. They were preparing for a final sortie and stood motionless. The *Valkyrie* wielded its katana to its right. The *Sygma*'s chainsaw was held up in front of Watanabe. Bloody Mary, and pretty much anyone within view, was watching. Their communications were on public channels, so anything they said could be listened to. Neither of them was speaking.

The buzz of the *Sygma*'s chainsaw signaled the final attack. It sprinted forward and attacked with a swing to the left. It actually hit the *Valkyrie* and it looked as though Nori was defeated. But the move had been a ploy by Nori to get in closer as the chainsaw got stuck on its belly plate (the sturdiest part of the mecha, since it shielded the BPG). Given a few more seconds, the *Sygma* would have destroyed the *Valkyrie*. But for Nori, it gave her the chance to strike with her sword and stab the *Sygma* through its neck. The impalement was swift and deadly.

"Your revolution is over," Nori said.

She removed the blade. All the connections to the bridge were severed, so control was lost. The chainsaw dropped. The *Sygma*'s arms went limp.

But Bloody Mary didn't seem at all unnerved or alarmed. She calmly turned toward Bishop and Reiko.

Was this to be the final stand with Bloody Mary? Bishop tightly gripped his Nambu heat pistol. To his side, Reiko had her missile knives hovering next to her.

"What can I do for you two?" she asked.

"You won't kill any more people," Bishop said.

"The wages of war are death, and my gift to the people is eternal knowledge of the bloody cost of civilized murder."

"No one asked for this kind of gift!"

"But I give it freely, since I want you all to feel my passion," Bloody Mary stated.

"I've seen your passion for killing before."

"'Unto whomsoever much is given, of him shall be much required.'"

Bishop raised his gun. "I'm willing to give whatever is required to stop you, including my life."

"I didn't ask for your life, or I would have already taken it," Bloody Mary said. "But if it's a fight you want . . ." She prepared her sword.

Bishop pulled the trigger on his gun at the same time as Reiko attacked, but it was in vain. All the bullets were absorbed by a directional plasma shield Bloody Mary wielded. She moved toward them. Bishop and Reiko raced to meet her, hoping if they could get close enough, the effectiveness of the shield could be minimized. But she was too quick and dealt with Bishop first, swinging in one stroke as she passed him by. At first, Bishop thought Bloody Mary had missed. Then he heard a clunk, looked over, and saw his arm and Nambu pistol lying on the mecha armor. Bloody Mary had sliced his arm clean off from the shoulder.

Reiko attacked with her missile knives, but Bloody Mary blocked using her arm, which was artificial. She was quick with her sword and sliced through one of the missile knives. Two struck from opposite sides, and Reiko charged at her with her laser gun. Bloody Mary's plasma shield still blocked Reiko's laser fire from the front, but its width didn't extend all the way around to her flank. One of the knives landed a blow on her shoulder, while the second lunged itself into the side of her torso. Reiko saw an opportunity and slammed straight into Bloody Mary. She took out the knife in Bloody Mary's side and tried to stab directly into her face. Bloody Mary blocked with her arm and then pushed her away.

"You've been practicing with your missile knives," Bloody Mary noted.

"Every day since we last met."

Reiko directed the two remaining knives straight at Bloody Mary. Bloody Mary propelled herself up, and her shield protected her from the knife missiles. Reiko had them attack again. Unfortunately, the plasma shield absorbed most of the kinetic energy of the knives and slowed them down to the point where they hit Bloody Mary and bounced right off—like throwing paper clips at an armored suit. Bloody Mary shot the knives out of the air. Reiko fired her laser gun rapidly and got a shot into her arm. Bloody Mary removed her burned gloves, peeled away the damaged skin, and revealed a gun arm that was actually more of a cannon.

"I've been preparing for this revolution my whole life," Bloody Mary stated.

She fired four times straight at Reiko, and the explosion was large enough to hurtle Reiko backward. She hit her head against the ground and fell unconscious.

Bloody Mary walked over to Bishop and put a sword to his neck, which caused his flesh to burn. It was electrically charged to give it a heat pulse and make it easier to cut metal. She kicked his knee, forcing him to the ground. Bishop's remaining hand was in his pocket, finger on the trigger to activate the bomb.

"Before you kill me," he said, "tell me what your real name is."

"Real name?"

"You weren't born as Bloody Mary," Bishop stated, refusing to let the sword at his neck get to his nerves. "And the records say you've been doing this for over forty years. I want to know the name of the person who's killing me."

"There have been many Bloody Marys in our history. The Bloody Mary that saved you in Texarkana is different from the multiple Bloody Marys that assassinated the Nazis in the past. Anytime one was killed in action, another took her place."

"What about you?"

She removed her mask.

Bishop could not believe the face underneath. But deep down, it all made sense.

"Akiko-san? W-what's going on?"

"I didn't want to kill you for your father's sake," she said. "But you're leaving me little choice."

"Can you tell me why you're doing all of this?" he asked, though the dots were connecting. A Tokko agent like his boss knew the real politics of the empire, not the fake propaganda that was perpetuated as truth. She could effectively use psychological warfare against the masses in ways most others couldn't and move furtively to gather her forces without triggering Tokko alerts. His finger was still ready to activate the bomb.

Akiko looked at Bishop. "I tried for years and toiled from my position to help bring change to the Empire," she replied. "But it was impossible with all the establishment figures wanting to maintain the status quo and their own power. You saw what happened to your father. I saw so many of my fellow agents arrested, or executed, simply because they stood up for what was right. The only way to bring about real change was with a revolution that would permanently wipe away the old in a baptism of violence."

From above, a tiltrotor aircraft landed at the helipad.

"I can't deny what you're saying," Bishop said. "But why kill so many civilians?"

"Your niece is safe, correct?"

"Yes. And I'm genuinely grateful to you. But many other people lost their family members, and I want to know why."

"Do you remember your first kill?" Akiko asked instead of answering his question.

"You already asked me that."

"I mean the real first. Mine was a young woman who believed she was fighting for the good of the Empire until she was ordered to attack a camp in the Quiet Border suspected of harboring Nazis. There were no Nazis there. Just refugees. But her officers lied to her, so she killed eight of them. In the morning, she found out that the people she'd killed weren't Nazis at all. She learned she hadn't been a warrior for a just cause, but a murderer, fighting for stupid old men high up in their castles who just wanted power for themselves. She vowed to kill them no matter what the cost. But she had to kill herself first. The person Bloody Mary was born as died long ago at my hands. She no longer has an identity. I throttled it out of her with my bare hands."

Bishop, who had lost a lot of blood from his arm, felt dizzy and blinked several times, fighting against unconsciousness and the idea of a young Akiko killing her old self. Pain hit him, but fatigue was trying to dispel the suffering. He removed his finger from the portical, and even if it was stupid, he accepted his fate. "I'm ready," he told her.

She raised her sword and was going to slice down. But instead of bringing it down, she sheathed her sword. "This is the third time I've spared you."

"Why?"

"Your family has lost too much. Go to your niece, Bishop Wakana. Leave the revolution to me."

Akiko put her helmet back on, walked toward the aircraft, and got on board.

Bishop crawled to Reiko, checked that she was okay. She opened her eyes and asked, "Bloody Mary?"

Bishop pointed at Bloody Mary climbing aboard the aircraft.

"I can get the *Kamakiri*, use the magnet gun, and—"

"Hold her in place while I run aboard and set off the Ulfhednar," Bishop concluded for her.

"I was more thinking we could shoot her from the ground."

"I had the chance to kill her," Bishop told Reiko.

"Why didn't you?" Reiko asked. But unlike a few days ago, her question wasn't from animosity or befuddlement.

"Because I finally found out Bloody Mary's real name."

The aircraft took off, taking Bloody Mary away. Bishop's world turned black.

II.

HE WOKE TO THE SOUND OF SOFT BREATHING AND PRESSURE ON HIS stomach. He was in a hospital bed. His niece, Lena, was sleeping on the chair, her arm and head using his belly as a pillow. There was violin music playing from the hospital lobby. He checked his right arm. Something was attached to his shoulder, but it wasn't his natural arm. He tried to move it. His augmented piece rotated up.

Lena got up, saw he was awake, and hugged him. He pushed a strand of hair hanging loose on her forehead out of the way. "You're finally awake!" she yelled.

Behind her, Reiko was on a chair. "You're lucky to be alive," she said.

"How *am* I alive?" Bishop asked.

"Because I drove you to Mitsuyasu Sakai Hospital and destroyed a lot of property on the way. Got you here just before you would have died from all the blood you lost."

Bishop smiled gratefully. "I guess I owe you one."

"You guess?"

"Thank you," he said. "I'll make it up to you somehow."

"I expect a lot of unique sushi rolls," Reiko replied.

"Definitely. What—what about the Ulfhednar?"

"Your friend Yasu helped the doctors remove it."

"How long have I been out?"

"Five days."

"Five days?" Bishop asked, surprised. "What have I missed?"

"Too much for me to tell you all right now," she replied.

"Can you sum it up for me?"

"We're under siege from all corners. Bloody Mary has declared the USJ dead."

"What happened to Bloody Mary?" Bishop asked.

"She's gone missing since that day," Reiko replied.

Bishop wondered if he'd ever see Akiko-san again.

"And the Empire?" he asked, but coughed from the strain.

"There's a lot to cover," Reiko said. "But they're sending attack mechas our way."

"How can I help?" Bishop asked.

"By recovering," Reiko replied. "And spending some time with your niece until you're healed up. We can talk more later."

Reiko left the room, and his niece began to tell him all that had happened to her during the past week. He laughed and asked, "Have you been having good food lately?"

"Mom tried to cook mapo tofu and fried rice, but it wasn't as good as yours."

"You need to get the spices and pork balance right or it doesn't work," Bishop said.

"I love your cooking," Lena said. "When can you leave?"

For a moment, Bishop looked out the door and wondered where Reiko was going, what she was doing next. But then his eyes turned back to his niece. "Hopefully soon," he replied.

REIKO MORIKAWA

★ ★ ★

LOS ANGELES

I.

A FEW HOURS AFTER LEAVING BISHOP, REIKO ATTENDED AN EMERGENCY meeting made up of the remaining members of the Sons of War. It had started to rain and the water was coming down hard, hammering the roof. Forty-seven of the senior members of the Sons of War were gathered. None of them were wearing masks. Reiko was not used to seeing all these high-ranking officials, generals, and politicians from the Empire present without a disguise.

Vice Minister Toyoda took the podium. Toyoda was previously second-in-command and had taken charge of the Sons. He was ex-military like Yamaoka, and they'd served together throughout the past two decades.

"Obviously, since Bloody Mary has publicly declared the USJ dead, the Empire has been mobilizing against us. But I'm more concerned about this new faction calling themselves the 'New Americans' who are quickly taking over. One of their leaders, Major Nori

Onishi, arrested eight of our ministers with her mecha legion. The public has lionized her for her battle with General Watanabe. Marshal Lanser has used this opportunity to lead a revolution of his own in the German Americas. Because of that, the situation could change at any time and we could have the Nazis breathing down our necks."

Reiko was amused to hear mention of the New Americans, the group she'd joined after the revolution ended. Although some in the press thought they were on the same side as Bloody Mary, they had no connection.

"We should put all the blame on Yamaoka," one of the generals stated. "Tell Tokyo Command that it was his idea and we had no idea about his desire to set himself up as a shogun."

"Yamaoka miscalculated! He's made us all vulnerable."

"How could he let Bloody Mary release all that private information?"

"If you surrender," Reiko stated, "we'll all be executed. Don't think you can squirm your way out of this. No matter what excuse you make, Tokyo Command won't let you off. The only chance we have is if we fight together."

"She's right," someone said.

"Don't be stupid and rely on their mercy. That isn't going to happen."

"But Yamaoka is gone. Who's going to take his place?"

"What'll happen to the Sons of War?"

Vice Minister Toyoda called everyone to attention and stated, "I've had personal assurances from the generals in Tokyo Command that if we blame it all on Yamaoka, they'll accept it and let us return to our former positions with our authority intact."

Assenting voices affirmed the hopelessness of resistance, as well as the hostility toward Yamaoka.

Reiko did not like it and shouted, "It's true, the Sons of War are over. But we can get through this if every one of you stands strong and defends your position."

"We can't fight both the Nazis and the Empire."

"Since when were we so afraid of Nazis?" Reiko demanded.

"A two-front war is suicide."

"We can't act rashly now."

The debate intensified. Reiko became frustrated with the way the cowards spun their arguments for surrender as common sense and reason. Her eyes drifted to a series of paintings in the hall that weren't very good. Each of them had business cards next to them with titles and suggested price range, which was a bit high considering their poor quality. The most interesting of them, Reiko noted, was closest to the vice minister. It depicted a woman eating a man who was in turn cannibalizing a woman who was also eating a man, all with sharp teeth in an infinite loop, struggling to break free.

She felt disgusted with the Sons of War for only caring about saving their own necks. They were vultures who'd been sycophantic around Yamaoka before his death, turning on him the moment he was gone. There weren't many people in the world who were really loyal. Then again, she assumed people could say the same about her.

The New American faction had promised her the chance to try to convince the Sons of War to join them. Reiko still felt they would be useful in the battle to come. But not if they insisted on the old ways.

As the group voted to censure Governor Yamaoka and publicly reassert their loyalty to the Empire, she felt sad that this collection of talented officials and generals couldn't understand that their ways were obsolete. They had to evolve.

Reiko had been wary of joining yet another political group after the Sons of War had failed. But Major Nori Onishi was one of the key members of the New Americans, and her word carried a lot of weight after the battle. What ultimately convinced her was that they hadn't invited Reiko to join as a member but as one of their leaders. The fact that they'd given her the chance to persuade the Sons of War, something the Sons of War themselves had never bothered to do with Governor Tamura's followers, encouraged her. They were also to be arrested, not executed.

Reiko looked again at the painting of the woman with the man inside her mouth. It was a surreal expression of suffering and interminable belligerence, drowning in the hunger of others. Hearing the Sons almost finishing their vote, she reluctantly gave the signal on her portical. When she heard the soldiers rush in, she closed her eyes and dreamed of a different kind of future in which she used mechas to explore the planet, not fight more wars.

It was a good dream.

Photo by Angela Xu

PETER TIERYAS is the author of *Mecha Samurai Empire* and *United States of Japan*, both of which won Japan's top science fiction award, the Seiun. He's written for Kotaku, the Verge, Boing Boing, *S-F Magazine*, Tor.com, and *ZYZZYVA*. He's also been a technical writer for LucasArts and a visual effects artist at Sony, and works in feature animation. He is currently warping between different alternate realities.

CONNECT ONLINE

Tieryas.WordPress.com
🐦 TieryasXu

Ready to find
your next great read?

Let us help.

Visit prh.com/nextread